CUT SHORT

Watch out for Leigh Russell's next two books

Road Closed and *Dead End*

And for further information go to:

Publisher's website
http://www.noexit.co.uk/cutshort

Crime Time online
http://www.crimetime.co.uk/publishing/ct54.pdf

Blog
http://leighrussell.blogspot.com/

CUT SHORT

Leigh Russell

NO EXIT PRESS

First published in 2009 by No Exit Press,
P.O.Box 394, Harpenden, Herts, AL5 1XJ
www.noexit.co.uk

ISBN 978-1-84243-271-6

4 6 8 10 9 7 5

Typeset by Avocet Typeset, Chilton, Aylesbury, Bucks
Printed and bound in Great Britain by Cox & Wyman, Reading

Dedicated
to
Michael, Jo and Phill

Acknowledgements

I would like to thank Dr Leonard Russell for his expert medical advice, William Goddard at South Harrow Police Station and Robert Dobbie of the British Transport Police for their suggestions, Matt Biggadike for his technical help, Hazel Orme and Keshini Naidoo for their guidance and, above all, Annette Crossland for her inspiring enthusiasm.

'Draw your chair up close to the edge of the precipice and I'll tell you a story.'

F. Scott Fitzgerald

PART 1

'pity this busy monster, manunkind,
not. Progress is a comfortable disease:
your victim (death and life safely beyond)
plays with the bigness of his littleness'

E. E. Cummings

1

Goodbye

He scrabbled at brittle leaves with clumsy gloved fingers then, crouching low, wriggled through the bushes. He glanced around to make sure no one was watching before he trudged away along the path. He'd been clever, careful to leave no clues. No one would find her in the park. It was his secret, his and hers, and she wouldn't tell. He had no idea who she was, and that was clever too. It meant she didn't know who he was.

He hadn't chosen her because she was pretty. He hadn't chosen her at all. She was just there. But she was pretty and he liked that. No woman had looked at him since school; she had stared into his eyes. She only said one word, 'No!' but she was speaking to him and he knew this was intimacy, just the two of them. It was a pity he wouldn't see her again, but there would be others. It was raining hard. He sang softly, because you never knew who was listening.

'Sweet the rain's new fall, sunlit from heaven, like the first dew fall, on the first grass, praise for the sweetness of the wet garden …'

The rain would wash her clean.

He faltered as he rounded a bend in the path because a woman was walking towards him. Then he saw she was older, and she wasn't pretty like the woman he'd hidden under autumn leaves. She asked him about a music shop called Bretts. He didn't know what to say so he walked quickly past. He wasn't allowed to talk to her.

13

'Never talk to strangers,' Miss Elsie said. The park was a dangerous place and he knew he shouldn't trust people who offered him sweets. He must never get in the car if they offered to take him home, not even if they called his name. The world was full of sin. The woman watched him hurry past. He was frightened.

'Don't worry,' Miss Elsie said. 'I won't let anyone hurt you.' He walked more quickly and he didn't look back.

2

Sophie

A shrill scream pierced the air. Judi gazed helplessly at her daughter. Sophie's fair curls shook furiously, her angelic face twisted in rage.

'Won't!' Sophie shrieked. She stamped her foot, ran to the table and flung her plastic bowl to the floor. Coco Pops and rusty milk splashed onto the Amtico tiles. Judi lunged forward, gripped Sophie's little forearm and slapped her hand. The child was shocked into silence before she crumpled. It took Judi nearly an hour to pacify her. No sooner had harmony been restored than the doorbell rang and Judi remembered she'd invited her neighbour round with her small son. She opened the door and saw Alice with two children in tow.

'Sorry,' Alice said. 'I completely forgot I promised to look after Jamie's friend. We can leave it for today, if you like.' Before Judi could reply, Sophie ran forward squealing with glee.

'Jamie! Jamie!'

Judi smiled. 'Don't be silly. Come in. It's fine. Gerta can take them all to the park.'

Judi and Alice settled down with coffee and slivers of cake while the three children trotted busily along the pavement behind Gerta.

'We're going to the park,' Jamie crooned and Otto repeated the words in a singsong chant.

The children's playground was on the far side of Lyceum

Park. Gerta hoped she might see the fit young gardener who sometimes worked there and smiled as she passed through the open gateway. Her eyes flicked round eagerly, but the park was deserted. It was ordinary enough, a typical urban park with scrubby grassland, and a lake boasting a half-hearted jet of water that could hardly be called a fountain. A few ducks pottered at the edge of the scummy surface alongside fat pigeons. They rounded a bend in the narrow asphalt path and saw the playground to their right, its ground covered in tree bark. As they approached the central bank of overgrown trees and shrubs on their left, the two boys raced past Gerta into the children's area. Sophie scurried fretfully at their heels.

Sophie always played with Jamie. They were best friends. They played on the slide in the park. Not the baby slide. They played on the big big slide. Mummy said they played nicely together. But Jamie was playing with Otto. Sophie wanted to push him off the slide, only Gerta was on the bench watching them. Gerta needed to go away so Sophie could push Otto off the slide and play with Jamie. She and Jamie took turns nicely on the big slide. Mummy said so. Mummy liked Jamie. Mummy didn't like Otto. Otto was horrid.

'Make Otto go away,' she wailed, but Gerta shook her head and told Sophie not to be silly. Sophie wasn't silly. Gerta was silly, and Otto was silly. Sophie didn't care. She'd go away and hide and they wouldn't be able to find her. Mummy would give Gerta a big smack and make Gerta cry.

Sophie flew with fairy wings across the path and into the magic trees. The leaves were red and yellow and brown and green. It was a good place to hide. She watched a hungry caterpillar crawling down a tree. It took a long time but no one came to find her. She picked up a stick and poked the leaves. Mummy never let her play with sticks but Mummy wasn't there.

'Sophie!' she heard Gerta's voice, rising with panic, and giggled.

'Sophie!' Jamie called.

'Thophie!' Otto echoed.

'Go away, Otto,' Sophie whispered. She was so quiet, no one heard her. Sophie wriggled further into the bushes. It was damp and scratchy. She saw a beetle scurrying along the ground and poked it with her stick. A bee buzzed by her ear. There was a hand in the leaves. She poked it and a cloud of nasty insects flew up. Sophie took no notice of them. She'd seen something worse, hiding in the leaves. The wicked witch was lying in the mud, staring up at her. Sophie didn't like it there any more. She wanted mummy.

'Mummy!' she yelled. She heard scrabbling in the bushes and saw Gerta peering down. Gerta looked like the dog with saucer eyes. Her mouth gaped wide open and she started to scream.

Sophie covered her ears. She didn't want the wicked witch to wake up. 'Go away, Gerta!' She wanted mummy. She wanted to go home.

3

Move

Flushed with excitement, Geraldine clutched the key. The sharp metal dug into her flesh. After months of anxious waiting she was finally taking possession of her new home. She suppressed an impulse to shout, 'Yippee!' The estate agent was watching her. She smiled while, inside her head, laughter bubbled.

'You're new to the area, aren't you?' the estate agent asked and she nodded, conscious of his bold eyes. 'What brings you here?'

'Work,' she replied.

'It's a very nice flat,' he remarked. 'What did you say you do?'

'I didn't.'

'Maybe I'll find out,' he smiled. Geraldine wasn't sure if he was flirting and felt like an awkward teenager. He obviously hadn't seen her details, as he didn't know she was a detective inspector. Accustomed to knowing about other people's lives, she felt unsettled. She hadn't even learned his name, and he was familiar with the interior of her bedroom.

The estate agent seized her hand in a warm, firm grip, congratulated her once more on her purchase and turned to leave.

'Is it a good time to buy?' As soon as she spoke Geraldine was afraid he'd see through her clumsy ploy but it worked. He spun round to face her.

'Property prices have been rising in the UK for fifteen years.'

'Will the trend continue, do you think?' She was tempted to invite him in for coffee, but she didn't have any milk.

'There are a lot of people saying the bubble's going to burst some time in the next two years.'

'What do you think's going to happen to property prices?'

'If I could predict the future of the housing market, I wouldn't still be working for a living.' He hesitated before scribbling on a business card. 'Here's my mobile number. Why don't you call me when you've settled in?' She reached out and took the card. 'I don't usually meet women like this,' he added, suddenly intense. Then he turned and walked away. Geraldine lingered in the doorway, watching his confident stride. She tried not to think about Mark.

It never occurred to Geraldine that Mark might leave her, until the evening she'd come home to find him in the hall surrounded by suitcases. Gazing past her, Mark announced that he was moving out.

'After six years,' was all Geraldine managed to say.

'We both know this isn't going anywhere.'

'This?' she echoed stupidly.

'Us. Our relationship. We've been taking each other for granted for too long. I hardly see you any more. You're always working. It's time we both moved on.'

Geraldine wanted to protest, to promise she'd change. She tried to speak but the words stuck in her throat. Mark had packed all his belongings. His silver letter opener had gone from the hall table. His coat wasn't on its hook. It went through her head that soon there'd be no trace of him in the flat apart from the rubbish he'd thrown in the bin, and the smell of him on her sheets. When that faded, she'd be left with nothing. They faced one another across the draughty hall.

'Where will you go?'

Suddenly brisk, Mark seized hold of a case. His eyes were fixed on a point just above her left shoulder. 'I'm moving in with a friend.'

'A friend?' she repeated, the word suddenly threatening. 'What friend?'

Mark hesitated then spoke gently. His features softened. 'Her name's Sue.' Geraldine clenched her fists until she felt her nails bite into the soft pads of her palms. Mark's face grew taut again. 'I'll pick up the rest of my stuff tomorrow,' he called out as he lugged his large suitcase through the front door. It closed behind him with a hollow clunk. Alone, Geraldine clutched the edge of the bare table and howled.

'He's not worth crying about. He's a lying toad. Forget about him, he's not worth it,' her sister raged on the phone later that evening.

Geraldine had been planning to spend the rest of her life with the lying toad. 'What am I going to do?' she wept.

'Forget about him,' her sister repeated. It didn't help.

Mark had always claimed he didn't believe in marriage. That was another lie. He just hadn't wanted to marry Geraldine. When she heard he was engaged, less than a year after walking out on her, she was consumed by an anger that left no room for self-pity.

'You'll meet someone else,' her sister assured her. Geraldine nodded, privately determined that she would never be emotionally vulnerable again. There was more to life than the future Mark had snatched away from her. He'd blamed her career for the failure of their relationship, but her job wasn't going to walk out on her. She managed to convince herself that she was happy to be single, devoted to her work.

Situated in a pleasant tree-lined avenue, her new flat suited Geraldine well, offering a haven from the stresses of her work on a mobile Murder Investigation Team based in the South East. As soon as she could, she took a few days off to paint her living room. Restful cream walls and beige carpet gave an illusion of space, enhanced by a large mirror above her small fireplace. She threw a critical look at her reflection. Dark eyes stared steadily back at her.

Once she'd finished decorating, she settled down to finish unpacking. Absorbed in boxes, she almost missed the doorbell. She ran to the entryphone. On a little shelf above the handset she saw a card: CRAIG HUDSON, RESIDENTIAL SALES CONSULTANT. Her glance lingered on the name.

'Washing machine,' a voice crackled over the entryphone.

'Come on in.' Geraldine pressed the buzzer for the gates. A few moments later her doorbell rang and she opened the door to a lanky man, his hair damp and his shoulders flecked with rain.

'Miss Steel?' She nodded and he consulted his paperwork. 'Your washer dryer,' he read aloud.

'Come in.' The man loped after her into the kitchen and sized up the space.

'Yes,' he confirmed, nodding his head. 'It'll fit.' He glanced hopefully at the kettle. 'It's a nasty day out there.'

Geraldine was keen to return to her unpacking. 'Can you bring it in, please?'

The delivery man sighed and walked slowly out, his large feet dragging at the fluff on her new carpet.

The two delivery men shuffled up the path in the drizzling rain.

'This way,' Geraldine said. Her breath caught in her throat as she glimpsed the second man and sensed that he recognised her. Standing aside, she scoured her memory to recall if she'd ever seen him before. She tried to picture him with a bald head or long straggly hair, instead of a grubby grey cap pulled low on his forehead.

Geraldine avoided meeting his eye again as, grunting and

nodding at one another, the two men manoeuvred the washing machine into the kitchen. She didn't put the kettle on while they plumbed it in. She wanted the delivery men gone from her flat as quickly as possible, so she could have the place to herself again, and was relieved when the front door closed behind them. She cleaned the kitchen thoroughly, wiping away all trace of the dirty wet marks they'd left on her floor.

Her housework done, she poured herself a mug of coffee and settled down once more beside a large pile of boxes. As she was ripping brown parcel tape off a box with a satisfying whoosh, her work phone rang.

4

Team

An Incident Room was being set up as Geraldine arrived at the police station. Woolsmarsh was a small town around half an hour's drive from her new flat, which meant she'd be able to stay at home instead of having to find accommodation locally. There was a buzz of activity as she walked in and she had to step aside smartly as two computers were carried past her along a narrow corridor. A harassed officer with a clipboard approached her as she hovered in the doorway.

'Hi, I'm Detective Inspector Geraldine Steel, MIT,' she said brightly.

'DS Peterson is on the Murder Investigation Team. He'll fill you in,' the other woman said, nodding with relief as a young officer came into view, hurrying purposefully along the corridor towards them. He wore a navy suit, crisp white shirt and sober striped tie, like a graduate dressed up for his first grown up job interview. His vigorous enthusiasm contrasted with Geraldine's first impression of the police station, thrown into disarray by the arrival of the Murder Investigation Team. The DS paused in his stride and smiled. A little over six foot, he was heavily built with huge shoulders. He looked as though he worked out. Geraldine liked him at once. She held out her hand, which was immediately seized in a strong grip.

'Ian Peterson, Detective Sergeant,' he said. Something about the eager way he announced himself suggested that he'd only recently been promoted.

'DI Geraldine Steel. What's going on?' As they watched a desk being manoeuvred into the Incident Room, Peterson told her they were there to investigate the murder of a local girl. That was all he knew. He shrugged apologetically as though he ought to know all the details of the case.

'That's more than I knew until you told me,' Geraldine fibbed and he smiled with relief, his blue eyes candid and friendly. They entered the Incident Room where a briefing was about to begin.

Desks for the three inspectors attached to the case had been set up in one corner, there being no accommodation in the small station for them to have their own offices. The room was packed and people were still arriving, milling about in the cramped space. As she made her way over to the inspectors' corner Geraldine recognised Ted Carter, a grey haired man with classic good looks who'd been her mentor during her year as acting DI when she'd been completing her training for the rank. He'd always treated her with gentle courtesy and she was pleased to see his familiar leathery face as she made her way over to the corner. Carter nodded and stood up to greet her, his long legs wedged awkwardly behind his desk.

'Small world,' she grinned. His brown eyes wrinkled in an answering smile.

Carter half turned and introduced the other DI on the case. 'This is Tom Merton, Geraldine Steel.' They shook hands. Merton's grip felt chilly after the young sergeant's energetic handshake. Soft wisps of ginger hair hovered like improbable candyfloss around his unpleasantly flushed pink face. Unlike Carter, Merton didn't return her smile as he enquired in a reedy drawl if she knew DCI Gordon. Geraldine shook her head. The other two inspectors on the case had both worked with the detective chief inspector before, and she hoped she wouldn't be at a disadvantage as the new girl on the team.

'The name sounds familiar,' she said uncertainly. With a nod, Merton retired behind his desk. Geraldine had the impression Carter was about to say something else, when a hush fell over the room.

'Speak to you later,' Carter whispered, 'DCI's here.' Geraldine made her way over to her own desk. She thought she caught Merton giving Carter a malevolent look as she turned to face the woman standing beside the Incident Board.

A jacket hung loosely on Kathryn Gordon's spare frame. Pale skin stretched tightly across her face but hung slack beneath her chin, and her eyes burned with determination. She wore no make up and her greying hair was cut in a severe bob along her jaw line. Her pallor contrasted with two red blotches on her cheeks, giving her a clown-like look, but there was nothing cheerful about her expression. Geraldine glanced round the room. All eyes were fixed on Kathryn Gordon.

'Now that I have everyone's attention,' the DCI said, 'let's begin. I'm your Senior Investigating Officer, DCI Kathryn Gordon.' She didn't speak again immediately. Instead, she turned to the Incident Board to look at a bruised face staring blankly into the room.

'We're here to find out who murdered this young woman yesterday. So far, her killer's not giving anything away.' Kathryn Gordon tapped at the photo with a rapid flick of her wrist and turned back to look round at the expectant team. On the periphery of her vision Geraldine was aware of officers straightening up and pulling their shoulders back. 'Her name's Angela Waters,' Kathryn Gordon went on. Apart from the rasp of her voice, the room was completely still. Only the hum of computer monitors could be heard. 'Also known as Angie or Ange. Twenty-two years old, slim, blonde, address 14a Marsh Crescent. She was killed about twenty-four hours before her body was discovered in

Lyceum Park this morning by a young child playing in the bushes. There's been a lot of disturbance. The child trampled on any evidence that might have been left on the ground, and her au pair went crashing in after her. In addition, the mud's been disturbed by animals: foxes, rats, squirrels, possibly a dog. Some kind of animal was there over night, tampering with what little evidence there might have been, before the child arrived on the scene to foul things up completely. She was probably killed in the bushes where the body was discovered but SOCOs haven't been able to identify individual footprints or movements with any certainty, due to all the mess at the scene.' She grimaced. 'The victim was strangled so we're not looking for a weapon but uniform are making a thorough search of the surrounding area. At the end of this briefing some of you will be joining them.'

The DCI paused and glanced back at the picture on the Incident Board before continuing. 'The victim's wrists were held together over her coat sleeves so it's impossible to say what was used to secure them. She was very thin so her assailant might have held her wrists with one hand just long enough to force her to the ground. We won't know more until we get a full forensic report but it seems nothing's been left at the scene to help us identify the killer. Any threads have probably been brushed off in the leaves, mud and animal faeces. From the pattern of bruising on the neck we believe the killer was wearing leather gloves, but there's no other trace, no blood from the victim or the killer, no saliva, no dandruff, no blood or skin under her fingernails. A fingertip search of the immediate area has revealed nothing so far. Hopefully we'll have more to go on after the full post-mortem report tomorrow but so far there's no sign of any defence injuries.'

The DCI looked around. 'We need a swift result,' she said. 'We'll interview all the usual suspects, and anyone who may have known the victim: boyfriend, family, acquaintances, anyone who knew her. We need to chat up the neighbours, check out the local shops and pub. Angela lived with a man, John Drew. Drew works in ...' she glanced down for corroboration, 'car sales. The Honda showroom on the Hinckley roundabout. We need to check out the workplace. Let's do it this morning, while he's not there. He went home, after we told him about Angela's death. See what you can dig up about him from his colleagues while he's out of the way and don't be too gentle. We're also looking for anyone with a history of violent assault. I want all the local hostels checked, and a thorough grilling of anyone recently released or out on parole. Whatever there is, find it.' Glancing round, Geraldine caught DS Peterson's eye and he grinned at her.

'Right, get your schedules from the duty manager. DC Mellor, can you get on to Rotherhithe where Angela Waters comes from? Ask them to speak to the mother, interview Angela's brother, and find out if there was a father around.' Sarah Mellor looked up from her notepad and nodded, her smile a welcome surprise among the tense faces.

Geraldine, sent to interview the child and the au pair, was pleased to find she was working with DS Peterson.

As the team dispersed, Kathryn Gordon stood for a moment gazing at the victim's face. It wasn't the image of death that worried her, but the prospect of a lucky killer. So far wildlife and a small child had obliterated any evidence. She glanced round the quiet Incident Room before slipping into her office. Closing the door firmly, she opened a filing cabinet and drew out a bottle of whiskey.

5

Gerta

There were two people in the porch. The man was broad shouldered, towering over the woman who stood very still and upright, her dark hair pulled back neatly from her face. Judi knew who they were straight away but she checked their ID carefully all the same. As police officers, she was sure they'd appreciate her responsible caution.

The woman's voice was low and soothing, well trained in calming nerves and situations. 'Mrs Judith Brightley? You spoke to Detective Constable Mellor this morning. I'm Detective Inspector Steel and this is Detective Sergeant Peterson. We've come to question your au pair, Gerta Hersch. I understand she can speak without an interpreter.'

'Yes, that's right. Do come in, Inspector Steel and … er …'

'Sergeant Peterson.'

'Yes. This way. Can I offer you anything? Tea? Coffee?'

She left them in the lounge and called from the bottom of the wide staircase. 'Gerta! Can you come down please?' For such a shrimp of a woman, she had a surprisingly loud voice, Geraldine thought. Glancing round, she smiled at the sergeant's grunt of appreciation as he sunk his bulk onto a large chintz sofa.

Gerta's eyes were bloodshot and puffy from crying as she came into the room, sniffing noisily. She sat down and began to sob quietly, twisting a handkerchief in her small fingers.

28

'Miss Hersch, did you know the dead woman? Was she a friend of yours?' Peterson asked brusquely. Geraldine noted with surprise that the sight of a woman in tears seemed to irritate him. A brief memory flickered into her mind, a snatch of conversation overheard at the station; Peterson was having problems with his girlfriend. Geraldine gave the au pair a sympathetic smile.

'No.' The sobbing stopped and she blew her nose noisily.

'Thank you. Now, perhaps, we can make a start. Please tell us exactly what happened this morning, Miss Hersch.' The DS had his notebook ready.

'Ja. I am in the park with my little girl Sophie, James and Otto also.'

'James and Otto …?'

Judi entered softly with a tray of tea and luxury biscuits, a small child in tow. She handed the visitors their cups, offered the biscuits, and sat down with the third cup. No tea for Gerta. The small girl, aged about four, stared at Geraldine with huge blue eyes.

'Jamie is my next-door neighbour's son,' Judi explained. 'Otto's his friend.' The child burst into a curious wail. 'Oh dear.' Judi set her cup down. 'What is it, my precious?' Geraldine almost choked on her tea at seeing how seriously Sophie's mother took the child's tantrum. Peterson coughed to cover a smile or a grimace, it was difficult to tell which. He put down his pencil and took a quick gulp of his tea. The china cup looked like part of a doll's tea set in his hand.

'Jamie's *my* friend!' the child blubbered. Geraldine saw the child dart a calculating glance from behind her fingers at her mother, who was clearly taken in by her show of grief.

'Yes, yes,' she crooned, 'Jamie's your friend. No one said he wasn't.'

'Perhaps you could take Sophie out so that we can talk to Miss Hersch?' Was that a touch of sharpness in Peterson's voice, Geraldine wondered? He was shaping up well, affable

29

but very quick on the uptake, and not afraid to speak his mind.

'Horrid, horrid Gerta!' Sophie shrieked, directing a look of such alarming gall at the au pair that Geraldine was intrigued.

'Why?' she asked, and noticed Peterson sit back, relieved. Doubtless she could rely on him to intimidate an intransigent villain, but a four-year-old girl was unfamiliar territory, and this four-year-old was plainly used to getting her own way. Geraldine sank to her knees and whispered confidentially to the child. 'Tell me about Gerta.' The tears vanished in a twinkle.

'Jamie's *my* friend. We play nicely. Mummy said so.' The nature of Gerta's offence soon became clear: she'd allowed Otto to play with Jamie. Geraldine took a deep breath. She had no special training in interviewing children, but she could be patient. 'Gerta's horrid and silly. She made Jamie play with Otto and she made me go under the leaves with a stick.' She glanced up at her mother. 'I played with a stick. A big stick. Gerta made me. And Gerta made me touch the hand. It got bigger and bigger until it was huge and I cried and cried because ...' she paused to check that she had their attention, '... it was the wicked witch!' She plopped her thumb into her mouth and reached out to her mother for reassurance.

'So, Miss Hersch,' Geraldine resumed as she rose from her knees and returned to her seat, 'the children,' she avoided mentioning their names, 'were playing and ...'

'Sophie is playing.' The au pair threw a fearful glance at her employer. 'She is hiding in the bushes. She knows she must not go in the bushes. It is not permitted to go in the bushes. I am telling her this.' Mrs Brightley sniffed. Geraldine wondered if this domestic drama would end in a dismissal and a call to the agency for a replacement. Or perhaps the cowed Gerta would be more amenable now she'd slipped up and allowed Sophie to run off, unsupervised.

'I am seeing at once she is gone,' Gerta continued. 'Quickly I look and I find her in the bushes.' She shuddered, back in the moment. 'And I am seeing something in the bushes. Under the leafs I am seeing the hand. It is the hand of the woman. I bring Sophie away from the leafs at once. I am cleaning her and I call at once Mrs Brightley and she is telling me go to the home. I bring Sophie to the home at once. And the little boys also. And Mrs Brightley is calling the policeman on the telephone.'

Peterson was scribbling furiously. Gerta slumped in her chair gazing disconsolately at Sophie who scowled back at her. A single tear flickered down the au pair's cheek and Geraldine thought how young she looked – eighteen, nineteen – to be so far from home, hemmed in by a foreign tragedy. She'd probably been looking forward to coming to England. Poor kid.

'Thank you very much, Miss Hersch. You've been most helpful.' With a polite nod at Mrs Brightley, she stood up.

'Thank you for the tea,' Peterson added as he rose to follow.

'We're looking at a quick, efficient murder, not a bungled assault,' Geraldine said, as they drove back to the station. 'What does that tell us?'

Peterson glanced across at her. 'Someone wanted to make sure she was dead?'

She paused. 'There's no sign of any struggle.'

'Perhaps she knew her killer,' the DS replied, 'and wasn't expecting an attack. But we know he approached her from behind,' he added, 'so it could have been a complete stranger, taking her by surprise.'

'It doesn't look like a frenzied attack,' Geraldine said, 'more a deliberate killing. Almost clinical. Was it planned? Did her killer just want her out of the way, for some reason?'

'Which would mean he knew her.' Peterson pulled up at a red light and turned to look at her.

'Does it point to that? That the killer hated her, enough to want to kill her?' She pondered. 'It was relatively quick. Hopefully she didn't even have time to realise what was happening. He came up behind her, grabbed her arms, pulled them behind her back, maybe tied them, just enough to immobilise them, although I don't know if he'd have had time for that, turned her round to face him – I wonder why? – and strangled her. He's a strong bastard. It was all over pretty quickly. But then, he had to be quick. He must've been afraid of being disturbed.'

'Oh, he was disturbed all right,' Peterson said.

Geraldine tried to imagine the scene. 'A sudden rush of fear and a frantic struggle, before she lost consciousness. It would all have been over in a couple of minutes. No time to shout for help.'

'She might have been too frightened to call out, or too surprised. Then again, we don't know she didn't shout for help,' Peterson pointed out. The traffic light turned green and he pulled away. 'Are you saying you think the killer wanted to finish the job quickly so she didn't suffer?'

'A considerate killer? It's possible, if he knew her. But so was the need to finish the job quickly. He strangled her in the park, remember.'

'Yes,' Peterson agreed. 'He'd have to be quick, whatever his feelings.'

'But why would he do it in such a public place?'

'Suggests an opportunistic killing. In any event, he wouldn't want to hang around.'

'So the question is: did he want to kill her? Or did he want her dead?' Geraldine asked intensely. Peterson frowned and she shook her head. 'It's not the same, is it? Not the same thing at all. Because if he simply wanted to kill … regardless of his victim's identity …' She fell silent and they considered the possibility. 'But the killer wanted to see his victim's face. He was checking he had the right girl,' she went on uncertainly.

'Or he was enjoying watching her,' Peterson said grimly. Geraldine winced as the DS voiced her own fears. They both knew that if the killer had strangled Angela Waters in pursuit of some perverse pleasure, he was likely to strike again.

The Incident Board had been updated. The names of Angela Waters' mother and brother were pinned up. Carter had taken a sergeant to the car showroom, a twenty-minute drive away, from where he would go on to question the neighbours. Merton was following up known offenders. Geraldine's next task was to visit the café where Angela had worked and then interview her boyfriend, John Drew. She tried to suppress her excitement. Statistically, she knew the boyfriend was the most likely suspect.

6

Café

A menu hung in the bay window of the Bella Cafe, alongside a notice advising customers that the café was open from '7 to 7, for the Best Cup of Coffee, with a Choice of Genuine Italian Pastries'. The fluorescent-lit interior boasted gaudy orange walls and tubular steel chairs with garish green plastic seats. It was empty apart from a girl dressed in black trousers and a white shirt who greeted them solemnly.

'Table for two?'

Geraldine held up her warrant card. Wordlessly the girl motioned them to a corner table.

'It's about Angie, isn't it? Is she in some sort of trouble? Only she didn't turn up for work yesterday and the boss is hopping mad. She still hasn't called in. I tried to phone but she's not answering her mobile. Has something happened to her?' She waited between them as they sat down.

'Please take a seat, Miss …?'

'Christina.' She fell into a chair and rested her chin on her hands. 'Boss'll be out soon.' She nodded morosely in the direction of a small white door marked 'STAFF ONLY'.

'How well did you know Angela Waters?' Geraldine asked her cautiously. She placed a tape recorder on the table. Peterson sat, pen poised. Christina looked up and the question hung in the air as a stout, balding man burst through the staff door and summoned her with a peremptory gesture. She rose and shuffled over to him. Although he spoke in

34

muted tones they could tell he was scolding her. Finally she remonstrated and his demeanour transformed. He switched his attention to the two detectives and advanced on them, his head inclined sideways in a servile pose. A black moustache bobbed on his upper lip as he spoke.

'Sir, I beg pardon.' His voice was incongruously high. 'I did not appreciate you are police. Please accept coffee. On the house.' He threw a perfunctory nod at Christina before smiling at Peterson.

Geraldine addressed him. 'We'd like to speak to Christina without interruptions, and then we'll talk to you, Mr . . .?'

'Umberto. Antonio Umberto is—'

'We'd like you to close your café while we talk to you, Mr Umberto. Please turn your sign round. We'll start with Christina. This needn't take long,' she added, as the proprietor stiffened. He scurried to the door, then withdrew behind the counter to eavesdrop.

Geraldine spoke quietly. Across the table, she saw Peterson struggling to catch her words as they dropped into the silence. Christina glanced nervously at her boss, busily straightening wilting sandwiches on a white plate.

'Christina, I'm sorry to have to bring you bad news about Angela. She was attacked in the park yesterday, and died there.' The girl looked down at the table. She didn't make a sound but her chin trembled and she pressed her hands together in her lap until her knuckles went white. Geraldine waited.

'Killed?' Christina repeated at last in a barely audible murmur.

Briefly, Geraldine outlined what had happened. 'She didn't suffer, but we have to find out who did this, so I need to ask you a few questions.'

Christina had worked with Angela Waters for seven months, but as far as information went, it was soon clear they'd drawn a blank. Christina knew little about her co-worker beyond what had emerged in idle chatter during quiet moments. The girls didn't socialise outside work and Christina had never met John Drew.

'Who?'

'Angela's boyfriend.'

'Oh, Johnny. Yeah. Sorry. I didn't know his surname. Ange never stopped talking about him. She was crazy about him. I told her she was too young to even think about marriage. 'Get out there and play the field,' I told her.'

'Had Johnny asked her to marry him?'

'I don't think so. It was just something she talked about, you know, how some girls do. I think she put up with a lot from him but they seemed to be working it out.'

'Working what out?' Peterson asked.

'His commitment phobia. The usual.' She shrugged. A single tear rolled down her cheek and she blinked. The reality of her colleague's death had hit her. Christina leaned her elbows on the table and shielded her face with one hand. The fleeting intimacy had slipped away.

'You said she put up with a lot from him. What did you mean?' Geraldine asked. Christina shook her head. 'Did she ever mention an argument? Did she complain that he drank? That he'd lashed out at her in a rage?'

'Look, I never met the guy. All I know is she said she thought he was the one, you know. He was always giving her flowers, which was sweet, but she was scared he wasn't the marrying type. The good ones generally aren't.' Mark darted into Geraldine's thoughts but she drove him from her mind and focused resolutely on what Christina was saying. 'She never said anything about any fights.'

'You said she put up with a lot from him?'

'Only that he wouldn't make a commitment. They never do.'

Geraldine carefully kept her voice even. 'Do you think one of them might have been seeing someone else?'

'You mean two-timing? Not her. She was crazy about him. And, anyway, she's not like that. I told you, she's … she was nice.'

'And her boyfriend?' Peterson pressed her, but the questioning had lost its force.

'Look, I want to help the police and all that, but I don't know anything about her boyfriend. I never met the guy. As for Ange, she was really nice, but I only ever saw her here. I don't even know where she lives.' Christina looked close to tears again.

'Thank you, Christina. You've been very helpful.' Geraldine pulled out a card and handed it to the girl. 'I'd like you to contact us if you think of anything else that might help us to find out more about Angela.' Geraldine looked up and caught the proprietor's eye, he was listening intently. He looked away quickly, and resumed fiddling with the food on the counter. 'Mr Umberto,' Geraldine called, 'we'd like to speak to you now, please.' He kept his eyes fixed sullenly on the floor as he walked to the corner table.

'Go clean the kitchen,' Umberto growled as he sat down. Christina jumped up and disappeared through the staff door.

Umberto looked apprehensively from Peterson to Geraldine. 'I been busy,' he said. 'My kitchen always sparkles like a pin. Only one of my staff, she's gone. Just like that. Not a word.' He threw his hands in the air, making a whistling sound through pursed lips. 'This is how it is with young girls today.' He shrugged. 'They come, they work a little, they go. Who knows where they go, one day she's here, next day she's gone. Not even a phone call. Not a word. Is not like Italy, the young women. Here no one cares, no one got family to teach them what is right and what is wrong.' He sighed. 'Now what am I going to do?'

Geraldine interrupted him. 'Angela Waters is dead, Mr Umberto.'

He looked shocked. 'Angela dead?' he repeated, his

nervous chatter silenced. He stared at Geraldine. 'She is dead, you telling me?' He crossed himself, and shut his eyes briefly.

Geraldine asked for Angela Waters' details and Umberto hurried through the staff door to fetch them. He ran on his toes, surprisingly light on his feet, returning a moment later with a slip of paper. Angela's name, address and mobile telephone number had been written in a childish scrawl in smudgy blue biro. After seven months' employment, that was all she'd left behind. Umberto had no other records. He'd paid her in cash. He assured them he kept scrupulous records, which were available for inspection at any time, but they weren't at the café just then. They were with his most honest accountant, a good man, more like a priest, who helped him.

Geraldine interrupted his earnest defence. 'We don't want to inspect your records, Mr Umberto, although I daresay the Inland Revenue would find them interesting.' Umberto was deeply sorry but his accountant was on holiday and 'all my papers are taken with him.' His protestations about Angela were equally insincere. He declared that the café would never recover from her loss. 'She don't complain. She is clean and always she smiles to see me.' The only thing that rang true was when he said, 'Always she gets good tips. Is good for everyone, yes?'

'We'd like to take a look around,' Peterson said.

Mr Umberto flushed. 'You want to look around?' he repeated, as though the sergeant had made an obscene suggestion. He followed them through the door marked STAFF ONLY. Christina wasn't there. As Geraldine turned to Umberto, the girl reappeared through the fire door. She smelt of cigarette smoke. Geraldine and Peterson exchanged a glance.

'I just been out for a breath of air,' Christina mumbled, and turned to the sink. She began to scrub it furiously. Mr

Umberto nodded and shrugged, as if to say, 'What can you do? You just can't get the staff nowadays. Is not like Italy.' They had a quick look around the kitchen.

'I'd like to speak to you again, Christina. In here.' Geraldine led the girl back in to the café and they sat down, out of earshot of Umberto. 'Just one last question, Christina. You were here at work, yesterday morning?' The girl nodded. 'What time did you arrive?'

'I was on the morning shift but Angie never turned up at one so the boss asked me to stay on. He was hopping mad. It wasn't the first time. She was always phoning in sick. Only yesterday she never phoned. The boss swore he'd sack her this time. I had to work a twelve hour day, without a break.' Peterson's eyes narrowed at that but Geraldine focused on her line of questioning.

'Were you busy here yesterday morning?'

Christina shrugged. 'The usual.'

'How does it work, then, Christina? You're serving at the tables, and Mr Umberto is where? In the kitchen?'

The girl laughed. 'Him? In the kitchen? Never. That's me, that is. In and out the kitchen, serving tables, clearing tables, washing up. All he ever does is stand behind the till and make sandwiches. He won't trust anyone else to do it. No one slices like he does, he says.'

'I bet he can slice cucumber thinner than anyone,' Peterson chipped in and Christina sniggered.

'You're right there.'

'Did he go out to the kitchen at all?'

'No. I told you. He never does. All he ever does is stand by his precious till, slicing, and grinning at people as they order their sandwiches.'

'Was he here all morning yesterday, Christina? He didn't go out for anything? Think carefully.'

Christina answered straight away. 'He never leaves the café when it's open. He doesn't trust anyone. Won't even go to the toilet. He won't give anyone else a key, or let us near the till.' Geraldine sat back. She had her answer. Antonio Umberto couldn't have slipped out to the park on Wednesday morning.

'The Food Standards Agency might want a chat with that charmer, after the Inland Revenue finish with him,' Peterson muttered to Geraldine as they climbed back in the car.

She nodded. 'Remind me to cross Bella Café off my list of places to eat.'

'What do you reckon on Umberto, ma'am? I think he's hiding something.'

'He's a slimeball all right,' Geraldine agreed, 'but the waitress gave him an alibi. And being crooked doesn't make him a suspect in a murder case. Where's his motive?'

'Umberto's accounts are fiddled,' Peterson said. 'Maybe Angela Waters found out.'

'Hardly a motive for murder.'

'She could have been blackmailing him?'

'Hmm. It's a thought, I suppose. Christina's given him an alibi, but we'll check out the possibility anyway.' Peterson grinned enthusiastically as she gave some credence to his theory, making her remember he'd only recently been promoted to DS. 'I'll have a constable put onto it straight away,' she promised. 'We can find out if there's been any unusual activity in his account, or any change in his takings or spending, although I'll bet a lot of it never reaches the bank.' There was a pause.

'What are you thinking, ma'am?' he asked.

'I'm thinking we should pay a visit to Johnny Drew,' she replied. 'And I'm thinking it's time you called me gov.'

'Right you are, gov,' he grinned again. Geraldine glanced in the mirror as they drove away. The sign on the door had been turned round. It was business as usual at the Bella Café.

7

Johnny

The flat Angela Waters had shared with her boyfriend was above a shabby parade of shops on the edge of a rundown estate. Dull white paint stained yellowy brown, like nicotine fingers, grimy shop frontages, litter blowing across the pavement: torn newspaper, food cartons, plastic bags like deflated balloons brought urban wildlife in the shape of foxes and rats scavenging the area. Yet the street possessed a vitality lacking in the more expensive areas of town; a community that screamed its commitment to life. However hard it might be, life was precious.

Geraldine heard the sergeant's feet thud above her on the concrete staircase. It formed a dismal passageway between a derelict printer's and a flower shop from which a dark-haired girl in a very short skirt stared curiously at them. The staircase stank. Geraldine reached the top and stepped on to a balcony that ran above the shop fronts. It was draughty and strangely quiet. Geraldine looked over the parapet on to the street where, far below, a group of boys in grey and brown hoods were kicking a can along the gutter. From her elevated viewpoint, she watched a diminutive old woman crawl along the pavement towards them. Geraldine tensed, but the youngsters were intent on their can.

She knew she mustn't let her judgement be clouded by intuition, but Geraldine had misgivings about Johnny Drew even before she saw him. He made them wait too long and when he finally came to the door, his woebegone expression was too fixed. Although he displayed all the signs of the shocked bereaved, she was convinced he was playing a part. Following him along the gloomy hallway, Geraldine sized him up from behind, noting his narrow shoulders and torso, his body skinny beneath a tight fitting T-shirt. He led them into a back room that smelt of stale beer and cigarettes, where they sat on a worn sofa and chairs that didn't match. Restless eyes in a sharp face flitted over her and away in motion as rapid as the movements of a trapped fly.

Frowning at her notebook, she struggled to keep up with Drew's pat answers. He had probably been rehearsing this scenario for hours. He must have known they'd be round. He spent his working week selling cars. Now he was selling his innocence. Geraldine hadn't believed his expressions of grief, but nor did she believe he had killed Angela Waters. Once again, she couldn't have said why, but something didn't feel right. His grief might seem insincere, but that didn't make him a murderer.

Angela had allegedly complained that Johnny wasn't ready to settle down, but that was hardly a motive for murder. His alibi was more interesting. It wasn't watertight, not by a long chalk. He told them he'd been busy arranging test drives on the morning of the 26th September. Details of cars rolled off his tongue, but he couldn't give a satisfactory account of his movements between ten and ten thirty. He said he'd been in the forecourt chatting up a punter. It might be true, but he couldn't recall the customer's name. He thought it might have been a Mr Shah. He'd only met Angela's mother and brother once and admitted he hadn't liked them much. Angela had never mentioned a father. He didn't know if her father was alive, didn't even know if she had one. They'd never talked about their families.

'Was she seeing anyone else?' Geraldine hazarded. Johnny actually snorted, oozing confidence. 'Arrogant bastard,' she thought.

'Did she have any enemies? Can you think of anyone who might have hated her enough to want to do this to her?' Peterson asked.

'Look,' Johnny burst out, anguish flaring suddenly in his eyes. 'I'm doing my best to get my head round all this. Not just losing my girl, as if that's not bad enough, but ...' He dropped his head into his hands. His shoulders shook. This was no act. He wasn't that good. Geraldine gave him a moment.

'I'm sorry, Mr Drew,' she resumed, 'but we're investigating a murder. If there's anything you can tell us, anything at all, we need to know. And your alibi ...' She tailed off pointedly.

'I'm not a fucking idiot,' he snapped, raising bloodshot eyes to meet her gaze directly. 'If I'd wanted to do her in – which I didn't so don't go getting the idea that I did – but if I had, don't you think I would've sorted out a story? Do you think I'm an idiot as well as a murderer? I can't remember what I was doing at ten o'clock on Wednesday morning. I was probably having a smoke. If there was an appointment at ten it would've been in the book. But I *was* at work. I never left the place that morning, I'm sure of that. And I didn't kill Ange. What the hell do you people think? That I'm some kind of perv that gets his rocks off killing girls? It wasn't me, but someone killed her. And what are you lot doing? Are you out there looking for the sick bastard? No, you're in here, harassing the one person who cared for her. I looked after Angie. She was just a kid, that's all. How am I going to manage now?' It could have been a cry from the heart, or a calculated bid for sympathy. Either way, they weren't going to get any more out of him.

'Is there anything else you can think of that might help us?' He shook his head. 'Thank you, Mr Drew. We'll be in touch.'

'Damn right you will. I want to know who the fucking

bastard is who did this to my girl. And if I ever get my hands on him, you'll have something on me all right.'

As they reached the bottom of the concrete staircase and emerged, blinking, into the sunlight, the dark-haired girl from the flower shop darted past them up the stairs. Geraldine watched the top of her head as it bobbed along the balcony and stopped outside Johnny Drew's door.

'I wonder what he does with all his money,' she muttered. 'He can't spend it all on this dump.' John Drew was dodgy, but Geraldine didn't believe he'd murdered Angela Waters. He hadn't felt comfortable expressing his grief, but he'd shown no signs of remorse, and although she wouldn't admit it out loud, he didn't fit the mental image she was forming of the killer. Intuition was useless without evidence, but Johnny Drew felt wrong. As far as Geraldine was concerned, the identity of the killer remained a mystery.

8

Chips

Jim was frightened. He didn't know why. People stared at him or pretended he was invisible. A woman turned her head away as she passed him. She knew what he was thinking. Women could do that.

'I done nothing to be ashamed of,' he muttered crossly.

'I know you do your best,' Miss Elsie said. He smiled because she'd come back.

'Miss Elsie!' He called softly, in case anyone was listening. A man glared at him and he walked more quickly.

'Don't panic,' Miss Elsie said. He fumbled in his pocket for the key to his room and threw it down a dark glistening drain. That was clever because now they'd never find out where he lived. Then he frowned. It meant he couldn't go home. That was a shame because he liked his room. He had a picture of Miss Elsie there, hidden in a box on top of the wardrobe.

'Put your thinking cap on,' Miss Elsie said, but that wasn't fair. He was hungry. He couldn't think when he was hungry.

'Is that all you got?' the girl asked when he held out a twenty pound note. She was stupid. Twenty pounds was a lot of money. He was only buying chips.

'I want chips please,' he repeated. He spoke as clearly as he could and thrust his twenty-pound note at her again. The girl scowled as she took it.

'I give you coins,' she complained, handing over his chips. The girl turned to the till. Jim saw a black ponytail dangling below her cap. The chips warmed his hands as he stared at her hair, swinging. If he lunged forward he'd be able to reach it. The sight of her hair made him forget about her funny voice. He grinned. 'What you laughing at?' the girl asked, spinning round suddenly to face him. He could tell she was cross. Their fingers touched as she held out his change. Her skin felt greasy and he nearly dropped his chips in fright. He turned and ran. 'Hey! You forget change!' the girl shouted half-heartedly.

He kept running. He ran until his legs ached. When he stopped, winded, he was round the corner from the park. The chips were cold but he ate them greedily, sitting on the doorstep of an empty house. When he'd finished eating he felt thirsty. He needed a drink and somewhere to sleep. He glanced around. No one could see him sitting there, concealed behind an overgrown hedge. Drawing his knees up to his chin he wrapped his arms round his legs and began rocking gently backwards and forwards.

'Clever boy,' Miss Elsie said and he laughed softly to himself. They'd never find her, hidden under the leaves. And they'd never find him.

9

Honda

DI Carter and his sergeant DS Black pulled into the forecourt of the Honda showroom on the Hinckley Roundabout.

'Nice,' Black said, looking around.

'Come on,' Carter answered. 'We're not here to look at cars.'

'Shame. Not that I'd go for a Honda, but even so. There's something about a brand new car, isn't there? They're so shiny and …' He paused, searching for the right word.

'Expensive?' Carter suggested. 'Come on, let's get on with it.' They entered a plush powder blue and white showroom where an attractive girl behind a white desk smiled up at them brightly. Everything in the showroom was gleaming.

'Can I help you?' she asked. 'A salesmen will be with you in a moment if you'd like to test drive one of the cars.' They smiled back, taking out their warrant cards. A young man approached them as she examined their credentials, his suit stylishly cut, teamed with an expensive looking red tie. He threw them the same professional smile that the girl had given.

'Marcus Morrissey,' he introduced himself. 'Sorry to keep you waiting, sir. We're short staffed this morning. Can I help you?'

'Yes,' Carter replied, turning so the salesman could see his ID card. 'We'd like to ask you a few questions about a colleague of yours, John Drew.'

'I'm afraid he's not here,' Morrissey said breezily.

'There was a phone call for him earlier on,' the receptionist added. 'He said he had to go. He wouldn't say why, but he looked pretty shaken.'

'Is Johnny in some sort of trouble?' Peter Morrissey asked.

'I'm afraid there's been a death,' Carter told them.

'Oh dear,' the girl said automatically. Her eyes fell.

Black stepped up to the desk. 'Were you working here yesterday morning?' he asked. She nodded, suddenly serious. 'And you, sir?' Marcus Morrissey confirmed that he'd been there every morning that week.

'Who else was here in the showroom on Wednesday morning?'

'Just us and the boss, Robert Lakeland.' He told them Robert Lakeland was away. He wouldn't be back until after the weekend. The receptionist thought he might be at home on Sunday and gave them her boss's address and telephone number.

'Should you be giving that out?' Morrissey hissed at her.

'Shut up, Marcus, it's the police.'

'Do you know where Mr Lakeland's gone?'

'Yes. He's gone to a meeting at Head Office in Swindon. He often goes and stays over. He's got a sister or someone he visits out that way,' Morrissey told them.

'His mother,' the receptionist corrected him. 'Robert goes to Swindon for a meeting every month. His mother lives there. He stays with her Thursday and Friday night, spends Saturday with his mother, and drives back down on Sunday. I think he goes to see his mother every weekend, actually.'

'And what about Mrs Lakeland?'

'She lives somewhere near Swindon. That's why he goes there.'

'His wife, I mean.'

'Oh, he's not married,' the receptionist said.

His colleagues confirmed that John Drew had been at

work the previous morning. He had no test drives in the book, and they definitely remembered him being 'around' but when pressed, neither of them could positively swear he'd been there all morning.

'Is it possible he might have slipped away for an hour or so? Left the showroom completely?' Carter asked the girl.

She hesitated. 'I didn't see him leave,' she replied.

'But it's possible?'

'I wouldn't have thought so, but I suppose he could have done.' She sounded doubtful.

Morrissey was equally vague. 'I was out myself,' he explained. 'I think you'll find I had a couple of test drives yesterday morning.' Black checked. Morrissey had one test drive booked for ten o'clock.

'How long were you away from the showroom?' Morrissey reckoned he'd been gone for about twenty minutes. He'd spent some time chatting to a customer. He thought it unlikely John Drew could have left the showroom for about an hour without anyone noticing his absence.

'I just can't promise, hand on heart, he didn't go out. I never saw him leave and I never saw him come back in. But I was very busy.'

'What about CCTV?'

Morrissey shook his head. 'The CCTV just covers the forecourt. It's only staff cars at the back.'

'One final question, Mr Morrissey,' Carter said. 'Did you know Angela Waters?'

'Doesn't ring a bell. Should I know her?'

'Mr Drew's girlfriend.'

'Oh Angie. Johnny's girl. Yes, he's mentioned her but I've never met her. Is this something to do with her then? She in some sort of trouble?' The two policemen exchanged a glance before Black explained the reason for their visit. Marcus Morrissey whistled. 'Jesus. So that's why Johnny's not in today. Do you think he did it?'

'We're just carrying out routine enquiries, Mr Morrissey. Is there any particular reason why you think John Drew might be responsible?'

Morrissey looked taken aback. 'Good lord no. It's just that you're here, asking questions. I thought, perhaps … Well, nothing. Just that you're here, that's all,' he mumbled in confusion.

'This is a routine visit, Mr Morrissey.' Carter handed each of them a card and asked them to be sure to contact him if they remembered anything about John Drew's movements the previous morning. He thanked them for their assistance and the two detectives left.

'They seem on the level,' Carter commented as they drove off.

'Not much help though,' Black replied.

'Perhaps Robert Lakeland will be more definite.'

Black grunted. 'Couldn't be less definite than those two,' he said. 'Shame people can't be more observant. Not much use, were they?' He sounded disappointed.

Carter smiled indulgently at his young colleague. 'You can't expect every interview to shed light on the case,' he said equably. 'It's early days. We haven't even got the post-mortem report yet.'

Black nodded. 'DCI's probably there now. What do you make of her, then?'

'DCI Gordon?' Carter grinned. 'I've worked with her before. She's bloody good. Formidable woman though. It doesn't do to get in her bad books.'

Black nodded. 'I'll remember that,' he said.

'And watch out for Geraldine Steel,' Carter added. 'She's one of those rare officers who seems to sniff out a villain by instinct.'

'Bloody women,' Black grumbled amiably. 'Too bloody clever.'

10

Mortuary

Geraldine saw at once why the pathologist was known at the police station as Dr Death. His emaciated features smiled at her in a ghastly grin, which stretched his skin tightly across his jutting cheekbones, a fitting death mask for his grisly work.

Gazing down at Angela Waters, she felt a familiar anger and a tremor at the responsibility. Someone had strangled the breath out of Angela Waters' young body with his bare hands. She glanced up at Peterson who was staring at the dead woman as though trying to memorise every sickening detail. Geraldine followed his gaze. At twenty-two Angela Waters looked about twelve. Her long blonde hair appeared natural but looking closely Geraldine saw the roots were dark. The dead girl had probably been a natural blonde who'd turned mousy as she grew up. She had heavy lidded blue eyes, a turned up nose and thin lips. In death, she'd acquired an ethereal quality, her skin implausibly pale above livid bruising on her jaw and neck.

Geraldine turned her attention to the pathologist. His eyes met hers above his mask, sharp yet compassionate.

'We know she was twenty-two,' he began, 'but physically she appears younger, slightly malnourished.'

'Anorexic?' Geraldine asked.

'Bulimic. You can see the discoloration on her finger joints.' He raised one of the dead girl's hands. 'See this rough skin on her knuckles, from making herself vomit.

Teeth are discoloured and beginning to decalcify. There are erosions and inflammation in the lining of the lower oesophagus.'

Geraldine heard Peterson groan softly but she didn't look up. She was focusing on what the pathologist was saying. At the same time, she was recording his voice. A copy of his detailed written report would lack the immediacy of his live commentary. In any case, Geraldine liked to record her own responses at the time. It helped her build a picture of what had happened.

'She's just a kid,' Peterson muttered behind his mask. Angela Waters had not been much younger than the DS, but she looked like a child.

'She was grabbed by the arms,' the doctor pointed to bruising on the dead girl's lower arms, 'and her wrists were secured.'

'Was something used to tie them?'

The doctor shook his head. 'Difficult to say. It's possible.'

'Do you think her attacker could've held her wrists together behind her back with one hand?'

He nodded. 'It's possible,' he said again. 'A man with large hands. She's got skinny wrists. They've been crushed together quite violently. It's possible.' He moved round the table to the victim's head. 'A hand over her mouth,' he indicated bruising on her jaw.

'One hand holding her arms behind her back, the other over her mouth,' Geraldine repeated.

'Bastard,' Peterson said vehemently.

'Strong and fairly large, I'd say,' Geraldine went on purposefully.

'She was dragged along the ground,' the doctor continued.

'Before she died?'

'Yes. There are scratches and grazes here, on the back of her legs. We found a thread under the nail of her right thumb,' the doctor went on. Geraldine looked up at him quickly. 'She seems to have managed to wriggle one hand out from beneath her. This little finger broke when she tried to grab onto something, probably after she was thrown to the ground.'

Geraldine tried to picture the scene in her head. Probably tall and certainly strong, the killer would have crouched down as he pulled the struggling girl into the bushes, her legs dragging along the ground. She must have reached out in panic with the one hand she managed to free when he seized her throat.

'You're saying they've found a thread from his clothes?' Peterson asked, excited. Geraldine waited.

'It's a cheap dark grey fabric, 75% polyester, 25% viscose. The sort of stuff you might find lining an anorak, or it could have come from a scarf or woollen gloves.'

'Any indication where it's from? Any traces of sweat or—'

The doctor interrupted him. 'Nothing so far. No blood. It's pretty old, that's all the initial analysis showed. Could be second hand. It was only one thread of fluff.' He shrugged apologetically. 'And there's nothing to prove it came from the killer.'

'You don't think it could've caught under her nail before the attack?' the sergeant asked.

Millard shrugged. 'There's no way of knowing.'

'Fuck,' Peterson burst out. The explosive syllable reverberated in the sterile air.

'There's more,' the doctor said, ignoring the interruption. Geraldine looked at him again. 'There are indications of physical abuse. A cracked rib,' he pointed at the right side of her chest, 'she's had a broken wrist, and there are scars from old cigarette burns.' He indicated several small marks on her shoulder and abdomen.

'How recent were these injuries?'

The doctor hesitated. 'In the past year or so, perhaps. I'm

afraid I can't be more specific. I doubt if these injuries were accidental, but they may have no bearing on the cause of death.'

'Then again, they may have,' Peterson replied grimly. Geraldine was silent. She was thinking about Angela Waters' attacker. He was probably tall, with big hands. He was wearing an old anorak with a dark grey fleecy lining, or a grey scarf. She frowned. It wasn't much, but it didn't sound like Johnny Drew.

11

Neighbours

Most of the shops below the flats where Angela Waters had lived with Johnny Drew were boarded up. Carter and Black were working their way through the others. They peered through the grimy window of an abandoned printers where a few broken shelves hung from metal struts on the walls. A pile of unopened mail lay inside the door, gathering dust. Apart from that the interior was bare. On the other side of the stairs leading up to Drew's flat a narrow florist's was more of a corridor than a shop premises. There wasn't enough room for two people to stand side by side between shelves of dreary plants without being poked by a protruding stick or frond. Everything looked neglected. A young girl with dark hair stood chewing gum behind a short counter at the far end of the shop. She stared at them blankly when the DI held out his warrant card.

'Do you know a woman called Angela Waters, lives upstairs?' Carter asked her.

'Knew her,' the girl answered. 'Dead, isn't she?'

'How do you know that?'

The girl jerked her head upwards. 'Told me, didn't he? Johnny. You lot ought to fuck off. Leave him in peace. Stop pestering him. You got no right.' She seemed faintly animated.

'How well do you know John Drew?' Black asked her. She shrugged and said nothing. He repeated the question with an exaggerated show of patience.

'Who says I know him?'

The DS sighed. 'You said he told you about Angela Waters. So, how well did you know him?'

The girl frowned. 'Customer,' she said. 'Comes in here, buys flowers on his way home.'

'Was he a regular customer?' Carter asked.

She nodded. 'One of the best, he is.'

'Do you know why he bought flowers? Was he feeling guilty about something? Did he and his girlfriend argue much?'

The girl shrugged. 'How should I know? He bought flowers, that's all I know. Perhaps he likes flowers. That's what I do, I sell flowers. I'm not a fucking mind reader. And I don't go round snooping on people.' She gave them a filthy look. Even if she knew something that might help their enquiry, she wasn't likely to talk to the police. All the same, Carter put his card on her grubby counter.

'If you think of anything that might help us—' he began.

'Fuck off, pig,' she cut in. She picked up the card and flicked it onto the floor, glaring at him as she did so. The card landed by Black's feet. Neither of the detectives bent down to retrieve it.

They climbed the dank concrete stairs and tried the flats on either side of Johnny Drew's. No one was in at number 15. A woman came to the door of number 14. She stared at them with the same glassy expression as the girl in the flower shop had worn. A man's voice yelled from somewhere inside the flat.

'Is it Billy?'

'Nah,' she called back over her shoulder.

'Do you live here?' Black asked.

'What's it to you?' She began to close the door. Carter showed her his warrant card. She barely glanced at it. 'It's the filth,' she shouted. From behind her came sounds of swearing, shuffling and thumping.

'We'd like to ask you a few questions about one of your next door neighbours,' Carter said.

'It's about them next door,' the woman called out. A man in a grubby white vest appeared in the hallway behind her, scowling. Carter explained they were making enquiries about John Drew who lived at number 14a.

'What you want to come bothering us for then?' the man demanded. 'Ask them next door.' He pushed past the woman. 'What you want to talk to them for, Cindy?' He shouted as he slammed the door.

Carter shrugged. 'There's something they're not telling us,' he said quietly.

'Something? They didn't tell us anything,' Black replied. He looked fed up. 'This is a complete waste of time. People who live on an estate like this are never going to tell us anything.'

'I grew up in a place like this,' Carter told him evenly.

'You ought to know then,' Black replied. Carter didn't respond; nothing seemed to rile him.

Cindy at number 14 turned on her partner as soon as the door closed on the two detectives.

'You could've told them, Jeff.'

'Told them what?' He scratched his chest through his vest and yawned.

'About him next door, that Johnny.'

'What about him?'

'About his hitting her.' Jeff snorted and turned away as she continued her tirade. 'It's not funny. At it all the time, he is. She had a broken arm one time, remember? He done that. And I seen her with a black eye more than once. He's put her in the hospital three times since we been here. It's not right. He shouldn't be allowed to get away with it.'

'So? What's it got to do with me?'

'Well, I just think you could've told them, that's all.'

'What the hell would I want to go and do that for?' he asked. He shuffled back along the hallway to the living room.

Cindy followed him. 'Because he's gone and done it this time, hasn't he?' She raised her voice. 'Why else are the filth coming round here asking questions? Use your loaf. He's topped her this time, for sure.'

'Don't be daft. Where's the remote? And don't you bloody shout at me,' he added, 'or you'll be getting a black eye and all.'

Jeff threw himself into a chair and picked up the remote control. He flicked through channels on the Sky box.

'Now my programme's finished,' he grumbled. 'Bloody filth. They got no right, disturbing decent people. Get us the dope, will you? It's under the floorboard.'

'What's it doing there?'

'I bloody put it there, you daft cow. What did you think I was going to do with it? Wait till they come in for a poke around? You should've told me what they were after straight away.'

Cindy didn't move from the doorway. 'You should've said something,' she repeated stubbornly, folding her arms 'I'm telling you, he done it.'

'Says you. Only you don't know what's happened. You don't know anything for sure. It's all in your mind, that's what. But let's just suppose you *are* right, for once in your life.' He twisted his head round to face her. 'We don't know, mind. We don't even know she's dead. But let's say she is, and it was him done it. He's still going to be living right next door us, all the same. Is that what you want? A murderer,' he said the word in a spooky voice, wriggling his fingers at her, 'living next door to us knowing you told the filth he beat her up. You want to go pointing a finger at that piece of shit? You might as well ask him to put you next on his list. Think of it, he might be right behind you one night, coming up the stairs, nursing a grudge against you. Because he's a nasty piece of work, make no mistake. You don't want to mess with Johnny Drew.'

'We can't just do nothing.' Cindy protested. Jeff stared at the television and she shrugged. 'I'll put the kettle on then, shall I? Poor cow,' she added under her breath. Jeff was right about one thing: Johnny Drew was a piece of shit. Cindy hoped they'd put him behind bars and throw away the key.

12

Pub

Carter and Black went to check out the rest of the shops. The dark-haired girl stared at them balefully from the doorway of the flower shop as they walked down the parade. Next door was a Chinese take-away. The DI brandished a mug shot of Johnny Drew at the girl behind the counter, who looked at it then thrust a menu at them. When Carter displayed his warrant card, the girl nodded and muttered something they couldn't understand. Black showed her a picture of the victim.

'She nice girl.'

'Did you know her?' the DS asked slowly. 'Her name's Angela, Angie.'

'Nice girl,' she grinned at him.

'Come on,' Black urged his companion. 'What's she going to tell us? That Drew liked chop suey?'

'Ah, chop suey, very good. You want order?' The Chinese girl nodded emphatically, and her ponytail bobbed up and down.

Their next stop was a newsagent's. The young man behind the counter peered short-sightedly at Johnny Drew's picture and nodded, rubbing his eyes with the back of his hand.

'Think he lives upstairs somewhere. Drives a flash car. Is that the guy?'

'Have you seen Angela Waters in here?'

'Who?'

'His girlfriend.'

'Sorry, mate. Didn't know he had one. I don't know the geezer. Just seen him around. She gone missing then? I can put a note in the window if you like. No charge seeing as it's police business.'

'No. Thank you, but no.'

A rundown pub on the corner was their last stop. The sergeant raised his eyebrows at the grimy exterior, but cheered up when they went inside. A gas fire with fake coals flickered a welcome in one corner and a warm smell of baking hit them as they reached the bar. A blackboard inside advertised 'Pie and Chips' as the special.

'What sort of pie is it?' Black asked. 'That smell's making me peckish.' He ordered pie and chips twice. Carter showed his ID at the bar and asked about Johnny Drew.

'Johnny Drew? Johnny Drew?' the barman mused aloud. The DI showed him a picture, which he recognised straight away. 'Yeah, I know the guy. Comes in here a lot. You with the drug squad then?'

Carter raised his eyebrows slightly and shook his head. 'We just want to ask a few questions about him, that's all. Did his girlfriend, Angela Waters, come in here with him?'

The barman's eyes opened wide. 'Angela Waters?' he repeated. 'That the girl was killed in the park?'

Carter leaned forward across the bar. 'Where did you hear that?' he asked softly.

All at once the barman was cagey. 'Couldn't say,' he answered, scratching his head. 'Just talk. I hear all sorts, standing here. Tell you what though,' he went on, suddenly inclined to be helpful, 'you might ask old Brian Burrows. He lives next door to Johnny Drew.' He nodded at a man sitting hunched at a corner table by himself. 'He knows most of what's going on round here. Don't believe all his stories though.' He laughed. 'Give him half a chance and he'll be telling you how he won the war single-handed. Won't say which war, mind.'

'Give us two halves and whatever the old guy's drinking,' Carter said. He carried two glasses over to the old man who glared up at him suspiciously from under bushy grey eyebrows. Carter sat on the only free chair at the table. Black pulled another one over.

'Here, what you after?' Brian Burrows asked. Bowed shoulders rose inside his filthy jacket and his head swivelled on his scraggy neck, looking from Carter to Black and back again. The detectives showed him their warrant cards and Black explained the reason for their attention as Carter put a drink in front of the old man. He listened, cupping arthritic fingers round the pint.

'Ah them next door,' he said, nodding his head. 'I been wondering when you lot would come round.'

'You know about Angela Waters?'

The old man tapped the side of his nose with one gnarled finger. 'Enough. I hear them, see. Always raising his voice, he is. And his fists. Oh yes, I hear him knocking her about. He might be small but he's vicious. Give her a black eye once. She said she fell over but I never believed it.' He shook his head knowingly and took a pull at his pint. 'Before that it was a broken arm. Accident prone, they said. Hmph.' He turned to face Carter. 'It's high time you lot did something about it. Noise pollution, that's what it is, all that yelling and screaming. No thought for the neighbours, and the walls as thin as paper. Gone and complained about him, has she? About time too. I would've been down to say something myself, only he's a right nasty one, that Johnny Drew. I wouldn't want to get on the wrong side of him. She should leave him. Young girl like that.' He shook his head. 'You ought to lock him up. Do us all a favour. Give us a bit of peace and quiet.'

The food arrived and Carter waited until the barman had gone. Black cut hungrily into his pie as the DI resumed. 'Mr …?'

'Burrows. Brian Burrows.' He watched the sergeant eating. 'You going to eat that or what?' he asked suddenly, indicating the DI's untouched plate. Carter sighed. He slid the plate across the table to the old man who tucked in eagerly. 'Do a nice pie here,' he said, his mouth full.

'Mr Burrows. I'm afraid Angela Waters is dead.'

'Dead? How did that happen then?' The DI gave a brief explanation and the old man nodded his head, still eating. 'Was him, mark my words. He'll tell you was an accident but he done it. It's as plain as anything.' Carter thanked Mr Burrows for his help and asked him if he would make a statement. The old man hesitated. A forkful of pie hovered in the air. 'All depends,' he said, casting a shrewd glance at Carter.

'On what, Mr Burrows?'

'On who would be moving in next door if he went down. I could be out the frying pan into the fire, couldn't I? Can't blame me for wanting to feel safe in my own home. I'm entitled, after all I done.' He nodded solemnly and shovelled another forkful of pie into his mouth.

PART 2

'Computers are useless. They can only give you answers.'
Pablo Picasso

13

Home

Carter caught up with Geraldine as she was about to leave and she agreed to join him for a drink before setting off home. Several of the team were already in the pub across the road from the police station. Merton was at the bar with Kathryn Gordon, who was buying a round. Peterson and Sarah Mellor were with them. Geraldine recalled hearing that the DCI had a reputation for 'drinking with the lads.' Here in the pub she looked comfortable and ebullient, a different person to the dour officer running the investigation. Her eyes smiled above cheeks that seemed less drawn. Even her hair, slightly unkempt, framed her face more softly. Everyone appeared relaxed apart from Merton, who always looked gloomy. He stood beside the DCI, tall and skinny, with an absurd potbelly. Geraldine joined the group. They were discussing the case in subdued tones.

'We'll certainly keep the pressure on the boyfriend,' the DCI was saying.

'Geraldine, let's catch up,' Carter suggested. He steered her over to a corner of the bar and smiled easily at her, his tone avuncular. 'We haven't had a chance for a proper talk. How've you been?' Meeting his sympathetic gaze, she was tempted to answer honestly and tell him how isolated she felt in her tidy flat. Carter was a good listener who had offered her consistent support as her mentor.

'I'm fine,' she replied.

'And how's that lawyer of yours? Mark, is it?'

'Not mine any more.' She looked down, vexed that she still found it difficult to talk about the break up.

Carter knew her too well – or perhaps not well enough – to let it go at that. 'Difficult break up?' he asked gently and she nodded. Geraldine stared at her glass, unable to meet his gaze. For a panicky instant, she was afraid her self control might slip, but she gulped at her drink and the moment passed.

'He walked out,' she confided and was surprised at how easily the words formed on her lips. She could have been talking about the weather. 'He met someone else,' she added and understood with a rush of emotion that it wasn't easy after all. 'He said—' She took a deep breath. 'He said I was married to my work.' She forced a laugh. 'How's your family?'

Carter nodded to acknowledge the change of subject and supped his pint, smacking his lips in satisfaction. 'Jenny's finished university now,' he said. He took another pull at his pint and stared at the pitted surface of the wooden bar as though trying to decipher a message in the scratches. 'She's nearly twenty-two.' The spectre of Angela Waters hovered between them. The DCI's laughter interrupted Carter's reverie and he raised his head. 'Kathryn Gordon's a bloody good detective,' he said. Geraldine nodded but before she could reply, a shadow fell across them.

'Cosy,' Merton commented, glancing from Carter to Geraldine.

Carter gave him a nod. 'Mine's a pint, you miserable sod.'

'Actually, I was just leaving,' Geraldine said.

'You haven't finished your drink,' Merton said. He made it sound like an accusation.

Geraldine shrugged and moved along to rejoin the group gathered around the DCI. Reaching her colleagues, she half turned and caught sight of Carter talking to Merton before her attention was caught by the discussion at the bar.

'He's the most likely,' Peterson was saying in an undertone and she guessed they were still talking about John Drew. Several other officers nodded their agreement. John Drew was automatically a suspect. Geraldine wondered aloud if a man accustomed to hitting out in anger would approach a girl from behind and strangle her.

'It's all violence, gov,' Peterson replied. Geraldine said she thought Drew would have been more likely to pummel Angela to death, or shove her down the stairs.

'More his style,' she concluded.

'There aren't any stairs in their flat,' Peterson pointed out. 'He's the most likely suspect. If you ask me,' he added quietly, glancing around the assembled officers, 'we ought to be pulling him in.'

'We've got no proof,' the DCI pointed out.

'How much proof do you need? He was violent. She never reported him, but you saw the previous injuries, ma'am. It must've been him. Why else would she have kept it to herself? That sort of abuse doesn't end with a picnic in the park.' Peterson made no attempt to conceal his impatience. 'I think we should bring him in.'

'It doesn't matter what we think,' Kathryn Gordon replied, 'or even what we know. Without evidence, our hands are tied. Any case will be thrown out before we even get started.'

'But the PM shows severe physical abuse over a period of time, ma'am. We can't ignore that. Surely that's our evidence, ma'am. It's staring us in the face.'

'You may be right, but this is all speculation. Any defence counsel would ride a coach and horses through it. Whatever we think, we're not the jury. And even if we establish he was violent, that doesn't prove he killed her. We need more than that. We need incontrovertible proof.'

A group of men came into the pub. The officers fell silent and drifted away to gather in small clusters round corner tables where they continued their discussion in low tones, leaning across their pints to hear each other speak.

'One for the road, gov?' Peterson asked. Geraldine shook her head. The pub felt stuffy and she was tired. It was a relief to step outside into the cool of the evening. She took a few deep breaths, trying to relax, but as she drove along dark streets the image of a white corpse kept flitting into her mind, and she was filled with anger. Angela Waters' killer might have been in the pub that evening, laughing with his mates. The DCI was rigorous and demanding, which was encouraging. Carter had worked with her before and he said she was a fine detective. But they still had nothing to go on.

By the time she reached the gate to her block, Geraldine felt completely washed out. She pressed the button on her remote control and watched the gates whirr open. She drove slowly along the cul de sac where each of the front doors opened on to a small entrance hall to two flats. Geraldine had bought a ground floor flat, the one before last in the row. Access to her garage was at the end of the cul de sac, round the back of the flats. An unofficial one-way system was in operation. Everyone drove up the close to reach their garage, driving out past the garages to the gate. There was a mirror image of the arrangement on the other side of the close; a total of twenty flats. Apart from the electronic entry gates there was no way in to the complex. The far end of the close was inaccessible without climbing over a high perimeter fence. It was a secluded and secure place to live, exactly what Geraldine wanted.

She cruised up the close, thinking about the discussion at the bar that evening, and approached the corner at the end. An untrained eye might have overlooked a motionless silhouette lurking in the shadow of the fence. Not yet familiar with her surroundings, she almost missed the figure as she drove past. She shook her head and carried on round the corner, locked her garage firmly and hurried through the back entrance to the building. The narrow passageway inside was eerily silent and she felt nervous, relieved to lock her front door behind her.

Geraldine only realised how exhausted she was when she kicked off her shoes and sat down. Too tired to mess about in the kitchen, she grabbed a hunk of bread and cheese and settled down with a stack of paperwork: reports to read, statements to study, files to scan through. In addition, she wanted to know all about the area where the murder had taken place.

Woolsmarsh was a town of contrasts. On the East side a neglected estate festered. Built in the sixties to house employees of a local ready-mix concrete plant, using raw materials from the gravel quarries South West of Canterbury, when the plant had closed down a generation later, those who hadn't moved from the area to find work had gravitated to the Chartwell Estate where prostitution and drug trafficking rapidly became endemic. To the West a very different picture emerged. Bordering an exclusive golf club, the only estates in the West were those belonging to wealthy individual households.

It was late when Geraldine finally undressed and fell into bed. She was worn out but slept fitfully, disturbed by images of Angela Waters. When she woke up she realised that the face of the body on the mortuary table in her dream had been her own.

14

Facts

There was a buzz of activity in the Incident Room as Geraldine went to her desk the following morning. She paused by the Incident Board to see what information had been added overnight. The board was tidy, everything presented in neat lists below the pictures, with arrows to indicate connections.

Carter came over and stood beside her. 'The Chief's a stickler for neatness,' he said and Geraldine murmured in agreement. 'And punctuality,' he added. Before Geraldine could reply, Kathryn Gordon swept into the room. Geraldine propped herself against her desk and focused on the DCI. Geraldine imagined the hardiest of villains might quake before Gordon's penetrating gaze. The genial woman of the previous evening had retreated once more behind a rigid mask, her hair a grey helmet, her eyes harsh slits. Geraldine felt immensely reassured that the investigation was in safe hands, but her optimism faded as Kathryn Gordon began to speak.

'We've got a series of negatives so far,' she said. 'Forensics haven't come up with anything new. The initial post-mortem report reiterates what we already know. We've found nothing at the site. No one's seen anything, and no one unusual's been spotted loitering in the park.' Geraldine glanced around. Everyone's eyes were fixed on the DCI apart from a constable who was busily making notes. 'We're probably looking for someone with a record. So far no one

local seems to fit the bill but according to one of the neighbours the boyfriend, John Drew, has a history of violence.'
She pointed to his name on the board and Carter related
what Brian Burrows had told them over a pie and a pint.

'I hear him knocking her about,' Carter read aloud, in a
passable imitation of a local accent. Someone giggled and
instantly fell silent. If the accent was amusing, the statement
wasn't. 'He gave her a black eye. She said she fell over but
I never believed it. Before that it was a broken arm. They
said she was accident prone.' Carter looked up. 'When we
told him Angela Waters was dead, he said he was convinced
John Drew had killed her.' A muted murmur hummed
around the room although no one appeared to be talking.

'This is all hearsay from a neighbour, quite possibly with
a grudge. We've had no other reports of Drew being violent
towards the victim.' As Kathryn Gordon spoke, the room fell
instantly silent. 'But for now John Drew is our main suspect.
Our only suspect so far.' She tapped at his weaselly face on
the board. 'The boyfriend. What about his alibi?' Carter
nodded at Black.

'He was at work,' Black said. 'No one saw him leaving
but no one saw him not leaving.' There were a few stifled
sniggers.

'Don't waste our time, Sergeant,' the DCI barked.

Unperturbed, the DS tried again. 'They didn't see him
leave and thought he was there the whole morning. But they
wouldn't swear to it.'

'What about the suspect?' Kathryn Gordon asked, turning
to Geraldine.

'He said he was at work all morning.'

'What was your impression? What did you think of him?'

'He's nasty enough, but I think he was telling the truth. I
don't think he killed her.' Kathryn Gordon nodded, studying
Geraldine's face.

After the briefing, tasks were allocated for the day. They

were spreading the net, looking for someone with a record, burrowing into John Drew's past, and finding out what they could about Angela Waters' short life. As Geraldine went over to check her schedule for the day, Merton approached her.

'Boss wants a word,' he said. Geraldine nodded to show she'd heard and made her way over to the DCI's office. Having been summoned, Geraldine tapped at the closed door and went straight in.

'Knock and wait for an answer before you come barging in,' Kathryn Gordon snapped. Geraldine hurried to comply. She wondered how Kathryn Gordon would react to a serious oversight and resolved to tread very carefully.

'John Drew,' Kathryn Gordon said when she'd summoned Geraldine back in. 'You don't think he's our killer, do you?' She leaned forward on her desk and listened intently as Geraldine explained her reasoning. 'It seems highly likely that he was responsible for some, or all, of the physical abuse the victim suffered before she died,' the DCI pointed out when Geraldine had finished.

'But we shouldn't assume—' Geraldine began.

'We should never assume,' Kathryn Gordon interrupted her. The two women's eyes met in a brief flicker of under-standing. Under pressure to achieve results, it was all too easy to jump to conclusions, as Peterson seemed to have done. 'Close the door on your way out, will you?' the DCI dismissed Geraldine.

'Yes ma'am.'

It was only a matter of hours since the media had begun to report Angela Waters' death but members of the public had already started phoning in. Additional clerical staff were being drafted in to take the calls. The majority would be spurious but they all had to be checked, all the cranks, the self-proclaimed guilty and the weirdo psychics who could hunt down villains in their dreams. Geraldine applauded Kathryn Gordon's thoroughness but wished she hadn't been given the job of monitoring messages, while they were waiting for more clerical staff to arrive.

The weekly *Woolsmarsh Chronicle* had come out that morning. Angela Waters' murder dominated the front page, which meant there would be a spate of calls. There was a small article in the nationals, briefly stating that a woman's body had been found. The local paper was more sensational. 'STRANGLER STALKS THE STREETS' the headline screamed on the front page, with several striking subheadings, including: 'CHILD FINDS BODY'. Geraldine scanned the article, frowning.

The police have launched a massive manhunt for the killer of blonde 22-year-old Angela Waters whose body was discovered in Lyceum Park by 4-year-old Sophie (*pictured below*). Emergency services were immediately alerted following a 999 call made by the children's mother. The park is still cordoned off this morning with officers in attendance. A post-mortem examination is expected to confirm that the victim was attacked in the park in broad daylight. Detective Chief Inspector Catherine Gordon, who is leading the investigation, said: 'This was a vicious assault and my team are working tirelessly to discover the identity of the killer as quickly as possible. We are currently following several leads.'

Geraldine turned from the pile of newspaper reports and picked up a tape. She knew that the smallest of details might prove crucial and was determined to be vigilant, but her heart sank as she listened to a woman's pathetic attempt to implicate her neighbour. The next caller accused his estranged wife.

My wife Jeanie hates blondes. I like blondes, see? The point is, Jeanie hates my girlfriend because she's a natural blonde. And that girl who was murdered, she was blonde too. You thinking what I'm thinking? Only I wouldn't put anything past Jeanie.

There were several messages from worried parents, and a call from a landlady whose tenant had disappeared.

I'm worried about my lodger. He's such a nice quiet man, on account of his speech impediment. He's not been back since Wednesday, so I thought the Woolsmarsh Strangler might've got him. Do you think I should let the room to someone else?

Then came a Mr Jack Ripper.

You'll never catch me. I'm Jack the Ripper. You didn't catch me last time and you won't catch me this time. Jack the Ripper. Remember the name.

Geraldine spent most of the morning listening to messages. For a break, she tried to read through statements from people who knew John Drew, but she couldn't settle. With an impatient sigh, she gathered up all her paperwork and deposited it in her drawer, which she closed with a bang. Turning to a new page in her notebook, she tried to think logically. Facts, she told herself, frustrated at having spent most of the morning listening to phone calls. Facts. She wrote the word in capitals at the top of the page, stared at it for a second then tore the page out, screwed it up and chucked it at the bin. Facts weren't enough. What was the point of listing what she already knew? It was all there in her head. She'd seen investigations held up by a colleague getting a fixed idea, which turned out to be a blind alley. The important thing was to keep an open mind and be prepared to change her internal account of events in an instant. But she had to have that inner vision directing her search.

The facts needed to solve a case might be staring them all in the face, but that was useless if no one had the wit to put them together so they pointed in the right direction. Geraldine was as dedicated to gathering information as anyone else, but she was driven by intuition. Not everyone appreciated that one didn't exclude the other. In her previous case, she'd spent hours trawling through reports. Only by memorising all the statements about a suspect who'd been cleared, and returning to question him again, had she picked up one possible inconsistency in his account.

'You did well to spot that,' her DCI had admitted with grudging admiration. 'What made you go back and inter-view him again?'

Geraldine had shrugged, embarrassed by the praise and the question. 'I just had a feeling something wasn't right, sir.'

The DCI had scowled at her reply. 'Don't waste time on airy-fairy hunches. The key to success is sheer slog, Geraldine, sheer slog and hard evidence. Fancy ideas can lead you up the garden path. You can waste a lot of valuable time following hunches, Geraldine,' he'd warned her adding, more gently, 'and they can get you into hot water if you're wrong.'

Geraldine sighed, opened her notebook, and began again. Everything pointed to John Drew. The report from Carter and Black had been interesting, alleging that Drew had been violent towards his girlfriend. The post-mortem confirmed the victim had sustained severe injuries in the past. The waitress at Bella Café hadn't mentioned anything about a black eye, but Angela had only been working there for just over six months. It was feasible that Drew had slipped away from the Honda show room, driven into town, killed his girl friend, and returned to work without anyone noticing. A DC had driven from the Honda showroom to Lyceum Park and back again in just over forty minutes. The whole exercise could have been accomplished in less than an hour. But she found it difficult to believe Drew had dreamed up such a farfetched plan, and even less likely that he'd met Angela by chance in the park in the middle of a working day.

Geraldine sighed and stared at her notes. It still struck her as improbable that Drew would have attacked his girlfriend in a public place when there was considerable risk of discovery. People often walked their dogs in the park, or jogged there, even in the rain. The body had been dragged into the bushes which afforded some cover, but the initial assault on the path would have been visible from several directions.

'In any case,' she argued with Peterson as they sat over a coffee in the canteen, 'how would Drew have known where she was at the precise time he arrived back in Woolsmarsh?'

'He might've followed her.'

'Not if he was driving back from Honda's. And why follow her to the park and kill her there? It's a risky place. Someone might've seen them. He could've taken her anywhere.'

'He would have wanted to kill her away from their flat, somewhere anyone could've done it,' Peterson said, but he agreed the exposed location suggested an unpremeditated attack. However, if John Drew had driven all the way back from work to kill Angela Waters, he must have had a plan in mind.

Drew remained their only suspect. They'd ruled out Umberto. Christina confirmed he'd been in the café all morning.

'Unless they're providing an alibi for each other,' Geraldine suggested, but neither she nor Peterson believed Angela Waters had discovered Umberto's irregular tax records, threatened to expose him, and been strangled by her boss to keep her quiet. To make sure, Geraldine had asked

Sarah Mellor to check their bank statements. No money had unaccountably left Umberto's account and his lifestyle hadn't changed. Maybe his books *had* been fiddled, but no one had been blackmailing him.

The DCI had Merton and Carter checking hostels, looking for someone with a record, but the boyfriend remained the most likely suspect. If he was guilty, Geraldine was confident they would wear him down, but she felt uneasy. She couldn't overlook his anguished protest, when they'd interviewed him the day after Angela Waters' death. That was the main problem: there seemed no obvious motive for John Drew to have planned to kill his girlfriend.

Back at her desk, Geraldine took out her notebook, then closed it with a sigh and shoved it angrily back into her bag. She knew they had to be patient, but it was hard to relax with Angela Waters' killer loose on the streets. She could have driven behind him that morning on her way to work, caught a glimpse of him standing at a bus stop, or walked past him on her way to the pub the previous evening. They didn't know who he was. He could be anywhere.

15

Suspect

By lunchtime they had made no progress. There were more inane calls from the public, including several from concerned mothers.

My daughter's gone out and she should've been home over an hour ago. Do you think something's happened to her? Oh, hold on, I can hear her now.

Nonetheless, Geraldine listened to the whole tape of messages, afraid she might miss a clue to the killer's identity.

That afternoon, the DCI decided to bring John Drew in and 'have another go,' as Peterson put it. Pleased to leave her desk, Geraldine led the way up the stale smelling concrete stairs. This time they didn't find the suspect alone. He peered round the door wearing nothing but a crumpled T-shirt and boxers and protested loudly when they pushed past him to see the dark-haired girl from the flower shop lying sleepy-eyed on the sofa, naked above the waist, her short denim skirt hitched up her thighs. Angela Waters' boyfriend hadn't wasted any time finding comfort in his loss.

'What do you want?' he growled.

'Get dressed, Mr Drew,' Peterson replied. 'We're taking a trip to the station. We'd like to ask you a few more questions.' The girl rose unsteadily to her feet, tugging at her skirt. She yanked a dirty T-shirt over her head.

'You arresting me?' Johnny Drew demanded.

'You arresting him or what?' the girl repeated sullenly. Her speech was slurred.

'Shut it, Millie,' Drew snarled. She hung her head, glaring up at the detectives through her dark fringe.

'You arresting me then or what?' He struck a defiant pose, legs apart, hands on hips.

'We'll arrest you for wasting our time, if you don't get dressed now,' the DS answered.

'Beat it, Millie,' Drew shouted over his shoulder as he disappeared into the bedroom, muttering about privacy, Peterson on his heels. The girl slammed the front door so hard the windows shook.

The suspect sulked in the car all the way to the station.

In the interview room, Peterson went in hard. 'You like beating up girls, don't you? It gives you a kick. That's right, isn't it? Makes you feel powerful.'

Drew wasn't cowed. 'What's it to you?' he countered, gazing levelly at the DS. 'None of your fucking business, that's what. I want a lawyer.' He leaned back in his chair, folded his arms and stared at Peterson. They left him to kick his heels while they sorted out a brief. Once they reassembled, Peterson resumed. Geraldine felt confident that if Drew *was* guilty the sergeant would crack him, but she wasn't convinced they had the right man.

'You were telling us how much you enjoy beating up girls, Johnny.'

'So? If a girl needs a bit of a slap now and again, what's it to you? Some women like a bit of rough.' He tried to wink at Geraldine but they could see he was scared. Too clever to deny that he'd raised his hand to Angela, Geraldine thought he must surely be too smart to risk discovery by attacking his own girl friend in broad daylight in public. She didn't feel comfortable with this line of enquiry.

'A bit of a slap?' Peterson was saying. 'A broken rib, a

broken arm. You think some women like that, do you? How would you like it?'

'Accidents. She fell and no one can tell you any different.' Drew flapped his hand dismissively but he was riled.

'Lose your temper a lot, do you, Johnny?' Peterson asked.

'Only with filth like you,' Drew countered.

'What about your girlfriend's black eye, Johnny? Was that an accident too?'

'She fell over,' Drew repeated stubbornly, his temper under control again. 'Look,' he said, sitting up suddenly. 'So there was maybe the odd time I raised my hand to her. But not as often as she'd have liked. She asked for it. I'm only human.' He appealed to Peterson. 'Don't tell me you've never been provoked, Sergeant? You know how a woman can get you all worked up. And Angie knew how to aggravate. It wasn't like she didn't know exactly what she was doing. She knew what was coming, but she never let up. I'd warn her.' He shrugged. 'Don't ask me why she kept on at me. You know how it is, Sergeant. What's a man to do? Then it'd be all tears and snuffling and apologies.' He didn't clarify who had apologised to whom and for what. The solicitor whispered in Drew's ear and the suspect nodded and shut up.

Geraldine glanced down at the report from Rotherhithe. The local CID had traced Angela's mother. Mrs Phelps no longer had any contact with her daughter. At fifteen, Angela Waters had run away from home when her mother remarried. Mrs Phelps had no idea where her daughter was living, and didn't care. It was a squalid but familiar story. Angela's father was an alcoholic who used to beat his wife and small daughter viciously. He'd made no attempt to find them when his wife had packed up and left and they'd never heard from him again. After that, Mandy Phelps had drifted from one violent partner to another.

'We heard you argued a lot with Angela,' Peterson said.

'Who? Me and Ange?' Drew threw back his head and

laughed. 'Don't give me that. Where did you hear that then? From the neighbours? Those walls are thin as paper. What did they hear then? What specifically did they hear? Interfering bastards. Ought to mind their own fucking business.' There was a pause. He seemed to have regained his confidence. 'No one heard me and Ange arguing. Couldn't have. She had a really quiet voice. No one told you that, did they?' He snorted. 'They couldn't say for sure it was me and Ange, could they?' He glanced at the solicitor sitting silently at his side. 'What they heard was shouting off the telly, that's what. She used to love her soaps, Ange did. That must be what they heard. We never argued. Not me and Ange. She wouldn't argue. Wasn't her style. You didn't know her.'

'She wouldn't answer back in case she got a beating?'

Drew glanced at his brief again. 'I never beat her, right? Like I told you, maybe a bit of a slap now and again, when she asked for it. That's all. Some women like a man to be in charge, you know what I mean. But she wouldn't have stuck with me if she didn't like it. Stands to reason.'

'Only it got a bit out of hand, that last time, didn't it, Johnny?' the sergeant persisted, getting nowhere.

Drew was all arrogance again. 'What are you on about now? You know you've got nothing on me. Nothing better to do than harass an innocent bloke who's lost his girlfriend. Kick a man when he's down, why don't you? How's that for abuse?' The lawyer sat mute. Drew turned his attention back to Peterson. 'This is harassment. I ought to complain about you, Detective Sergeant.'

'You went too far, didn't you?' Peterson pressed on. Geraldine could hear the exasperation in his voice but Drew was a cool customer. 'It was more than just a slap wasn't it? You didn't mean to kill her, did you? What happened, Johnny? Did she struggle? Fight back this time? Enough to provoke anyone, isn't it?'

Drew stood up suddenly. 'I've had enough of your

fucking crap, Sergeant. Are you going to charge me or what? I told you, I was working on Wednesday. Ask anyone. There's no way I touched her. You're barking up the wrong tree, and it's doing my head in. You should be out there, looking for the bastard that killed her, not hassling me.'

'Why did you do it, Johnny?' Peterson asked.

'I keep telling you, I never done it.' Drew rolled his eyes.

'*WHY*?' Geraldine wrote on her piece of paper, frowning.

Peterson persisted, but it was clear they were making no headway. In the end, even the sergeant had to concede they had nothing on Drew, and they let him go. He darted out of the door like a rat out of a trap.

'Now where's he off to in such a hurry?' Peterson wondered aloud.

Johnny ran out of the police station as though a bomb was about to explode. Back on the street, he slowed down with an effort. He needed something to calm his nerves. His heart was thumping; he could hear it pounding in his ears. He slipped along an alley and reached the pub by an indirect route. No one was tailing him but he was jumpy as hell after the day he'd just had. He was taking no chances, not with the filth on his case. He sat hunched over a pint in a dark corner of the pub, waiting. As soon as his dealer arrived, Johnny slunk over. The dealer never hung around for long. He looked up but didn't invite Johnny to join him. His eyes flicked round nervously. He could tell something was wrong.

'I just seen you, Johnny, legging it out of the cop shop.' His voice was low and angry. 'What's going on? You got a problem or what?'

'No,' Johnny was quick to reassure him. 'Not a problem, exactly.'

'What then?'

'Well, yeah, in a way. I had to flush the gear down the

kazi.' The dealer frowned as Johnny perched on the edge of a chair.

'What the fuck you gone and done that for?' the dealer's eyes were restless, skimming round the bar.

'Had a visit, didn't I?'

'Shit.' The dealer wasn't laughing any more. His posture shifted as his legs tensed under the table. 'Busted?'

Johnny stared at him, wondering what he'd brought. He shook his head. 'Nothing like that. It wasn't a bust.'

'What then?' The dealer was losing interest in Johnny. His eyes continually browsed around to see who else was in the pub.

Johnny explained. He'd been at home, all set, his gear laid out ready, when he'd heard a loud banging at his door. Looking out he'd seen two of them on his doorstep. 'Filth.'

'What they come for, if it wasn't a bust?' The dealer narrowed his eyes.

'You're all right. I flushed it away like I said. Only I needn't have bothered. It wasn't the drug squad.' He looked down. 'It's Angie. Some bastard done her in.' The dealer stared at him. Johnny made a whishing noise and pulled his hand across his throat.

'They think it was you what done it?' the dealer asked. He was interested now.

Johnny shrugged miserably. 'What do you think? She was all right, my Ange. She was a good kid.' He sighed. 'So, what you got? I don't suppose you could do us a discount, seeing as it's the second time this week. It's been a bloody nightmare. I can't believe I panicked like that. Good gear too.'

'Only the best.' The dealer agreed. He considered. 'Shame about Angie,' he said at last. 'She was a good kid.'

'Yeah.'

'Still, least it wasn't Ballard's mob,' the dealer added.

'Yeah, that's one good thing, I suppose. It wasn't Ballard's lot. They wouldn't have found anything, mind. I flushed it all away.'

'Those bastards always find something,' the dealer told him. 'Even if they have to bring it themselves. Special delivery. You know that. How's about you get us a pint, then?'

Johnny grinned in relief. 'We're all right then, are we?'

'Sure thing. It's not your fault the filth come calling. Only you should lay low till it's blown over. Because they'll be back. You can count on it. Once they get hold of you, there's no knowing when they're going to stop poking their fucking noses in. Best to lie low, is my advice.'

Johnny swallowed nervously. 'I'll be fine. They won't be back. Honest. They're done with me. So what you got for me?'

The dealer stood up. 'See you around some time, Johnny,' he said softly, moving away.

'What about that pint?' Johnny swore under his breath, furious with the filth for screwing everything up. It wasn't right. Now he needed to score and he was getting the cold shoulder. He spat angrily on the floor.

'Oi!' a voice yelled at him.

'Oh shut it,' he muttered, getting to his feet. 'I'm leaving.'

He called in at the Chinese for a portion of greasy chips on his way back to the flat. He had no Angie to cook dinner for him now. He swore. Angie's death was causing him no end of grief. Back in the flat, he noticed a photo she'd put above the fire. He remembered when they'd taken it, the two of them together on the front at Blackpool the weekend they met. She looked so happy he was startled.

He picked it up and stared at her smiling face. Her long fair hair had fallen across her eyes like a veil. She had a habit of brushing it off her face with the back of her hand. With a curse, Johnny chucked the photograph in the bin. He winced as the glass smashed, and fell to his knees. Carefully he picked at the photograph to extricate it from the cracked frame. A shard of glass slit his finger. He sat back on his heels and stared in dismay at a trickle of blood that slid across the photograph obscuring Angela's smile.

16

Terry

Melanie Rogers flicked her long blonde hair off her face. She was humming, stirring the beans, and didn't hear footsteps creeping up behind her. Suddenly she felt arms around her, squeezing all the breath out of her lungs.

'Stop it, Terry!' she squealed. 'You nearly made me spill it!'

'Give us a kiss then,' Terry laughed, nuzzling her neck with questing lips. Melanie enjoyed cooking for Terry in his grotty little kitchen. The first time, she'd experimented with a Gordon Ramsey recipe. Her cherry and port sauce had turned out perfectly but Terry had toyed with it and asked if she couldn't cook normal food.

'What do you like then?' She'd tried not to look crestfallen.

'Apart from you?'

She'd giggled. 'You know what I mean.'

'How can I think about food when you're here? But give me sausage and mash any day.' Melanie didn't mind. Simple food was a lot easier to prepare. It left more time for the bedroom.

Melanie's parents had never thought much of Terry. In the end, it was their disapproval that had prompted her to pack her bags and turn up, uninvited, on his doorstep. Her parents had broached the subject when she got home from work one evening. What had started as a 'quiet word' had quickly escalated into a noisy quarrel until Melanie had driven off in a rage. Throwing her arms around Terry on the doorstep, she hadn't seen his eyes light up when he caught sight of her car over her shoulder or heard him whistle under his breath.

'Are you for real?' he'd asked, his eyes on the silver Porsche as he grasped Melanie in a tight embrace. She'd pressed her body against his and smiled.

Melanie loved being with Terry. Her parents' disapproval didn't bother her but she felt let down by her friend Lucy.

'You're moving in with him? You've only just met him. You don't know anything about him, Mel.'

'I know as much as I need to know. You sound like my mother,' Melanie replied crossly. 'And before you ask, no, he doesn't know who my dad is. Seriously, Lucy, you should see him. He's drop dead gorgeous.'

'That's all right then,' Lucy replied and they laughed.

Peter Lamprey, head gardener at Lyceum Park, clicked his tongue disapprovingly on the roof of his mouth. His new assistant, Terry, was late for work again even though the boy only lived a mile or so away. He would have to have words with him. He'd seemed a pleasant enough lad when he'd first come along, but he'd turned out too easygoing for his own good. Peter had seen his type before. He selected a rake, and as he locked the tool shed saw the boy running lightly along the path towards him.

'Sorry I'm late,' the boy panted. He didn't look sorry. 'My alarm didn't go off.'

Peter raised his eyebrows. 'Well you're here now,' he grunted, and unlocked the shed again. 'Wasting my time,' he muttered under his breath. The boy paid no attention. 'Fetch yourself a rake,' Peter said, 'we're collecting leaves. First we'll rake the grass, then you can take the leaf blower to clear the path.'

'Can't I just use the blower?'

Peter shook his head without a word and they set off,

rakes in hand. Rounding a bend in the path, they met a group of girls on their way to school.

'Morning ladies,' Terry called out, with a wink. The girls giggled and simpered. Peter scowled. There was no denying Terry was a handsome boy and he certainly had an eye for the girls. Terry paused in his stride and turned to watch the schoolgirls strutting past.

'He's watching us,' a voice shrilled to a chorus of laughter.

'Come on, get a move on. And make sure you're here on time in future. There's more than enough to do, this time of year.' Peter carried on grumbling as they walked. 'You keep turning up late, you're wasting my time. You listening to me?' He stopped abruptly. Terry carried on walking, oblivious. Peter hurried after him and tapped him sharply on the shoulder. Terry looked round, startled. He pulled tiny earplugs from his ears and drew a small machine from his pocket.

'What do you think?' he asked. 'My girlfriend gave it to me. It's the latest one.'

'What the hell is that then?'

'It's an Iphone. What do you think?'

Peter snorted. 'New fangled gimmick,' he muttered. Peter didn't approve of all those new fiddle faddles. Computers, Ipods, mobile phones, he was having none of it. 'Now you get yourself over to the far side of the lake, and I'll start this end. Break for tea at eleven, and not a moment before.' Peter stood for a moment, watching the boy tramp cheerfully across the muddy grass whistling a jaunty tune. 'He won't last long,' Peter thought to himself. He gave him a month, tops. Gardening was too much like hard work for a loafer like young Terry. He walked around like he owned the park, when he bothered to turn up at all.

It was a bright morning, fresh after an early shower, and the grass seemed to sparkle. Peter gazed around the park, paying no heed to the dratted police who'd erected a tent over the poor dead girl, and were scurrying round it like ants at a sugar lump. The air was growing chilly under a glowering sky. Weathermen were predicting heavy showers but the clouds were too high for rain. Peter paid scant attention to forecasts. He'd spent too many years working outdoors to need some smooth talking git in a fancy suit to tell him what he could see with his own eyes. He scanned the sky and shook his head knowingly. The rain would hold off until nightfall. He checked his watch and scowled. One thing was sure: the boy would turn up when it was time for a break.

He looked round again. On the far side of the lake he saw Terry tramping across the grass. That boy was Trouble, Peter thought grimly. Trouble with a capital T.

'Trouble,' Peter muttered darkly to himself as he began to rake the leaves. 'Nothing but trouble since he came. And never on time.'

17

Secret

Jim stared through the railings and watched the old man as he raked the leaves. There was a young man and an old man. He'd heard them talking and he knew the old man's name was Peter. It didn't mean they were friends, but Jim liked knowing his name. Peter was a friendly name. Jim wanted to speak to Peter. He wanted to tell him they were the same. Jim did his work in the park as well.

Peter put down his rake and started pulling up little plants. He looked around, scowling, but he didn't see Jim watching him from the other side of the fence. Jim wanted to ask Peter why he was pulling up the little plants when it made him angry.

Miss Elsie was worried. 'I'm telling you to keep quiet,' she said.

'I'm only going to be his friend,' Jim told her.

'People like that aren't worth trying to make friends with,' she answered. She was trying to sound kind but he knew she was annoyed. 'Don't even think about him,' Miss Elsie said but Jim took no notice. He closed his eyes.

When Jim looked for him again, Peter had disappeared. He was hiding in the bushes. Jim giggled. He knew that game. He shut his eyes and counted to ten but he didn't go into the park to look for Peter. He was afraid of the policemen guarding the gate, even though he hadn't done anything bad.

'Keep out of trouble,' Miss Elsie warned him and he

nodded. He walked along the pavement beside the park and saw Peter through the trees. He was leaning on his rake, smoking. Jim grinned. He liked cigarettes as well. Now they had two things in common. But Peter wasn't good at hiding. He was standing in the middle of the grass where anyone could find him.

'I can teach him,' Jim suggested. 'I'm good at hiding. I'm the best,' he boasted.

'He doesn't want to play with you,' Miss Elsie said. She sounded sad.

'You don't know that,' Jim answered. Peter looked up, scowling, and Jim stood completely still so Peter wouldn't see him.

Miss Elsie was talking again. Her voice buzzed in his ear. 'You can't make the others be friends with you,' she said. 'You have to be nice to them so they like you.'

'They're not nice to me,' he told her crossly.

'I am,' she said and she smiled.

Peter picked up his rake in both hands, holding his cigarette in the corner of his mouth. Jim watched a thin wisp of smoke curl upwards. It skirted round Peter's eyes without making him blink. Jim wondered how he did that. When they were friends, he was going to ask Peter about it.

Suddenly Peter looked right at him through a gap in the trees. Jim was scared. Miss Elsie began to shout in his ear. He turned and ran along the pavement, away from the policemen, and Peter, away from the park, all the way to the end of the road. He was panting so hard his chest hurt but Miss Elsie wasn't even out of breath.

There were things Miss Elsie didn't know. When he told her she'd be pleased with him. She'd stop telling him what he could and couldn't do. He thought of the girl hiding in the trees and giggled. There was a lot about him Miss Elsie didn't know.

'I've got a secret,' he whispered. She didn't answer. 'With

joy we hail the secret day, which God has called His own,' he sang. He looked for her, but Miss Elsie had gone away.

18

Media

Heather Spencer glanced at her watch. Living so near the school she could hardly arrive late, but there was time to finish her coffee before she left. The local radio station spun its early morning mix of jingles, debt consolidation, world affairs, sport, celebrity hype and the weather. She wasn't listening, but thinking about the day ahead, when the radio suddenly caught her attention.

'... so if you were in the vicinity of Lyceum Park in Woolsmarsh on Wednesday morning, the police would like to hear from you. Now over to Nick for the latest weather report...' Heather frowned. She'd been in the park on Wednesday morning on her way to visit a pupil doing work experience in the music shop, Bretts. She'd missed the beginning of the item on the radio, but whatever it was had nothing to do with her. There were more pressing demands on her time, like what to do with her year nine class who were driving her up the wall. Four weeks until half term, she reminded herself, as she hurried out of the house.

It wasn't until break time that Heather learned what lay behind the police appeal on the radio. When she reached the staff room, she helped herself to coffee and picked up a copy of *The Times* that was lying on the table. The front page reported that world powers were delaying until November any further decision about imposing tougher sanctions on Iran over its controversial nuclear programme. She didn't bother to read the whole article but flicked through the paper. Suddenly a corner headline screamed up at her and she felt the hairs on her arms prickle.

POLICE APPEAL AS WOMAN'S BODY DISCOVERED IN PARK

A park was sealed off yesterday after the discovery of a woman's body. Police were guarding access to a public park in Woolsmarsh as forensic experts examined the area. Detective Chief Inspector Kathryn Gordon, leading the investigation, said the victim had been identified as 22-year-old local resident Angela Waters. A post-mortem examination will take place shortly. 'We cannot speculate on the cause of death. However, at this time the death is being treated as suspicious. Lyceum Park is a popular park that is generally busy, especially with people walking their dogs or passing through. We would like anyone who has been in the park to come forward as they may have unwittingly seen or heard something that may be of importance to this inquiry. We are particularly interested to hear from anyone who was in the area on Wednesday morning.'

Beneath the article was a small blurred picture of a girl with long blonde hair. Heather saw the paper quivering and put it down quickly. It was none of her business, she told herself, but she knew she'd been crossing the park just before ten on Wednesday morning. Did that make her a witness? An image flashed into her mind of the odd-looking man she'd encountered on the path. She wondered if she should go to the police, but was reluctant to get involved. She didn't want to waste police time.

All afternoon Heather was distracted. While she'd been in the park, struggling to control her umbrella, had another struggle been taking place only a few feet away from her?

'Get a grip,' she told herself sharply, and, when that didn't help, she tried being kind. 'Hang on in there. It's nearly four o'clock.'

Heather had never been inside a police station before. She hesitated outside the square brick building with its elegant blue signs that reminded her of Victorian gas lamps. She expected to see people rushing along corridors, as they did on The Bill, and was surprised to find it hushed inside, like a library. A solitary uniformed policeman was sitting behind the front desk. He looked up and Heather smiled awkwardly. She wished she'd changed her shoes and put on some make-up, or at least brushed her shaggy hair. She felt scruffy and implausible, and she wanted to be taken seriously.

'Er … I have … I may have some information for you,' she began.

'Yes, madam?'

'Er …' she glanced around as if the murderer might be lurking in the atrium. '… I may have some information …'

'Yes, madam?'

'… about the body in Lyceum Park.'

She'd said it and she couldn't back out. The policeman reacted instantaneously, as if she'd flicked a switch to set him in motion. He ushered her into a small waiting room, and invited her to sit down. It felt like a cell. Before she had time to read the notices on the walls, the door was dashed open and a smartly turned out young woman entered, closely followed by a tall man. The woman took a step towards Heather and smiled.

'I'm Detective Inspector Steel,' she said as they all sat down, 'and this is Detective Sergeant Peterson. I understand you may have some information for us, Mrs – Miss –?'

'Heather Spencer. Mrs.'

Heather took a deep breath, and launched into her carefully rehearsed story. 'I'm a teacher,' she began, keen to establish herself as a credible witness. 'Last Wednesday I'd arranged visits to some of our pupils out of school on work experience. Most schools arrange their work experience at the end of year eleven, but we do ours at the start of year twelve. I had an appointment at nine fifteen, in the High Street.' At first she felt embarrassed. It sounded trifling, but the detectives' eyes were riveted on her. Their interest couldn't be misinterpreted and Heather wondered why she'd hesitated to come forward. The police were very pleasant about it and encouraged her to tell them everything she could remember.

'Where was the appointment?' Heather saw the sergeant was taking notes. She was childishly excited to think they might check her story. She knew it would be corroborated.

'My first appointment was with Mr Proctor at Miles and Proctor, number 7, the High Street.' The inspector nodded. 'He had one of our year twelve boys there for a week. Andrew Marsh.' The sergeant was busy writing. 'My next appointment was at Bretts, the music shop in Waverley Street, with Mr Williams, the manager. I was due there at ten.' The inspector's chair creaked. 'I was crossing the park,' Heather said. The inspector stared at her, unblinking, as though willing her to speak. 'It must've been around nine forty-five. There was no one about.' It was raining, she explained, and went on to describe her encounter with the man on the path. 'It's so difficult to be sure now,' she concluded apologetically. 'I remember thinking there was something odd about him – I mean, apart from his not speaking. I wondered if he was deaf, actually. I think there was something strange about him, but I can't be sure that's not hindsight, because I've been wondering if he could have been the man you're looking for. The one who murdered the girl in the park.'

The inspector nodded, searching her face. 'Where do you teach, Mrs Spencer?' she asked at length, sitting back in her chair.

'Redhill School.' The inspector thanked her for coming forward and nodded at her colleague. Heather grinned in relief. 'I just felt, on balance, that I should tell you, in case it might be useful. I mean, that's not for me to decide, is it? And I often pop into Waitrose on my way home …' She tailed off lamely, regretting her reference to the supermarket a block away from the police station. It must sound as though she thought helping to catch a murderer was something to be fitted into her busy schedule when it was convenient, like doing her weekly shopping.

'Mrs Spencer,' the young sergeant said, 'can you describe the man you saw in the park on Wednesday morning?'

Heather tried to picture him in her mind: around forty, tall and muscular. 'He was wearing a baggy grey jacket so I couldn't see his build clearly. It's just an impression. I don't know why, but he seemed – energised, somehow. When I spoke to him he sort of jumped back, like I'd startled him. And he stared at my lips when I was speaking, not at my eyes. That was when I wondered if he might be deaf. Although he seemed to be listening to me. It was odd. As though he couldn't quite understand what I was saying. Or didn't like my talking to him.' The sergeant asked if he had any distinguishing features. 'Oh dear, I'm not very good with faces. He had funny eyes, I think.'

'Funny?'

Heather sighed. 'I'm sorry. I wasn't really paying much attention. But there was one thing that might help. He had a scar just above his top lip. It looked as though it had been split open in a fight a long time ago, or perhaps he'd had an operation on it.' The sergeant looked up from his notebook. 'I'm afraid that's all I can remember. Do you think it was the man you're looking for?'

'It's a possibility.'

'That's what I thought. I wish I could remember more about him. I didn't look too closely, I'm afraid. I wasn't paying him much attention.'

'Of course not. Why would you? You've been very helpful, Mrs Spencer.' The inspector gave her a card and asked her to be sure to call if she remembered anything else. Then the sergeant took her to see an E-Fit Officer who patiently attempted to reproduce the face of the man Heather had seen in the park, but Heather could only really picture a scar and peculiar eyes.

'Does that look more like it?' the officer asked each time she adjusted the image.

Heather shrugged and apologised. 'I'm sorry,' she kept repeating, 'I really can't remember what he looked like.' All she could recall was that he made her feel uneasy, and that wasn't something that she could define in a picture.

19

Review

Geraldine stared at the e-fit until the image went blurry. She picked it up and held it at arm's length then replaced it on her desk. Shaking her head, she pulled her notebook out of her bag. She'd never believed John Drew was guilty and Heather Spencer's statement seemed to confirm her reservations about him. Reading what she'd written about him, she put a question mark by John Drew's name and added to her notes.

WITNESS Heather Spencer TIME 9.45?
odd
watching lips – deaf? foreign?
funny eyes
scar – top lip, vertical, old fight?
About 40? Muscular?
E-fit – too vague?

She put her pencil down and sighed. Too many question marks.

Heather Spencer was a credible witness. It was a pity she didn't have better visual recall of the man she'd passed in the park. Geraldine followed up the leads from her description, searching for a man with a scar on his top lip. If it was a relatively recent injury, and he was local, she hoped they'd be able to trace him quickly, although she knew it was a slim chance. The local hospitals were co-operative, but it turned out to be a predictably wild goose chase. They widened the search but she knew it could take months. Even if they succeeded in tracking down the man Heather Spencer had seen in the park, he might have nothing to do with Angela Waters' murder.

'Can you describe the nature of the injury? Where exactly was the scar? How old was it? Was the injury sustained in a fight? Could it have been due to a congenital abnormality?' The hospital administrators spoke rapidly, rushing the constables through a list of questions.

The impression that the man in the park hadn't understood Heather Spencer suggested he might be a foreigner. Perhaps he was just passing through the area, leaving a gruesome calling card. Geraldine frowned at her notes, rejecting the idea that they might never identify this murderer who had slipped away, leaving no clues. Something was buzzing in her brain, a feeling she'd seen or heard something that might help lead them to the killer, if she could only remember what it was.

Closing her eyes to clear her head, she saw a pale thin form lying on a mortuary table, imagined Angela's terror, silenced by a hand slapped over her mouth, her helplessness at being dragged off her feet, the dread she must have experienced at the end. Thinking about the victim's history of abuse, Geraldine was consumed by a rage to discover who had committed the final atrocity. Nothing could restore Angela Waters' chance of a better life, but at least her killer could be punished. There had to be some justice for Angela.

As she sifted through her memory, the DCI came to fetch her for a meeting with the press. None of Angela Waters' family were available to join them for an appeal so they weren't being televised. Nevertheless, it was a daunting prospect. Geraldine nervously patted her hair in place.

'Ready, ma'am.'

'The nationals are here,' the DCI said. They were all

pleased at the coverage. The more publicity they generated, the more co-operation they could expect from the public. Geraldine thought of the tapes she'd been forced to sit through. No doubt there'd be plenty more spurious calls and misinformation. But, somehow, they would find him. If there was a chance an appeal through the newspapers might produce results, she was glad to do it. She'd read through endless statements and listen willingly to any number of tapes, if it helped. She owed it to that silent figure in the mortuary. Gritting her teeth, she marched into the briefing room.

The press conference passed in a blur.

'What are the police doing to find Angela Waters' killer?'

'We're doing everything we can,' Kathryn Gordon assured them. 'We're leaving no stone unturned.'

Geraldine remembered playing on a pebble beach as a child, lifting up stone after stone looking for crabs. She'd never found one. She felt like that child on the beach now, hunting through numerous documents. Somewhere there had to be a clue to the killer's identity, if they could only find it. But there was so much information to search through. She kept up her resolve and stayed at the station for hours after her shift ended, reading through reports and witness statements.

She arrived back at her flat that evening too tired to cook. As she was scavenging in the kitchen, her sister phoned.

'You're always busy,' Celia complained when Geraldine said she had no time to chat. Geraldine tried to explain the demands of her work. 'You could at least get a girl in to clean, once a week,' her sister suggested. 'That would save you a bit of time, and it's not as if you can't afford it.'

'Great idea. I'll make sure I'm always here at the right time to let the cleaner in, shall I?' Geraldine snapped. 'Or maybe you'd like me to give a key to some stranger?' She regretted her answer immediately. Her sister was only trying to be helpful. 'I'm sorry. It's just that I've got a lot on right now. I'll call you soon.' She hung up, opened her briefcase and pulled out the files she'd brought home. The memory of that small pale figure in the mortuary wouldn't let her relax. Over a solitary supper of cheese and crackers, she settled down to work.

20

Melanie

He'd only met the boy once, but Ron was suspicious of his daughter Melanie's new boyfriend.

'You assume everyone's after your money. This Terry probably doesn't even know who you are,' Lynda protested. They both knew that was unlikely. Ron Rogers had been a huge rock star in his youth and still made frequent appearances on television. His ravaged features were familiar from award ceremonies and charity events on both sides of the Atlantic along with his wife, former international fashion model, Lynda Clare.

'He knows who I am,' Ron retorted testily. 'His eyes were on stalks all the time he was here.'

'It's not like she's planning to marry him,' Lynda said, dismissing her husband's concerns. 'It's just a fling. She'll soon get bored of him.' They lapsed into moody silence as Nora knocked and came in to announce that dinner was ready.

Nora liked to have everything perfect for Mr Rogers and his wife. He'd given up his music career years ago, but Nora still remembered Ron Rogers in his heyday. She'd been a devoted fan, buying all his records. She'd even seen him live in concert once, screaming along with all the other girls whenever he waved his electric guitar at them. Ron Rogers strode into the dining room, his wife at his heels.

Nora couldn't help overhearing snatches of conversation at the table as she flitted in and out. She was fetching coffee from the kitchen when the front door slammed and Melanie ran in, her long blonde hair flying. She resembled her mother and would have been just as beautiful had her looks not been marred by a hint of her father's horsey features. Even so, her face was almost perfect, with her mother's striking green eyes, full lips and upturned nose. As a child, Melanie had idolised her father. He had that effect on people. Even now, with his grey hair and lined face, the effect of his presence in a room was electrifying. Nora smiled at Melanie and carried the coffee tray into the dining room.

'I'm hopping over to Le Touquet,' Ron Rogers was saying. He pulled on his cigar.

'That's a good idea,' Lynda nodded her golden head at her husband who waved his cigar at the coffee pot. Melanie's feet pounded across the wide hallway. Lynda glanced at her husband over the coffee pot and carried on pouring. Ron Rogers gave no sign he'd heard his daughter as Melanie flung the door open and hurried in. She sat down without an apology and looked up expectantly. Despite her furious scowl, her resemblance to her mother was remarkable.

'Don't suppose there's any dinner?' she asked Nora, without a word to her parents.

'Thank you, Nora,' Ron said firmly. 'You can go.' Nora dutifully withdrew.

'But Ron,' she heard Lynda protest, 'she must be hungry.'

'Should've been here on time, then,' came the peremptory reply. Nora retired to the kitchen. Even at that distance she could hear raised voices from the dining room. All that money, and they were never satisfied.

Melanie was seething. Her father never listened to her. He always thought he knew better than everyone else. She hated the school he'd chosen for her, and the college he'd packed her off to had felt more like a prison. Now she was a working adult, her father had to stop thinking he was running her life. She was determined to stay with Terry and prove to her father that he could no longer control her every move.

'You don't even know him,' she fumed. 'You don't know the first thing about him. You think he's only interested in me for my money.'

'Your money?' her father repeated. 'It's not your money, is it?'

Melanie stared at him. 'And what exactly is that supposed to mean?'

'Oh Melanie,' Lynda interrupted with a sigh, 'don't go upsetting your father.'

'Terry doesn't care about your money,' Melanie insisted. 'He's an independent man. He earns his own money, not like some.' She slumped in her chair, biting her lip.

'I'm glad to hear he's not a complete sponger. What does he do?'

'He works in a park. It's a perfectly respectable way to earn a living. Healthy too.' She glared pointedly at her father, who had notoriously indulged in alcohol and drugs in his youth.

'A gardener,' Ron relit his expensive cigar. 'Good for him.'

Melanie pushed her chair back and stood up. 'You never care about what I want, do you?' she grumbled. 'Well, I'm not going to give him up just to make you happy. Why should I? What do you know about love? All you think about is money. What about my happiness?' Ron's eyes slid away from his daughter's face. He nodded at the coffee and Lynda picked up the pot. It shook slightly as she poured.

They all knew Melanie didn't earn enough at the chic art gallery where she worked to fund her extravagant tastes. Ron picked up his coffee and gazed levelly at his daughter over the rim of his cup. His fat cigar smouldered gently in his other hand. Melanie turned to appeal to her mother but Lynda sat immobile and stared at her lap, refusing to take sides.

'See if I care,' Melanie bleated. 'You're nothing but a bully. You think you're a big shot, but you can't buy me.'

'I think we're done here,' Ron Rogers said evenly, indicating the table, but his eyes remained fixed on his daughter. Flicking her long blonde hair off her shoulders with a violent twist of her head, she slammed out of the room and out of the house. She roared off in her Porsche, along the empty road that led back to Terry.

21

Lakeland

The DCI wondered if Heather Spencer could have been mistaken.

'She struck me as a reliable witness, ma'am,' Geraldine said, glancing round the room. Peterson stared at the Incident Board.

'A reliable witness who can't remember anything,' Merton muttered.

'The boyfriend's profile fits,' the DCI said, tapping the board, but she sounded unconvinced. John Drew had previous form. At eighteen he'd been accused of GBH but the trial had been thrown out when a key witness disappeared. Kathryn Gordon underlined the information on the board.

'That was years ago,' Geraldine protested, 'and he wasn't found guilty.'

'Because someone cocked up the prosecution,' Kathryn Gordon replied. She turned to Carter. 'We need to speak to the Honda manager. Find Lakeland and see if he can shed any light on Drew's whereabouts on Wednesday morning.'

'Yes, ma'am.'

No one at the Honda showroom knew where Robert Lakeland's sick mother lived and he wasn't answering his mobile phone. A constable telephoned the Honda Head Office at Swindon and established that Lakeland had left early to take his mother to a hospital appointment that afternoon. By the time the DC was connected to the right department, Robert Lakeland and his mother had left the hospital. He still wasn't answering his mobile and there was no answer at his mother's house.

'Swindon want to know if you want them to look out for him?'

Carter decided there was no point. They would make contact with Lakeland before long. 'Just keep trying his mother's phone. They have to turn up there sooner or later.'

The DC finally got hold of Robert Lakeland's mother. 'She says he took her out for tea after the hospital appointment.'

'Put him on,' Carter said, reaching for the phone.

'He's not there any more, sir. He dropped her off and left straight away.'

Carter nodded. 'We'll wait till he gets home then. At least he's on his way. I don't suppose he'll talk to us while he's driving. Leave a message on his mobile and on his answerphone at home, if he's got one. Tell him to call us as soon as he gets in, it doesn't matter how late. Say it's routine, but we need to hear from him straight away.'

When Robert Lakeland phoned the station at seven on Friday evening, DS Black had already left for the night. Carter picked up his keys.

'Want to come along?' Geraldine heard him ask Peterson. The sergeant hesitated. 'You don't have to if you don't want to,' Carter said. 'It's not a problem.'

'Of course I want to come.' Peterson sounded vexed. 'I'll just call my girlfriend.'

'If you've got plans, I don't need you ...' Carter began but Peterson was already on the phone. Geraldine tried not to listen.

'I'm going to be late again ... Yes, as soon as I can ... I told you, I'll be back when I can ... You'll just have to manage without me ... I can't promise but it shouldn't be long ...' He moved out of earshot.

'Coming?' Carter asked.

Peterson nodded, frowning. 'Look, Bev, I've got to go.' He hung up. Geraldine observed his long face thoughtfully out of the corner of her eye.

Robert Lakeland was a small, bald, energetic man in his late forties. He opened the door straight away and ushered them in.

'Good evening, Mr Lakeland. I'm Detective Inspector Carter and this is Detective Sergeant Peterson.'

'Yes, come in. I've been expecting you.' He bustled around them. 'I'm sorry I couldn't get back to you sooner. I'm afraid my mother's not a well woman, Inspector. As an only child it falls on me to take care of her. I'm trying to move her closer, but it's not easy. Since they moved me here from Swindon it's been very difficult. Very difficult.' He sat down. 'Now, Inspector, what's this all about? It's not this fuss about my dog again, is it? Only—' Carter interrupted him to explain they were investigating the death of Angela Waters.

'Ah yes, I read about that in the papers. A dreadful business. Right here in Woolsmarsh too!' he added, as though that somehow made the crime worse. He was shocked to learn that the victim had been John Drew's girlfriend. 'My goodness. I had no idea. I knew he had a girl but she never came to the showroom.'

'You've never met her?'

Lakeland shook his head. 'My God, poor Johnny. What a terrible thing to happen.'

Carter leaned forward. Peterson sat, notebook and pencil at the ready.

'Mr Lakeland, it's very important you answer accurately. If you can't be precise as to times, say so. Were you at the Honda showroom last Wednesday morning?'

'Wednesday morning? Yes, I believe so.' He sounded uncertain.

'Are you sure?'

'I'm always there all week or sometimes till midday Thursday when I drive over to Head Office in Swindon. This week was a Swindon week.'

'Can you tell us,' Carter paused and took a deep breath, aware how much hung on Lakeland's next syllable, 'was John Drew at work on Wednesday morning?'

'John? He's always there.' Lakeland's eyes flittered nervously from Carter to Peterson, busy writing.

'Are you sure he was there all Wednesday morning?'

'He's in every morning. Never misses. I've got a good sales team, Inspector. They don't mess about. That's why we're one of the most successful Honda—'

'Could John Drew have left the showroom at any time on Wednesday morning?' Carter interrupted.

'I'd need to double check the book to see if he was out on a test drive.'

'We checked. He wasn't. Could he have left the showroom for any other reason?'

'There wouldn't be any other reason.'

'Are you sure?' Carter pressed him.

A flicker of annoyance crossed Robert Lakeland's face. 'Inspector, I'm not going to be pushed into saying something that's not true. If John Drew left the showroom on Wednesday morning, I presume that would make him a suspect. I take it that's what you're driving at. If that was the case, why would I want to protect him?'

'Can you be sure he didn't go out?' Peterson added his voice to the interrogation.

'I run a tight ship, Inspector,' Lakeland blustered, but he squirmed uncomfortably in his chair. 'My staff don't leave the premises without good reason. If they go off site, I know about it. And they have every reason to stay. They're not going to sell cars anywhere else.' Lakeland rubbed a chubby hand backwards and forwards across his mouth and tried to smile.

Carter leaned forward and spoke quietly. 'Mr Lakeland, we need to eliminate John Drew from our enquiries. Are you able to confirm his whereabouts on Wednesday morning or not? It's a simple enough question. I need a definite answer from you, an answer you'd be prepared to swear to in court, if necessary.' Lakeland crumpled suddenly, like a balloon deflating. He wiped the sweat from his forehead with the back of his hand.

'I can't say,' he admitted. 'I was called away. My mother had a relapse. It happens more and more often. I'm at my wit's end with her.'

'Thank you, Mr Lakeland, you've been very helpful.' With the usual request that Lakeland contact them if he thought of anything else, the two detectives left.

'Which leaves Drew in the frame,' Peterson concluded as he told Geraldine about the interview with Lakeland.

She nodded uneasily. 'Just because Drew's vicious doesn't make him a murderer. No one saw him leave work that morning and, in any case, what about Heather Spencer's statement?'

Peterson groaned. 'It's getting us nowhere, that's for sure. She's given us a lead of sorts, but who is this mysterious man she happened to see in the park?'

'It's not much to go on,' Geraldine admitted, but the killer was out there somewhere. She hoped he'd been motivated by hatred or jealousy. If he was driven by darker impulses, Angela Waters might not be his only victim. She saw her own apprehension reflected in Peterson's eyes and an uneasy silence fell between them.

22

Celia

At the briefing they went over what they'd learned so far. It wasn't much. They had pieced together the last hours of Angela Waters' life. They knew where the attack had taken place, and had painstakingly reconstructed the sequence of actions at the scene. Geraldine had gone over it again and again until she could see it playing in her mind like a film. But the soundtrack was missing.

It was frustrating that they knew so little about the man Heather Spencer had seen in the park. After all their efforts, they were no closer to finding him. Kathryn Gordon had put a large red question mark by Heather Spencer's name.

'I see the DCI's not crossing Drew off the list,' Geraldine muttered to Peterson.

'He was violent,' Peterson whispered back. The briefing was about to begin.

'Let's hope it jogs someone's memory,' Kathryn Gordon said. They had enough to make a reconstruction on the television worthwhile. 'And there's the e-fit in the papers,' she added.

'D'you think there's enough in that image for anyone to recognise him?' someone asked.

'It's a shame the teacher didn't get a better look at him,' Kathryn Gordon replied tersely.

'Not easy when you just walk past someone in the park. Specially these days,' someone else said.

'True.' A line appeared between Kathryn Gordon's heavy

brows. 'John Drew's still in the picture, but we need to keep up a wider search. We can't overlook any possibility. It could be a previous boyfriend who's never been in any trouble before.' She looked around the tense faces gathered in the room and smiled suddenly. 'Whoever it is, we're going to catch him, make no mistake. We've got a good team together here, and we'll crack this case. We'll find him.' Geraldine felt her spirits lift as the DCI finished speaking and left the room. She squeezed back between the desks to type up her report.

'Fancy a pint?' Geraldine asked later as she passed Peterson in the corridor.

He shook his head. 'Best be going straight home,' he said and she felt unexpectedly let down.

Geraldine gazed at her copy of the picture that had appeared in the morning papers. It was little more than an artist's impression. There was no point in speculation, but it was infuriating to feel they might be close to a description of the killer, and yet no closer to discovering his identity.

'How about that, Mrs Spencer? Is that more like it?' the E-Fit Officer had asked the teacher.

'Um ... maybe ...'

'How about if we lengthen the nose? Or shorten it? We can make it wider?'

'I'm sorry, I really can't remember his nose at all.' All they knew was that he had a scar on his top lip, but that could be enough. Geraldine scanned the faces of men she drove past in the street. Once the picture appeared in the paper he was bound to hide his scar but by then it might be too late. Someone might have phoned in with a positive identification. She imagined discovering a previous boyfriend of Angela Waters had just such a scar.

'So if you couldn't have her, you made sure no one else could,' she said in her imaginary interview with a faceless suspect who crumbled and confessed.

When she arrived home, her phone was flashing to indicate there was a message. Her sister's number came up on the call screen.

'It's me. How are things? Call me back when you've got a moment. You haven't forgotten it's Chloe's birthday party this Sunday? She's six! I can hardly believe it. Speak soon.' It wasn't clear if her sister was reminding her to send a present, or inviting her to the party. Geraldine wondered whether to go. She hadn't seen her sister for weeks.

While Geraldine devoted her life to strangers, trying to either protect them or lock them up, Celia was equally busy transporting her daughter to endless ballet, swimming, and tennis lessons. In her spare time, she did voluntary work in a local charity shop. Geraldine tried not to envy her sister for living the conventional married life Geraldine had once planned to enjoy with Mark, although she now knew she would never have left the force.

She'd been surprised when Celia had once confessed to feeling jealous of Geraldine's career. 'It must be great to feel you're doing something useful and important.'

'And bringing up a child isn't useful and important?' Geraldine had tried not to sound bitter.

'Is something the matter?' Her sister had looked concerned. 'You are happy in your work, aren't you?'

'Of course I am. It's just funny that we're envious of each other. I never realised.'

Celia had smiled, gazing through the window at her daughter, playing in the garden. 'I wouldn't change places, though. Not for anything.'

'Me neither.'

If Geraldine had been less caught up in the investigation, she would have sent her niece a birthday present. If she'd even remembered to post a card, she might have got away with it. As it was, she fibbed when she returned Celia's call.

'Of course I haven't forgotten Chloe's birthday. I haven't

sent her present because I was planning to bring it round in person, but I'm in the middle of—'

'Of course Auntie Gerry remembered your birthday. She's coming to your party,' Celia's voice shouted away from the phone.

'Hurray!' a child's voice shrilled faintly in the background. It was one of the rare moments when Geraldine would gladly have traded places with her sister. In any case, she hadn't seen Celia for weeks and Chloe's birthday was an ideal occasion for a visit.

When she left home, a driving rain intermittently blurred her windscreen. Her hair was damp and the bottoms of her jeans were wet from the short trip between her back door and the car. She'd been so immersed in the investigation, it felt strange to be driving in the opposite direction to Woolsmarsh, as though she was travelling away from her life. She turned on the radio. For days, she'd been thinking of nothing but Angela Waters, Johnny Drew, and the mysterious man with a scar. When she'd been assessed in post during her year as acting inspector, Carter had advised her to pace herself. But what he considered a sensible schedule seemed half-hearted to Geraldine.

'Don't forget, you don't get paid overtime any more,' he'd reminded her with a smile. They both knew that wasn't the point. Geraldine tried to explain her compulsion to throw herself into work. It was only way she could keep everything fresh in her mind. She rarely missed a discrepancy between witness statements. In her previous station, she'd earned a reputation for her recall of detail.

'Did one of the witnesses say they saw him in the pub at seven fifteen?' a colleague would enquire, and the answer was always the same: 'Ask Geraldine.' Her memory hadn't failed her yet. It was the way she liked to work, engrossed in the case to the exclusion of everything else. Mark had resented taking second place until she returned to what he called 'real life'. Since Mark had left her, there was no other life but as long as she was working, Geraldine could forget the void.

The radio music played on, but Geraldine barely noticed. She stared at the dark road ahead and thought about Angela Waters' pale face, her skinny torso and raw hands. The further she drove, the more drained she felt. For days the adrenaline of work had been keeping exhaustion at bay and now a wave of tiredness threatened to overwhelm her. She stopped a few times and stepped out of the car. The cold air revived her. When she arrived, a bevy of expensive cars were parked outside Celia's house and she had to leave her car round the corner and run back in the rain, clutching Chloe's tissue-wrapped present beneath her coat.

Geraldine caught a whiff of perfume as Celia kissed her on both cheeks. Celia leaned her head back, her hands resting on her sister's shoulders, and studied Geraldine's face before delivering judgement. 'You look awful.'

'I'm fine. A bit tired, that's all.'

'Well, take it easy. You're not going to be any good to anyone if you make yourself ill. Difficult case?' Geraldine nodded.

Celia knew better than to ask more questions. She turned and led Geraldine into a room packed with children all screaming at once. A woman in a bright red and yellow jumpsuit was clapping her hands and screeching into a microphone above the beat of loud music.

'No!' she yelled and a roomful of histrionic voices answered, 'Yes!' Geraldine felt a headache starting at the top of her skull.

'Chloe! Look who's here!' Celia shouted. Her voice was swallowed up in the din. 'Chloe! Aunty Gerry's here!' Chloe didn't turn round. Celia guided Geraldine out and closed the door. 'You won't get any sense out of Chloe while Party Pantomima's here,' she apologised. 'She's horrendous, as you saw, but the kids love her. Or think they do. They follow the herd at that age. We only managed to get her because she had a cancellation. Honestly, Gerry, it's a nightmare arranging these bloody parties. And it costs an absolute bloody fortune too.' Geraldine nodded, trying to look interested. 'Come on, let's join the girls.'

Geraldine was about to remonstrate, but Celia led her away from the screaming children to the dining room where a dozen women were sitting round the table drinking red wine.

The woman beside her smiled politely at Geraldine. 'Is your daughter at the Maltings?'

'No, I'm Chloe's aunt.'

'So where do yours go to school?'

Geraldine bridled at the assumption. 'I haven't got any children. I'm not married,' she replied, vexed by the defiance in her own voice.

The other woman gave her an encouraging smile. 'Plenty of time. So what *do* you do?'

'I'm a police officer.'

'A police officer? Really? I've never met a police officer before. Not socially. I don't suppose you dealt with a break-in in Rowley Grove last month, by any chance?'

'I don't work around here, I'm afraid, but I do work in crime detection, yes.'

'I've always thought that must be really interesting.' She turned to the woman sitting on her other side. 'This is Chloe's aunt. She's a police woman.'

'DI,' Geraldine corrected her pettily. 'I'm a detective inspector.'

'Cool,' the other woman replied, her smile too sudden to be genuine. There were a few jokes about minding their Ps and Qs and not making off with the silver, before the conversation reverted to husbands, children and school. As long as the police kept a lid on things, most people preferred not to think about them. Geraldine sat dumbly, torn between wanting to see Celia, and hoping the DCI would summon her urgently back to the station.

The afternoon dragged on. When the visitors finally left, clutching party bags, Celia turned to Geraldine. 'You're staying for supper, aren't you?' With uncanny timing, Sebastian arrived home just as Celia announced the lasagne was ready. Geraldine smelt fresh rain on wool as her brother-in-law embraced her. She smiled into the warmth of his familiar features before he turned and kissed Celia lightly on the lips and swung Chloe in the air. His daughter screamed in delight, his wife in protest.

'Put her down. There's no room in here,' Celia remonstrated, laughing.

Driving away from the warmth of her sister's house, Geraldine felt lonelier than ever. Her mood didn't improve when she arrived home to see that someone had sprayed graffiti on the fence at the end of her close. *FILTH* was written in red paint that had streaked so that the huge letters seemed to be weeping blood. Geraldine was faintly troubled. One of the main attractions of her block of flats was its security, but vandals had gained access to the premises and amused themselves defacing the fence. It was raining so she scurried from the car to the back entrance of her block and fell into bed exhausted.

Preoccupied with Angela Waters, she closed her eyes. Instead of the small pale figure that haunted her, the graffiti flashed across her mind. With a shock she realised it must have been put there just for her.

23

Newspaper

Jim didn't recognise the picture at first. It was above an article about Angela Waters in one of the national papers. The police had found her. That made him angry because he'd left her in a very secret hiding place. The police had no business sticking their noses in there. He barely glanced at the headline: 'DO YOU KNOW THIS MAN?' When he'd finished reading the description of Angela Waters' death, he looked at the picture again and the truth dawned on him. It was meant to be his face.

He choked on his sandwich. Tiny wet crumbs spattered on the page. Someone must have seen him in the park and told the police about his scar. That was how he knew it was a picture of his face. With confusion came a gathering rage that had to be controlled. He needed to think clearly. It wasn't a good likeness, but he knew it was supposed to be his face. The scar was the clue. Someone else might recognise it and go to the police. He licked his lips nervously and his fingers wandered to his face, feeling their way around the familiar crease on his lip.

He knew he should leave Woolsmarsh and go far far away so he'd be safe. But Miss Elsie lived in Woolsmarsh. Ever since he'd seen her picture in the newspaper he'd made Woolsmarsh his home. Once he'd seen her drive past very fast in a black car. Every day he went out looking for her and sometimes she came and stood right beside him. If he went away, he might never see her again.

121

He stared at the picture and his fingers explored his face. He'd have to hide his scar. It was a pity, but he'd have to stop shaving.

'Long hair is dirty,' Miss Elsie said, but she understood it wasn't his fault. He didn't have a choice. He licked his top lip and felt himself quiver. No space in his brain for anger. Not yet. He thought about what to do until his head hurt. He'd seen different pairs of glasses in the chemist's. A beard, a moustache and glasses. That would be a good disguise. His thoughts kept drifting, getting jumbled and angry.

Calm down, he told himself. He read the article again, mouthing the words to make sure he didn't miss anything. They hadn't discovered his hiding place. They would have come poking around asking questions if they knew where he was. Maybe they were looking for him. It was lucky he'd hidden himself so cleverly. But someone had linked him to the woman in the park. He stared at the grey image in the newspaper.

'Calm down,' he told himself out loud, 'it's alright. Miss Elsie won't let them hurt me.'

He sat down on the floor to think. He was used to managing. He'd got used to it early on, trapped in a grimy flat when he was too small to open the front door to the dubious freedom of the streets. Life was full of menace when you were small and your face didn't fit. There were always bigger kids jeering and spitting, slapping and kicking. And his mother would be at home, waiting for him, violent in her affections, and her rage. He never knew which was worse.

Now it was his turn to be strong. No one would ever hurt him again. His memories made him tremble but he knew his rage would have to wait until it was safe to go back to the park. He knew what he had to do. He was going to make it safe to walk around without women putting dirty thoughts in his head all the time.

'It's bad to be dirty,' Miss Elsie said. When he had dirty thoughts he had to be punished. God didn't want him to be dirty. But they were everywhere, giving him dirty thoughts. He had to stop them, all of them, one by one. He was going to be very busy doing God's work and Miss Elsie would be pleased with him. He smiled and then he remembered he was supposed to be thinking. He had to be very clever.

Now they knew what he looked like, they'd be looking for him. It was lucky he hadn't gone back to his room. No, not lucky. He'd been clever. They were probably there now, waiting for him. They were going to be disappointed. He smiled to think how cross they'd be when he never went back there. It made him sad too, because he'd liked his room. The lady there was nice. She'd give him his picture if he went and asked her, but he wouldn't go back for it now. That was what they were expecting him to do. Miss Elsie warned him they'd be there, waiting for him, but he was too clever for them.

He was very clever. He knew lots of places to hide. He'd found a shed in a garden where no one would find him because all the houses along the road were empty. Someone had put wooden boards across the windows. He could peep between the cracks and see the street. No one could see him looking out. He never saw anyone and no one saw him creep along the side passage across the overgrown garden. The path was hidden under grass but he'd found it.

'God leads us in the path of righteousness,' Miss Elsie had said when he found it and he knew God had brought him safely to the shed. It was his shed now. No one would find him there, but he could go out and find them. That was very clever of him. He giggled to himself at his cleverness. He clapped his hands softly so no one would hear.

Someone had told the newspaper about his scar to get him in trouble but he was too clever to be caught. He was like David who beat a giant even though he had his arm in a sling. He had a sling once but it never made him strong. And it never helped him fight anyone.

'Don't pick on him. He's got his arm in a sling,' Miss Elsie said, and the other children ran off laughing.

He sat in his shed and made a plan. First he had to find out who had told the newspapers about him. Then he'd make sure they never told on him again. It wasn't nice to tell on people. God would give him the strength to defeat his enemy. He sang to himself under his breath:

> 'Make, then, our task to match our strength,
> Our strength to match our task,
> And make us unafraid to do
> Whatever Thou wilt ask.'

Miss Elsie taught him the words. He could hear her voice now which was funny because he couldn't see her although he looked everywhere for her. But he knew it was her voice, singing. He loved Miss Elsie because she had golden hair and she never shouted at him, even when he was dirty. She said he couldn't help it.

'Are you an angel?' he asked her. She was as beautiful as an angel. All the children said so. They made him angry. She was his angel, not theirs. The teacher told him he had a garden angel and he chose Miss Elsie.

His shed was in a garden. It reminded him of the park. Thinking about the park, he realised who'd told the newspaper about him. It must have been the stranger who spoke to him even though he didn't know her. She'd asked him about a music shop. He wasn't allowed to talk to strangers. It wasn't his fault she spoke to him. Now he had to find her and shut her up. He could do that. She was a problem but he knew what to do because he was clever.

His moustache grew quickly. It made him look like someone else and that made him chuckle, even though he hated the feel of it, itchy and dirty on his face. He was going to buy some glasses to hide his face. He wouldn't go back to his usual chemist for them because the woman there was trying to poison him. She thought he didn't notice when she gave him the wrong pills, but he wasn't stupid. He was wise to her tricks. He was too clever for her. He never swallowed her pills. He didn't even want to touch them. He threw them down the drain and serve her right.

Jim sprinted past the chemist's window. No one saw him. He raced round the corner and slowed down. There were other shops he could go in. Along a narrow turning on the outskirts of town he found what he was looking for. He glanced up and down the deserted street before he slipped into the chemist. The shelves were packed with plastic bottles and jars, packets and boxes, brushes, hairpins and combs, a bewildering array of containers displayed in neat rows.

He was afraid the woman in there would see through his disguise. Women could do that.

'Didn't I see your picture in the paper?' she might ask, worry plastered across her face.

'Can I help you?' Jim turned with a guilty start. She had a nice voice, but she was old. Her grey hair was cropped in short tight curls all over her head. As he looked round in alarm, he caught sight of what he wanted.

'Those,' he said hoarsely, pointing at the stand of glasses. Lenses winked horribly at him like empty eye sockets.

'The reading glasses?' she asked. 'What strength?' Jim fought to control the panic rising in his throat like sick. The woman was staring at him. Her smile vanished. She turned and shuffled along the aisle to the counter where a fat woman in a brown coat was waiting to be served. Jim watched her hurry away from him. She knew what he was thinking. He dashed over to the stand, grabbed a pair of glasses, and thrust them across the counter.

'Excuse me,' the fat woman said loudly. Jim turned to face her and she backed away with a hurried mutter. 'It's all right, you can go first.'

Jim didn't know what to say. He shook his head and held out the glasses.

'Don't you want to try them first?' the woman behind the counter asked. She pretended to smile at him. He shook his head again and held out his money. He had to get out of there quickly. She knew what he was thinking. Two more women came in, chattering loudly. Their voices dropped to a whisper and he knew they were talking about him. If he ran away they'd know he was scared and they'd run after him.

'Cowardy cowardy custard,' the children shrieked when they chased him. He looked at the floor and waited for his glasses.

'You mustn't let them upset you,' Miss Elsie said.

The woman handed him his glasses in a little brown bag. 'Would you like …' she began to ask, but he turned and darted away without waiting for his change. A woman was standing in front of the door. He had to push past her to get out of there. They were all staring at him. The woman behind the counter was shouting at him. He ran along the pavement without looking back. He was shaking and sweating by the time he reached his shed.

He looked in all the newspapers he could find. He picked them out of bins. Sometimes they were dirty. That was how he found Miss Elsie again. She was getting into a car and she looked very cross. Under the picture it said: 'TROUBLE IN PARADISE'. He read all the words but it didn't make any sense. He kept the picture. He wished she was smiling in it. He tore it out carefully and put it in his pocket.

Hidden behind his glasses, Jim went out looking for Bretts Music Shop. He knew he had to go out the back of the park to find it. He was following her trail. At the far end of all the shops he saw Bretts Music.

'Well done,' Miss Elsie said. He was very clever. He stopped thinking for a moment because his head was hurting and it made his eyes feel funny. He had to concentrate. He couldn't remember what he was doing there. 'You have to do it by yourself,' Miss Elsie told him. She was cross because he'd forgotten.

'I haven't forgotten,' he told her but she knew he was lying. The stranger in the park had told the newspapers about him and now she'd got him in trouble with Miss Elsie. He was going to find that dirty bitch and stop her mouth once and for all.

'You have to try,' Miss Elsie said and she smiled. 'I know you can do it.'

A little bell rang as he opened the door of the music shop and he looked around. Everything was fuzzy.

'Don't look nervous,' Miss Elsie told him. 'They don't know you're scared unless you show them.'

'Are you looking for anything in particular?' He hadn't heard the girl coming up behind him and he jumped. He looked at her long blonde hair and wished it was the other way round. Him creeping up behind her. He didn't know what to say. Miss Elsie had gone away.

'No,' he stammered. The girl looked worried. She went behind the counter. She never stopped looking at him. He was scared. He wished she'd turn her back on him. By the till, he saw a desk diary and God sent him a revelation. He knew about diaries. You mustn't ever read them because they were private. That meant secrets. He needed to know a secret.

'Let's not get our hopes up,' Miss Elsie warned him, but he knew it would help him because God had shown it to him. God loved him but he had to be careful. And clever. He had to help himself. He walked over to the counter. His eyes never left the girl's face. She looked worried. Seizing the diary, he spun round and ran out of the shop.

'Hey!' the girl's voice followed him out on to the street as he fled. She didn't follow him. He was going to shut the bitch up so no one would ever find out what he'd done in the park. Then he could go out and do it again. There were lots of dirty women in Woolsmarsh. He was going to find them all and make the streets clean. Miss Elsie would be pleased. 'I'm doing God's work,' he whispered, and he giggled to himself. It was his work too.

It was dark by the time he reached the shed. The glasses must have fallen off when he was running but it didn't matter. He didn't need them any more. He had to use his torch to read the diary. He wished he had pyjamas to wear in bed. He knew better than to sleep in his day clothes. That was dirty. It worried him that the tracksuit he wore in bed wasn't real pyjamas, but he never put it on in the daytime. There hadn't been any pyjamas in the bag of clothes he'd found on the pavement outside a shop.

'Just do your best,' Miss Elsie told him and he nodded his head gravely, like a good boy.

He heard rain drumming on the roof of the shed as he opened the diary. Slowly he read it out loud: Order this. Order that. Deliver this. Deliver that. He couldn't decipher some of the words and what he could read made no sense. He felt stupid and that made him cross. He threw the diary across the shed and kicked a pile of jumpers he'd found in a bin bag. Red, blue and green, they fell in a jumble but he didn't pick them up. He kicked them again, anger building in his head.

Thinking about Angela made him feel better. He knew her name from the papers. Angela Waters. The papers said Angela had a boyfriend. That made him sad. Her boyfriend might be nice. They could have been friends. But her boyfriend wouldn't want to be his friend now. He picked up the diary and tried again. He still couldn't understand it so he dropped it on the floor and went out into the cool of the evening. He put his gloves on before he went out.

'Always be prepared,' Miss Elsie said.

The rain had settled into a steady downpour and daylight was fading early. He thought about Angela as he walked towards the park. He liked to walk in the park. It helped him think. He liked it best in the rain because he had the park to himself then. He needed the park to be empty, so when he saw her he would be free to do God's work.

PART 3

'we have gone on living,
Living and partly living,
Picking together the pieces'

T. S. Eliot

24

Meeting

Tiffany wasn't going to say anything to the other girls until after she'd done it. Best to keep it quiet or, knowing them, they'd all turn up, just for a laugh. Only it wasn't funny. It was dead serious because it was going to be her first time.

'I been with loadsa boys, loadsa times,' Holly boasted. 'You should see what I got just for doing it. You ought to try it, Tiffany. Only I don't suppose you can get anyone to do it with.'

'Could if I wanted,' Tiffany muttered. She should have made up a boy, someone out of school. 'I got a boyfriend,' she imagined herself saying. 'He's seventeen and he's got a car.' But they would have known. They always knew. They'd have laughed at her even more. Even smelly Della had done it. She only went with Harry, but still, she'd done it. Tiffany hadn't ever done it. Not yet, at any rate.

Tiffany's face had burned on Valentine's Day when she didn't receive any cards. She suspected some of the girls had sent cards to themselves, just so they could show them off. She should have thought of that. She could have jacked herself a huge one, maybe with a red love heart on it.

'This one's my best,' Holly had said, waving a card in the air so the whole class could see. It was pink with a big fat squishy red love heart on it. Some of the boys sniggered but the girls were impressed.

'Who's it from then?' Tiffany had asked without thinking, and the other girls shrieked with laughter.

'They don't tell you, thicko.'

Tiffany didn't care that she hadn't been sent any cards. She was used to the other girls laughing at her. She knew she'd never be like them. Her clothes were all wrong, for one thing. But she wished she'd got herself a really big card, just to make them think someone fancied her. No one ever did. Holly was right about that. All the boys ignored her. She might as well have been invisible.

It was worse when people did notice her.

'I can't believe you've not done your homework again, Tiffany May,' the new maths teacher complained one morning. He sounded so surprised, she laughed out loud. He must have got her mixed up with someone else. Mostly the teachers left her alone. No point putting her in detention. She had better things to do, especially now she'd been given a working telly off the social for her mother. As if her mother was ever going to sit up and watch the telly. That stupid fucking social worker didn't have a clue, but Tiffany had persuaded them to give her a telly anyway. Result! It was better than the crackly old one that never worked properly. At least she had something to go home for now.

When she was little, Tiffany had wanted to be a hairdresser, like Auntie Jean. But you couldn't do anything without the qualifications the teachers were always going on about. Tiffany didn't care. She never wanted a stupid job anyway. She had a better idea. Before long she'd have her own place like Della next door. She'd be like Carrie Bradshaw and the girls she watched on the telly. That would make the other girls sit up and take notice. Because Tiffany was going to have a baby to love her like no other and she'd be given a place of her own. She was going to take the telly with her too. Her mother wouldn't know.

His name was Pat; Pat the Pratt, the girls at school called him. It wasn't that Tiffany fancied him. She didn't like anything about him. He was short and fat, and he smelled of farts.

'That's his sexy stink when he sees our Tiffany coming,' Holly said and the other girls doubled up, laughing. Tiffany was sorry she'd ever told them about him. She'd have preferred almost any other boy in her class, but it didn't matter who it was. The baby would be hers, whoever she did it with, and a baby was her ticket to a better life.

Pat told her to meet him at six o'clock by the park gate that evening, but when she set off, she wasn't sure which gate he meant. There were two. She decided to get there early, and wait by the main gate. That way, if he didn't show up at six, she could take a short cut by legging it across the park to the other gate. Her spirits rose as she hurried along the wet pavement to have a baby and start her new life. Mrs Rutherford said they weren't allowed in the park because of some dead woman, but Tiffany didn't give a fuck about the headmistress and her stupid rules. All she had to do was wait until six o'clock. She hoped Pat wasn't going to chicken out. With any luck he'd be there, waiting for her in the park.

25

Women

When Melanie was invited to join the Woolsmarsh Women's Group, she introduced herself as Melanie Tillotson. She liked using Terry's name. It was hard to meet normal people when you were Ron Rogers' daughter. The other women had known each other for a long time, but they welcomed her into their group. Melanie watched one of them slop milk into chipped cups, which clattered softly on the tray as it was carried round the circle.

'Biscuit?'

'I know I shouldn't.'

'Sugar?'

'Shhh.'

Julie launched into a speech. Melanie stifled a yawn. She wished Julie would stop talking about the park. Melanie had come to the meeting to discuss social inequality in the area. The previous week Julie had made a speech about lobbying the council to help the poor. It wasn't something Melanie had thought about much, but since she'd moved in with Terry it occurred to her that someone should be concerned about raising living standards for the disadvantaged. It was appalling how often Terry's hot water didn't work, and there were many people living in similar conditions, or worse, some of them with young children.

'It's a poverty trap,' Julie had declared. 'Do you know how many women are living on the minimum wage, here in Woolsmarsh? And what are the council doing to help them?'

Melanie had liked the sound of that. She wanted to hear what the council were going to do to help people on low incomes. But this week, they all seemed obsessed with the park. Julie was very strident, and she had an unpleasant nasal voice. Melanie tossed her head cautiously, so as not to spill her tea, but her long blonde hair fell back over her face again.

'And if the police aren't doing anything,' Julie was saying, 'then it's about time we did.'

'What do you suggest we do?' one of the women asked.

'You're the one who should be on the council, Julie, not that husband of yours,' someone else called out. Melanie joined in with the murmurs of agreement. She couldn't care less about the council, but she did want to be part of the group. Her family home had been in West Woolsmarsh all her life but she'd never really mixed with people from the town centre before.

'It's time we women took action,' Julie declared firmly. Melanie saw two of the women exchange a smile, as if to say, 'She's off again.' Other women nodded. 'If a *woman* was in charge, they'd have caught this killer by now. He's been roaming the streets for nearly a week. It's all right for the men, they're OK. He only attacks women. But we can't step outside our homes without fearing for our lives. We know all about the sexism that's rife in the police force. It's everywhere—'

'I think you'll find it's a woman who's in charge of the investigation,' someone butted in.

'Well, that just proves my point. Why haven't they put their top man on the case? Because it's only women being attacked, that's why.'

'Perhaps this woman *is* their top detective,' someone else pointed out.

Julie frowned impatiently. 'You're all missing the point. What I'm saying is, as women, we want to feel safe on the streets, don't we? As women? It's not fair. It's all right for the men.'

'But what can we do?'

'We'll start a campaign.' There was a brief pause as Julie gulped her tea. 'We'll mobilise the women of Woolsmarsh, get everyone out on the streets, and protest about police inaction. It's an insult to women. We want something done about it, and we want it done now. We can't just sit around waiting for someone else to be murdered! Nice cup of tea, by the way.' Melanie thought the police were probably doing their best, but she went along with the idea of a campaign. It sounded like fun.

'You know Julie Master's married to the leader of the local council?' Terry asked her when she told him about the project.

'They've split up,' Melanie said. 'He doesn't want people to know in case it puts them off voting for him. Julie told us.'

Terry whistled. 'I feel quite sorry for Jonathon Masters, not much chance of keeping his problems quiet with you lot gossiping for England.'

'That's not fair. We don't just gossip. We talk about other things too, like the sink estates no one's doing anything about, and what the council should be doing to help people living in poverty. Anyway, Jonathon Masters doesn't deserve sympathy. He's brought it on himself by neglecting his wife. All he cares about is his political career. He's not 'poor old Jonathon' at all.'

'You only heard his wife's side of it.'

'She says he's pathetic. He's going nowhere,' Melanie said, with an eloquent glance at Terry, but he just threw his head back and laughed.

'He's the leader of the council, for fuck's sake,' he spluttered. 'What more does she want?' Melanie sighed and followed him into the bedroom.

*

Ironically, since his wife had threatened to leave him, Jonathon Masters' life had become more complicated than ever. Of course, it would happen at a crucial time in his political career with the local council elections only a few weeks away. Julie couldn't have made her announcement at a worse time. It was typical of her.

'I don't know what you're getting so worked up about,' his sister responded unsympathetically when he told her. 'She's been threatening to leave you for ages. It's time she made up her mind to pack her bags and go. You don't need her. Just think what your life'll be like without that self-obsessed bitch driving you mad.' She offered him a cigarette and lit one for herself. 'It's not as if she makes you happy. Anyone can see that. She only married you because she thought you'd end up in the senior partner's chair. Money, that's all she's after. Tight arsed bitch.' She grimaced, and blew smoke at him. 'If you want my advice, get a quick divorce. You'll meet someone else, Jon. Someone who cares about you.' She made it sound simple, but she didn't know his wife, who had a way of making his life difficult.

Much as he courted publicity, the last thing Jonathon wanted in the run up to an election was his name splashed all over the papers for the wrong reasons. He could understand his sister's annoyance. It wasn't as if he'd behaved badly. The situation was entirely of Julie's making. She had nothing to complain of in his conduct and had gained considerable personal wealth through their marriage, milked him shamelessly in fact. But he couldn't entirely blame her. She hadn't always been like that. Julie denied that his infertility was the cause of her resentment towards him, but he wasn't sure he believed her. It wasn't his fault, but he still felt guilty for not giving her the child she so desperately wanted, and Julie had been quick to take full advantage of his consequent generosity. In spite of her coldness towards him, he couldn't help feeling sorry for her.

His sister was right of course. If he was honest, his marriage had been over for a long time. But before he could start discussing a divorce, he had to get through the election, and Julie was well aware of his precarious position. The problem was that Jonathan had declared himself a passionate champion of traditional family values, and a large proportion of his support came from older women. By orchestrating a smear campaign against his twice divorced rival he'd managed to persuade the voters that a steady, married man was more trustworthy than a fly-by-night divorcé. To be publicly exposed as a hypocrite could mean the end of his political career – and Jonathon had worked too hard to give up without a fight.

He knew how important it was to remain on friendly terms with the media. *The Woolsmarsh Chronicle* was the most influential paper in the area. He wined and dined the editor carefully, aware that his strategy might prove counterproductive. The editor was a hard-headed journalist who could smell a desperate man from a hundred yards, but the Woolsmarsh Strangler was keeping the press busy and the editor only wanted to know what Jonathon was planning to do to safeguard the streets. It gave Jonathon a little breathing space while he tried to manage his wife. He even agreed to consider her outrageous claim on the house.

'It's with my solicitors,' he told her, careful not to put anything in writing.

Julie was in the dining room when he got home.

'Had a good day?' he asked. She didn't answer. A roll of wallpaper lay on the floor at her feet and he went over to see what she was doing. A length of paper, about six feet by three, was sellotaped to the tablecloth to prevent it curling up. Julie was writing on it in thick black marker pen. 'Close the park', he read aloud over her shoulder as she finished. 'What's this all about?'

Still with her back to him, Julie told him about her campaign. 'Since the police don't seem to be doing anything about it.'

'Oh, the police.'

'And the council,' she added sharply. 'This is a perfectly legitimate political protest, and I wouldn't try to stop it, if I were you.' She swung round to face him, eyes blazing angrily. 'That would be an interesting story for your precious newspapers, wouldn't it? The councillor who doesn't believe in free speech.' Jonathon sighed. That ridiculous accusation was just the sort of nonsense the papers found irresistible. Of course he believed in free speech. He just wanted his wife to keep her mouth shut until he was re-elected. Thank goodness the papers were preoccupied with the Woolsmarsh Strangler, he reflected, and was instantly ashamed of himself for such a wicked thought.

26

Row

It was unusual for Geraldine to oversleep, especially when she was working, but the long drive to see her sister on Sunday had taken its toll on her. She had no time for breakfast and rushed to the station, arriving in a panic with barely five minutes to spare. As she was quickly checking the latest updates, Peterson strolled over to enquire about her weekend. He was holding the remains of a bacon roll in one hand, a steaming mug of coffee in the other. Geraldine was starving, and desperate for her morning shot of caffeine. The mingled smell of bacon and coffee goaded her unbearably, but the briefing was about to begin and there was no time to dash to the canteen. She snapped at the sergeant just as the DCI walked past them. Peterson's eyes widened in surprise and Geraldine instantly regretted her flash of temper, not only because the DCI must have overheard her. It wasn't the sergeant's fault she'd driven for two hours to visit a six-year-old who hadn't even noticed she was there, and then two hours back again through driving rain. Before she had a chance to explain, Kathryn Gordon spoke.

'We're five days into the investigation and I don't need to remind you we're no closer to making an arrest,' the DCI said. 'With every day that passes the trail grows a little colder. We can't afford to waste another moment. I expect everyone to give this case their undivided attention. We'll work round the clock if necessary. No leave till we nail him.' Her face was grimly determined.

Geraldine struggled to clear her head and focus on the briefing. Not much had come up over the weekend.

'We're going to recheck everything. Don't forget this could be a first offence,' the DCI concluded.

'Don't you think there'd be a record of assault at least, ma'am?' someone asked.

Kathryn Gordon shrugged her shoulders wearily. 'All I'm saying is, don't fall back on stereotypes. John Drew remains our prime suspect, but we need to keep an open mind.' There was a general sigh of agreement. 'Carter, check with forensics again. I agree it's unlikely, but it's quite possible this could be the work of a first offender. Every criminal has to start somewhere.' Glancing round the room, Geraldine saw that several officers were nodding their heads.

'No peace for the wicked,' Carter muttered as they broke up.

The DCI always seemed to have her feelings under tight control. Geraldine thought wretchedly about her own outburst. She never normally lost her temper. It wasn't as though she'd even been angry with Peterson. She glanced up and saw him and Sarah Mellor conferring together. As she lowered her eyes, she heard Sarah laughing. They were probably talking about her. Peterson was a good sergeant and Geraldine had lost her temper with him for no reason. Much as Geraldine regretted her behaviour, she wasn't sure how to put matters right. She told herself it wasn't cowardice or pride that held her back from apologising, but a proper sense of her dignity as his superior officer.

As the team dispersed, Kathryn Gordon asked Geraldine to follow her into her office, which was too small to fit her desk and filing cabinets comfortably. Geraldine noticed the drawers weren't labelled and wondered how anyone else would be able to find anything in there if the DCI were away from her desk. A window was open despite the cold, but a faint whiff of a familiar aroma permeated the chilly air. It seemed the DCI didn't restrict her drinking to the pub. Geraldine hovered as the other woman sat down.

'Is there a problem with DS Peterson?' Kathryn Gordon asked. 'Well?'

'No, ma'am.'

'It takes a certain sort of woman to cope with the pressure of serious crime investigations,' the DCI continued.

'Like you, ma'am?' She hadn't intended to sound impertinent.

Kathryn Gordon glared. 'Don't try to be like me, Geraldine,' she retorted. She took a deep breath and gestured for Geraldine to sit down. 'We have a responsibility towards our fellow officers, Geraldine, particularly to those younger and less experienced than we are.' Geraldine wondered which of them Kathryn Gordon was talking to. 'This is a difficult investigation. Murders are. You know that. We're all feeling tired and frustrated. But we can't allow our feelings to work against us. We have to pull together, because we're a team. And if we're a team …' She paused, losing her place in a familiar speech.

'Yes ma'am.'

'Am I making myself clear?'

'Yes, ma'am. I get the message.'

'All I did was have a few words with a DS,' Geraldine grumbled to Carter later as they sat over lunch in the canteen. 'He wasn't bothered. And she goes and makes a fuss about it. Gave me a bloody lecture about working as a team. It's all right for her to take a pop, but if I say anything to a DS, I as good as get a warning. It's outrageous. The DCI's definitely got it in for me.' Carter began to remonstrate but Merton joined them and the conversation moved on. The knowledge that she was being petty did nothing to improve Geraldine's mood, but she wasn't alone in her agitation. Everyone was growing edgy as time passed without any new leads, and tension turned to anxiety.

The media weren't helping. Five days had passed since Angela Waters' murder, and some of the papers were already asking questions. *The Woolsmarsh Chronicle* had been openly hostile.

Blonde Angela Waters (22) was murdered in broad daylight beside a children's playground. *What are the police doing to safeguard our children?*

They published their questions without bothering to look for an answer, interested only in sensational headlines, not the arduous daily slog of the investigation. Most crime detection work was too dull to be newsworthy, so they filled their pages with hysterical claptrap, aping the worst campaigns of the national tabloids.

'Who killed Angela Waters?' the paper screamed at her. Geraldine wished she knew. The headlines were useful in raising public awareness and it was true the articles might encourage a witness to come forward, but she resented their ill-informed criticism of the police. Journalists thought they could print anything with impunity. At least the *Chronicle* had put the picture of the man with a scar on the front page.

Suddenly aware she was hungry, Geraldine glanced at her watch. It was six o'clock and she hadn't eaten since one. Wearily she packed her bag and made her way home where she spent a miserable evening studying reports. After midnight she finally sank into bed, hoping she wouldn't be disturbed by nightmares.

It wasn't long before she found herself wishing she *had* been woken by a bad dream.

27

Witness

Geraldine groped for the snooze button, but it wasn't the alarm.

Merton's thin voice slapped her awake. 'We've got another one.'

She switched to speakerphone. 'Go on!' she yelled, tugging at her trousers, fumbling with buttons, and scanning the floor for her shoes.

'DCI thinks it's the strangler.'

'I'm listening.'

'Young girl. Blonde.'

'How young?'

'Twelve? Thirteen? Approached from behind. Probably strangled, if the last one was anything to go by.'

'What do we know?'

'Not a lot. Possible sexual assault. Pathologist's on his way. Millard.' Merton sounded out of breath, as though he was running.

Geraldine grabbed her keys. 'I'm on my way. Where to?'

'Lyceum Park.'

Geraldine gasped. The forensic tent had only just been taken down in the park after Angela Waters' murder. She felt as though she was dreaming as she passed between tall Gothic gateposts to the scene where a second body had been discovered within a week. It was barely daylight. Trees looked black and menacing in the background and the lake gleamed coldly in the early morning light. It was a setting for a cheap horror movie. She half expected to hear sinister music as she walked along the path. By the time she reached the scene, the Murder Investigation Team had taken over a large patch of scrubby grass beside the children's playground. Peterson was already there and Geraldine nodded at him glumly. The DCI was standing by the catering truck, her gloved fingers wrapped round a steaming polystyrene cup, flanked by the two other DIs. Carter gave Geraldine a brief nod and Merton glowered at her as she hurried over to join them. They stood watching as a second white forensic van drew up. They collected their suits, masks, and gloves. A dog handler jumped down from one of the people carriers, and joined the throng around the catering truck.

'Don't put your overshoes on until you reach the tent,' the girl dispensing suits called out. Scrambling through muddy undergrowth, bent nearly double to protect her head from overhanging branches, Geraldine could see why. Brambles and protruding roots would have destroyed their flimsy overshoes before they were even near the tent.

Her skin looked very white. Lights flashed like buzzing insects as she was photographed from every angle. Geraldine doubted if the dead girl had ever received this much attention when she was alive. Her grey skirt was pulled up to her stomach, tights and knickers half-way down her thighs. A skinny torso made the exposed area of pubic hair look obscene, and unutterably sad. She was only a child. Gloom hung like a pall over the white-coated activity. With a time of death around seven p.m. she had been lying there overnight, not reported missing yet. Her absence wouldn't be noticed now until the day began. It was only six thirty. Geraldine gazed down at the pointed little face and hoped her last moments had been painless, not degrading.

'Was she raped?' Kathryn Gordon enquired curtly, her words cutting the air. 'She's intact,' the doctor replied.

Geraldine swallowed, relieved beyond words. 'Seems he was just looking, or disturbed.'

She couldn't have put up much of a fight. She looked as if a puff of wind would blow her over. Her hair was like straw, her clothes shabby. An old brown satchel lay nearby.

'Anything in the bag?' Carter held up a dirty pink purse containing three pounds and eleven pence. Scrunched-up tissues, a mucky pot of concealer, a clogged mascara brush that had come loose from its tube, a pink comb and a small round mirror had been photographed and bagged. Geraldine was handed a school diary, dog-eared and covered in doodles. She flipped through it. On the inside page the dead girl had filled in her personal details.

Name	Tiffany may
Address	
Telephone No.	
Mobile No.	
Date of Birth	22nd march 1994 so get me a presant if your reading this
Doctor	Docter membery
Dentist	non
Next of Kin	non

Geraldine calculated her age: thirteen. Unlucky for some. The rest of the book was filled with scribbles and doodles: 'TIFFANY 4 ROBBY', and other childish jottings. There was no timetable or record of any school work.

'Who found her?' Merton asked.

'Old chap, walking his dog early. We offered him a lift home but he said he'd wait in case he could help.' Kathryn Gordon pointed through the branches and creepers to an elderly man sitting on a bench a little way off. A small white and brown dog was jumping up and down by his side. The DCI nodded sombrely at Geraldine who ran the gauntlet of the brambles again, hands scratched and ankles blistered with nettle stings.

'Remember to bring a machete next time, ma'am,' someone called out.

'There won't be a next time,' she heard the DCI reply sharply, an edge of nerves behind her stern tone.

They should have been prepared. He'd struck a second time in the same place and they'd let him slip away. Tiffany May, thirteen years old, had been in the park alone after dark. It was unforgivable. They should have done more to raise public awareness. Announcements had been broadcast on the local radio station and warnings had appeared in the papers but a child like Tiffany probably only watched American TV shows. They should have double-checked that schools were issuing regular reminders. Now they needed to act quickly to find out what the victim had been doing in the park, and whether she'd come alone.

Geraldine sat down on the bench and introduced herself. The old man's name was Fraser Duncan, although his accent wasn't Scottish, but slightly Welsh.

'I don't sleep well these days,' he wheezed. 'Not since my Jeanie passed away. All on my own, see. The girls come and visit, but they're not local. I get lonely. That's why they got me Betsy. For the company.' And the guilt, Geraldine thought, as the dog scrambled to its feet. 'Down, girl.' Betsy obediently sat at his feet again, her tail beating a tattoo on the ground. 'I often wake up early. I might get up and make a cup of tea, like I did today. And then Betsy, she nags for a walk, so I think, why not? Might as well keep the dog happy. I got no one else to think about.' He nodded at the shrubbery where the body was concealed. 'It wasn't me, Officer. I was with Betsy all the time.' Geraldine was too despondent to smile at the alibi. She pulled out her note-book.

Mr Duncan described his struggle to penetrate the dense

shrubbery. 'I could hear her, see? Moaning and whimper-
ing —'

'She was still alive?' Geraldine sat forward.

'What? Oh, the poor girl. No, I don't think so. I'm talking
about Betsy.' Duncan Fraser could shed little light on the
murder. The girl lay as he'd found her. 'I didn't touch
anything. I seen enough shows on the telly to know not to
tamper with the evidence at a crime scene. And Betsy, well,
she's only a dog, when all's said and done. I pulled her off,
soon as I saw what it was. I don't think she …' He wrinkled
his nose and sighed. 'Then I used the mobile telephone to
call you lot. Moira gave it me for Christmas. 'You take it
with you any time you go out, dad,' she told me. 'You never
know when you might need it.' Geraldine gave the old man
a card. He refused a lift home. 'She needs the exercise,' he
said, nodding at his dog as he rose unsteadily to his feet.

His dog frisking at his side, the old man began walking
slowly away. Geraldine watched his stooped progress, sharp
pity making her eyes water. She knew what it was to be
alone.

Peterson bounded up to her. 'The boss wants us to come
back later and speak to the two gardeners,' he told her. 'It
can't be coincidence, gov, both incidents in the same place.
It's got to be something to do with the park.'

They turned to watch the doors of the mortuary van open
for the stretcher. A chilly morning mist hovered over the
lake as Tiffany May set off on her penultimate journey.

28

Name

Jim was sensible. He changed into dry clothes before he lay down and closed his eyes, to remember his latest triumph. She wouldn't give him dirty thoughts again. He'd seen her walking quickly, hunched forward in the darkness and the driving rain, her collar turned right up. In the beating of the rain she hadn't heard him, moving swiftly behind her. He smiled. Inside his head it was happening again.

'It's your turn,' Miss Elsie said.

'You're it!' he mouthed, reaching for her arms She was thin and he caught her easily, her skinny wrists gripped in one hand, the other slapped over her mouth. It was lucky for her he was holding tight or she might have had a nasty bump when her feet slipped on the wet mud. Her eyes bulged in her scrawny face. She looked like a bushbaby. That was funny because he was carrying her, like a baby, into the bushes. She didn't laugh when he told her, gabbling under his breath in his excitement. Above his hand he watched her eyes widen as he turned her round and flung her down. He never let go of her mouth. He clutched her throat fiercely, shaking her until her fingers stopped scrabbling at his sleeves and her head flopped.

He shut his eyes and counted to ten because that was the rule. He had to whisper in case they were listening. She was staring up at him, ugly and cross. He didn't care. Her flimsy grey skirt had lifted up at the front when she fell. Curiously he pushed it up as far as he could. Through her tights he was surprised to see tiny flowers. Wondering, he pushed his hand between her legs. It was warm and damp. Encouraged, he tugged at the top of her tights. Her knickers came down with them. The strip of hair felt scratchy. He tried to push the thin thighs apart but they were held together by her tights. She smelled of wee and that was dirty. He wished he hadn't touched her. Rage exploded in his head. It wasn't fair. It was all right for her. The rain would wash her clean. But she'd made him dirty with her wee. She knew he didn't have a washbasin so he couldn't get properly clean. It was all her fault. He smacked her head and the sound echoed in his ears, frightening him.

Without pausing to cover her up, he fled, brushing wet leaves from his legs and chest as he ran along the path. He was careful not to touch anything with his dirty hand. He held it stiffly so it wouldn't touch his body. He was going to scrub it and scrub it until it no longer smelt of wee. He noticed a figure in the distance, across the lake, but he kept on running. He was sobbing, his heart thumping so fast it was difficult to breathe but he ran and ran. It wasn't safe in the park any more. It was all her fault, the stranger who'd asked him about a music shop. He'd done his best not to speak to her, and now she'd gone and spoiled everything. He had to find her and shut her up before she told anyone else about him.

Back in the shed, he picked up the diary again. He'd find her because he was clever. Wednesday, 26 September, was in the diary. That was the day he'd seen Angela Waters in the park. Among the notes and numbers he saw '*10.00 teacher Heather Spencer (Mrs).*' He thought until his eyes ached because he knew it was a clue. The papers said Angela Waters died at about nine thirty. *Teacher Heather Spencer (Mrs)* was going to the music shop at ten, so she would have been in the park, on her way, at half past nine. That was when she'd asked him where the music shop was. He knew her name. He felt a huge rush of cleverness in his head and laughed.

'Use your brain,' Miss Elsie said. He stared at the page as though it might tell him where to find her. At the top of the page it said '*9.00 Shelley Wigan (work experience) Redhill School*'. He knew about work experience because he'd done it. They said it was going to last a week. But after the first day, they told him he didn't have to go back again. He didn't mind. He didn't like work experience.

They sent him to a bakery. He had to wear a white hat and a white coat. He had to wear the hat at all times, in case his hair fell out. A woman told him and she said it again because it was important. He didn't want to go back there. He didn't want his hair to fall out. They told him to be careful not to burn his finger. The teachers said it was good for him but he thought it was stupid. He didn't want his hair to fall out and he didn't want to burn his finger.

Shelley Wigan (work experience) must be at school because she was doing work experience. He grasped at an idea. He kept thinking he understood something and then it went out of his brain. He knew the thinking bit of his brain didn't always work, but this was important.

Miss Elsie told him to think hard. 'Stay on the topic,' she said, 'and you can work out the answer all by yourself.' It went together, like a jigsaw where all the pieces fitted in their holes. His teacher had been to see him at the bakery to check he was being good. *Teacher Heather Spencer (Mrs)* had gone to see *Shelley Wigan (work experience)* at the music shop to check she was being good. It all made sense.

Miss Elsie smiled. 'Clever boy,' she said. 'I knew you could do it.'

Now he knew where to find her. She was a teacher at Redhill School. He'd seen a school near the park but that wasn't the right school. He had to find a school called Redhill. He wondered if it was on a red hill but that didn't help. He asked a girl in school uniform where to find Redhill School. She shook her head and ran away. She looked scared but he'd only asked her where to find a school. It wasn't a bad question. He hadn't asked her to get in a car with him. He hadn't offered her sweets.

He tried again and a boy told him. 'It's the other side of the park, innit?' Jim walked across the park but when he got to the other side he couldn't see Redhill School. He didn't get angry. Instead, he had another clever idea. It was better to be clever than angry. He came back early in the morning and waited until he saw some children going to school. He followed them. They didn't see him because he was clever. He was going to find Heather Spencer.

He found the school on the corner of a busy street. The main entrance was on a bus route. There was a big sign on the fence: REDHILL SCHOOL. He'd found where she worked. There was another way in round the corner. He watched and waited. No one saw him. She never went in the main entrance, so he stood round the corner and waited again. He was a good spy. It could be his job. No one knew he was there, watching. He was 'it' and no one could catch him. It was his turn.

He saw the stranger who'd spoken to him in the park. She walked quickly up the side street and into the school. She didn't see him watching her. Now he could move on to the next stage of his plan. It was easy to be clever. He was clever. Miss Elsie said so. The police had found Angela Waters and written about her in the paper. They didn't know about the other one. He didn't want them to find her or he'd be in trouble again. But they would never find her because he'd hidden her so well. All he had to do was find Heather Spencer (Mrs) and he would be safe to carry on his work. Miss Elsie would be pleased with him. He was doing God's work.

'Cleanse me from ev'ry sin and set me free,' he sang to himself and smiled.

29

Gardeners

Peter Lamprey had worked as a gardener at Lyceum Park for seventeen years. Blue eyes sparkled in a face weathered from decades spent outdoors. He seemed to take the two women's deaths as a personal affront.

'I never saw anything like it,' he told them, 'not in my park. In all the seventeen years I've done here, I never saw anything like this. I'm sorry I can't help you track down whoever it was did for those poor girls, but I wasn't here last Wednesday. Never here on Wednesdays. We do Mondays, Thursdays, and Fridays here. Wednesdays is a day off. I do other jobs on Wednesdays. So I wasn't here.' His gaze seemed drawn to the far trees. 'There was no one here on Wednesday. Never is. So you can just let me get on now. I've got work to do. Always busy this time of year.' He turned to go.

'Mr Lamprey,' Geraldine said, 'we don't want to keep you from your work. But we do need to eliminate you from our enquiries. This is a murder investigation and it would be best for everyone if you co-operated with us by answering a few more questions.'

Lamprey turned back and inclined his head. 'Go on then,' he said. 'Ask away.'

'Can you tell us where you were last Wednesday morning?'

'Yes I can. I started over at Mrs Merriott's this week, weeding beds, raking leaves …' He reeled off a list of chores.

Peterson interrupted him. 'Can you give us her address?'

The old man scratched his head. 'It's Wisley Street, one of the big houses on the West Woolsmarsh estate. It's the one next to the letterbox, with a magnolia in the front garden. Doesn't look much at this time of year, but it's a lovely tree. You want to see it in bloom.'

'What time were you there?'

Lamprey told them he started at Mrs Merriott's about eight thirty. 'She's up early, that one. Always has a cup of tea waiting. We call it our breakfast. She likes a bit of a chat. They all do. I look after the gardens for a few old ladies on the estate and they all like to stop and chat. I see to the gardens and do a few odd jobs outdoors. Fixing the fences, and the gates when they slip and start to bang in the wind. I don't work inside. Only in the gardens.'

'What time did you leave Mrs Merriott's?'

He shook his head. 'Must've been just before ten. Next one was old Mrs Creakey. She makes me tea at ten.'

'And you were at Mrs Merriott's until then?'

'Yes.'

'Have you seen anyone unusual hanging around the park lately?' Geraldine asked.

'We see some odd characters in the park, yes.'

'Have you seen a man with a scar on his upper lip?'

'A scar? No. No one with a scar, not that comes to mind. But I'm usually seeing to the plants. I don't pay much attention to people passing through.'

Geraldine frowned. 'Anyone unusual? Any strangers?' she persisted. There was a pause.

'Was a tramp,' he replied thoughtfully. Geraldine waited but Lamprey was silent.

'Can you describe him?'

'Just a tramp. Dirty.'

'Where did he sleep?'

'Don't know.'

Geraldine asked if Peter Lamprey had a coat. He looked down and held his arms out to display his navy parka. Geraldine asked if he owned another coat, or a scarf, and he shook his head to both questions.

'What do I need another coat for?' he asked. 'This one not good enough then?' He scowled at her. 'It'll do well enough.'

'What can you tell us about Terence Tillotson?' Peterson asked.

Lamprey shrugged his wiry shoulders. 'He's only been here a few weeks,' he replied, 'and if he lasts a few more it'll be a miracle. Work shy, that one.' The two detectives exchanged a glance.

'When exactly did he start working here?' Peterson continued.

Lamprey pursed his lips, thinking. 'Second week in September,' he said at last. 'He started that Monday and if you ask me, I was better off on my own. Never had any trouble here until he came along. Nothing like this ever happened before. He turns up and suddenly some young woman goes and gets herself murdered. He's got an eye for the girls, that boy has. I'm not saying he did it, mind, only it looks suspicious, if you ask me.' He narrowed his eyes and spat on the damp earth. Geraldine didn't react. She knew Peterson had noted the coincidence. Geraldine thanked Lamprey and asked him to let her know if he thought of anything else. He nodded, his head turned away, his thoughts already back among the trees and shrubs.

The second gardener, Terry Tillotson, told them he'd lived in the area all his life and had been working in Lyceum Park for three weeks. Geraldine studied his cheerful young face. He claimed to be twenty-four but barely looked old enough to be out of school. He was blond, with eyelashes any girl would covet and dazzling blue eyes. He was wearing a hooded grey jacket.

Before Geraldine could begin, Tillotson spoke. 'I reckon I saw someone, last night,' he told them. 'About six o'clock.'

'Why didn't you report it?'

The boy shrugged, nonchalant. 'Guess I didn't think of it.'

Geraldine wondered what else he was keeping back. He was probably up to some scam in the park, meeting young girls, or dealing drugs. She wondered if it could be something more vicious. He'd admitted being in the park the previous evening, when Tiffany May was killed. He'd been working late to make up his hours, he explained, sweeping the paths and emptying the bins. It was mainly litter this time of year.

'Not been bad the last week. Quietish, like. Pete reckons it's because of that dead girl. It's keeping them away, specially the kids. They're the ones drop most of the litter.' He was little more than a kid himself. He'd finished his work and was locking his equipment in the shed, when he realised he was missing his litter spike. He retraced his steps and found it near the pond. It was past knocking-off time but he sat on for a bit and had a smoke.

'Go on,' Geraldine said quietly.

Tillotson told them he'd been enjoying the quiet of the evening. 'Had the place to myself. It was nice. Like it was my own private estate.' It was a starry night, Terence said. He was interested in stars. He knew all about the 'consolations' up there. Geraldine didn't believe that for a moment. He'd finished his smoke, stubbed it out carefully, and tossed his cigarette butt into the nearest bin on his way back to the shed.

'Very public-spirited,' Peterson sneered.

'If you had to go round collecting up all the fag ends people leave lying around, you'd be careful. And it's not only fag ends, I'm telling you.' While he was traipsing across the sodden grass in his wellies on the far side of the lake, he'd spotted a figure in the moonlight, hurrying along the path in the direction of the High Street. It was too dark to make out much, but he was sure it was a man. He described how the figure had 'a dead arm' hanging limply at his side as he loped along.

'Was it him? The Woolsmarsh Strangler?'

Geraldine gave a noncommittal grunt. 'Is there anything else you can tell us, Mr Tillotson?'

'No.' He shook his head vigorously.

'Where were you last Wednesday morning?'

'Me?' He looked surprised. 'I was at home. Don't work Wednesdays. It's a day off.' Peterson noted down his address.

'Can anyone confirm you were there last Wednesday morning?' Geraldine asked. She saw a glint in the gardener's eyes.

'My girl, Melanie Rogers. Ron Rogers and Lynda Clare's daughter,' he boasted. They couldn't rule him out, but somehow Geraldine doubted if he was their man. She gave Tillotson a card in case he remembered anything else and thanked him for his co-operation, and he swaggered off, whistling jauntily.

'He's fit,' Geraldine remarked.

'He's only twenty-four, gov,' Peterson laughed. Geraldine turned away. Inside her head she still felt the same age as the sergeant, who hadn't reached thirty. It was galling to be reminded that he viewed her as older. The difference between them couldn't be much more than five years. Without thinking she raised her hand and smoothed the lines on her forehead, making a mental note to avoid frowning. And smiling. And raising her eyebrows. With a sigh she switched her thoughts back to the case.

'What did you make of the wounded man?' Geraldine asked Peterson as they walked back to the car. The DS shook his head.

'I don't buy it, gov.'

She nodded. 'He made the whole thing up, didn't he? But do you really think *he* could be our killer?' It seemed unlikely.

'He's certainly here a lot, I'll grant you that,' Peterson conceded cautiously.

'That's because he works here.'

'Which gives him the opportunity, but no more than anyone else walking in the park. It's not as if it's locked at night. I hardly think he'd murder two girls right here, so soon after he arrived. But why put himself in the frame like that?' Peterson asked.

'In case he was seen? He might think that by telling us he was here he's making himself look innocent. Or perhaps we caught him off guard? He's got the grey jacket. It fits. And you said yourself his story of a man with a disabled arm is fabricated.'

Peterson nodded. 'He didn't strike me as stupid. Immature, yes, and dishonest, but not a violent type. Then again, it could be an impulse he can't control. Or maybe he just thinks he can get away with it.'

The murderer *is* getting away with it, Geraldine thought angrily. 'Still,' she said, 'it's a coincidence, isn't it, his starting work here just two weeks before Angela Waters was killed? And he's lying about something. Could be just another bored youngster with a lively imagination, but let's check him out carefully.'

There was something shady about Terence Tillotson, but he struck her as an improbable suspect. Whichever way she looked at it, she doubted that such a good looking boy would attack strange women in the park where he worked, when he could easily pick up girls further away from home. Peterson agreed.

'Just because someone's around a lot, it doesn't necessarily mean they're up to something,' she went on. The DS scowled and Geraldine remembered having heard a couple of WPCs gossiping in the toilets. They'd fallen silent as soon as Geraldine came out of her cubicle, but she'd heard enough. Someone had been visiting Peterson's house while he was out at work.

'Turned out it wasn't only the heating he was servicing,' one of the WPCs had said, erupting with laughter. She'd caught sight of Geraldine in the mirror, and fallen silent.

Geraldine lowered her eyes. If Peterson was having personal problems, she'd have to tread carefully. They couldn't afford to allow anything to distract them from the case.

Later that evening she reread all her notes, alone with a bottle of chilled white wine. Tillotson's statement was puzzling. A man couldn't hold a girl down and strangle her with only one arm. It didn't make sense, unless he'd been injured during the attack, but forensics had found no evidence of a struggle. There were no scrapings of skin under Tiffany May's fingernails, no blood, just dirt and grease. Then again, if Tillotson had intended to mislead them, he would surely have come up with a plausible description of an imaginary figure. Geraldine closed her eyes and a picture of a man began to form in her mind. He didn't understand English, or couldn't hear well, or he disliked being spoken to. He had an injured arm and slunk about in the park waiting for solitary women. She opened her eyes. The arm didn't fit. She bit her lip in frustration. There were too many unanswered questions.

30

Carer

The atmosphere was tense at the morning briefing.

'John Drew is out of the frame for Tiffany May,' Kathryn Gordon said. She nodded at Merton who stood up and cleared his throat.

'Drew was involved in a brawl on Saturday night outside the Dog and Duck in Wilberforce Street,' he said. Several local officers shook their heads, murmuring darkly. The Dog was a notorious trouble spot on Saturday nights. 'He was admitted to Woolsmarsh General at eleven fifteen on Saturday night,' Merton's voice droned on. He glanced down at his notes. 'Concussion. He lost consciousness at the incident and was taken in for observation.' Everyone knew where this was leading. Merton carried on remorselessly. 'They did a scan yesterday afternoon and kept him in for observation. They're still waiting for the results. So Drew's out of the frame for the murder of Tiffany May.'

'Bugger,' a voice exclaimed loudly. Someone else muttered a weary crack about a scan finding nothing between Drew's ears but no one smiled.

'We'll keep an eye on Drew,' the DCI said. 'It's possible Angela Waters and Tiffany May were killed by different people.' Everyone knew that was grasping at straws.

'One step forward, two steps back,' someone mumbled. They'd lost their suspect. The atmosphere was subdued as they set off on their day's tasks.

Geraldine parked the car on the dilapidated Chartwell

Estate. Identical four and five storey brick blocks hemmed them in on all sides. Although the air outside was fresh, she felt claustrophobic and her eyes searched for the driveway that led back to the road. The flat they wanted was located in one corner. A narrow strip of grass grew feebly by the entrance to each block, and someone had planted a few daffodils in front of Tiffany May's doorway. Geraldine wondered who had taken the trouble to put them there; someone young enough to feel that life still held the promise of something better. She scrutinised the motley assortment of vehicles parked there. Next to the unmarked police car a filthy white van displayed a two-year-old tax disc. On the other side, a rusty red Skoda sported a slashed tyre. Peterson raised an eyebrow and she shook her head. Better not advertise their business. He put the police notice back inside the car and closed the door.

Tiffany May's flat was on the ground floor. They heard the bell ring, but no one came to the door. It was eleven o'clock. By now everyone would have gone out for the day. No one had reported the girl missing. If Geraldine had disappeared overnight when she was thirteen, her mother would have been on the phone to the police station at once, demanding urgent action, but Tiffany's absence had gone unnoticed. A mother so careless of her young daughter's whereabouts was probably blind drunk or too far gone to worry about anything beyond her next fix.

'Let's try the school,' she muttered. Peterson looked relieved as he climbed back in the car. They hadn't seen a soul, had heard no sound, no muffled television, no distant music. Driving off the estate, she glanced in her rear mirror and glimpsed indistinct figures emerging from doorways and passages. The residents had been watching them. At least one of them probably knew exactly what had happened to Tiffany May.

'Someone there knows something,' the DS muttered at

her side, as though reading her thoughts.

The school resembled an abandoned prison block, with cracked window frames and a fenced in concrete yard littered with gum and cans, scraps of paper and scrunched up crisp packets. The head teacher, Mrs Rutherford, was a harassed-looking woman, prematurely grey. She acknowledged them with an air of resignation.

'Let's get this over with quickly. I have a million and one things to attend to this morning,' her eyes said. She gasped silently when Geraldine explained the reason for their visit.

'Tiffany?' Mrs Rutherford repeated, as though the police had mistaken the name. 'Tiffany May? Are you sure?'

'No one's reported her missing. Did anyone telephone the school about her absence?' Geraldine enquired. 'We called at her home, but there was no reply.'

'There wouldn't be,' Mrs Rutherford replied. 'Mother's incapacitated. Virtually bedridden. Tiffany took care of her. Tiffany is – was – a carer …' She broke off, eyes glittering with tears or anger, it was impossible to tell which.

'Carer?' Peterson echoed.

'That's why there was no answer at home. Tiffany's mother can't get to the door. She doesn't get out of bed. Clinical depression. She has bouts in hospital, but they always send her home. Social services keep an eye. Apart from that, Tiffany looks – looked after her mother. Mother's comatose, on a good day. So, no. No one at home to report her missing.' Mrs Rutherford sat silent for a moment, staring with a vacant expression. When she spoke again, her tone was brisk. 'Knock next door. They have a key. Either side. They'll let you in. You'll need to tell her, won't you? But don't expect too much. She probably won't react and if she does want to speak, you'll need to be patient. I suppose you'll notify social services?'

They drove back in silence to Kings Close, parked in the same spot as before and tried next door. A stale smell wafted out as a young woman opened the door. She was holding a baby with dirty smudges on its cheeks.

'Yeah? Whadya want?' Geraldine showed her warrant card and explained they needed to speak to Mrs May. The neighbour barely glanced at the card. Instead she stepped back, glaring at them.

'Whadya want?' Mrs May was known to her neighbours only as 'Tiffany's mum'. 'Oh her. Why didn't you say? Who's he then?' Peterson displayed his ID card, which the woman scrutinised with an exaggerated show of suspicion. 'Dunno about him,' she said finally. Geraldine gave her a sharp warning about obstructing the police in their enquiries and the woman capitulated. 'Only being careful of our Tiffany's mum.' She gave an aggrieved sniff. 'No need to get so fucking shirty.' She sloped off down the hallway, grumbling to herself, and returned with a Yale key dangling from a greasy piece of string. 'Here,' she said, tossing it at Geraldine, 'and mind you bring it back.' Slam. They heard the baby bawling. As they turned away, its cries stopped abruptly.

Geraldine opened the front door and peered cautiously into the semi-darkness.

'Mrs May?' Silence. The narrow hallway stank of vinegar and body odour. Geraldine almost gagged when she breathed in. Empty crisp packets littered the floor. Chewing gum and cigarette stubs had been trodden into threadbare carpet. The sitting room was strewn with magazines, several clearly labelled 'School Library' and 'Doctor's Surgery' and 'DO NOT REMOVE'. Glamorous figures smiled up from the covers, mocking the squalor around them. In the tiny kitchen a clutter of soiled plates and half empty cups covered every surface. Empty pizza boxes were piled along one wall, next to a bin overflowing with greasy newspaper, chips, ketchup and tea bags. 'Hope we never have to search this lot,' she muttered.

They found Tiffany's mother lying in bed, staring at the ceiling. At first Geraldine thought she was unconscious. A bluebottle darted round and round in a crazy configuration, the only sign of life in the room.

'Mrs May?' There was no response, then the woman blinked. Her head moved and she looked past Geraldine blankly. Her mouth opened. As if it was all too much effort, she resumed staring at the cracked ceiling. Her mouth closed slowly. She showed no curiosity about her visitors. Geraldine waved her ID card without prompting any reaction. Speaking slowly and clearly, so there could be no mistaking her meaning, Geraldine explained that Tiffany was dead.

'I'm so sorry for your loss, but I'm afraid Tiffany won't be coming back here any more.' The woman didn't move. Tentatively, Gerry reached out and touched the fingers bunched on top of a grubby pink blanket. They were cold. As the woman inched her hand away, Geraldine wished she could be anywhere else but here, in this gloomy room. They would alert social services. There was nothing more they could do for Tiffany's mother.

On the way back to the station, Peterson wondered if there might be a connection between Angela Waters and Tiffany May. Geraldine doubted there was anything to link the two victims.

'They grew up in different places, weren't the same age, lived in different areas of town, and had different tastes and friends. Where could they have come across one another?'

'But think about it, gov. Why these two women in particular, when it could've been anyone?' Geraldine rather thought that was the point, but she considered the possibilities with him anyway.

'I'm nothing if not open minded,' she said and was pleased out of all proportion when the DS agreed.

They both knew that if there was nothing to connect the

two victims it meant the killer was striking at random, making his movements virtually impossible to predict, or track. Back at the station, they explored the idea. Geraldine jotted down a list as they spoke: young, long fair hair, alone in the park.

'What about the rain? Could that be a trigger for him?' Peterson suggested.

'He has to strike when there's no one else around. The park's not going to be so busy when it's raining.'

'Long fair hair,' Peterson read out. 'He likes long fair hair.'

Geraldine nodded. 'We ought to make sure that's stressed in the press release,' she said. 'The hair and the rain. Sarah, can you see that's added, suitably worded.'

Sarah Mellor nodded. 'Shall I run it past the DCI?'

'Yes,' Geraldine replied.

'Women with long fair hair shouldn't walk in the rain,' Peterson said lightly and Mellor slapped him playfully on the arm. Geraldine was taken aback by the intimacy of the gesture and annoyed with herself for noticing.

Geraldine left Peterson following his hunch; she was afraid the only link between the two victims was that they had been alone when they encountered the killer.

'That's two bodies in a week,' the DCI had fumed in the early morning briefing. 'Why the sudden hurry? What's triggered it?' Everyone listening shared her sense of urgency. The killer had struck twice in quick succession. The spectre of a third victim hung in the air.

31

Mellor

Geraldine left Peterson searching for a possible link between the two victims. Crouched over a keyboard, he looked very different to the dapper young officer she'd met on her arrival at Woolsmarsh police station only a week before. He'd removed his jacket; her glance took in armpits stained with sweat, a crumpled shirt and slipping tie, tousled hair and eyes shadowy with fatigue. Geraldine and DC Mellor drove in silence to the school where Mrs Rutherford had compiled a short list of Tiffany's friends: Holly Denning, Amy James, and Patrick Purvis.

'We don't know anything about her relationship with Patrick,' the head teacher said, 'but the girls have told us he was Tiffany's boyfriend. He denies it, of course, but I thought you'd want to have a word with him. You can use my office. There isn't anywhere else. The deputy's accompanying the children.' Geraldine thanked the head teacher who led them to her office and then rushed away to deal with her daily round of petty crises.

The deputy brought the children in one by one.

'Will we be on telly?' each of the girls asked on entering the room. They must have been discussing the question while they were waiting. Cynical about adult vice, Geraldine found their youthful narcissism depressing. Neither of the two girls appeared to be upset. They had plenty to say about Tiffany, but their comments were irrelevant or incomprehensible. Tiffany May hadn't been popular, even with those who claimed to have been her friends.

'She stinks,' one of the girls said haughtily, pursing glossy lips. Both girls mentioned Pat and giggled.

Geraldine felt awkward quizzing the boy. He looked about ten. The deputy head, a mealy mouthed woman, sat watching stony faced.

'Was Tiffany your girlfriend?' Geraldine began, smiling encouragement. The boy looked at her blankly. He didn't answer. 'Do you know why Tiffany went to the park on Monday?' she asked him directly. The boy shook his head, eyes suddenly wary. A fierce blush tinged his cheeks. Geraldine glanced at Mellor. The DC had seen the boy's reaction and was making a note. 'Were you meeting her there? It's very important you tell us,' Geraldine urged. The boy mumbled something unintelligible about Tiffany wanting to.

'It's all right, you haven't done anything wrong,' Geraldine said gently, but the boy flatly refused to say any more and was taken away.

'Looks like she went to the park to meet that boy,' Geraldine said to Mellor as they trudged across the dismal schoolyard.

'Sad,' the constable replied. 'Resorting to that for a boyfriend.'

'Not exactly a boyfriend. They're only thirteen.'

'Old enough.'

'And her mother ...' Geraldine sighed. 'She'd been caring for her mother since she was eight.'

'It's not like she had a choice.'

They drove off in silence. Geraldine wondered how she'd react if she were ever called on to care for someone. Being godmother to Chloe was a formality. If anything happened to Celia and Sebastian, Geraldine wouldn't have a clue what to do with her niece. She'd grown used to her own routine. Spending her working life in the service of her fellow man, since Mark had walked out on her she'd grown used to thinking only of herself in private. A glorious, bitter freedom. Sometimes she thought it was lucky she and Mark hadn't had children. But a child would have changed everything.

'Maybe Peterson's come across something,' Mellor suggested brightly as they drew into the station car park.

'Maybe,' Geraldine answered, remembering a time when she herself had been young and optimistic.

32

Rogers

As soon as Geraldine caught sight of Peterson's face she knew he hadn't come up with anything new.

'Nothing so far, gov.'

'Nothing at all?' Geraldine realised she'd been clinging to the faint hope that he would find something to connect the two victims and give a clue to the identity of the killer.

He shook his head. 'Only that they both walked through Lyceum Park, on different days at different times, and were strangled there in the bushes. Apart from that, I've found nothing in common. My guess is, they must have met the killer in the park.'

'Have you gone right back?' she asked. 'What about school?'

'Angela Waters lived up North until two years ago, remember? She only came down here after she met John Drew in Blackpool. He was on holiday there and she was working in some sort of men's club. He brought her back here, gave her somewhere to live and a better life.' His bitterness was almost palpable.

'What about the café? Did Tiffany ever go there?'

'I checked. Umberto said he doesn't encourage school children. It's not that sort of place. And Tiffany May was hardly the sort of girl to go out for coffee and pastries. She wouldn't have had the money. Neither he nor the waitress recognised her picture.'

'What about a hairdresser?' Geraldine knew she sounded

desperate. Tiffany May had probably never seen the inside of a salon. 'There's still some work to be done on it, but let's leave the rest of the cross checking to Sarah,' she said at last. 'Now, let's see what the young gardener was up to on Wednesday morning, when he wasn't at work.'

Peterson nodded, brightening up. 'Here's hoping he hasn't got an alibi and falls apart when we pull him in for questioning,' he said breezily, his good humour restored. He liked to be out and about, not stuck behind a desk. Geraldine shared his need to be doing something.

Peterson rang a bell on imposing wrought iron and gold gates. A bronze sign announced the name: PARADISE. A buzzer sounded and a voice challenged them to state their names and display their passes for the entry camera. A moment later the gates swung soundlessly open and they drove up a climbing tree lined avenue that led to Ron Rogers' palatial house. To their left they glimpsed tennis courts behind massive rhododendrons and azaleas as they drove up the sweep of the drive. Rounding a bend, they caught their first glimpse of a red brick building. It looked like an exclusive country house hotel.

Geraldine had read all she could about Ron Rogers. He'd been a big name in the music industry in his youth. He'd long since given up performing, but not before amassing a huge personal fortune. His wedding to an international fashion model had been a media circus, earning the couple the predictable nickname, 'Beauty and the Beast'. They retired from the limelight in the 1980s, hoping to bring their daughter up away from the paparazzi, but in a backwater like Woolsmarsh they'd inevitably become celebrities in the area. The local press seized on anything Ron Rogers did and often reported on his daughter's activities too: her outings to London and her fashion faux pas. There was a picture of blonde Melanie Rogers on the file, in a shiny ball gown: a pretty twenty-one-year-old seeing a man of whom her father disapproved. Geraldine felt a little envious.

Wealthy people aspired to live close to Ron Rogers' estate. The surrounding area was on the route of regular police patrols and there were numerous security systems in place on the property itself. Ron Rogers had electronic gates in his high fences, security lights, cameras, and guards with dogs. The property was defended like a fortress to protect his magnificent art treasures and his wife's jewellery collection. The Rogers hosted fabulous events attended by an assortment of household names. Geraldine scanned the list of media personalities, pop singers and film stars who visited them. No wonder the local constabulary patrolled the area conscientiously. It was a target for professional burglars and the slightest hint of trouble on Ron Rogers' estate would throw the media into a frenzy.

Peterson parked beside a beautiful carved fountain: a tall figure of Neptune holding a trident, surrounded by mermaids. Water streamed from shells they held out to him. In the distance they could see a golf course as they ascended a wide stone stairway to the double front door. They were ushered into an oak panelled hallway lit by concealed lamps. Ron Rogers came down a broad staircase to meet them. He was a tall man, round shouldered and lean. He wore his thinning hair long, tied in a ponytail. Geraldine had never met him before, but his ravaged face was familiar.

'Inspector?' He extended a huge hand in welcome. 'How can I help you?'

'We'd like to speak to Melanie.'

Ron Rogers' convivial smile drooped. 'She's with her boyfriend. I've got the address here somewhere if you'd like to wait a moment. Somewhere in East Woolsmarsh.'

'Do you know the name Terence Tillotson?' Geraldine asked.

'Melanie's seeing a young bloke she calls Terry. I've only met him once. I'm afraid I don't know his other name. I can tell you that he works in a park.'

'Thank you.'

'Is this Terry in some sort of trouble? I'd be very grateful if you could keep my daughter's name out of any embarrassment. You know she's not like most young people. Any story's all over the papers like a rash.' He gave an apologetic smile. Geraldine assured him that, as far as they knew, Terence Tillotson wasn't involved in any illegal activity. She wasn't sure whether Ron Rogers looked pleased or not.

'This is merely a routine enquiry,' she said. He looked at her sceptically but made no comment. They thanked Ron Rogers and took their leave.

'Nice place,' Peterson muttered as the gates swung closed behind them.

They drove through the centre of town and drew up outside a rundown block of flats in East Woolsmarsh where Terence Tillotson lived.

'Let's hope she's here,' Geraldine said, screwing up her face at the smell of rotting vegetables and damp that clung to the air.

'And confirms he wasn't, last Wednesday morning,' Peterson added. He sounded suddenly tense. No one came to the door when they rang the bell. The DS knocked loudly but there was no answer.

'We'll have to try later,' Geraldine said, turning away. Peterson nodded and followed her to the car.

Their next visit was to Mrs Merriott in Wisley Street. They found the house beside the letterbox easily. A tall bare tree stood in the middle of a sloping front lawn. Mrs Merriott peered beady eyed at Geraldine's warrant card before opening the door wide.

'Oh yes,' she said, 'come in, come in. It's about Mr Paul is it?'

'Mr Paul?'

'Mr Paul, leaving his bins out the front all week. I've asked him not to. But it's very good of you to come along. How did you know?' Geraldine explained they'd come to ask about her gardener, Peter Lamprey. Mrs Merriott frowned. 'Peter the gardener?' she repeated, in surprise. 'Yes, he looks after things for me. He's a lovely man, Inspector, so obliging. He comes every week and does for a couple of hours. It's not really enough, but it's better than nothing. Keeps the weeds at bay.'

'Was he here last week, Mrs Merriott?'

'Oh yes. He never misses.'

'Did he arrive on time last week?'

'Yes. He's never late.'

'And did he leave at his usual time?'

'Yes, he did. Same as always. He comes week in, week out. Even when it's raining. He knows I rely on him. And there's always something to do in the garden. Or he can work in the green house if it's raining. He always stops for a cup of tea and a chat. Such a nice man. He's not in any trouble is he?'

'No, and thank you, Mrs Merriott.'

'Now, you'll stop for a cup of tea, won't you? It won't take me a minute to put the kettle on.'

'Thank you, Mrs Merriott, but we have to get on.' The old lady nodded, crestfallen. Their visit had probably been the highlight of her day.

'Melanie Rogers again?' Peterson asked as they climbed back in the car.

Geraldine nodded.

Melanie was on her own in the flat when the doorbell rang. She didn't recognise the man and woman standing outside and began to close the door when the woman held out a police identity card.

'You can check with the police station,' she said. 'We'll

175

wait.' There was an air of determination about the two strangers.

'Did he send you?' Melanie asked suspiciously.

'He?'

'My father.'

'We're here on police business, Miss Rogers. This has nothing to do with your father.'

'You'd better come in then.' Melanie led them into the front room where she'd been tidying up. Clothes were heaped everywhere. She cleared two chairs for them. She had no idea what the police could possibly want with her and wished they would just go away.

'Does Terence Tillotson live here?' the sergeant asked. Melanie looked at him. He had cute blue eyes, and was amazingly fit, but he looked way too serious. And boring.

'Yes.'

'We're interested in Mr Tillotson's movements last Wednesday.'

'Why do you want to know?' Melanie demanded.

The inspector cut in swiftly. 'Just answer our questions please, Miss Rogers.'

Melanie swallowed. 'What is it you want to know?' she amended her question.

'Can you tell us what were you doing last Wednesday morning?'

'I was at work.' She gave them details of the art gallery where she was employed and confirmed that Terry didn't work on Wednesdays.

Melanie wanted to finish tidying the flat before Terry came home, but the detectives kept on questioning her about Wednesday.

'Think about this carefully, Melanie. It's important.' Melanie stared at the woman, disconcerted by her stern tone. For the first time, it crossed her mind that this could be serious.

A vague memory flashed into her mind. 'This isn't about those women who were murdered in the park, is it?' she asked. 'That had nothing to do with Terry. He doesn't go to the park on Wednesdays.'

'We need to eliminate him from our enquiries.'

'You mean he's a suspect? That's crazy. Terry wouldn't hurt a fly. He's the gentlest person I've ever met. Tell me he's not a suspect? He can't be.'

'Please calm down, Miss Rogers, and just answer the questions.'

Melanie nodded. She thought about her answer. 'I was with Terry on Tuesday evening. We went shopping, and then we went out to eat. We were out late and Terry had a skinful.' She giggled suddenly. 'He told me he stayed in bed most of Wednesday morning. Hung over.' She shrugged. 'I had to get to work but I called him to check he was OK. When I popped home at lunch time he was still in bed.'

'Could he have gone out during the morning, while you were at work?' the sergeant asked.

Melanie shook her head. 'I wouldn't have thought so really, he was pretty sick.' She tried not to giggle.

'But you can't be sure Terence Tillotson stayed here in this flat throughout the whole of last Wednesday morning?'

'Well, I suppose he did. I wasn't here. But he was pretty sick. You can't really think he had anything to do with those women?'

The detectives looked at one another and then rose to their feet. Neither of them answered her. They thanked her for her time and moved towards the door.

Melanie was glad they were going. Terry would be back soon and she wanted to be ready for him. She'd been waiting all day to see him. But as the front door closed on the two detectives, an alarming suspicion entered her mind. Her father had warned her that Terry might sell her story to the papers, but what if he was hiding a more sinister secret?

Thinking about it made her feel sick as she realised she didn't really know Terry at all. She'd been at work on Wednesday. Terry could have faked his hangover, knowing she'd provide him with an alibi. She tried to dismiss her fears, but kept coming back to the same thought. How could she be sure he hadn't gone out on Wednesday morning?

33

Reporter

Laurie Jackson didn't care about the low pay. He loved his job, and he was ambitious. He'd already worked on another local rag and was impatient to get on.

'I won't be stuck on a local paper for ever,' he boasted to his colleagues. 'London, and the nationals, that's where I'm headed.' It had been a stroke of luck discovering that his landlady, Nora Mayberry, worked for the rock star Ron Rogers and his wife, former model Lynda Clare. To be first with a story about them would be a real scoop. It might get him a by-line in the nationals, with maybe even his picture alongside his name, 'our reporter, Laurence Jackson'.

Laurie set to work on Nora Mayberry. He had to tread cautiously. His landlady knew he was a journalist, and when he'd found out who her employer was she'd told him in no uncertain terms what she thought about intrusive reporters.

'Always pestering Mr Rogers, they are. And poor Mrs Rogers. Sometimes they can't even go out the front way because they're hanging about out there, with their cameras. Not that you'd be so ill-mannered, Mr Jackson, I'm sure.'

'Oh, no,' he lied, smiling broadly. 'I've never been involved in the gossipy side of things, ferreting around in celebrity's dustbins and chasing after them in the street, and all that vulgar stuff. I'm a serious journalist, Mrs Mayberry. Believe me, I have a social conscience. Some of us do, you know. I investigate serious moral issues, how we can support young people, and so on.' The old bat swallowed it. 'Please,' he added, smiling confidentially, 'call me Laurie.'

'And you can call me Nora.' He was not much younger than her son and she took a shine to the boy. She liked a friendly presence in the house.

Laurie worked his socks off to charm the old lady. He always had a ready smile for her and sang the praises of her dull breakfasts. He even let her show him her albums of family photos. In return she sometimes shared news about the Rogers, but she was careful. She only ever told him what was already public knowledge. She was no fool, and loyal to her employers. Laurie bided his time and did everything in his power to earn her trust, just in case anything interesting came up. When it came, the story was well worth the wait. Nora had let slip a comment about Melanie Rogers' boyfriend. Laurie seized on the snippet of information and worried away at her gently. Finally, in desperation one evening Laurie succeeded in getting her tipsy by insisting she have a drink with him to celebrate his 'birthday'. That was when Nora confided that Mr Rogers flatly refused to allow his daughter's boyfriend in the house.

'Although what's so wrong with him being a gardener, I don't know. It's a very respectable profession. But he's said he'll cut her off without a penny to her name, and I've no doubt that's what he'll do. He was never one to mince his words. So she's upped sticks and gone to live with the boyfriend.' She stopped suddenly. 'But I shouldn't be telling you all this, should I? You won't go printing it in your paper, now will you?' Laurie hurriedly reassured her of his discretion before running to his laptop to type up the story.

PROBLEMS IN PARADISE
By our reporter Laurence Jackson

In an exclusive, the Woolsmarsh Chronicle *uncovers a dramatic local crisis!*

Melanie Rogers, beautiful daughter of rock star Ron Rogers and stunning international model Lynda Clare, is to lose her share of the family fortune. Blonde Melanie (22) has run away from home to live with the man she loves, our inside source reveals. Ron Rogers is threatening to disinherit his only child whose boyfriend works as a gardener.

The story didn't come out in the other local paper. The nationals picked it up the following day and Laurie was noticed by his editor, who called him in for a chat. At last, Laurie was on his way. Having to find new digs was a small price to pay. He packed his bags straight away and found a dingy room near the park. His new landlady had one vacancy up on the top floor. She gazed anxiously at him with beady bright eyes as Laurie assured her he didn't mind sharing a bathroom with the tenant on the floor below.

'That won't bother me, Mrs Lewis,' he told his new landlady cheerfully as he paid her a month's rent in advance. 'As long as there's a lock on my door.' He didn't add that he wasn't intending to stick around for long.

'You're lucky,' Mrs Lewis said, 'I've just finished doing it up after my last gentleman left. The whole room's been freshly painted. It's all ready now. It's a nice room on the top floor with a view right over the park. My last tenant used to sit for hours by the window, looking down into the park. You've got a lovely view from up here, Mr Jackson.'

Laurie gazed round at magnolia walls and thin rust coloured carpet and thanked his landlady. Her footsteps faded away down the stairs. He couldn't be bothered to unpack straight away. Instead, he pulled a chair up to the window and watched the daylight fade over the park.

34

Garage

The sun was setting as Geraldine approached her garage that evening. As she rounded the corner at the end of the building, she slammed on her brakes in shock. In large untidy red letters someone had written one word, *FILTH*, on the door. If the paint hadn't dripped, it would have been quite well executed. She took a deep breath, and controlled her fury, but she couldn't stop trembling. There was no longer any doubt that this was personal. She wondered who else had seen the message. Graffiti on her garage door was hardly likely to endear her to her new neighbours. She'd seen the man from the flat above hers twice. The first time he'd scurried past her along the corridor, head lowered. The second time he'd thrown her a worried smile but they'd never yet spoken. He was walking out of the adjoining garage as she approached hers. Their eyes met and she rolled down her window.

'We've never had anything like this before,' he told her. It wasn't clear if he was apologising, or accusing Geraldine of bringing trouble to the flats. 'It's shocking.' He nodded at the garage. 'You with the police then?' Geraldine told him she was. 'That's all right then. I suppose your people will sort it out.' He turned and walked away without a backward glance.

Geraldine rang the caretaker's bell.

'Oh aye,' he said, scratching his head, when Geraldine explained. 'You'll be wanting me to clean it off, will you?'

Geraldine hesitated, uncertain whether to offer him a tip.

'I appreciate it's not one of your normal duties—' she began.

'It's all part of the maintenance,' he interrupted her and she nodded. She paid enough in maintenance charges. 'Only I hope this is the end of it,' he went on. He was keen to report the vandalism to the police. 'It's the second time this has happened,' he grumbled.

Geraldine informed him she was a police officer and her colleagues were too busy to investigate graffiti. 'It's not as if we don't have good security measures in place. I'm sure the properties are quite safe with you on site.' She smiled ingratiatingly at him.

He gave her the security tape, relieved to pass on the responsibility. Geraldine took it up to her flat and scrolled through to Sunday evening. A shadowy hooded figure emerged out of the darkness, its face averted from the glare of security lights. She watched as one arm waved and letters appeared on the fence. With a vigorous run and leap, the figure grasped at the top of the fence with gloved hands and pulled itself up and over. She watched the film over and over again, searching for clues, but the image was too blurred to give much away and she was reluctant to hand it in at the station for analysis. She didn't want anyone else to know, as though it was somehow shameful.

'I'm the victim here,' she reminded herself sternly, but it didn't help. She fast-forwarded to Tuesday night. The same figure dropped to the ground, and ran out of sight in the direction of the garages. Geraldine knew a message was being painted on her garage door, out of sight of the camera. A moment later the figure reappeared, tucking what could have been a can of spray paint into its pocket. It was visible only for a second before hauling itself quickly over the fence. The face remained concealed.

Geraldine considered her options. Of the few people who

knew where she lived, someone was nursing a grudge against her. She must have colleagues who didn't particularly like her, but she couldn't think of anyone who'd stoop to such stupid scare tactics. She wracked her brains. As a detective she'd put away some nasty characters. She wouldn't be doing her job if she hadn't. But none of them knew where she lived. She was careful. Her flat was discreetly tucked away, protected by electronic gates and hidden security cameras. She would have noticed if someone was following her. She decided against discussing the problem with any of her colleagues. They might report the incident. The DCI might even want her taken off the case and removed to a safe house until the matter was resolved. She had to get to the bottom of it herself. She was a detective, after all.

That night, pondering in the darkness, Geraldine recalled how one of the men who'd delivered her washing machine had appeared to recognise her. Within a week, the graffiti had started. If he held a grudge against her, his chance discovery of her address might have proved an irresistible temptation. She resolved to find out who he was. She closed her eyes and pictured him, hovering behind Bert. He was called Arthur. Small, wiry and strong, he'd been wearing a cap pulled down over his brow. She remembered he'd pulled it further down over his face as Bert stood talking on the doorstep, until his eyes were a mere glint beneath the brim. His build was similar to the figure captured on film, strong enough to have pulled himself up and over the fence.

Now that she had something to go on, Geraldine felt relieved, as though she'd somehow regained control of the situation. With returning confidence, she dared to hope that was the end of it. When the current case was over, and Angela Waters' killer secured, she'd deal with her stalker. Until then nothing was going to divert her attention from the murder investigation.

Everyone at the flats seemed to know about the second incidence of graffiti. People Geraldine had never seen before appeared in the morning with sympathetic smiles and comments. They were all incensed, although not everyone seemed to understand the message.

'It's not as if it was even dirty!' one woman said indignantly. Geraldine kept quiet but when another neighbour asked, she admitted to being a police officer.

'Everything all right, gov?' Peterson asked, giving her a curious stare as she walked in.

'I'm fine. And you?' She knew who'd been vandalising her property, someone called Arthur who'd delivered her washing machine. When the time came, she'd make it clear to this Arthur, whoever he was, that she wouldn't be intimidated by inane scribbling on her fence and garage door. In the meantime she wasn't unduly worried. It wasn't as though he could gain access to her flat.

35

Departure

'What d'you mean, they were here? In my flat? Who were they?' Terry gripped Melanie by the shoulders so hard she couldn't wriggle free. She stared at him, shocked at the fury in his eyes. She'd never seen Terry lose his temper before. Clearly this wasn't the right time to suggest they spend a romantic evening at her favourite restaurant.

'An inspector and a sergeant, like I said,' she repeated, barely able to speak for fear. 'They showed me their ID, it was all above board. They said I could phone the police station if I didn't believe them.' She tried to twist out of his grasp. 'Let go, you're hurting me.'

'Yes, but what did they want?' He was shouting at her now, still holding her fast and shaking her. Melanie whimpered, terrified. She thought about the questions the police had asked and wondered what Terry was going to do to her.

Suddenly she found her voice, letting him know the police were on to him. 'It was about that woman who was killed in the park. They wanted to know where you were last Wednesday morning.'

'Last Wednesday morning?' He looked puzzled. 'What did you tell them?'

'I told them you were here, and they left.' Terry let go of her and turned away. After a few seconds he heaved a loud sigh and looked at her, shamefaced, his head lowered.

'I'm sorry, love. I just don't like the police coming round here, that's all.' Melanie backed away from him, her eyes narrowed and brimming with tears. 'What are you looking at me like that for?' He took a step towards her.

'I was wondering why you're so terrified of the police.' And what you were doing last Wednesday morning, she thought.

Terry forced a grin. 'Me? Terrified? You're having a laugh. I'm not terrified of anyone.'

Melanie edged further away from him as she repeated her question. 'Why are you scared of the police?'

'Aren't we all?' he asked her. 'Aren't you?'

'No, not really. Why should I be?'

'That's where you and me are different, Mel,' he said with an exaggerated sigh. 'You're fun to be around, but it's a different life you lead. It's like a dream. The car, the restaurants, the clothes. But you're not real, are you? You're not …' He paused and scratched his head, struggling to explain what he meant.

'Not normal?' Melanie asked. She didn't know whether her voice was shaking with rage, or disappointment. Or fear.

'Yeah. That's it.' He smiled uneasily, taking in the expression on her face. 'Come on, it's not important, is it? They've gone now. It's over. I reckon it was your old man put them onto us. Let's forget about it. Life's too short to quarrel. Let's have a beer and chill.' As he came towards her she took an involuntary step back.

'How can we just go back to how it was before?' she asked in a low voice.

'It's only words, innit? Come and give us a kiss. Come on. Let's go to bed and forget all about them.' Melanie shook her head. 'Come on, let's have some fun together.'

'Fun,' she repeated, fighting back her tears.

'Come and give us a kiss then,' he repeated, wheedling, but she turned away.

'I think I'd better go,' she said quietly. He didn't reply. 'I'm leaving,' she repeated, more loudly this time.

Terry grunted but didn't try to persuade her to change her mind. 'Tell you what, I'll make myself scarce shall I, so you can pack up in peace?' If anything, he sounded relieved. 'Only I can't bear to hang around with you snivelling like that. Never could bear to see a girl cry. Specially not a pretty girl like you. Why don't you go to the bathroom and sort your face out, for fuck's sake.' She ran into the bathroom and locked the door.

He didn't come after her, or plead with her to come out and make up. She listened for ages. When she finally came out, Terry had gone out. Good riddance, she told herself ferociously. She pretended he'd gone out to buy her flowers. In a moment he'd return, full of remorse, clutching thousands of red roses, to tell her he couldn't live without her. But she knew that wasn't going to happen. She'd been an idiot to let herself fall for him in the first place. She didn't ever want to see him again. He expected her to be gone from his pokey little flat by the time he returned. Fine. She'd go. The sooner the better. She wasn't going to risk being there when he came back. Sobbing, she pulled her suitcase down from the top of the wardrobe and rammed her clothes into it, careless of creasing them. It didn't matter. Nora would iron them.

She looked around for her handbag. It was nowhere in sight. She searched the tiny flat, coolly at first, then frantically, but her bag had vanished. A horrible suspicion crossed her mind; there was no denying that her handbag had gone, along with her phone, her Ipod and her purse stuffed with cash and most of her credit cards. Her leather jewellery case had also vanished with her diamond pendant and earrings, her black pearls and all of her rings and brooches set with precious stones. Terry had taken the lot, along with his own wallet and Ipod, the one she'd given him, his rucksack and his clothes.

Melanie was alone in the flat, abandoned and humiliated.

She'd been a complete fool. A search through the kitchen cupboards produced three cans of beer and a bottle of gin, three quarters empty. There was no milk so she couldn't even make herself a cup of tea. She threw herself on the bed, her anger giving way to a torrent of furious tears. But as she wept, she felt a flicker of relief that he'd gone. Terry had lied about his feelings. And if the police were right in their insinuations, she'd had a lucky escape. She blew her nose fiercely and went back to the kitchen where she poured a generous measure of gin into a cracked mug and thought about what to do next.

PART 4

'My innocence begins to weigh me down'
Racine

36

Party

'Is there really going to be alcohol at Ella's party?' Shema asked. Rusty rolled her eyes and laughed loudly. Shema laughed too. Even though her friends were all girls, Shema didn't dare tell her father about Ella's party. Since the recent murders he'd been even more protective than before, if that were possible. She knew he'd never allow her to go to a party after school.

'Muslim girls don't roam the streets after dark,' he'd say, and that would be that.

Shema and her father had moved to Woolsmarsh over the summer. It wasn't easy starting a new school in Year 10. The other pupils in her year all knew each other. She was aware of the boys watching her at first. After a few days their eyes slid past her as though she was invisible. The girls were worse. Only the teachers took any notice of her, praising her for her work.

Shema could remember exactly when Rusty had first spoken to her. The maths teacher had been away and the cover teacher had allowed them to work in pairs.

'Can you understand these?' Rusty had turned to Shema in despair. And that was how they became friends. Rusty was really nice and always said, 'Thank you,' when she copied Shema's homework before class. Rusty was in the cool gang. Once Shema would have been appalled by their obscene language, but everything was different when you were included, and being Rusty's friend meant Shema was accepted into the gang whatever the other girls thought.

Ella was having a party and they were all invited. Shema knew her father would never give his permission.

'Of course I'm coming,' she told Rusty. 'But my dad's working at home on Friday so can I come back with you to get ready?'

'Sure. But I'm not going home first. We're all going straight round to Ella's so we can get ready together.'

Shema told her father she was staying for an after school revision session and another girl's mother was going to drop her home at nine o'clock. 'There's no point in you coming out too.'

'All right, you can go because I know you'll work hard, Shema, but you will be home by nine.'

Shema crossed her fingers behind her back. She didn't like lying to her father, but even as she was struggling with her conscience, she was plotting her evening of freedom. Her father would never know. This was the most exciting thing that had ever happened to her.

'What did you learn at school today, Shema?'

'I learned that life is better for you when you are good at your school work, father.' It was true. After all, she'd only become friends with Rusty because she was good at maths.

The four girls rushed to Ella's house after school. It was only a few stops on the bus and they chattered excitedly all the way. Rusty let Shema use her make-up. Alice helped her and they all agreed she looked fantastic but she was embarrassed when she saw what the others were wearing. Shema was the only one in a dress that covered her arms and hung to her knees. When they started talking about boys who'd been invited to the party, Shema felt sick with excitement.

The party was a nightmare. Music blared so loudly Shema couldn't hear what anyone was saying. It was like stepping into a different world, and she hated everything about it. The boys were wild and loud, unrecognisable, although she knew some of them went to her school. They were shouting and cursing, drinking from cans and bottles, and smoking. Rusty had promised to hang out with Shema but she couldn't see her friend anywhere. Ella was snogging a spotty boy up against the wall in full view of everyone. Shema looked away in shame. A tall boy came and stood in front of her, leering. Shema panicked and pushed past him. He rocked unsteadily on his legs, cheerfully mouthing obscenities at her retreating back.

Shema pushed her way upstairs to look for a quiet room where she could phone her father, but there was no signal. It was almost nine o'clock. She had to leave. Looking for her blazer, she finally found Rusty stretched out on a bed, partially concealed by a boy on top of her. Rusty was lying on a pile of coats, her hair fanned out round the boy's dark head. Shema could see her school blazer beneath Rusty's spread-eagled legs but she couldn't get to it. She stared at them in horrid fascination. Suddenly Rusty opened her eyes wide and looked straight at Shema. She pushed the boy away and sat up, pulling her T-shirt down quickly. The boy rolled over onto his back but didn't sit up.

'Who's the weird gash?' he asked indifferently.

'I'm her friend,' Shema blurted out.

'Is that why you're watching us get off?' he asked. He raised his head, lit a cigarette and let his head flop back on the coats as he inhaled deeply.

'I wasn't watching,' Shema stammered, 'I was waiting to retrieve my blazer which you're lying on.' She could feel her face burning as she turned and ran.

'Oh Christ! Maths coursework,' Rusty muttered obscurely at the boy beside her. Grabbing the only school blazer from the pile of coats, she hunted for her shoes.

Shema fled, hot and disgraced. How would she explain this to her father? She passed a strange boy on the stairs. He grabbed her round the waist and kissed her full on the lips.

His wet slobbery mouth tasted sour and he stank of cigarettes and beer. Shema shoved him away as hard as she could and he relinquished his hold at once with a casual shrug. She pushed past him, fighting off her tears. She manoeuvred her way past several clasping couples in the hall and found the front door. Tears were streaming down her cheeks. It was a huge relief to close the door behind her and breathe in fresh clean night air.

Shivering with cold and shock, she set off at a brisk pace. If only she could remember the way back to the bus stop. Everything looked so different in the dark. On the way to the party she'd just followed the others. She needed to find a bus route. It was twenty past nine. She'd never been out this late before by herself. Her phone started ringing. Trembling, she answered it. Her father was angry but he sounded curiously grateful.

'Shema, tell me you're all right, please,' he begged and she felt ashamed. Promising herself she would never cause her father to worry again, she told her lie. Her friend's mother had been delayed.

'But why didn't you call me, Shema? I would have come straight away. Where are you now?' With difficulty she put him off. She told him the car had broken down, and she was waiting with her friend and her friend's mother. The AA were on their way. She was perfectly safe. She'd be home soon. She wasn't sure where they were, exactly. And, in the end, she gabbled, 'I'm losing my signal. Don't worry daddy. I'm quite safe.' Then she switched her phone off. She had to get home. She hoped her father wouldn't smell cigarette smoke clinging to her and shook her head violently as she walked, feeling her hair flap around her face in the cold night air.

It was eerie walking along a strange street by herself at night. She was frightened but also wildly excited. What an adventure! She was lost and alone. And what she had seen at the party! It made her blush just to think of it. She reached a crossroads and hesitated. Behind her she thought she heard footsteps. She turned in what she hoped was the direction of a distant hum of traffic, and walked faster. Behind her, all was quiet. Until she heard footsteps again, faster now. Someone was following her.

She hurried along until she was almost running. The footsteps were getting closer, echoing inside her head. Desperately, she fumbled inside her bag for a weapon. She clutched at her keys, adjusting them so they stuck out between her fingers when she made a fist, as they'd been shown how to do in self-defence at school. It was better than nothing. If he attacked her, she would punch him in the eyes and blind him. She knew the most important part of self-defence was running away but she was out of breath and didn't know how much longer she could keep going. The footsteps were gaining on her. She could hear someone calling out. Fearfully she turned, still stumbling along, and saw Rusty, half a block behind her, trying to run in her high heeled sandals. Shema stopped, panting.

'Shema! Shema! Stop for fuck's sake, you daft cow. I've got your blazer!' Rusty held it up. 'You deaf or what?'

Rusty handed over the blazer. Shema put it on and thanked her friend profusely. They walked on together.

'Where we going?' Rusty asked. Her voice was slurred. She walked erratically in her high heels, and laughed a lot. She seemed really happy to see Shema who explained that she had to get home. Between bouts of uncontrollable giggles, which started Shema laughing too, Rusty walked with her. She was a very good friend and Shema's nightmare fears vanished in a twinkling. They looked up at the stars and bitched about Alice's boobs and Ella's bright red thong. Rusty whooped, collapsing in another fit of giggles until she could hardly walk. Shema hurried her along urgently, almost regretting the company.

The walk seemed to take forever, but finally they found the main road and followed it back to a bus stop. Shema nearly cried with relief when she saw her bus turn the corner.

'What about you?' she asked Rusty with a sudden stab of conscience. 'What are you going to do?'

'Party, party,' Rusty replied. She broke into a gawky jig, right there on the pavement. Shema giggled. 'I'm going to a party,' Rusty crooned. She winked at Shema, and her shiny blue eye shadow glittered in the approaching headlamps.

'Will you be OK, walking back on your own?' Shema asked, as the bus pulled up. She was so pleased, she no longer felt scared about facing her father. She even had her blazer, thanks to Rusty.

Rusty lit a cigarette and blew smoke into Shema's face. 'I'm fine,' she replied, teetering on her heels. 'Don't you worry about me. I'll see you on Monday.' Shema climbed aboard and leaned back in her seat, shivering with relief, as the bus pulled away. She wished she could be more like her friend Rusty who went to parties and knew lots of boys and could stay out late without getting into trouble.

37

Alone

That evening Carter caught up with Geraldine as she was leaving and arranged to meet her in the pub over the road. She was keen to mull over the case with a colleague and Peterson had gone home mumbling about having to visit his girlfriend's parents. The dimly lit bar was deserted when she arrived. Pint in hand, she gazed around and almost missed Carter behind his newspaper.

'I'm not interrupting your reading?' she asked as she took a seat. He looked up with a ready smile. 'Be my guest. I've been wanting to have a word, Geraldine.' He folded his paper carefully and put it on the bench beside him, avoiding her eye. She started to talk about the investigation but Carter clearly had something else on his mind. 'I hear you've been staying late, working long hours,' he said softly. Geraldine suppressed a sigh. She glanced around but there was no one else seated nearby. She nodded. 'Does the boss know?' he asked.

'Sure she knows,' she answered circumspectly, staring into her pint. 'She knows everything that goes on.'

Carter leaned forward and spoke in a low undertone. 'I'm concerned about you, Geraldine. There's nothing wrong with being keen, but you don't want to burn yourself out. You've got to pace yourself. Remember Fielding?'

Geraldine nodded into her glass. 'Fielding was a workaholic,' she muttered.

'Who ended up in hospital.'

'I'm sure we're missing something so I've been reading through some of the old files again after my shift, that's all.'

'I hope you've been eating properly.'

Geraldine laughed. 'Don't worry. I'm a big girl. I can look after myself. But I can't see the problem with working late. Apart from losing my overtime, now I'm a DI. It's not as though I've got anyone to rush home to,' she added, thinking of Carter's long-suffering wife with a twinge of envy. 'What else am I supposed to do? Sit at home on my own while a maniac roams the streets killing young girls? He could be stalking another victim right now and we're sitting here doing nothing.' She stopped as her voice rose in agitation. Carter must have noticed it too.

'You sound like a reporter from our favourite local paper,' he said and Geraldine smiled sheepishly. 'Take it calmly, Geraldine, that's all I'm saying. You know these things take time. And trust the DCI. I've worked with her before. She's tough, and she likes things done her way, but she gets results.'

'She's a control freak,' Geraldine conceded.

'Aren't they all?' he answered, a bitter grin twisting his agreeable features. 'But she's got every right to do things in her own way – she's in charge. Just be careful, Geraldine. You've got your career to think of. It doesn't do to go getting yourself all worked up. You don't want to go making your-self ill over the investigation. You have to keep a certain distance from it. After all …' He paused. For a horrible moment, she was afraid he was going to tell her it was only a job. 'There are cases which don't reach a – satisfactory conclusion. It happens and we have to deal with it. You have to stay detached.'

'Is that it?' she asked shortly when he finished speaking. The prospect of failure was too depressing to contemplate.

Carter gave her a tired smile. 'One more thing,' he said and she groaned. 'Don't let Merton get to you. He's a depressing bastard, but he's thorough and reliable. He's a good officer to have on the team, even if he is a bloody misery most of the time. Don't take it personally, and you'll find he's OK. It's just his manner.' Carter scrambled to his feet, gathering up his paper and his empty pint glass. 'Remember, stay detached,' he repeated and he sauntered off to join a group of colleagues who had just arrived.

Geraldine sat gloomily over her pint, considering what Carter had said. She hoped he didn't think the investigation was heading for failure, but that seemed to be what he'd implied. She glanced up and saw him deep in conversation with Merton. They looked over at her and nodded. She decided she ought to join them for a while before she left, when Kathryn Gordon walked in.

'All on your own, Geraldine?' she asked, adding pointedly, 'don't you want to join the rest of the team?'

'I was just going to the bar,' Geraldine replied, but as she stood up, she realised she was too tired to make any more effort that night. Instead, she mumbled her excuses and left.

Geraldine punched in the code on her alarm, slid her feet into her slippers, and went through to the kitchen. She poured herself a generous measure of chilled white wine, and sank on to her new leather sofa. Leaning back, she studied the yellow liquid in her glass. Her slim strong fingers curled around the glass and put another image in her mind.

Celia would have advised her to switch off. 'Drop everything and take a break,' was her answer to any problem. But not even Celia would have been able to switch off from the responsibility that fell on her sister's shoulders. Not if she'd seen the victims. Geraldine had joined the force with the intention of stopping evil people preying on the weak and vulnerable. Only now, when her dream had been realised, was she was discovering how hard the reality was. The sheer slog of searching through records was endless. There was no challenge and excitement of heroic pursuit, only repeated disappointment and the sick fear of failure. If there was one small detail that would help crack the case, they had to find it. She'd studied the case until she was familiar with every sentence of every document. But she couldn't shake off the feeling that she'd overlooked something.

Sipping her wine, she scanned through her notebook again. The two victims had been killed by the same method in the same place. It had to be the same killer. No one apart from the police and the killer knew the details of the Angela Waters' death, so Tiffany May's couldn't have been a copycat murder. The only difference was that the second assault appeared to have been sexually motivated. Each attack was likely to increase in brutality, to give the assailant the satisfaction he needed. And they still had no idea who he was.

Resolutely, she pulled a pen out of her bag and listed the differences and similarities between the two fatalities. At school she used to enjoy comparative essays, but they hadn't been a matter of life and death.

= *victim: long hair, blonde, young*
attack: from behind, arms secured, strangled,
location: park, shrubbery, body poorly concealed
rain

victim: ages 21 (1st), 13 (2nd)
attack: sexual? (2nd)
location: time of day – morning (1st) evening (2nd)

She went to the kitchen and poured herself another glass of wine. She knew she ought to eat something but instead she sat, staring stupidly at her notes.

'We must be missing something,' she'd insisted to Carter before he'd started on his lecture in the pub.

'It's not always there to be found,' he'd warned her, but Geraldine refused to stop looking. Pumped with adrenaline, she couldn't relax. The thought that the killer might be on the street stalking another young girl kept her awake at night. She poured herself one last glass of wine and settled down to work.

The investigation was going nowhere. John Drew had an alibi and Merton had found no record of violence in Tillotson's history. Geraldine pulled his report from the pile.

'He's not local,' Merton had told them at the briefing. 'That much we know was a lie.' Tillotson came from Portsmouth where he'd received a non-custodial sentence for shoplifting when he was sixteen. He'd been put on a Youth Rehabilitation Programme, and duly carried out his community service. The report from Portsmouth was on the file. Geraldine had glanced through it already, after Merton had given them the gist of it. Tillotson was a liar, but that didn't mean he was a murderer. In addition to his petty thieving in his home town of Portsmouth, he'd been cautioned in North London for a minor drug offence. There was no mention of any violence on his records. His probation officer had described him as 'a charmer' and emphatically rejected the idea that he might be a killer.

'Terry's motivated by money,' the probation officer had told Merton. 'He's an opportunist, but he's not violent. He'd talk his way into anything he wanted, con his grandmother for a tenner. He wouldn't use his fists. He's too proud of his good looks to risk a broken nose.' She described Tillotson as 'shallow and narcissistic,' but said 'he wouldn't hurt a fly.'

'Just because he's got no history of violence, doesn't mean he didn't kill them,' Merton had concluded bleakly.

Geraldine looked at the piece of paper in her hand, and tried to think. It didn't make sense for the killer to choose a public place for his attacks, but that line of enquiry had led them nowhere so far and the killer wasn't likely to frequent the park any longer. He'd been seen both times, if Heather Spencer and Tillotson were to be believed. Meanwhile, the council were busy cutting back shrubs and pruning trees, as though that would help. The reporter who had led the campaign to clear the bushes would cover himself in glory. *The Woolsmarsh Chronicle* was going to be all over the story: 'Killer Copse', milking the recent murders to boost sales. The editor would reassure readers that the paper was taking steps to protect them. But cutting back shrubs in the park would make no difference. The killer was still out there. He would find other places and other victims.

She searched again for something she'd overlooked, only there wasn't just one loose end that didn't fit. Nothing made sense. Geraldine finished her glass of wine and returned to the kitchen to find something to eat. The shelves were neatly stacked, every surface sparkling. An image of Tiffany May's kitchen flashed across her mind and she shuddered. Dirt and disorder. A serial killer prowling the streets was part of that. They had to find him, or there would be another victim, and another. She poured a final glass of wine, positively her last one, but it didn't help her relax. She couldn't sleep, knowing the killer might be out on the streets in the gathering darkness, stalking his next victim.

38

Mermaid

Jim pushed his hair wretchedly out of his eyes. It felt dirty and itchy.

'We keep our hair and fingernails short to keep them clean,' Miss Elsie said, but it wasn't his fault. He couldn't cut his own hair. He was in the front room of the house where he kept some of the clothes he found outside charity shops. In the half-light from the street lamp he poked his finger through a small hole in a jumper. The jumper felt soft. He pulled it over his head. It was lucky he was looking out between the gaps in the boards over the window as she went by, weaving her way between the street lamps, long hair swinging from side to side like a mermaid.

He ran along the hallway, across the kitchen, out the back and along the side passage to the street. She was still there, walking unsteadily in high-heeled shoes and singing in a high voice. She didn't hear him, creeping like a panther. In a flash his hand was in place. He didn't even flinch when she kicked him as he lifted her off her feet and hurried back, his hand still clamped over her mouth. It was awkward, holding on to her as he ran. She was annoying him with all that wriggling but it didn't matter because he knew what to do. It was soon over.

He didn't want to take her into his shed but he needed to think what to do with her.

'Be careful!' Miss Elsie warned him. It was dangerous. He was getting dirty ideas because he had a girl in his shed and no one could tell him what to do with her. Giggling with excitement, he felt around for his torch and switched it on. The light played on her hair and face. He closed her eyes, which were staring crossly at him. He didn't want her watching him. She had shiny blue stuff on her eyelids and he wiped it off with his fingers, careful not to get any on his clothes. He was too clever to leave any clues. The beam moved past the ugly red marks on her neck, across her sparkly top. It was beautiful. It glittered at him as he waved the torch in the air above her. The mound of her breasts made him chuckle. No one could see him looking at her. No one could tell him not to be dirty. She was the dirty one. There were big black smudges on her face. He picked up a sock and rubbed at them.

The light moved down her body. If he leaned over he could see right up inside her short skirt but he already knew what it looked like there. He'd seen a girl's fanny before. He'd pulled her knickers down in the park. He smiled. Miss Elsie didn't know that.

The torch moved on down the girl's legs and sudden fear gripped him. She only had one shoe. The other one must have fallen off when he was bringing her to the shed. If they found it, they'd know she was there. Reluctantly leaving her alone in his shed, he ran back to the street. He found her shoe easily, shiny and winking in the lamplight. He shoved it into his trouser pocket where he felt it knocking against his leg as he jogged back to the shed where she was waiting for him. He had to hurry. She had to be gone before daylight, but he didn't know where to take her. He sat next to her, stroking her hair. He wanted to take her to the park, where he could hide her in the bushes. She'd be safe there.

They'd been cutting down trees in the park. That was mean. Now he had to find somewhere else to hide her. She had to go away, because she was dirty. She had no clothes on. That was her punishment for dropping her shoe. She'd wanted to get him in trouble, leaving her shoe behind as a clue. So she had to take off the other shoe and all her clothes. He had to be sure she couldn't leave anything else lying around for them to find. It served her right. He wasn't scared of her. She thought he was scared, but he'd seen girls before. He wanted to do sex to her, only he didn't know how and she wouldn't help him. She just lay there refusing to move.

He didn't like her in his shed. She was dirty and she made him think dirty. He didn't like her any more. He searched for his thinking brain. He made a picture of the park in his head. Miss Elsie told him to throw her in the pond, like a stone. That would make her clean and he'd have his shed to himself again. It was a very clever idea.

'How do I do it?' he asked, but Miss Elsie wouldn't say. He wished the girl on his bed would go away. He squeezed his eyes tight shut. When he opened them she was still there but Miss Elsie had gone.

He couldn't get the girl inside a black bin bag. She wouldn't help him at all. He began to panic. He needed to get her to the park. Angrily he pushed her off his mattress and sat down. She fell to the floor with a thump. It served her right. He was in big trouble. He needed help. She thought he was going to cry but she was wrong. He wasn't weak. And he knew where to go for help.

Kneeling down by his bed, he began to pray to his father, the one who gave him his daily bread on earth as it is in heaven. The one who'd brought her to him to be made clean. He opened his door a little and stared out into the darkness. He wished he was back in his room. There were no girls there. He used to sit at his window and watch people in the park. They couldn't see him and he'd liked that. He stared into the darkness and wondered what to do with the girl in his shed.

39

Missing

Geraldine hadn't slept well and left the house early. As she sped along the motorway she glanced in the mirror and caught herself frowning, but she was too preoccupied to care about her worry lines. She couldn't shake off the niggling conviction that she'd seen something significant, if only she could remember what it was. At the station she went straight to the Incident Room where she found Merton rifling through a pile of documents on her desk.

'What the hell are you doing?' she yelled. He looked up, startled, pale eyes stretched wide, and explained he was looking for his pen.

'I took a call on your phone while you were out yesterday and thought I might've left my pen on your desk. Is that a problem, Geraldine? We're supposed to be on the same team.' He took a step back and Geraldine sat down.

'Sorry. I'd just prefer you to ask before you go rummaging through my things,' she mumbled. 'I had these in a certain order, and now they're all mixed up,' she added untruthfully. Merton slunk back to his own desk, where he sat muttering about her being a control freak. Geraldine was riled at hearing her own criticism of Kathryn Gordon thrown back at her. Her resentment didn't diminish when she calmed down sufficiently to acknowledge she'd overreacted. The case was unsettling her, but that was no excuse. Five minutes later, she moved a folder and saw a Parker ballpoint that had rolled underneath it. Merton reclaimed it with relief.

'It's part of a set my daughter gave me.' He scowled at Geraldine, as though accusing her of wanting to steal his pen. Remembering what Carter had told her, Geraldine smiled at him but Merton just grunted and walked away. Geraldine ignored him and soon she was too preoccupied with developments on the case to remember Merton's rudeness, or worry that she'd provoked it by her unreasonable behaviour.

A hysterical woman arrived at the station to report a missing girl. Mrs Ross had flaming red hair, grey at the roots. Her face was lined with worry, her bottom lip bitten raw.

'She's not a bad girl, Inspector,' she said, as though that might persuade Geraldine to take her concern more seriously. Geraldine looked down and flipped through her notebook to hide her own alarm. Quickly regaining her outward composure, she began her questions.

'Try and calm down, Mrs Ross. It's important we get these details right.' She paused and the woman nodded, twisting a soggy tissue in her fingers. 'How old is your daughter?'

'Fourteen.'

'Have you brought a photograph?' The woman shook her head. Tears spilled from her swollen eyes but she didn't wipe her face. 'That's not a problem, Mrs Ross. A description will be fine for now.' The distraught woman nodded and took a deep breath.

'Jacqueline's a very pretty girl. She's got my hair, only hers is long and wavy, when she hasn't straightened it. She's got blonde highlights, but her friends have always called her Rusty on account of her hair. She's got lots of friends, Inspector. They're always calling round for her. She's popular with the other girls.' She gave a faint smile, picturing her daughter. 'Her eyes are a kind of bluey green and she's tall. She's always been quite thin, but well developed. She's got that sort of build. She's sporty. Likes netball, and she can swim …' She sighed heavily and sniffed. 'I don't know what else to tell you, really. She's a good girl.'

Mrs Ross hadn't seen her daughter since Friday morning. 'She left for school as usual, only she was dead excited …' She stopped suddenly, and swallowed hard.

'She was excited,' Geraldine prompted her.

'Because one of the other girls was having a party after school.'

Relief flooded through Geraldine but she suppressed it and spoke in a level tone. 'Was it a sleepover, Mrs Ross?'

'No, nothing like that. It was just a few of the girls getting together for an evening, getting dressed up together, you know.' Geraldine said she did. 'I told her she couldn't stay over. She had to be home first thing this morning because of her tutor. She has a maths tutor comes on a Saturday morning. She's got her GCSEs next year and we thought …'

Geraldine nodded. A teenager who failed to come home for a maths lesson wasn't exactly cause for panic. Even so …

Mrs Ross voiced Geraldine's thoughts. 'It's just that, with that strangler, well, I'm worried about her, Inspector.'

'Did she want to stay at her friend's house? Did she mind having to come back home?'

'She was fine about it. The maths tutor's made a huge difference already. Jacqueline's been getting much better marks for her homework. Even the midweek ones he doesn't help her with. She promised to be home by one o'clock the latest. She knew I'd wait up for her.'

'How was she getting home?'

'I gave her money for a taxi. It's not far, only my husband won't wait up that late. He gets tired, you see. He's an early riser. If Jacqueline's home before eleven he'll fetch her, but any later – which is unusual – and I give her money for a taxi. I don't want her out by herself at night. Not with a killer loose on the streets.'

Geraldine asked about the girl who had hosted the party.

'I phoned the house and spoke to her when Jacqueline didn't come home. I waited up all night. I thought she must've fallen asleep round at her friend's and then ...' Geraldine, scribbling down the details, looked up as Mrs Ross's voice rose in pitch. 'She said Jacqueline left her house yesterday evening. She said she tried to find her at about ten thirty. She wanted to tell Jacqueline something, only she couldn't find her. She didn't know what time Jacqueline had gone, but she was sure it was before ten thirty. And Jacqueline left her bag behind, with the taxi money and her keys and phone.'

Geraldine struggled to sound unperturbed as she assured Mrs Ross they would set a search in motion immediately. 'A constable will take a list of all Jacqueline's friends. And try not to worry, Mrs Ross. Most children who disappear like this turn up safely. You'll probably find she's been at another friend's house all the time.' Mrs Ross nodded but she looked about as convinced as Geraldine felt. The image of a small pale body on a table in the mortuary slipped into Geraldine's mind as she comforted the anxious mother facing her across the table in the interview room.

After reporting the incident, Geraldine went straight to the house where the party had been held. It stood at one end of a row of Victorian terraces. She walked up a crazy paving path, slippery in the rain. The sound of shouting floated out to meet her and she heard a girl's voice, hysterical with rage, as she pressed the bell. She rang again, trying to time the peal to coincide with a gap in the clamour inside. A woman opened the door.

'You'd better come in. You certainly picked your moment,' she said as Geraldine held up her ID and explained the reason for her visit. She turned and called over her shoulder. 'Norm! Norm! Come here!' A gaunt man in shirtsleeves and slippers emerged from a door at the far end of the hall, his bald pate shining under the hall light. A teenage girl hovered behind him, her face puffy from crying.

'Who the hell's this, now?' he demanded angrily. Geraldine flashed her warrant card and the man whipped round to yell at the girl. 'Now see what you've done! Only gone and involved the police! Some of these nice friends of yours brought drugs into the house, did they? You stupid, stupid …' He stopped as the girl vanished through an inside door.

'Norm, it's about that girl gone missing,' Ella's mother hissed at him, 'the one whose mother phoned this morning.' Geraldine was quick to reassure them that she'd come to ask Ella a few questions about Jacqueline Ross and they led her into the front room where their daughter sat hiccupping and sulking.

'We're following up a report on a missing girl. She never returned home last night. We understand she was at a party here, after school.'

'Her party,' Norman Hooper growled, jerking his head at the girl. 'I said it was a mistake. But would you listen?' He turned on his wife who shrugged. She looked close to tears herself.

Geraldine questioned the girl. Had Jacqueline Ross, nick-named Rusty, been at the party? Did she stay overnight? What time did she leave? Did she leave alone? Did Ella know where she was now? Was she sure? Did Jacqueline have a boyfriend? Could she have gone home with anyone? Ella didn't show much interest. Her fit of sobbing over, she appeared listless, probably hung over. Rusty might have gone home with a friend. No, she hadn't seen her leave. Yes, she had a boyfriend. No, she couldn't remember his name. Mike? Andy? She was picking names at random, refusing to look at Geraldine.

'It's not like it's always the same one.' The girl was truculent now she'd regained some self-control but she was clearly very frightened about landing herself in more trouble with her parents.

'They're only fourteen,' Mrs Hooper explained. 'Too young for serious boyfriends.'

'Mum!' Ella protested.

'Too young for boyfriends at all, serious or not,' Mr Hooper interjected.

'Oh, Norman, she's said she's sorry.'

'Sorry? Did she clear up the mess in the bathroom? Well, did you?' Ella muttered an expletive under her breath. Her father threw her a black look.

'We only wanted a bit of fun,' the girl burst out suddenly. 'Is it a crime to have some fun once in a while?' She appealed to Geraldine, looking her in the eye for the first time. 'It's all work, work, work, with them. And it's the same at school. All they do is bang on about bloody GCSEs, like the universe depends on it.' She turned on her father. 'Why can't you just leave me alone? I'm going upstairs. Homework!' She leapt up and ran out of the room. They heard her feet stamping on the stairs. Geraldine made her escape, as domestic conflict threatened to start up again and the sound of shouting followed her until she had passed through the garden gate. Geraldine tried to quell her unease, but visiting Ella's house had confirmed her suspicion that Rusty had lied to her mother. More than just a few girls had attended the party.

The DCI said she wanted the missing girl to be treated as a priority. 'We've got to find this girl, wherever she is. Where did she stay overnight? Let's assume she stayed with a friend, or at some man's flat. Drop everything else and start looking,' she barked. 'Geraldine, I want a full report on my desk now!'

'Taking a risk there, gov,' Peterson smiled, crouching down by Geraldine's desk. She looked up, startled, and closed the notebook she'd been staring at. 'Postponing your report,' he scolded, making a tutting sound and grinning broadly.

Geraldine smiled back. 'Typing up my report will have to wait,' she replied firmly, 'and the boss'll have to lump it. I've given the duty sergeant the gist of it. I want to get on with the real work.'

'Finding Jacqueline Ross.'

'Exactly.'

'She could well have left the party with some boy or other,' Peterson said, straightening up.

Geraldine voiced her doubts. 'It's nearly six o'clock now. Wouldn't you expect her to have been in touch with Ella at least, to find out if she'd left her phone there?'

'Maybe she can't contact her, because she hasn't got her number.'

'True. She's probably only got the number saved on her phone. Which reminds me, have we got anything from the numbers on her phone yet?'

Peterson shook his head. 'Just kids from the school so far. Look, gov,' he leaned forward, lowering his voice. 'Don't you think the DCI's jumping the gun a bit? I mean, if it wasn't for Angela Waters and Tiffany May, we wouldn't be getting all het up over some fourteen-year-old who goes to a party and doesn't come home straight away, would we? It's not like it doesn't happen all the time.' His confident assertion turned into a plea. 'We're only jumping through all these hoops because of the strangler.'

'Yes,' Geraldine agreed. 'We're doing all this because of the strangler. And yes, as it happens, I think she's right.'

'My guess is she'll go back to her parents when she's ready,' Peterson insisted, but his face was drawn with tension.

'Fancy a drink on the way home?' she asked him. The DS shook his head and mumbled something about needing to get home.

Geraldine drove back to her flat early. She could have stayed on at the station but she needed a break. Perhaps a girl going missing when there was a killer abroad was no more than an appalling coincidence. Carter was right – she *was* letting the stress get to her. She needed to be more detached. Catching sight of the estate agent's card propped up on the shelf in her hall she wondered whether Craig Hudson might offer her a brief distraction from the haunting images of Angela Waters and Tiffany May. Any company would be better than none during this interminable waiting. And by some miracle the missing girl might even have turned up by the morning.

40

Return

Melanie hesitated on the doorstep. At least her keys had been in her pocket, or Terry might have taken her car. And the keys to her parents' house. Bracing herself, she turned the key in the lock and breathed in the clean scent of home. Roman came running along the parquet floor, paws sliding in a wild rush. He barked once. Melanie sank to her knees and buried her face in his warm fur, grinning with relief as his tail thumped a welcome tattoo on the floor. Nora came out of the dining room, holding a tray.

She caught sight of Melanie and a smile rose to her lips. 'Melanie!' Nora turned and scuttled back into the dining room. Melanie heard a murmur of voices. She had barely clambered to her feet, when she felt her mother's arms around her shoulders and the warmth of her body. Then her father was smiling and patting her awkwardly on the back as though she'd just given birth.

It was tough confessing to her parents that Terry had taken her jewellery, including some of her mother's heirlooms. Her father narrowed his eyes but said nothing. She listened to her parents discussing the situation later, when they thought she was out of earshot.

'Are the police going to be interested, Lynda? The boy could claim they were a gift.' Melanie heard the gentle buzz of her mother's voice but couldn't make out what she was saying. 'It's her word against his,' her father replied. 'I'd rather leave it, Lynda. Let's just take it on the chin and move on or it'll turn into a whole media circus. Just drop it. It could be a lot worse.' She heard her mother crying and her father conceding. 'All right, I'll get onto the police in the morning. But they'd better be discreet. And I don't want that little shit mentioned in front of Melanie. She's suffered enough. Let's not make it any worse for her.' Melanie crept upstairs, for once grateful for her father's protection. As far as she was concerned, that was the end of the affair.

Later that evening Lucy phoned and Melanie agreed to go out with her friends. She'd cried long enough over Terry. He wasn't worth it. But as she drove through the high wrought iron gates, a posse of journalists sprang from nowhere to surround her, blocking her car in every direction. Somehow they'd got wind of her affair and had been waiting to grill her. Melanie swore out loud. On top of everything else, she was going to be late to meet the girls. If she didn't hurry, Lucy and Hannah would set off to London without her.

'Melanie! Can you confirm your parents have disinherited you?'

'Miss Rogers, what are your plans for the future?'

'Are you getting married?'

'Where's your boyfriend?'

'Tell us his name, Melanie. Just give us a name.'

Melanie gritted her teeth as cameras flashed. She'd forgotten how intrusive journalists could be. If her father threw a party it was reported as a key event hosted by a major force resurfacing in the UK music industry. He had only to sneeze in public and the media suspected terminal pneumonia for an ageing rock star from a bygone era.

'Miss Rogers, what has your father got to say about your love affair?'

'Melanie!'

'Melanie! Can you tell us anything?'

As it happened, she had a story that would make their keyboards crackle. She could just imagine the headlines in the tabloid press: 'Melanie Rogers Ripped off by Cheating Lover'. The thought of her private humiliation being made public made her cringe. She bit her lip, and turned away from the cameras.

'Miss Rogers!'

'Melanie!'

'Have you got anything to say?'

'Anything to tell us, Melanie?'

'Yes,' she thought furiously, 'I can tell you lot to fuck off,' but she answered primly, 'No comment,' her voice drowned in the camera clicks and shouting. She gave a wonky attempt at one of her mother's gracious smiles as she put her foot down and reversed back through the entrance and a security guard closed the gate. Melanie hurried into the house, cursing. She knew she wouldn't be able to hide away indefinitely but she wasn't ready to face the reporters yet.

She dialled Lucy's number. No answer. If she'd thought to ask where her friends were heading, she could still have joined them, but they were probably on their way to London by now.

She tried Hannah's number. 'Hi this is Hannah. Leave a message and I'll call you back.'

Melanie's mother came out into the hall. 'I thought you were going out,' she said.

'Changed my mind,' Melanie smiled. She didn't want to upset her mother any more. At least those bloody reporters had taught her how to hide her feelings.

41

Lake

Jim was good at hiding things. Leaving the girl under his mattress, he went out into the night. He didn't find Miss Elsie but he had a clever idea. He knew how he could move the girl without being seen. She'd be safe in the park. He watched a car go by and grinned. He'd never passed a test so they wouldn't give him a car but he knew what to do. He knew how to watch and learn.

'You see, you're good at lots of things,' Miss Elsie said. He loved Miss Elsie but she didn't like it when he told her so, even though she let him sing it with everybody else.

'Close by me forever and love me I pray.' Miss Elsie taught him that. That was when he'd known she wanted him to love her. Even his mother had never asked that of him.

It was easy to borrow a car. He had to check a lot of doors until he found one he could open. He was looking for a van but he found a car instead. He drove slowly up the road. He bumped into the kerb and laughed uneasily. The wheels on the car went round and round. He had to be careful not to hit them too hard or they might burst. He shut his eyes tight and giggled.

She was heavier than before but he carried her down the passage all by himself. It wasn't easy because she wouldn't help him.

'Don't be put off when it isn't easy,' Miss Elsie told him. 'You can do it if you try.' He had to make sure no one was watching. 'Look right, look left, look right again,' Miss

Elsie told him, but he stared straight ahead and hurried to the car with the girl in his arms. If anyone asked, he'd tell them she was his girlfriend and she was drunk. His mother couldn't walk when she was drunk. Men carried her.

He'd wrapped the girl in a coat but she was still cold. It was dark. No one saw them hurrying from the passage way to the car. That was lucky because she struggled a lot. She didn't want to go in the car. He wanted her to lie down on the back seat of the car but she made herself all stiff and refused to move, even when he made his gloved hand into a fist and hit her, hard. He had to bend her and twist her until she fitted in and he could shut the door. It was hard work but he didn't want to drive with the door open and her head sticking out.

'We mustn't draw attention to ourselves,' Miss Elsie told him and he nodded. He knew that.

Once he got her in the car, she lay as good as gold on the back seat while he drove her to the park. The streets were mostly empty. He passed two cars but no one paid him any attention.

'We're OK,' he told her. 'Soon be there.' She wanted to know where they were going. She was always asking questions. 'I'm taking you to the park, and I told you that before. It's so you can be clean.' He told her and told her but she never listened. No one listened to him. 'I don't know why I bother,' he said. 'You never listen.'

He drove right up to the gates and stopped the car with a sudden jerk. He was too clever to drive into the park because he knew the car would leave secret clues on the mud. He'd seen on the telly that cars left patterns on the ground. The police were clever at finding clues, but he was clever too. He was getting more and more clever every day, with all the thinking he had to do.

It was difficult getting her out of the car. Now he'd brought her all the way to the park, she didn't want to move.

She was awkward and heavy but there was no one about. No one saw them. He had to pull her and pull her to get her out and it wasn't easy, but he didn't care. He was happy to be back in the park where she'd be safe.

'You can't have a bath in a coat, silly. Now be careful. The water's very cold, but it's clean.' She didn't want to get in. He had to push her. She didn't splash much. The moon came out. He looked up and saw a fox staring at him, silent in the silvery light.

'Go away,' he said, 'it's private.' Without a sound, the fox turned and trotted away into the darkness. She bobbed about on the water, swimming. He put her coat round his shoulders because he was cold.

He couldn't remember where he'd found the car so he drove it slowly back up the road and left it somewhere. It didn't matter where.

'No one will know unless you tell them,' Miss Elsie said. He was very pleased when he got safely back to the shed. 'Well done,' Miss Elsie said, 'you get a merit star for being clean.'

'And one for being clever?'

'Oh, all right then,' she agreed and he smiled. He was getting very clever at this game. That night he slept well.

42

Protest

Geraldine was confused when she came to, naked, in a strange bed, feeling as though a ton weight was pressing down on her head. The sound of someone breathing startled her into wakefulness. A man was lying next to her beneath an unfamiliar duvet, the back of a tousled head plainly visible on the pillow. One of her shoulders ached and she explored it carefully, wondering if she'd fallen, or stumbled into a wall. Stretching her legs, she tried to recall the previous evening. She'd phoned Craig who had obligingly taken her out.

She vaguely remembered laughing a lot and drinking herself silly before returning to his flat. She had no memory of arriving in his bed and wondered if he'd carried her up the stairs. Her memory of the ensuing intercourse was disappointingly hazy although she recalled insisting he used a condom, so she hadn't been completely wasted. Then she must have passed out. It was embarrassing behaviour in a woman her age. Her face burned just thinking about it. She'd have to make sure no one found out. But Craig knew. Craig was the first man she'd been to bed with since Mark, and she'd ruined her chances with him on their first date. She remembered he'd made her feel like a giggly teenager, although that had probably been due to her drinking so much. Whatever the reason, she'd played the part with a vengeance.

'Is it a crime to have some fun once in a while?' Ella had

222

complained after her party. Geraldine had gone out looking for some fun. Now she had to get through the day with a thumping headache. She was lucky there hadn't been any calls in the night.

She glanced down and her breath caught in her throat. There was no signal on her phone.

'What?' Craig muttered.

'Where can I get a signal?' She blinked fiercely. Her head pounded.

'Oh, signal's crap, yeah.' He was barely stirring, eyes still closed. 'Reception's crap. Use landline.' He turned over.

'Craig!' she shook him roughly and he growled in sleepy protest. 'Where can I get a signal in this house?' She was already out of bed, pulling on her dress. She'd have to go home and change. She must have been completely out of her mind the previous night.

'It's Sunday morning, for Christ's sake,' Craig grumbled without opening his eyes. 'Go to the bathroom.'

'What?'

'Bathroom. Signal.' He rolled over, snoring gently.

Geraldine pulled her fingers through her hair as she hurried to the bathroom. She examined her drained face in the mirror and dashed cold water on her eyes while she waited for her phone to pick up a signal. She held her breath and then relaxed. There was a signal and no messages. She hadn't blown it after all. Trembling with relief, she sat down on the toilet and tried to decide if she was going to throw up.

When her phone started to beep, she thought it would never stop. Seven missed calls and one message. She didn't pause to say goodbye to Craig. Grabbing her coat from the banister, she tore out of the flat.

As soon as she reached the park, Geraldine realised her mistake. She should never have turned up looking as though she'd slept in her clothes. A group of women stood outside the main gateway, several of them waving handmade placards:

KEEP OUR STREETS SAFE
PROTECT WOOLSMARSH WOMEN
CATCH THE KILLER

Geraldine was shocked. A sudden flash of envy shook her.
She wished she could join those women, united in their
anger. How easy it was for them. They could think up
slogans, strut about shouting, and then go home feeling
socially responsible.

She opened the car door and a strident voice assailed her
ears.

'They keep us out of the park, but what about the killer?
What are they doing about him? Why target us?' and a wild
chant started: 'Catch the killer, catch the killer, catch the
killer!' followed by another refrain: 'Close the park, close
the park, close the park!' Geraldine glanced in her mirror
and paused, one leg already out of the car. Men might not
notice her high heels and smeared face, but these women
wouldn't miss a trick. She grimaced at her reflection in
harsh daylight, but there wasn't time to go home and
change.

She climbed back into the car, closed the door softly and
rummaged in her bag for a tissue. There weren't any. Her
mouth tasted like sour milk but she licked her finger and
rubbed at a smudge of mascara under one eye. It was
supposed to be waterproof. She wished she'd checked her
face after splashing it with cold water in Craig's bathroom.
Her reflection in the rear-view mirror looked dreadful.

Her phone rang. 'Where are you, gov? There's a protest of
some sort going on here, and the press have just turned up.'

'Great!'

'What?'

'Look, I'm here, on my way. I'm outside the park. Only I
look a mess.' She wished she hadn't said that.

Peterson sounded surprised. 'Not as much of a mess as

the girl we just fished out of the lake, gov. Where the hell have you been?'

Her face burning with embarrassment, clutch purse concealed under her arm, Geraldine pushed her way through the throng of women at the gate. Quickly she held up her warrant card and a poker-faced young constable stood aside to let her in. A camera flashed as a journalist spotted her. Too late, she ducked her head.

'Who's she then?'

'Must be a reporter.'

'No, they're letting her in.'

'Hey, you! Are you in charge round here?' Dressed in her work clothes she would have paused to answer their questions, but today she walked swiftly past.

'She doesn't look like a police woman ...' a woman's voice reached her.

'I don't feel like one right now,' she felt like saying, 'but I can't take a day off.'

Geraldine hurried towards a tent she could see on the grass beside the lake. The copse of trees where the other two bodies had been concealed was just visible, the children's playground out of sight round a bend in the path.

Peterson brought her up to speed. The body of a young girl had been found in the lake at eight fifteen that morning. A couple of early joggers had spotted her in the water.

'They thought she was a dead swan,' he said. 'To make matters worse, there's a coven, mostly women, kicking up a stink nearby. Talk about bad timing. We've closed the park and no one's told them about the latest vic yet. You must've seen them out there, making their protest. The boss wants you to deal with them. She asked for you, said she tried your phone, but I told her you were on your way and would call her. I tried to call you. Where were you?'

Geraldine took a deep breath. 'Is the DCI still here?'

'No, she's headed back to the station.' Geraldine breathed

out, thankful for small mercies. The women at the gate could wait and so could Kathryn Gordon. For once she was relieved to pull a white suit over her clothes, and cover her shoes. 'Death the Leveller,' she muttered bleakly.

Millard was on his knees in the forensic tent, more informative than usual before removing the body to the mortuary, because the girl had been pulled naked from the water. No clothes had been found at the waterside, and no bag. Geraldine shivered. Like the women at the gate, she believed this was the work of a serial killer. What the public didn't yet know was that with each attack the killer's sexual aggression was escalating.

Millard had done as much as he could in situ and a white-coated forensic team were busy hunting for evidence.

'She was naked,' the doctor said. 'No clothes, no jewellery. Pierced ears but no earrings or studs. She's been in the water overnight. Possibly longer.'

'Someone would probably have seen her if she was here yesterday,' Peterson pointed out. Ghoulishly, the park had become popular since the first two killings. Only children were kept away by anxious mothers.

'Quite possibly. So let's assume overnight.'

'How did she die?'

'I really can't say until I've examined her. Presumably she entered the water last night but it doesn't look …' The doctor paused, frowning. 'She looks a bit battered and bruised, but … no, I'm not going to speculate. This kind of head trauma can be sustained ante or post mortem.'

'You don't think she was strangled? She's not like the others?'

Millard gave a wary frown and refused to divulge any more. It was a macabre sort of wish, hoping a girl had drowned and not been strangled. Either way, it made no difference to the victim. The mortuary van was on its way but Geraldine didn't wait for it to arrive. She barely had time to rush home and change as it was. She hoped Peterson hadn't smelt her stale breath, and was glad they'd been talking out in the open air.

'Don't forget to call the DCI, gov.'

'I'm onto it,' she lied. She had to scurry back past the chanting women to get to her car and cringed at the flashing cameras. She pulled her coat collar up to her chin and shuddered as she felt it tight across her throat. Three victims in eleven days, and she was worrying that her mascara had smudged. Full marks for detachment from the case. Carter would be very proud.

43

Exclusive

Settled in his new digs, Laurie Jackson finally started unpacking on Sunday morning. Most of his clothes cost more than he could afford, but he liked to look the part when he was working. He was hanging up his Paul Smith jacket when he heard a commotion outside. Yanking his window all the way up, he heard several voices all talking at once. He craned his neck sideways and looked down on a cluster of people gathered by the park entrance. Two policemen marched up the path, out of sight round the bend, followed by a couple more. Laurie made out a group of women milling about by the gate with placards. The sound of an approaching siren jolted him into action. Whatever was going on down there Laurence Jackson, reporter extraordinaire, would be first on the scene. Grabbing his camera, he locked his door and charged down the stairs, two at a time, almost barging into his landlady at the foot of the stairs.

'Going somewhere nice, Mr Jackson?' she asked.

'Hope so,' he called out over his shoulder as he hurried along the hall.

'Would you like me to give your room a bit of a go—' she started to ask, but her new tenant had already slammed the front door. She shook her head, smiling. He was probably out to meet a young lady, she thought. He had that sprightly look about him.

Two uniformed policemen were standing at the entrance to the park, which was closed off by blue and white tape.

There were about twenty protesters, mainly women, packed on the pavement and spilling out onto the road. Laurie hovered on the edge of the group, watching.

One woman appeared to be in charge. 'What do we want?' she yelled and her companions answered in a hectic chorus: 'Safe streets!'

'When do we want them?'

'Now!'

From the chanting and the banners, Laurie gathered they were protesting about the recent murders in the park. He turned to a man at his side and asked about the police presence, which struck him as an extreme response to a bunch of women shouting slogans. When he heard the answer, Laurie felt his heart race. This was even bigger than Melanie Rogers. Another victim had been discovered in the park, and he was the first reporter on the scene. He knew it wouldn't be long before the whole pack arrived. Even the nationals were following the story of the Woolsmarsh Strangler. He tried to think of a way to turn his early arrival to his advantage.

A pale woman made her way through the crowd, her coat collar turned up. When she reached the entrance, the uniformed constable stood aside to let her through. Laurie snapped her just in time, before she hurried away up the path. At least he had that. He'd read that a woman was running the murder investigation and wondered if he'd just seen her scuttling into the park. He turned his attention back to the woman leading the chanting, an idea forming in his mind. He guessed she was in her early twenties. Ash blonde hair fell in a smooth cascade over one side of her face and her leather jacket looked expensive. As he drew closer, Laurie revised his opinion. She was closer to late forties.

He made his way through the throng and bided his time. As soon as there was a brief hiatus in the racket he stepped up and introduced himself to the woman in charge of the protest, throwing out his suggestion as though he was doing her a favour.

'In any case,' he concluded, raising his voice against the noisy crowd, 'I'd be happy to warn you which papers aren't sympathetic to your campaign. My paper supports you, of course. That's why I'm here. We think you're doing a great job. But unfortunately some of the more conservative editors regard you as ...' he gave an apologetic smile, 'a bunch of hysterical women.'

'My husband's supporters,' the blonde woman said with inexplicable venom – but she'd swallowed his story. The protest wouldn't be a scoop, but at least he'd have an exclusive interview with the leader of the Woolsmarsh Women, Laurie thought as he jostled with other reporters to get a decent picture of the mortuary van leaving. If only he could get a shot of the dead girl inside it. Now *that* would make the editor sit up and take notice. He followed the van with his eyes, wondering what the latest victim looked like, and wishing he could be the one to break the story.

44

Body

Millard was on the phone in his office. Geraldine peered through the open door and saw him sitting on his desk, thin legs swinging.

'I'll try to be home early. I'm waiting for the police now.' He glanced up and smiled at them. 'Oh, they've arrived. Well, call if you want me to get anything on the way home. I shouldn't be late.' He sketched a little wave at the DCI. It was funny, but Geraldine had never imagined the pathologist having another life outside this house of death. She'd pictured him spending solitary evenings in his office, poring over dusty anatomy books, piecing skeletons together like gruesome jigsaws.

There was little doubt about the dead girl's identity. Jacqueline Ross's parents hadn't formally identified the body yet but the victim matched the description of the missing girl.

'You couldn't have found the killer while my phone was playing up. Just another victim,' Geraldine grumbled to Peterson as they pulled on their gowns. Under bright electric lights she saw him scrutinise her face: skin pasty, eyes faintly bloodshot and clogged with vestiges of last night's make-up. He made no comment but Geraldine could guess what he was thinking. She looked away, embarrassed. Being a grown woman, and a DI, wasn't turning out to be easy. Right now, she seemed to be making a hash of both.

Her mood didn't improve when she followed Peterson

inside and saw that Kathryn Gordon was already there, waiting for them. The DCI turned and looked coldly at Geraldine. Just as both women were about to speak, Millard began.

'She's not a pretty sight,' he warned them. Geraldine stealthily fingered the pouches below her own eyes. She glanced up and saw Kathryn Gordon looking at her. The DCI dropped her gaze, but not before Geraldine had seen an expression of disapproval cross her face. 'She's been in the water all night,' Millard continued. It was difficult to establish the time of death, but the doctor estimated she'd been in the water for approximately nine hours. 'I'll let you know if there were any drugs in her system, when the tox report's back.'

'Not exactly a distinguishing feature among the kids, these days,' Peterson grumbled.

'It wasn't the Strangler?' Kathryn Gordon asked.

'That's what I thought, initially,' Millard said grimly.

'Thought?'

'Her lungs confirm she didn't drown,' the pathologist explained. Kathryn Gordon gave an involuntary groan. Geraldine felt sick as Millard's voice rumbled softly on. 'There are the typical signs of submersion, swelling and wrinkling of the skin, and discolouration, which occur from immersion before or after death. But there's no sign of froth or foam in the airways, no fluid in the trachea or bronchi, and none in the stomach.' He looked up. 'All of which confirm death occurred prior to submersion.' He glanced down at the body again. 'There's haemorrhaging in the middle ears which can indicate drowning, but it's also present in victims of asphyxiation.'

'Was she strangled?' Kathryn Gordon asked bluntly. Millard nodded and continued to reveal his findings in a low, steady voice. The state of her lungs and airways confirmed that Jacqueline Ross was already dead when her body entered the water. The marks on her neck indicated that she'd been strangled, about twenty-four hours earlier. Bruises on her arms indicated where she'd been grabbed from behind. Discolouration on her jaw was consistent with a hand having been pressed over her mouth before she died.

Peterson was staring at Millard as though he wanted to hit him. Geraldine felt slightly concerned, yet reassured, by the young sergeant's fervour.

'What else do we know about her?' the DCI asked. There was no immediate means of identification except her face, bloated and discoloured.

'She died maybe a day before she entered the water. And she was thrown in the water naked,' Millard repeated.

'So she was killed somewhere else, the body was deposited in the lake, and her clothes were left behind,' Peterson said.

'She was killed on Friday night?' Kathryn Gordon asked.

'It's difficult to say with certainty. She's been in the water too long to be precise but I'd say so, yes. Friday night sounds right. But that's an opinion.' He stressed the final word carefully.

'After the party, on her way home, probably drunk. If we can find out exactly where she went, we might start to close the net … We have to find out where she went,' Geraldine said.

'Was it a sexual assault this time?' Peterson asked quietly.

Millard shook his head. 'She's still virgo intacto.'

The atmosphere was despondent when they returned to the Incident Room. A number of senior investigating officers preferred not to display pictures of victims after death when other photos were available. There was a feeling in some quarters that such morbid images lowered morale. Kathryn Gordon had no such qualms. Mrs Ross probably had albums full of pictures of her daughter, but none as recent as the photo on the board, which resembled a medieval gargoyle.

That evening, Geraldine left at the end of her shift intending to drive straight home. Instead she ate fish and chips in her car and returned to the station.

'Is the DCI in?' she asked.

The desk sergeant shook his head. 'She left over an hour ago,' he said. 'She'll be in the pub.'

'Do you know if Ted Carter's with her?'

He shook his head again. 'You might catch him, but he's probably gone home by now.' Geraldine thanked the desk sergeant. She hesitated, then made her way to the Incident Room and picked up a pile of papers from the floor. She could still work for a few hours before she grew too tired to concentrate. Even then she knew she'd be unable to relax, haunted by the feeling they'd missed some detail that might identify the killer. But although she'd gone over and over the statements, she'd found nothing to move the case forward. Meanwhile, the man the papers had dubbed 'The Woolsmarsh Strangler' had struck again. The newshounds were going to have a field day.

45

Interview

The newsroom was humming as usual the following morning, but inside the editor's office it was relatively quiet.

'Come in, take a seat.' The editor, Bill Hardy, didn't so much as glance at Laurie as he sat down. Bill Hardy had barely exchanged two words with him before the Rogers story broke. Since then, he'd given him a nod, or a 'Morning, Jackson,' as he passed through the newsroom, making Laurie feel like he was on his way at last, destined for better things than local charity events with wilting pot plants and homemade cakes. The paper had been going wild with strangler stories over the past fortnight. Laurie was desperate to get a look in but as he waited he began to regret having requested a meeting. At last Bill Hardy looked up, eyes bright with energy in his creased face, his dishevelled bush of grey hair springing up from his head in every direction.

'Well, Jackson? What is it this time? Another scoop up your sleeve? It's a gift, being able to sniff out a lead.'

'Yes, sir.'

'Well, come on, out with it. What've you got in mind this time? Another story?'

'Yes, sir, I think so.'

The editor rubbed his hands together briskly. 'Let's have it then.'

As Laurie described the increasing local unrest about the serial killer, he could see Bill Hardy's attention starting to wander. He went on too long, trying to build up to his exclusive.

After a minute, the editor interrupted him. 'Well, have you come up with a plan to catch the killer? Where's all this going, Jackson? Get to the point.' Laurie mentioned his report on the protest, playing up the fact that theirs was the only paper to print a photograph of the detective inspector entering the park, as well as leaving. He wondered whether Bill Hardy had noted the significance of the picture, which showed that Laurie had been first on the scene. He pointed it out, tentatively.

'Yes, nice work. What's next?' He spoke with a hint of impatience. Laurie told him about the protest. 'Yes, a group of local women. Nothing better to do with their time,' the editor said dismissively. 'What of it?'

Laurie hesitated. Suddenly his exclusive interview with the leader of the protesters didn't sound very impressive but he couldn't very well back down so he ploughed on awkwardly.

There was a very brief silence when he finished speaking. Bill Hardy was studying his screen again.

'Fine, fine. Do the interview and let's see what comes up.'

'I think this unrest is going to escalate, sir,' Laurie said, in an attempt to interest the editor in his idea.

Bill Hardy glanced up. 'I daresay, but we're here to report the news, not speculate about it, Jackson,' he said. That was a bit rich, considering the headlines he'd been running: MORE DEATHS LIKELY, for one.

'What do you suggest I do then, sir?'

The editor leaned forward, staring straight into Laurie's eyes. 'Do what all reporters do, Jackson. Find a story and report it.'

Laurie nodded and scrambled to his feet without a word.

Julie Masters lived on the West side of town on the way to Ron Rogers' estate. The further West you went, the more expensive property became. Laurie knew all about the price of property in the area. Not that he was thinking about buying. He barely managed to live within his means as it was. But he'd done some research on local housing for a story. Julie Masters' house would be worth a packet, he thought, as he passed between high hedges and caught sight of the landscaped garden leading down to a wide double fronted house.

The aroma of fresh coffee met him as Julie Masters opened the door. Her hair had been swept back off her face but a few tendrils fell artfully over heavily made up eyes. Her top was low cut, her jeans skin tight. Mutton dressed as lamb, Laurie thought uncharitably but was glad he'd worn his black chinos and Paul Smith jacket. She led him along a hallway, past closed doors, to a kitchen that stretched in an L shape along the back of the house. Through the huge window, the garden looked beautiful, but it didn't match his view of the park, Laurie thought smugly. Julie Masters didn't offer him coffee so he launched into his questions straight away.

'Mrs Masters,' he leaned forward, smiling affably. 'I understand you're one of the founder members of the women's protest group?'

'Well, yes, it was my idea.' The interview progressed slowly. Julie Masters answered his questions monosyllabically, seeming a different person to the fired up speaker he'd seen leading the protest outside the park. Laurie persevered, struggling to hide his disappointment. Some exclusive this had turned out to be. Exclusive, because no one else would waste their time on a bored housewife with nothing to say. Yet she had agreed to the interview. He wondered if she wanted to discuss something other than her women's movement. Laurie pressed on, but she kept glancing at her watch. If she had anything interesting to say, he'd have to discover it soon. He tried a more general question, to see where it led and she started complaining about the council. Her main gripe centred on the serial killer's activities in the park.

'But surely it's down to the police to catch him, Mrs Masters. What can the council do?'

'What can the council do?' she repeated, suddenly animated. 'That bunch of hypocrites? The council are our elected representatives and they're doing nothing to protect us. They sit in their fancy offices and do nothing to make our streets safe so women can walk freely around Woolsmarsh without fear of murderers and rapists.'

This was a bit more like it. 'What would you like to see the council do?' he asked again.

'They should set up surveillance of the park and the streets around it for a start. The killer must be living some-where nearby.'

'You want the council to set up surveillance of the park?'

'Yes. That's where he's killing all these poor girls. If they watched the park, they'd catch him, wouldn't they? It's hardly rocket science.'

'You don't think he'd just move on somewhere else?' For a moment, Laurie had thought he was onto something, but the interview degenerated into a pointless debate, with Mrs Masters insisting the killer be 'hounded out of Woolsmarsh.'

'By a posse, you mean? A lynching?'

'Well, no, of course not, but something's got to be done to protect the ordinary women going about their daily lives.'

Laurie was relieved when she told him she had another appointment and he thanked her for her time.

'How did your interview with Julie Masters go?' a colleague asked when he returned to his desk.

Laurie shook his head despondently. 'Complete waste of time,' he griped. 'Might fill a gap on the women's page, but that's about all.' It was hardly the front page feature Laurie had envisaged.

'Did you get a chance to pump her about her husband?'

Laurie tried not to react. 'Huh?' he said casually, fiddling with his keyboard, as though he hadn't heard the question.

'Jonathon Masters.' Laurie recognised the name of the controversial leader of the local council, always in the news with his radical statements. *That* was the story behind the interview with Julie Masters – only Laurie had been too poorly prepared to find it.

'No,' he said flatly, 'she refused to say anything about the council.'

His report appeared the following week. It was only a short article, as he'd predicted, and didn't make the front page. It had been heavily ghosted.

JONATHAN MASTERS' WIFE IN SAFETY CAMPAIGN

Jonathan Masters' wife is leading a campaign to make the streets safe. The wife of the council leader has stepped up in support of local women. The movement, Women of Woolsmarsh, of which blonde Julie Masters (29) is a founder member, is spearheading a protest against police inaction over recent brutal murders in the town.

Details of the victims followed, with the identikit picture of the killer, showing his notorious scar. The article concluded with a comment from Jonathan Masters in bold type.

COUNCIL LEADER SPEAKS OUT

In an exclusive interview with the *Woolsmarsh Chronicle*, council leader Jonathon Masters said: 'The council fully supports this movement and we urge everyone to be vigilant in helping the police with their enquiries. We are looking into the proposal for a temporary closure of Lyceum Park.'

The article outlined Jonathon Masters' defence of traditional family values and quoted him calling for 'a decent society where everyone can freely go about their daily business without fear.'

'What d'you think?' someone asked Laurie.

'Julie Masters hasn't seen twenty-nine in a long while,' he replied spitefully.

46

Car

The post came early next morning. There was a small pile of envelopes on the hall mat when Geraldine left her flat. She flipped through them quickly. Most were for her neighbour upstairs. She put them on the window ledge. There was only one personal letter for her, a pink envelope with her name and address carefully inscribed in childish handwriting. She slit it open and pulled out a pink Thank You notelet, written in the same immature script. A chubby little dog winked up at her from a bed of pink daisies.

Dear Aunty Geraldine
Thank you for my birthday present.
With love from Chloe

Geraldine wondered if Chloe even knew what present Geraldine had given her, among the pile of gifts she'd received. Stuffing the card and pink envelope in her pocket, she hurried along the corridor to the back door.

A fierce wintry sun was shining through biting wind. Overhead, the sky loomed dark and heavy. Geraldine thrust her hands into her pockets and hurried over to her garage. As she drew near, her eyes widened in dismay. The lock appeared to have been tampered with during the night. The handle was hanging loose, the new paintwork around it scratched. Careful not to touch the damaged lock, Geraldine nudged the bottom of the door with her foot and pushed.

The door swung open. Her alarm subsided as she saw her car was still inside.

'No harm done,' she muttered, but her relief was short-lived. A message had been scratched on the back of the car. In spidery, uncontrolled letters, the word was clearly legible: *FILTH*. Her stalker had forced his way into her garage. The implication was clear: his next step might be to force his way into her flat. 'No harm done,' she repeated unsteadily under her breath. It was just silly scare tactics. If the intruder intended to harm her, he would have attacked her by now, not alerted her with warnings. She told herself she was perfectly safe. There was no reason to take any of this seriously. She'd have to change her car, that was all. She couldn't drive around in a vehicle marked like that. But her hands were shaking so much by the time she climbed in that she struggled to insert the key in the ignition.

Geraldine prided herself on her powers of concentration, but driving into work that morning she found she couldn't focus on the case. Every time she blinked, the crudely scrawled message flickered into her mind: *FILTH*. Locking her car, she averted her eyes from the ugly scratch.

Peterson, arriving at the same time, spotted it straight away and whistled. 'What happened there?'

Geraldine was startled by the animosity in his voice. 'Nothing.' It was a stupid response. Peterson stood blocking her way. She waited for a second in silence. 'Excuse me,' she said and sidestepped to pass him. For an instant, she thought he was going to take a sideways step to block her path again but he didn't move. She hurried inside, utterly humiliated. Peterson had been genuinely angry, resentful at having to answer to a senior officer who clearly wasn't in control of her own life, let alone her work. Geraldine bit her lip and wished the sergeant would just mind his own business.

*

Peterson watched the DI studying her screen, unaware she was being observed. Geraldine was a conscientious officer, maybe a brilliant one, and he bridled at the possibility that someone was threatening her personal safety. He wasn't a man to look the other way when confronted with a challenging situation and, in any case, harassment of a DI was an attack on the whole team so he was involved whether she liked it or not. He pushed his chair back suddenly, his mind made up. It took him a few seconds to discover the number of the caretaker in her block of flats, slightly longer to break through his reserve. Geraldine had told the caretaker the police wouldn't be interested in the graffiti that had appeared, first on the fence, then on her garage door. The caretaker didn't seem to know about the damage to her car.

'And you've got no idea who's behind it?' Peterson persisted.

The caretaker grunted. 'That's your job to find out, isn't it?' he said gruffly. 'I've been busy enough cleaning up the mess.'

'That's fine,' Peterson replied confidently. 'You can leave it to us to find out who's behind it all and make sure it doesn't happen again. Just tell me one thing: have any deliveries been made to Geraldine Steel's flat?'

'Deliveries?'

'Yes. Has anything been delivered recently?'

'I'm not saying any more. You can ask her what that was,' the caretaker replied, inadvertently answering Peterson's question. 'I thought you said you work with her.' He hung up. Peterson narrowed his eyes thoughtfully. The caretaker wasn't the only one harbouring suspicions.

The Incident Room was quiet. Officers were studying documents or discussing theories before the morning briefing. The phones had not yet begun ringing but it wouldn't be long before they started. The public were increasingly agitated about their safety. Children were being escorted to and from school, and women were reluctant to go out alone. The press had been quick to take advantage of the situation. They claimed the public had a right to know the truth, but some of their sensational headlines smacked of deliberate attempts to whip up hysteria. The DCI had decided to give a press briefing in an attempt to placate the press and ensure their reports were at least reasonably accurate and she wanted Geraldine present to help scupper rumours that the police were ignoring women's fears. With a female DCI heading the investigation, and a female DI on the team, it would be hard to level accusations of police misogyny.

Geraldine had dressed with care, still mortified at her recent photograph in the *Woolsmarsh Chronicle*. 'WOMEN DEMAND ACTION', the headline declared above a picture of a group of well-groomed women brandishing placards. By contrast, Geraldine could be seen skulking in the bottom right hand corner of the picture, looking as though she'd been dragged out of bed. Even in the grainy black and white picture her make-up appeared smudged around panda eyes as she stared into the camera.

'They still cling to their bloody stereotypes,' Kathryn Gordon grumbled. 'According to them the force is riddled with bigotry, run by sexist white male racists.' Geraldine was surprised to see the DCI's hands were trembling; she hadn't expected her to be nervous too. This was Geraldine's first televised appeal. She greeted Mr and Mrs Ross sombrely and led them to the briefing room. The table was in place, microphones ready, and the backdrop fixed. All Geraldine had to do was remember her carefully rehearsed lines.

Gazing out into the faces and camera lenses, she felt a shiver of trepidation and was glad she was sitting down. The appeal wouldn't be transmitted until that evening but it would be broadcast unedited. She hoped she wouldn't make a fool of herself on camera and did her best to look confident. She pictured the headlines if she were honest about their progress: POLICE CLUELESS AS MORE WOMEN DIE! All she could tell them with any certainty was that the man they called the Woolsmarsh Strangler had claimed a third victim.

Cameras flashed and Geraldine tried not to blink in the bright lights as Kathryn Gordon read out her statement slowly, pausing frequently to look around at the assembled reporters. Geraldine wondered if she was deliberately trying to spin it out, to leave less time for questions.

'We regret to confirm that the body of a teenage girl was found in the lake in Lyceum Park early yesterday morning. She has been identified as Jacqueline Ross, a local school-girl.' At her side, Mrs Ross gave one loud sob. A subdued groan rippled round the room. The DCI paused and a few reporters shouted out questions. Cameras flashed. Voices heckled more loudly. 'At least we're trying to find the bastard,' Geraldine thought angrily. 'The investigation into these tragic deaths …' Kathryn Gordon resumed, raising her voice but outwardly unperturbed, and the reporters fell silent, listening to the end of her prepared statement. Geraldine was shocked by the questions fired whenever the DCI paused.

'What are the police doing?' a voice called out. This was not a personal attack against the police, Geraldine reminded herself.

'We are following several leads and more information is reaching us daily. The co-operation of the public, and members of the press, is vital to our enquiry.' There was a muted mumbling that rose to a roar as Kathryn Gordon finished. The room fell respectfully silent when she intro-duced Mr Ross. He gave an emotional appeal for members of the public to come forward with any information. When he finished, the reporters began calling out again, demanding more answers.

'That's three murders in less than two weeks. What are the police doing about it?'

'Do the police support a curfew?'

Geraldine wished she hadn't been given the job of fielding questions. She wondered if the press officer always looked so grim on these occasions. She suspected it might have been different with a man in the hot seat, although the most aggressive questions came from the female journalists. She pulled her shoulders back and looked out at the faces with a display of confidence.

'Why is the park still open?' someone called out and a host of questions followed, all clamouring for attention.

'Is this the strangler's doing?'

'Why hasn't there been an arrest yet?'

'It's almost two weeks since Angela Waters' murder. Are the police any closer to finding her killer?'

'Is there a suspect?'

'Was the drowned girl connected with the recent stranglings?'

'Can the police confirm that this is the work of a serial killer?' someone yelled and there was a mutter in the crowd. The reporter who had called out the question continued: 'There's been no official confirmation yet from the police on that point.' Geraldine did her best to remain calm. The reporters were only doing their job, sniffing around for a dramatic soundbite.

SERIAL KILLER CONFIRMED

The headline would be followed by an 'in-depth' analysis, beginning with a rhetorical question:

What are the police doing to keep our streets safe?

And all the police could offer were timeworn formulae about pursuing enquiries and following leads. For an instant Geraldine was worried they were going to start heckling again. Then the briefing was over and she led Mr and Mrs Ross away. It was time to face her next audience.

47

Monday

Monday morning started badly. Rusty wasn't in school. The other girls hadn't seen her since the party.

'I was wondering if she said anything about me,' Shema said as they gathered in their form room before class began. She didn't understand why Alice and another girl looked at each other and burst out laughing.

'She says plenty about you,' Alice called over her shoulder as she walked away to join a group of girls gossiping about who they'd pulled on Friday. Shema asked around. Someone said Rusty was bunking because of the Maths test but, as it turned out, there wasn't a test that Monday. Sir told them to line up and go to the hall.

'Why?' someone called out but sir wouldn't tell them.

The whole school assembled in the hall, laughing and chattering. The head and both deputies were on the platform with two visitors, a woman and a man. They all looked solemn. Shema heard Alice's braying laughter and hoped the other girls weren't bitching about her. She remembered how Ella had sniggered at her dress on Friday. Rusty had told her not to worry about it. She was in the gang with Alice and Ella, but they made her feel uncomfortable. It was no fun without Rusty. Mrs Galvin stepped forward. The word was spreading that Mrs Parker, head of year ten, had been crying.

Everyone fell silent as the head teacher began to speak. 'The police have brought us news of a terrible tragedy. There is no easy way to tell you this. One of our year ten pupils sadly died at the weekend.' She paused before saying the name, 'Jacqueline Ross. The death of this popular girl, who was a valued member of our school community, touches us all. Jacqueline was full of life and high spirits and I know we will all miss her. There will be a full school service in here straight after lunch and Father Bembridge will lead us in our prayers for Jacqueline. A committee will be set up to decide what more we can do in her memory.' She paused. 'The police are investigating the cause of Jacqueline's death and are here as part of a murder enquiry. Now the police would like to say a few words.'

There was silence for a moment, then Shema moaned, the sound lost in an outcry that echoed round the room. A girl fainted, and was carried out stumbling between two teachers. Mrs Galvin introduced the two visitors and when the woman spoke, everyone listened. Someone sobbed quietly at the back of the hall.

'We're very sorry for your sad loss. We can understand how shocked you must all be feeling, but we need you to help us catch whoever killed Jacqueline. Anything you can tell us about her would help us. We're particularly keen to hear about Jacqueline's movements on Friday evening. We know she went to a party. If anyone saw her after school on Friday please come and speak to either myself or Detective Sergeant Peterson. We'll be …' she whispered to Mrs Galvin, 'in the Etherington Room all morning.' The woman carried on speaking softly into the microphone. She looked strict, but she had a kind voice. 'We also need to know about any friends Jacqueline had out of school. We need your help to build a picture of Jacqueline's last hours, where she went and whom she might have seen. So if you can tell us anything about Jacqueline, however unimportant it seems, please come and talk to us in the Etherington Room. Anything you tell us will be treated in confidence.' Dismissed, they returned to class and sat in stunned silence.

Even Sir didn't know what to say. Then a prefect came in with a request for Shema to go to the Etherington Room.

Shema knew she had to be careful. She couldn't imagine the consequences if her father found out she'd lied to him and gone to a party after school on Friday, and that she'd been on the streets alone after dark. She was probably the last person to see Rusty alive, apart from the killer. She remembered leaving Rusty alone at the bus stop, drunk, but there was no point in admitting that now. It would only land her in trouble and it wouldn't bring Rusty back.

The two police officers smiled sadly at her as she sat down. The woman explained that they needed to establish where Jacqueline had gone after she left the party, so they could work out her route. Shema explained that she'd left the party at about nine. No, she hadn't seen Jacqueline at the party. No, she didn't know who Jacqueline's boyfriend was. She didn't know she had one. She was quite sure she hadn't seen Jacqueline after she left the party. She didn't know anything about a witness who'd seen two girls at a bus stop at around half past nine. No, she knew nothing about a girl leaving the party wearing a school blazer, accompanied by an Asian girl. Lots of girls wore their blazers out of school.

Shema thought they must know she was lying, but their questions changed. No, she didn't know if Jacqueline had been with a boy at the party. She didn't know if Jacqueline had met anyone that evening. She had no idea if there were any strangers at the party. There were loads of people there she'd never seen before. She didn't know how old they all were. No, Jacqueline Ross wasn't a special friend of hers. Shema felt her face go hot with shame. The woman gave her a little card with a telephone number on it and asked Shema to be sure to call the police if she remembered anything else.

Shema was shaking by the time she left the Etherington Room. Was there no end to the terrible consequences of going to that awful party? She had lied to her father and now she'd lied to the police too. As soon as she was out of sight she sidled up to a bin in the yard, and dropped the card in it. Then she turned and ran as fast as she could towards the toilets where she threw up, trembling and sobbing. At last she stopped puking, splashed cold water on her face and made her way unsteadily back to her classroom. Now maybe life could return to normal. But she knew it never would, because she would never have another friend like Rusty. Jogging back along the corridor, she began to cry again. She'd wanted to tell the policewoman everything she knew, but she couldn't risk her father discovering her shocking secret.

48

Ramsden

The firm that supplied the station's unmarked vehicles replaced Geraldine's car discreetly but it was impossible to keep the graffiti a secret. Gossip spread fast, and soon everyone at the station knew about it. The paperwork had been a further time consuming irritation she could have done without. At least there wouldn't be an official investigation, although she had to report the incident as a random act of criminal damage. As she drove her new car out of the school, Geraldine didn't head straight back to the station. First she had an informal investigation of her own to conduct. Homeware was a large store on the bypass where she'd bought her washing machine. As luck would have it, the store was only about twenty-five minutes' drive from Woolsmarsh.

Tall and slender, Miss Clarke in Human Resources rose to her feet and smiled pleasantly at Geraldine. 'Please come in, Inspector. How can I help you?' Miss Clarke sat down and leaned back comfortably in her chair. Her smile failed to conceal a nervous tic in the corner of her eye.

'I'd like a list of all your delivery personnel, and a list of all your local deliveries on the 27th of September.' The HR woman didn't move. Instead she enquired what the investigation was about. 'I'm afraid I can't discuss that with you. Now, can I have the list, please?'

'If there's been a complaint against one of our staff …'

'There's no complaint, Miss Clarke, but I do need sight of

that list right away. This really can't wait and I'm afraid you're wasting time. I'd appreciate your co-operation.' Geraldine rose to her feet. 'If there's a problem with compliance, I'll have to close your store and ask you to surrender all your records to the police. But that would be taking a sledgehammer to crack a nut. All I require is a list of your delivery personnel and your deliveries for the 27th.'

Miss Clarke's smile vanished. 'Of course,' she said quickly. 'Can you wait one moment, please?' She hurried away to fetch the information and Geraldine sat down again. As soon as the HR manager left the room, her phone rang. Geraldine waited impatiently, half listening to the message.

'You're through to Miranda Clarke in Human Resources. I'm not at my desk at the moment. Please leave a message and I'll return your call as soon as possible.'

'Miranda, it's Lynne in accounts. Can you pop up and see me before the end of the day? Thanks.'

The caller hung up and almost immediately the phone rang again. Geraldine glanced at her watch and yawned as she listened to the Miranda Clarke's message for a second time. A memory flickered in the back of Geraldine's mind as a muffled voice came on the line.

'Miranda, it's Anne. Call me when you get this. We need to talk.' Geraldine wondered who Anne was. Then Miranda Clarke scurried in.

Geraldine scanned the list quickly and found it straight away. On Thursday 27th September Bert Whalley and Arthur Ramsden had delivered a washing machine to her address. About two years earlier, Geraldine had apprehended a Norman Ramsden in the course of a violent robbery.

'What can you tell me about Arthur Ramsden?'

Miss Clarke shrugged. 'What do you want to know?' She turned to her monitor and typed in the name. 'He started working here three months ago. He's been very reliable. It

LEIGH RUSSELL

was lucky for us we found him when we did. His predecessor left us literally overnight.' She looked up at Geraldine with a rueful smile. 'Your lot picked him up, in fact. He's awaiting trial for a spot of burglary on the side. Are you sure he's not the one you're looking for?'

Geraldine thanked Miss Clarke for the information and drove back to the station, puzzling about how to deal with Ramsden. Back at her desk, she telephoned her previous station for information. 'Can you look up Norman Ramsden. I need to know if there's a brother or anyone else called Arthur. Arthur Ramsden. Soon as you can … Thank you.' She replaced the handset and looked up. She hadn't heard Peterson approach. He was standing beside the desk, watching her.

'Who's Arthur Ramsden?' he asked quietly.

Geraldine frowned. 'It's nothing.' Peterson was about to speak when her phone rang. Geraldine learned that Norman Ramsden had a younger brother, Arthur. Her former colleague added that Arthur hadn't been seen since his brother had been sent down. Geraldine replaced the handset thoughtfully. Arthur Ramsden was persecuting her maliciously, but it was a relief to put a name to the figure she'd seen on the security tape.

49

Attention

The strangler's third victim had whipped the media into a frenzy. Whenever members of the Murder Investigation Team set foot outside the station, reporters were waiting to quiz them about their progress. Geraldine resented having to field their questions but at least the police didn't have to respond to the reporters, and certainly not in any detail. The DCI was trickier to fob off, as she exerted pressure on them for a swift result, even though she knew how laborious these cases could be. There were notes and witness statements to read, reports to type up, photos to study and phone calls to make. Geraldine had worked hard for her rapid promotion to DI. Once she'd thought she might rise higher. Now she wasn't sure she wanted this any more. If they ever managed to draw the case to a satisfactory conclusion, she decided to think seriously about handing in her resignation.

It wasn't the demands of the investigation that worried her so much as the nagging fear that she wasn't up to the job. People depended on her and she was floundering. She'd rushed headlong into her career without giving it much thought. Now she wondered whether this was really what she wanted to do. There must be more to life than this gruelling slog, and constant anxiety, eating away at her. She could find a job in a bar, with no responsibility at all, and look forward to a good night's sleep at the end of each simple day. But then she'd not only have to give up her flat, but her identity as well, along with everything she'd worked for. Being a detective was all she knew. She didn't really want to give up her career, she just didn't want to fail. She sighed and turned over in bed.

Kathryn Gordon wasn't helping. She'd bowed to pressure, wasting valuable resources manning a twenty-four hour patrol of the park.

'We have to maintain public support, Geraldine,' Kathryn Gordon insisted when Geraldine voiced her reservations at the morning briefing. Geraldine didn't need reminding of that. She'd read more than enough harsh criticism of the police in the press over the past week, and witnessed near hysteria on the street. There were rumours of local residents forming vigilante groups.

'It's not the first time this has happened,' the DCI said. There was a murmur of assent. They all knew the press profited from stirring people up. 'We've already had those bloody women marching around with their placards: keep our streets safe, and so on. We have to keep a lid on it all,' the DCI went on. 'The last thing we want now is problems with public disorder. The media go to town on things like that, stories galore, it's easy pickings for them, and it's important to keep them focused on the investigation. Anything else is a distraction. We have to keep the case in the public eye. That's our only chance of getting information that can move us forward.'

'But standing guard over the park isn't going to help,' Geraldine protested. 'Putting all our available manpower into the investigation might. House-to-house enquiries. Following up all these people coming forward with information. It's all got to be covered with limited resources.' Kathryn Gordon bowed her head for a second then raised her eyes.

'We've all heard what you have to say, Geraldine,' she responded tersely before she continued.

Geraldine wasn't surprised when the DCI asked to see her

after the briefing. This time Kathryn Gordon invited her to sit down. Geraldine waited. The older woman sighed.

'You worry me, Geraldine,' she said at last. 'Frankly, your last DCI's report wasn't altogether flattering.' She quoted, without looking at the file, 'Tendency to lateral thinking.' She paused. 'You're a bloody good officer, and God knows the force needs strong intelligent women. But be careful. Lateral thinking,' she repeated. She sat forward and spoke very quietly. 'The force won't tolerate maverick officers.' Geraldine was startled by the bitterness in her voice. 'You have to understand, this isn't a power game, Geraldine, it's a necessity, if we're to get the job done. And we will get the job done. But only if everyone pulls together. And that includes you.' Geraldine nodded dumbly. 'You're an able officer, with great potential,' the DCI went on, 'but you have to play by the book, Geraldine. I can't afford to lose good officers, but the needs of the team have to override every other consideration. Remember your place in the team.' Geraldine was shaking by the time she left the DCI's office.

Her shift over, she didn't want to spend the evening alone so she went to the pub. Carter was at the bar and she bought him a pint.

'What did Kathryn Gordon want with you?' he asked. Geraldine shrugged, and didn't answer. 'You think it's hard for a woman to get to the top. Well, it was a whole lot harder back in the nineties. Your rapid promotion owes something to the DCI and women like her. Pioneers in their day. But it takes a certain sort of woman to get to where she is. Determined, single minded, ruthless.' He took a swig of his pint.

'Egotistical, self aggrandising,' Geraldine added under her breath. Carter smiled sadly and shook his head. 'I think she resents me,' Geraldine confessed, staring into her glass.

'That's bloody daft, and you know it,' he chided her and she nodded miserably.

'I guess I'm just feeling undervalued.'

'That's down to you, isn't it?'

'You mean I have to prove myself? Because *she* had to fight to be respected, every woman has to?'

'We all have to earn respect, Geraldine,' Carter said sharply but Geraldine wasn't so sure. For all the talk about equality, the gender divide ran deep, and it wasn't only men who treated women unfairly. The DCI seemed to be going out of her way to prove she wasn't giving Geraldine any special treatment; all Geraldine wanted was to be treated the same as her male colleagues.

That night Geraldine lay awake, while the frustrations of the day raced through her mind. She could feel tension in her neck as she moved her head on the pillow, and realised she was biting her lip. It was hard to believe that less than two weeks before, she'd been moving into her new flat, eager to be sent on another case. She got out of bed but was too wound up to work, so she busied herself tidying and dusting the flat. She could think more easily when she was active, and at least she had the comforting illusion she was doing something useful. When she'd finished on the living room, she tidied her bedroom. There was always something out of place. With so many disturbing loose ends in her life and her work, she needed the repose of an orderly home.

She dusted her bedside cabinet and replaced her clock. Opening her top drawer she was startled to see Mark's photo grinning up at her. She touched the shiny surface, tracing the line of his lips, and felt unbearably lonely. Peterson had joined her for a drink a few times, but he was usually in a rush to go home to his girlfriend. They spent a lot of time together, and she liked him, but it wasn't the same. Apart from Craig, there were no single men in her life and she'd managed to ruin things with him. All the men she met were either married, much younger or older than her, or sitting on the other side of the interview table trying to blag their way out of a prosecution.

She went into the kitchen and set about scrubbing her tiny kitchen worktops. She could bear any amount of solitude, if only she could have the satisfaction of success in her work. But another girl might die that night, and all she could do was clean her flat until every surface gleamed.

PART 5

'the gift of fantasy has meant more to me than any talent for abstract, positive thinking'

Albert Einstein

50

Boyfriend

The following morning, Geraldine was thrilled to receive a text from Craig, asking if she was free for dinner that evening. She was on early shift. Perfect.

'Love to' she keyed in, then deleted the message and changed it to 'Sounds good.' Craig replied straight away with the name of a restaurant, suggesting they meet there. Geraldine smiled. If the fiasco of their first date hadn't put him off, he must genuinely like her.

'Either that or he's desperate,' Celia chuckled when Geraldine called her.

'Thanks a lot.' Geraldine said. She thought about Craig and sighed. It was easy for Celia to make light of her sister's relationship problems.

'Seriously,' Celia added, 'you know what not to do this time.'

'Don't worry, I won't touch a drop.'

Returning to her desk, Geraldine was surprised when Sarah Mellor approached her.

'Fancy a drink at lunch time, gov?' Mellor looked so uncomfortable, Geraldine thought the young DC must have a reason for wanting to talk outside the station. She could hardly refuse.

'Just a quick one then,' she said. 'I've got a lot on. I'm going out later.' She resisted the temptation to tell her about Craig. There was no reason for Sarah Mellor to be interested in Geraldine's love life, such as it was.

When she arrived in the pub at lunchtime, Sarah wasn't there. Peterson was. 'Sarah couldn't make it,' he said, pushing a pint across the table.

Geraldine hesitated, recognising a set-up.

'I'll get straight to the point,' Peterson said. 'What's going on?'

Geraldine sat down heavily. 'I was going to ask you the same question.' She didn't touch her drink.

'I asked you here because I want to know what's going on with your car.'

'Just kids, messing around in the night.'

'How do they know where you live?'

She realised her mistake, and shook her head. 'They don't. It's just coincidence.' She didn't tell him it had happened three times.

Peterson put down his pint. 'I'm not an idiot, gov.'

'Well neither am I,' Geraldine retorted. 'And if I thought there was any cause for concern, I'd deal with it. So drop it, Sergeant.' She rose to her feet and swept out of the pub wishing she felt as self-assured as she sounded. At least she had a date that evening. It might take her mind off the case for a couple of hours.

Geraldine left the station on time, for once, and was home early. After showering, she smiled uncertainly at herself in the mirror. Her eyes were her best feature, so dark the pupils were swallowed up by her irises which were almost black against her pale skin. She dragged her gaze away from her reflection with a sigh. She still had a report to type up for the morning before her day's work was over and by the time she'd finished, it was nearly time to go. Even though she'd arrived home in plenty of time, she still ended up rushing. Soon her clothes were spread out over the bed; she couldn't find the one dress she'd decided might be suitable. Finally, only twenty minutes behind schedule, she turned on her alarm, closed the front door and hurried to her car. She had to make a conscious effort not to glance over her shoulder as she unlocked her garage, but couldn't stop her eyes flicking nervously from side to side as she drove down the close. There was no sign of Arthur Ramsden.

Her destination turned out to be a fairly expensive restaurant, and Geraldine was glad she'd chosen to wear a smart dress, simple but clingy in the right places. Craig was sitting at a corner table, his eyes fixed on the door. He half rose to his feet and raised his hand as she walked in. She waved back to let him know she'd seen him and he broke into a smile that flickered in the flame of a table candle. With a rush of pleasure she realised Craig was relieved she'd turned up. She called in the number of the restaurant, just in case, and checked her mobile in her bag. After that, she concentrated on trying to relax and enjoy dinner by candle light with a good looking man, in an expensive restaurant, with romantic music playing softly in the background. Suddenly it wasn't difficult to silence her worries and focus on her evening, doing normal things like normal people did. It couldn't last.

Craig was even more attractive than she remembered and the conversation flowed easily. The more she found out about Craig, the more she liked him. Their initial disastrous date had broken the ice between them, and she was surprised to find herself laughing about it without any embarrassment. She had a vague recollection of being carried upstairs, virtually unconscious, but Craig was able to add a few shameful details about her drunken performance that night. Beneath his superficial bravado, he was warm and funny.

'You can't be shy,' he warned her at one point. 'Remember, we've spent the night together.' Geraldine grinned. She rather liked being called shy. It made a change for a ballsy thirty-seven-year-old DI. For the first time since Mark left her she felt feminine and desirable.

Everything was fine until Craig started telling her about his week. He was a skilled raconteur, and made her laugh with his anecdotes. But she was aware of an invisible gulf yawning across the table. She dreaded the inevitable question.

'What about you, Geraldine? You must see lots of interesting things in your job.'

She hesitated. It wasn't classified information, but any account of her week would jar with the light-hearted atmosphere of their evening. She was trying to find a serial killer who'd strangled three girls. He'd stripped the third one and dumped her naked body in a dirty pond. He was likely to kill again if he wasn't caught and the police hadn't the faintest idea who he was. She couldn't share the details of her work with Craig. No one outside the force could understand. It would be the usual fake interest: 'How do you cope?' and 'How can you stand seeing all those dead bodies?' She was afraid he'd be repulsed by her work and she no longer just fancied Craig. She was really beginning to like him.

This was the reason why so many relationships failed on the force. It wasn't the gruelling shifts and unpredictable hours, the stress and absorbing nature of the work, the phone calls in the early hours, that eroded any chance of intimacy with another human being. It was this chasm of experience. However close they grew, they would always look on horrors from different sides of the abyss. She could describe her current case to Craig, but his shock would be a natural reaction she could no longer afford to feel. To switch from her professional detachment into a woman with normal emotions was a demand too far. It would be more than stepping out of a role. It would affect her ability to do her job if she considered the hideousness of what she'd seen. Shock numbed. It slowed reactions, and clouded judgement. She couldn't allow herself to feel that kind of compassion. But if she gave a simple factual account of one of her cases to the accompaniment of soft background music, she'd sound like an inhuman monster. How attractive would that be?

She decided to pre-empt his questions. 'I can't talk about my current case, and, if you don't mind, I'd rather not talk about my work at all.' She knew she sounded rude. If he agreed too readily, it might mean he wasn't interested to hear about her life; if he protested, he was insensitive.

Craig responded with disarming honesty. 'I'm not sure I understand, Geraldine, but OK. But if you ever want to talk about it, I'm a good listener.' She couldn't ask for more than that. 'I can be very patient,' he added, pouring more wine. He held the bottle motionless for a moment, allowing it to drip into her glass. Together they watched the blood red surface ripple in tiny concentric circles.

'How about telling me something about your life outside of work?' Craig suggested.

Geraldine hesitated. 'What do you want to know?'

He smiled and shrugged his shoulders. 'You could start by telling me about your family?'

'My family,' she hesitated. 'They're not very interesting. My parents split up when I was eighteen. My mother still lives in the house where I grew up, although it's far too big for her. My father married an Irish woman and moved to Dublin, so I don't see much of him.'

'Did you fall out?'

'No. It's just that he's a long way away.'

'It's not that far.'

'No, but it seems a long way. It's not just that he moved away. He's moved on. His wife had three small children when they met and he's got his hands full with all of them.'

'So he doesn't have time for you?' Craig smiled sympathetically.

Geraldine shook her head. 'It's not like that,' she protested. But of course Craig was right. She resented her father's desertion, although she hadn't been angry at the time. 'When he left us, my sister had just met her husband and was busy planning her future, and I'd gone off to uni. My mother was the one who felt abandoned. It was hard for her.' She shrugged. 'It's all a long time ago.'

Craig filled up her glass. 'What about you?' he asked. 'Have you ever been married?'

She shook her head. 'I was with someone for six years, but it didn't work out. You?'

He grinned. 'Never even close,' he replied. 'I'm still looking,' he added and he stared straight at her.

Geraldine's spirits lifted. His comment about patience must mean he wanted to see her again. She smiled. It was hard to restrain the seed of hope. Not everyone on the force was single or divorced. Some people made relationships work. Maybe it would happen for her.

The evening lost its romantic glow as soon as they stepped out of the restaurant. Geraldine's buoyant mood deflated at the sight of two uniformed constables. Craig stared at a youth being questioned and tightened his grip on Geraldine's arm. Following his gaze, she saw a boy with a bloody nose and split lip trying to speak. The police constable was having difficulty understanding him.

'Fah Firriff,' the boy said.

'Sam Phillips, is that?' the officer interpreted stolidly. 'And where do you live, Sam?'

The boy shook his head, spattering blood from his dripping nose. 'Mo,' he insisted with belligerent despair, 'Fah Firriff.'

'If they're like this on a Monday evening, what the hell are they like on a Saturday night? I hope you don't have to deal with that sort of trouble,' Craig said as they hurried past.

'No,' she smiled. 'That's for uniformed officers.'

'Good,' he said, taking her hand.

'I just deal with serial killers,' she thought grimly. But she was relieved that the evening had gone well and pleased when Craig asked to see her again.

'How are you fixed for Saturday?'

'I'll have to check my schedule. All weekend leave's been cancelled and I may be on nights. But as long as I'm not working, I'm free on Saturday.' Craig raised his eyebrows and said he'd call her. Geraldine wondered if he would. At work, she was skilled at distinguishing truth from lies. In her personal life, her past judgement had been disastrous, but maybe this time would be different.

Craig's goodnight kiss was gentle. Geraldine responded and for an instant his arms tightened around her before he released her and walked her back to her car. She felt a pang of regret when he didn't invite her home with him, but there was no rush. Although she felt as though she'd known him for a long time, in reality this had been the first evening they'd spent together properly. She didn't really know him at all. As she drove home, she made up her mind she wouldn't be disappointed if he didn't call. Craig had distracted her from work for an evening. That was all. She wouldn't allow him to become an additional problem for her to try and forget. When she reached home, she fell into bed, exhausted. She didn't even think about doing any work.

She was standing in a vast church hall. An icy wind blew through a broken window. She moved to one side but the cold draught followed her. A man stood facing her across the empty hall. A silver sword gleamed in his left hand. She wanted to warn him of danger, but every time she tried to speak, the wind carried her words away. She struggled to call out to him, but she couldn't remember his name. She had to speak to him, but the wind was howling. Her eyes filled with blood as the silver blade carved an indelible mark on her face. She woke with a start to find her cheeks wet with tears.

She glanced at her watch. It was two thirty in the morning. She knew she wouldn't get back to sleep so she got up to read through some more reports but couldn't concentrate. She put her laptop away, made herself a cup of tea and sat back in her armchair to think about her evening. She grinned, recalling Craig's shock when they'd come out of the restaurant and seen a youth with a bloody face. He'd have a huge black eye in the morning. His lip was split and he'd been struggling to give his name. 'Fah Firrith'. She smiled. He reminded her of something but she couldn't grasp what it was. She thought about Heather Spencer's description: 'He had a scar just above his top lip. It looked as though it had been split open in a fight a long time ago.' But there was something else. She knew it was important. Wide-awake now, she threw some clothes on and drove to the station. She had to find out what was stirring at the back of her mind.

She arrived at the station at three a.m. The desk sergeant gave her a sleepy grin and went back to his paper. He was used to officers on the Murder Investigation Team wandering in and out at odd hours.

Geraldine hurried to her desk and began rummaging through files. It was disheartening. Some of the recent accounts by so-called witnesses reminded her of stories she used to read when she was a teenager. Most were plagiarised. The killer had been seen roaming the streets with a chainsaw ... with scissorhands ... with steel teeth ... She could have been judging entries in a competition for a horror story. Once the papers raised the spectre of a serial killer, people's imaginations went wild, fanciful stories interspersed with spiteful claims from people venting personal feelings. All the searching around the park, the questioning of local residents, and investigation of medical records had led them no nearer to the killer. Geraldine lowered her head in despair.

The DCI had covered everything. She'd arranged a reconstruction on national television. The broadcast had concentrated on the strangler's first victim. Tiffany May had gone
to the park after dark on a wet evening and might not have
been seen before she was killed, but someone must have
noticed Angela Waters going into the park in the middle of
the morning. Regular appeals were read out on the local
radio: 'Have you seen anything unusual in the park over the
past fortnight? Anyone acting suspiciously?' Specially
trained officers had visited all the local schools to talk to
children and display posters. Young women were advised
not to wander the streets alone after dark. Notices were
posted at both entrances to the park: FATAL ASSAULT
CAN YOU HELP? And, of course, the local papers had gone
crazy.

The trouble with public appeals was they kicked off a
wave of responses, every lunatic in the area reporting their
crackpot visions. It fell to the police to roll up their sleeves
and trawl through the tittle-tattle and delusion, to search for
a clue to the mystery. Sometimes they found it. Geraldine
had heard two constables laughing together at some of the
more bizarre statements. She didn't envy them.

She flung down the report she was looking at. It was a
pointless exercise. Every interview had been scrutinised. She
wasn't going to come across anything new. They were
working through all the information, cross referencing every
possibility, chasing up any and every lead, and rereading the
same reports over and over again, hoping to find some magic
key to unlock the mystery – but it was never that simple. The
endless slog took time. And while they dedicated hours and
hours of police resources to following up specious statements, the killer was free to roam the streets. He could be out
there now, hunting for his next victim. Geraldine closed her
eyes. She could almost sense his stealthy footsteps, his
gloved hands reaching out …

Sipping tepid coffee, she wondered what it felt like to have a job where the worst that could happen was that you were fired. No one else suffered. No one died. In most professions, projects were routinely written off but they couldn't pull the plug on their investigation as though it was a flagging television show.

Geraldine worked relentlessly on through the night, pushing through her exhaustion, unable to shake off the feeling that she'd overlooked something. She decided to go right back to the beginning, start with the early statements and make her way through them all over again. She'd read through the files so many times she knew passages from the statements by heart. Where else might she have seen something?

She leaned back, casting her mind over her day. Thinking about the voice messages Miranda Clarke received, she thought back to the second day of the investigation, when she'd been asked to monitor phone messages received at the station. They hadn't struck her as significant at the time and she hadn't listened to them again but now she sprang to her feet, energised by the possibility that had opened up. She checked the date in her notebook and went to ferret through the tapes, trying to rein in her expectations.

She found the right one near the bottom of the pile and decided to start with the first call and check them all again. Humdrum voices droned on, stumbling, accusing. Listening to one woman's hesitant voice, Geraldine felt a sudden pounding in her chest and a rush of blood in her ears. She listened to it again.

I'm worried about my lodger. He's such a nice quiet man, on account of his speech impediment. He's not been back since Wednesday, so I thought the Woolsmarsh Strangler might've got him. Do you think I should let the room to someone else?

*

'He's not been back since Wednesday … on account of his speech impediment … I thought the Woolsmarsh Strangler might've got him …' Geraldine rewound the tape. '… on account of his speech impediment …' the muffled voice repeated. Geraldine felt a strange tingling at the back of her neck as she wondered where the missing tenant had come from. And where he'd gone. She stared at the tape and took several deep breaths, but couldn't keep her excitement in check. She told herself it was bound to be another dead end. But she was already rewinding the tape. She found the address. Mrs Edna Lewis had a small B & B at 17 Lyceum Park Road. Geraldine glanced at her watch. She made a half-hearted attempt to catch up on some of her outstanding paperwork, and paced the floor impatiently. Finally she snatched up her keys and set off for Lyceum Park Road.

51

Room

'Off for some breakfast?' the desk sergeant called as Geraldine hurried past.

'Yes,' she replied without thinking. She decided not to stop to report what she'd found. It was probably another wild goose chase. Yet her heart raced with a wild excitement as she made her way across the car park. The sun had just risen, lightening the sky behind its coating of grey cloud. It was still only seven thirty. After running on adrenaline and coffee for four hours, her hands were shaking as she climbed into the car and she forced herself to drive slowly. The front entrance to the park would be visible from the top floor of 17 Lyceum Road. She waited in the car. At a quarter past eight Geraldine rang the bell. The door opened a crack and a face peered up at her.

'Mrs Lewis? I'm Detective Inspector Steel. You called the station two weeks ago to make a statement about a missing tenant.' She showed her identity card and the door opened cautiously to reveal a mousy little woman. Scared button black eyes blinked at her above a faded pink dressing gown.

Mrs Lewis led the way to a small square sitting room furnished with worn but comfortable arm chairs. 'Have you found him?' Geraldine told her they didn't know where her lodger was. 'It's very good of you to be concerned about him,' Mrs Lewis said uncertainly.

Once they were seated, Geraldine began her questions. The missing tenant had lived quietly at the B & B for seventeen years. 'He had a nice room at the front,' Mrs Lewis said, 'up on the top floor. It's my best room. He had no call to go off like that. He liked it up there. It's a nice room with a lovely view of the park. He used to sit in there for hours, staring out the window. I'd see him when I went out to the shops, sitting up there looking out.'

Geraldine felt her scalp crawl. 'You mentioned your lodger had a speech impediment. Did he have a scar on his lip, Mrs Lewis?'

The landlady shook her head. 'Well,' she said apologetically, 'it's not something I like to mention. I think he was embarrassed about it.'

Time hung suspended in the still air.

'He told me he was born with a hare lip,' Mrs Lewis went on placidly. 'I was never quite sure what he meant. He wasn't all there, if you get my drift. He said they operated on his lip when he was very small, but it left a scar. It wasn't very nice. I tried not to look at it. I felt sorry for him.'

'A scar?' Geraldine repeated. 'Do you read the newspapers, Mrs Lewis?'

The landlady smiled wistfully. 'No. My eyes aren't what they used to be. Not that I was ever much of a one for the newspapers, even when I was younger. All that news, it's depressing, isn't it? Life's difficult enough, I always say, without reading about all the muggings and murders and I don't know what. And it just gets worse, doesn't it? I used to like magazines, when my eyes were stronger.' She sighed and fluttered her hands in her lap.

Geraldine fished in her pocket. 'It's terrible what goes on in the world,' Mrs Lewis continued. 'I watch the telly, of course, but I always switch over when it comes to the news. It's too depressing. All those wars and famines. I know I should take an interest, and not bury my head in the sand, but it's not for me. And all this trouble in the park now. It makes you nervous to step outside your own front door.'

275

Geraldine pulled a crumpled picture from her pocket. 'Could this be your missing lodger?' The delicate paper trembled in her outstretched hand. Mrs Lewis stared at it. She screwed up her eyes, then went to fetch her glasses. She took the picture from Geraldine and held it at arm's length, peering at it. Geraldine waited.

'No,' the landlady said finally, handing it back, 'that's not him.'

'But he had a scar like this one?' Geraldine asked, concealing her impatience.

'Well, yes. Something like that. Only his scar was smaller than that, and more crooked. It's a bit like him, mind. It looks like one of those street artists drew him, you know? The five-minute portraits. They never get it right, do they?'

Geraldine swallowed. 'What was your missing lodger's name?'

'Jim Curtis.'

'I'd like to take a look at his room.' Geraldine stood up.

Mrs Lewis explained that soon after Jim Curtis had disappeared, she'd let the room to another tenant. 'I might have kept it vacant for him, only this young man turned up on the door step looking for somewhere to stay and he seemed a nice young gentleman. I'm—' she broke off, aghast, and pressed a hand to her lips. 'I tried to tell the social straight away, only I haven't had time to get down there and it's impossible to get them on the phone …' Geraldine wasn't there to investigate Mrs Lewis defrauding the Social Services of a week or two's rent. 'I'll get that sorted …' the landlady added, gazing fearfully at her visitor.

'Yes, I'm sure you will. Now, would it be possible for me to see the room Jim Curtis rented?'

'The problem is, like I said, it's been let. A very nice young man turned up, and he needed somewhere straight away. Some mix up with his last digs. My son-in-law had just redecorated the room for me – it needed it after seventeen years. Would you believe it, that's how long Jim Curtis lived in that room, and then he just upped and left, without a word. That's what made me think maybe something happened to him. Just as I had it looking very nice, all newly decorated, this young man turned up and agreed to pay extra for the view. It's got a lovely view up there. I didn't see any point in leaving it empty. I would show you the room, only now Mr Jackson's moved in it makes it awkward, doesn't it? He wanted to move in straight away. He works for *The Chronicle,* so I knew there'd be no problem with the rent. It's never a problem when you know where they work.'

Geraldine swore softly under her breath. It would be a journalist. If Jim Curtis's name appeared in the papers, he might leave the area. Disappear. Change his name. They'd lose track of him and somewhere else more girls would die until, in time, a new investigation would begin.

'Did Jim Curtis leave anything behind when he left?'

'That was the funny thing. He left all his clothes behind, even his coat. He was very proud of that coat. Used to wear it in all weathers. That's why I thought something must've happened to him. It's not normal, is it, to go off like that leaving everything behind? I mean, he was a strange man, but you'd think he'd want to take his things with him.'

'Strange?' Geraldine queried.

'Quiet. Kept to himself. He hardly ever left his room. And he wasn't all there, if you know what I mean.'

'Have you still got his belongings stored?'

'No. What would I be wanting with all his rubbish? Clothes, and some sour milk in the fridge. I threw it all out. And his bits of newspaper. He had a picture of that rock star's daughter, Melanie something or other. Pretty girl.'

'Did you keep anything he left behind?'

'No, I told you, I threw it all out. His clothes were no good to anyone. If he wants to come back for them, I'll tell him straight, I just had to get rid of them. I can't be expected to store things when people leave. If he'd given me any sort of notice, we might've come to some arrangement. But he left me without a word. What was I supposed to do with his stuff? I can't keep everything people leave behind when they go. I run a B & B, not a lost property office—'

'Of course, Mrs Lewis,' Geraldine interrupted. 'Now, I'm going to ask you to be very discreet and not mention Jim Curtis to anyone. It's very important. You say his old room has been let to a reporter. If Jim Curtis's name got into the papers, it would cause a lot of trouble.'

Mrs Lewis looked worried. 'Trouble for poor Jim?' she asked. A gnarled hand wandered to her lips and she blinked nervously at Geraldine.

Geraldine nodded. 'Serious trouble, and not only for Jim Curtis, for you as well. I don't need to point out the difficulty you could find yourself in for renting the room privately while still collecting rent for Jim Curtis. If you co-operate and keep quiet, and notify the authorities straight away, we won't pursue it.'

Mrs Lewis nodded. 'I will,' she said. 'I'll be down the social first thing tomorrow.'

'Good. And remember, not even your family must know I've been here asking about Jim Curtis. Not a word to a soul, Mrs Lewis.' The landlady nodded dumbly. 'Now, I'd like to take a look at the room, if your new lodger doesn't object.'

Geraldine followed Mrs Lewis up two flights of stairs. The landlady knocked at a door on the top landing and a dapper young man opened it.

'Thank you, Mrs Lewis,' Geraldine said. 'I won't trouble you any further. I'm sure you're busy.' With an anxious nod, the landlady turned and made her way back down the stairs.

Laurie Jackson was almost jumping up and down with excitement when Geraldine introduced herself.

'I thought I recognised you,' he said as he led her into his room. 'What's this about, Inspector?' As if by magic, a tiny recording device appeared in his hand. Geraldine took it from him and switched it off. Still holding the dictaphone, she crossed the room and looked out of the window. 'What's this about?' he repeated, with slightly less exuberance.

'I wanted to see the view,' she replied.

'Yes, it's a very good view,' he agreed, joining her by the window. 'Now, what's this about?'

'Is it a comfortable room?' she asked, glancing round. She wasn't sure what she was hoping to find. The old fashioned wardrobe was closed. An electric shaver and toothbrush mug perched on a narrow glass shelf above a chipped sink. A towel hung on a ring beside it. A small side table and chair stood in front of an old fridge that hummed annoyingly in one corner. Geraldine turned back to the window.

'It's a great view,' the reporter repeated. 'You can look out of the window and watch the world go by, and no one knows you're here.' Geraldine nodded, gazing down at the park. She glanced up and saw the young reporter staring hungrily at her, desperate for a story. He saw her hesitate.

'Look, Inspector,' he spoke firmly, arms folded, legs apart. 'This is my room, you know. You come barging in, without any reason, and all you can say is you want to know if it's comfortable. I think you owe me an explanation.'

'An explanation?'

'Yes. What are you doing, here in my room?'

'You invited me in.'

'I'm not trying to accuse you of trespassing. I just want to know what you're doing here.'

She nodded, reaching a decision. 'All right, Mr Jackson. I'll tell you. But it's off the record for now.' He let out an exaggerated sigh and nodded to indicate he understood. Geraldine sat down on the chair and he sat on his bed. 'We had a request from Ashford station. They think the previous occupant of this room received some stolen goods. They can't trace them and asked us to check if he'd left anything here. Did you find anything when you moved in here?' She was making it up as she went along.

He shook his head, puzzled. 'What sort of thing are you looking for, Inspector?' He narrowed his eyes, calculating. He was wondering why an inspector was making this visit in person.

'I can't tell you that. Would you mind if I had a quick look around?'

'Be my guest.' He explained that Mrs Lewis had cleared and decorated the room before he moved in. 'If anything had been left, she would've found it.' Geraldine saw him watching her closely as her eyes roved round the room. She knelt down and looked under the bed. She had no idea what she was looking for. She just wanted to find some clue to link her to Jim Curtis. She didn't find anything. She couldn't look inside the wardrobe or the chest of drawers. They'd be full of Laurence Jackson's things.

'Thank you, Mr Jackson.'

'Is that it?' He sounded disappointed. 'You're working on the hunt for the Woolsmarsh Strangler, aren't you?' he asked abruptly, obviously trying to catch her unawares.

'It's a huge investigation, Mr Jackson,' she replied evenly. 'The whole station is involved and a lot of officers have been brought in.' She smiled at him. 'But I'm involved in it, yes. And I won't forget your co-operation over this small enquiry from Ashford.' She handed him back his recording device and he stared at her, unconvinced.

Geraldine ran down the stairs empty handed, but in her mind she held a picture of a muscular man with big hands and a scarred lip, sitting up there watching, hour after hour. She imagined him hidden away somewhere else, still watching. Wherever Jim Curtis was, they'd find him. In the meantime, she was late for the morning briefing.

Geraldine raced to the station. At a zebra crossing in the

town centre a woman with a pushchair seemed to move in slow motion across the road. After that, the traffic lights were against her. She nearly accelerated regardless but thought better of it, which was just as well as a cyclist careered unsteadily across the road directly in front of her. At last she screeched to a halt in the police station car park, nearly ten minutes late for the briefing. The door to the Incident Room squealed in protest as she pushed it. Everyone turned to look at her as she attempted to sneak in unobtrusively at the back, behind the constables.

'How nice of you to join us,' the DCI commented frostily. 'Now perhaps we can get on.' Embarrassed at holding up the briefing, Geraldine was relieved she hadn't missed anything.

'Thank you for waiting, ma'am. I'm sorry, I had to—' she began, but Kathryn Gordon silenced her with a raised hand and nodded at Merton.

'We've traced Tillotson,' he said and everyone turned to him, Geraldine forgotten. 'But he's in the clear.'

'It seems he has a cast iron alibi,' Kathryn Gordon chipped in grimly.

'Tillotson was in a holding cell overnight in Portsmouth,' Merton informed them. 'Picked up at six o'clock on a charge of theft. Seems he nicked his girlfriend's jewellery and ran off back to Portsmouth with it.'

'So we're back to square one,' the DCI said sourly, as she crossed Tillotson's name off the board. Disappointment seemed to permeate the air, spreading from face to face like a contagion.

'Maybe not,' Geraldine stepped forward. For the second time that morning, everyone turned to stare at her. 'I never thought Tillotson was our man,' she said, glancing round, suddenly unaccountably nervous. She could feel her legs trembling. Someone gave a faint groan. Kathryn Gordon's eyes narrowed but she didn't speak.

Merton shrugged. 'Hindsight's a great gift …' he began, but the DCI's eyes met Geraldine's and she held up her hand for silence.

'Go on,' she said, looking at Geraldine. There was an almost palpable buzz of expectation at the excitement in Kathryn Gordon's voice.

Geraldine took a deep breath. 'I remembered hearing a call we received, on the 28th September.' She flipped through her notebook. 'Here it is. 'I'm worried about my lodger. He's such a nice quiet man, on account of his speech impediment. He's not been back since Wednesday, so I thought the Woolsmarsh Strangler might've got him.' Wednesday was the 26th. The missing lodger disappeared on the day Angela Waters was killed and,' she raised her eyes from her notebook and looked straight at Kathryn Gordon, 'on the strength of Heather Spencer's statement, we've been looking for a man with a scar on his lip who seemed reluctant to talk. Possibly someone with a speech impediment.'

'Go on,' the DCI urged.

Geraldine resumed. 'I've just come back from visiting the caller, Mrs Edna Lewis, at 17 Lyceum Park Road.' The room crackled with tiny sounds of rustling paper and scratching pens. The significance of the address wasn't lost on the listeners. 'She confirmed the e-fit from Heather Spencer's description was probably her missing tenant, name of Jim Curtis. He rented a room with a view of the park.' Geraldine consulted her notes again. 'The landlady described him as 'a quiet man', born with a harelip, operated on when he was very small, leaving a scar.'

'Didn't she see his picture in the papers?' Merton asked.

Geraldine shook her head. 'When I showed her the image she said it was a pretty poor likeness. Only the position of the scar linked it to her lodger. In any case, she said her eyes aren't good any more. She doesn't read the papers and doesn't like watching the news. Says it's too depressing.'

'She's right there,' someone chipped in.

For a second no one spoke. Then the DCI nodded briskly. 'Get on with it then,' she barked. 'Report back to me as soon as you find Jim Curtis. Bring him in and let's see what he's got to say for himself.' She turned and conferred with the duty manager. Before she disappeared into her office, she wrote JIM CURTIS in large letters on the board. With a quick grin at Peterson, Geraldine set off on her allocated task as the duty sergeant added details below the e-fit picture and began writing up Jim Curtis's last known address.

52

Records

The introductions were swiftly made. They were both busy.

The young social worker peered anxiously through her glasses at Geraldine. 'You asked about Jim Curtis,' she said. 'You're lucky. Someone had his mother's file sent on and we kept it. She died in 1980, so I suppose it's OK for you to have it.' She handed Geraldine a dusty folder and started tapping at her keyboard. 'Jim Curtis,' she muttered under her breath, scanning the screen. While she waited, Geraldine glanced through the mother's file.

> Carole Curtis: prostitute, two arrests for soliciting … addict: amphetamine, crystal meth, smack, solvents, alcohol … abusive relationships … one brief stay in a refuge … Three abortions … Died 1980 … James born 3rd May 1964 … Claire born 15th September 1969. Died 1972 …

The social worker accessed Jim Curtis's records and hesitated. 'I'm not sure I should let you see his personal details.'

Geraldine did her best to look puzzled. 'We've never experienced any difficulty with co-operation from the Social Services. We've always found you very efficient,' she lied shamelessly, banking on the social worker's inexperience. 'We're two arms of the same organisation really.' The social worker looked uncertain but she complied, reading aloud from her screen as the document was printing.

'James Curtis. Is this the one you're after? Born in Lewisham 3rd May 1964. Hospitalised at fifteen weeks to correct a congenital left sided unilateral cleft lip and cleft palate. No child abuse on record, but hospital visits for various injuries. An accident prone child.' The social worker glanced up at Geraldine with a sceptical jerk of one eyebrow before continuing her litany. Her printer whined crankily in the background. 'He was taken into care in '73. One period of fostering when he was eleven, for about three months. Foster parents reported aggressive behaviour. No educational achievement to speak of. Low IQ. Not much detail on his educational needs, I'm afraid. He was on the list for an assessment, but there's no follow up on record. Typical. He's on medication for paranoid schizophrenia.'

'A cleft palate,' Geraldine repeated. 'He had an operation for a cleft palate.'

'Yes. But I wouldn't say that's the worst of his problems.'

Geraldine nodded, brisk again. 'How long's he been on medication for paranoid schizophrenia?'

The social worker referred to her records again. 'He was diagnosed in 1984.'

'That's over twenty years ago.'

'Yes. He moved here in 1987. No reason for the move is mentioned in the records. He was transferred from depot injections to anti-psychotic tablets nearly two years ago.'

'Meaning his medication has been self administered for two years,' Geraldine said slowly. 'What would happen, now, if he stopped taking his tablets?'

The social worker looked up, her pale eyes faintly troubled. 'He wouldn't. Why would he?'

'He could have stopped taking them at any time over the past two years.'

'In theory, yes. But he would've been kept on injections if he couldn't be trusted to take his medication orally. The change wouldn't have been made without a full psychiatric assessment. There are strict procedures. They would have to be sure he's a hundred per cent reliable. And he still has to check in every month to collect his prescription. It would be followed up if he didn't show. The notes say he was compliant.'

'You mentioned aggressive behaviour.'

'As a child, yes, but he's been sorted out. He's fine on his medication.' Their eyes met. Neither woman spoke for a moment.

'So,' Geraldine repeated her question slowly, 'if he *did* stop, what would happen?'

'You'd have to ask his doctor that.'

'Has he been collecting his medication recently?' Geraldine asked quietly.

'He collects it every month.'

'But we don't know he's been taking it.' There was a longer pause. The social worker looked down and resumed reading from her notes.

'He's a loner, been living in the community since he moved to the area. Current address …' she scrolled down.

'17 Lyceum Park Road. Landlady Mrs Edna Lewis.'

'Yes.'

'He left that address at the time the first girl was murdered in Lyceum Park.'

The social worker swore under her breath. 'They never let us know what's going on. So where is he now?'

'That's what we're trying to find out.'

'He could be in a hostel? Or sleeping rough?'

Geraldine shrugged. 'We've checked all the usual haunts. Asked around. No one's seen him.'

The social worker sighed wearily. 'Let's hope they put him back on injections when you find him and monitor him properly this time.'

'What he needs is to be locked up in a secure institution,'

Geraldine retorted, exasperated.

'That's a bit harsh, isn't it?' the social worker gave a disapproving frown. 'You're talking about a seriously disturbed man. He should never have been left to wander the streets unsupervised but the trouble is, once they're out in the community it's so hard to keep track. They slip away. He needs help, not punishment.' Geraldine wondered if the social worker would have been so charitable if she'd seen Jim Curtis's victims.

'We have to keep the streets safe,' was all she said. 'That's got to be the priority, for all our sakes.'

'What's he done?' the social worker asked, suddenly uneasy.

'We're not yet sure ourselves.'

'We can't watch these people twenty-four seven, is all I'm saying,' the social worker insisted wretchedly. 'It's a huge burden on resources and …' she sighed. 'We keep making the case for more funds, but …' There was nothing more to say.

'No one can hold you personally responsible,' Geraldine assured the dejected social worker, as she took her leave.

Theoretically *everyone* was accountable, but no one was ever held responsible. The social services were doing their best but they could only provide crisis management. When the system failed, there was no one around to pick up the pieces. Sometimes, no one even saw the pieces until it was too late. Too late for Angela Waters, Tiffany May and Jacqueline Ross. Geraldine was almost certain she'd discovered the identity of the Woolsmarsh Strangler, but all she felt was a sick despair. The deaths of those three women had been an insane waste of their young lives and, whether she was right or not, the killer was still at large. Nothing had changed.

Peterson accompanied her to the doctor's surgery where the practice manager ushered them into a small white waiting room.

'The doctor will be with you shortly,' she said as she left them, an anxious smile hovering around her mouth. A few moments passed before they heard her voice outside in the corridor.

'I don't know what it's about, Dr Callum.' There was a muffled buzz. 'They didn't say.'

Geraldine stood up and opened the door. 'Dr Callum? I'm DI Steel and this is DS Peterson. We'd like to speak to you in private.'

The tall grey haired doctor led the way into his consulting room and waited courteously for Geraldine to sit down. He glanced pointedly at his watch as he told them he could spare them a few moments.

'I have patients waiting,' he added apologetically. Without explanation, Geraldine asked him about Jim Curtis.

'I'm afraid all the information I have about my patient is confidential,' he replied. He sat with his arms folded, and met Geraldine's gaze steadily.

'We'd appreciate your co-operation, sir.'

'Might I ask what this is about?' the doctor asked.

'We need to know as much as we can about your patient—' Geraldine began.

'It's a murder investigation,' Peterson interrupted bluntly. The doctor glanced at the DS, suddenly apprehensive.

'We know he's a paranoid schizophrenic,' Geraldine resumed, 'on medication since 1984. We know he moved to Woolsmarsh and became your patient in the late eighties, and was transferred from injections to tablets two years ago.'

'You seem to know a lot about him already.'

'It's not enough.' The doctor frowned at the urgency in Geraldine's voice. 'We need to know everything about him. We're investigating a triple murder.' She stared at the doctor who returned her gaze levelly. 'We're looking for a serial killer.'

'And you think my patient might be the man you're looking for? Your serial killer?' he asked slowly. His voice didn't waver, but Geraldine saw his eyes widen in alarm. She inclined her head.

'Since you've indicated this is a matter of serious concern to public safety,' the doctor said gravely, 'I'm prepared to give you whatever information I can, Inspector. I can't advise you, but I will pass on what I know.' The doctor turned to his computer. 'Jim Curtis is prescribed anti-psychotic medication, administered orally, as you say, for the past two years. He goes to a specialist unit every six months where his treatment's monitored. Drugs are tapered off under supervision and the dosage adjusted as necessary. He's due for a psychiatric assessment in three weeks.' He paused. 'He should be back here before then.'

Geraldine sat forward. 'When did you last see him?'

The doctor glanced at his screen before he replied. 'You seem to know …' he began.

'When did you last see him?' Geraldine repeated.

'He sees the practice nurse once a month.'

'The nurse?'

'Yes. To collect his prescription. He doesn't use our normal procedure for repeat prescriptions. We have a box in reception and some of our elderly patients have an arrange-ment with the local chemist who collects the prescriptions on their behalf. We like some of our patients to come to the surgery in person. Jim Curtis falls into that category. He's what we'd consider vulnerable—'

'When did Curtis last come in to collect his prescription?' Geraldine interrupted.

Dr Callum checked his screen. 'Three weeks ago. On Wednesday, 12th September.'

'Supposing he didn't take his medication. What if he took his prescription, went to the chemist and collected the pills as usual, but didn't take them. What would happen?'

Geraldine asked. The doctor raised his eyes to meet hers but didn't reply. 'Might he suffer delusions?' The doctor shrugged. 'Could he become violent?' The doctor still declined to answer.

'We're trying to find him,' Peterson said brusquely. 'Do you have any idea where he might be?'

Dr Callum shook his head. 'I'm sorry,' he said. 'I assume he's not at his current address?'

'Could he be the serial killer we're looking for?' Geraldine asked, her voice suddenly rough with impatience. 'And if so, is he likely to attack again?' She heard the urgency in her own voice but the doctor merely shrugged and refused to give an opinion.

'In these circumstances I can only supply you with the facts. I'm not an expert witness, Inspector. You'd need to approach his psychiatrist for an opinion on his mental state.' He paused then looked straight at Geraldine and added carefully that it was impossible to predict the behaviour of a delusional paranoid schizophrenic. Geraldine nodded. She understood. Jim Curtis was at liberty. He'd already killed three women and, in his current state of mind, would probably feel the urge to kill again. He might already be closing in on his next victim even as she sat with his GP, solemnly discussing that very possibility.

53

Contacts

Heather Spencer reminded herself that her pupils' belligerence wasn't personal. Sometimes she took a step back and tried to view herself through their eyes: a strident, bad tempered old woman, wasting their time with her boring drivel. This morning, she was struggling through poetic imagery with them. It was like ploughing rocks (simile).

'Ow Miss, he flicked paper at me!' The outcry provoked boisterous laughter. The aggrieved boy clutched his neck and stared at her in exaggerated outrage.

'Miss, he jacked my pen.'

'I need a black pen.'

'Miss, can I ask Joe for his ink eraser?'

'No you can't, prick.'

Heather ignored the unconscious metaphor and continued with her lesson. 'Can anyone find an example of a metaphor in the poem?' she asked. They were beginning to settle down and even appeared attentive for a few minutes. 'Look at line seven,' she suggested.

'What page are we on, Miss?'

'Page 102. Line seven. What do you notice?'

'It comes after line six, Miss?' someone called out, to an accompaniment of tittering.

Heather tried again. 'Brandon? What do you think?'

'What was the question, Miss?'

She forced herself to hide her irritation. 'Page 102. What do you notice in line seven? And please don't tell us it comes after line six. Remember we're looking at metaphors. It's on your sheet from last week. And it's on the board,' she added before the boy could complain he didn't have a sheet. 'So, Brandon, can you find anything to comment on in line seven?'

Brandon studied the page seriously before replying. 'It comes before line eight, Miss?' The class hooted with laughter. Heather smiled, seething. Once she lost her temper, she knew that would be it for the rest of the lesson. Game over.

'Homework diaries out, please,' prompted a predictable chorus.

'Miss, I got no homework diary.'

'Mine's at home.'

'I lost my homework diary, Miss.'

'I can't find my homework diary.'

'It's not homework tonight, Miss.'

'I'm not doing homework. It's a joke, innit?"

At last the bell shrilled joyous release. Heather was set free for coffee and biscuits and civilised adult conversation.

'Bloody year nine,' she grumbled amiably to a colleague who grunted in sympathy.

There were the usual national curriculum-endorsed leaflets and brochures in her pigeonhole: Shakespeare Made Easy, Spelling Made Easy, Everything Made Easy. If teaching was easy, why was it so bloody hard? Among the commercial promotions she saw an envelope addressed to her in hand written capitals. Hoping it wasn't a complaint from an irate parent, she ripped it open and gaped. She folded the letter quickly and replaced it in the envelope. Controlling her voice with an effort she asked the staff room secretary for an A4 envelope.

'You OK?' the secretary asked, 'you're as white as a sheet.' Simile, Heather thought automatically, cliché.

'Fine.' Carefully holding the letter by one corner, she

dropped it into the larger envelope and hurried away. Her hands shook as she fumbled in her handbag for the card the detective inspector had given her. Relieved that she'd kept it with her, she dialled the number. The telephone rang three times before the inspector herself answered, her voice business-like.

'DI Geraldine Steel.' Her tone softened when Heather introduced herself. There was a pause. Heather didn't trust herself to speak straight away.

'Have you remembered something else?' the inspector prompted her.

'I received a letter,' she blurted out, 'an anonymous letter.' She glanced around nervously, checking she was still alone in the staff toilets.

'Ah,' the inspector said. 'And do you think it might be from the man you saw in the park?'

Heather recited the horrible note verbatim. She'd only glimpsed the short message once but could recall it word for word. She didn't think she'd ever be able to forget it. She explained how she'd placed the letter in an envelope, to preserve any fingerprints.

'That's excellent, Mrs Spencer. Now, how soon can you bring it in to us?' Heather was still shaking when she hung up. After school, she handed the A4 envelope in at the police station and went home.

That evening the telephone rang and Heather froze. 'Don't be silly,' she told herself, watching her hands trembling in her lap.

'Get that, can't you?' William called, rustling his newspaper in irritation. Heather breathed deeply as she heard her sister's cheerful voice on the line.

'Heather, how's it going?' Heather was grateful it was a rhetorical question. 'We've finally got our roof finished and, guess what?' Dee continued. After a lengthy diatribe against roofers in general and her own roofers in particular, Dee said she was calling to confirm a dinner arrangement for Saturday.

Heather's heart sank at the prospect of an evening of forced conviviality. William would sit taciturn, or else discuss sport with the other men, a dull drone at the far end of the table. Heather imagined the conversation at her end of the table.

'What's your news, Heather?'

'Oh, same old same old, although I do have one piece of news: I received a death threat this week. But don't worry, the police are dealing with it. It's just some maniac who goes around strangling women. You probably read about it in the papers. They call him the Woolsmarsh Strangler. Well, it seems he's chosen me as his next victim.'

'Thank God for you and William,' Dee gushed, before Heather had a chance to conjure up an excuse. 'Jeanie and Michael can't come, which is a shame, she's such good company. But Mandy and Phil are coming. I don't think you've met them. He's a teacher too – history or something – so you'll have a lot in common.'

'Sounds lovely. We're looking forward to it,' Heather lied feebly. William glanced up from the sports pages. She covered the handset and mouthed, 'Dee … Saturday …' William nodded and retreated behind his paper again.

'I think it's our turn to invite them,' he muttered from behind his paper after she hung up. Heather shrugged. She couldn't be bothered to get drawn into that discussion again. Dee enjoyed entertaining. Heather didn't. She looked over at William, and hesitated. She knew that she ought to mention her visit to the police and now this business with the threatening letter.

'William …' she began and stopped. She couldn't think what to say. Dull middle-aged schoolteachers didn't get themselves involved with serial killers. In any case, the police were taking care of it. There was no point in worrying

William when his father was deteriorating and becoming difficult. 'I'm going upstairs,' she said, 'for a bath.' William grunted and turned the page.

Heather always felt better after washing her hair. Only two days to go until the weekend, she told herself, but the thought didn't brighten her up.

William looked up from his paper as she went downstairs again. 'You all right, love?' he asked unexpectedly as Heather sat down.

She started. 'Why d'you ask that?'

'You look a bit peaky,' he said, and at that she almost broke down and told him everything, but he turned back to his paper and the moment passed. She didn't want to make a fuss. It was better not to worry him. She settled down to her knitting, and the quiet of her domestic life.

54

Information

The Incident Room was a maelstrom of activity. Charts and rotas were pinned up on the wall beside the Incident Board, files and photos covered every available horizontal surface, another computer had been installed, and a table had been set up for two more clerical staff to help with the phones, which rang incessantly. Geraldine was energised by the commotion, everyone focused on the same goal.

'There's a girl here to see you, ma'am. Her father says she's got something important to tell you.' With a frown, Geraldine put down the statement she was reading. She had so many case files out, she couldn't stack them all on her desk so she'd made two further piles of documents on the floor below her desk. It was difficult getting in and out without knocking over one of her precarious towers of paper and card.

'Who is she?'

'Her name's Shema Malik. Says she was with Jacqueline Ross when she left the party in Queen Street last Friday.'

'Yes,' Geraldine interrupted, already on her feet. 'I know when it was. Where is she?' She kicked over some files and swore as she bent down to restack them.

Summoning Peterson, she hurried to the interview room where Shema Malik sat huddled in a chair beside a stout man with a shiny bald pate.

'I am Shema's father,' he explained, nodding as though his head was on a spring. Geraldine introduced herself and the DS. 'My daughter has something she wishes to tell you.' Mr Malik spoke with an easy formality, but his eyes were guarded. The girl stared at the floor.

'I understand you've remembered something about last Friday night? Would you mind if we taped what you have to tell us? It would help,' Geraldine prompted her. The girl gave no sign she'd heard the question.

'Go on, Shema,' her father encouraged her. 'It's all right. She doesn't object to the tape. She wants to help,' he insisted. Shema raised her head. She looked frightened. She spoke in a low monotone so Geraldine had to strain to catch the words. Out of the corner of her eye she could see Peterson leaning forward in his chair.

'I went to Ella's party,' she began. She hesitated and looked up at her father who nodded again.

'It's all right,' he coaxed. 'Now tell the police what you told me. Tell them, Shema.'

The girl took a deep breath. 'I left Ella's party at nine. I'd promised to be home for nine so I had to call my father and I couldn't get a signal on my phone. I left my blazer behind because … because I couldn't find it.' She began to cry, her chest heaving with shallow sobs. Geraldine waited patiently while Mr Malik patted his daughter's hand. After a moment the girl stopped weeping and resumed her narrative. 'Rusty came after me with my blazer.'

'How did she know—' Peterson began but Geraldine shook her head to silence him.

'Go on, Shema,' she urged.

The girl looked uncertainly at her and then continued, tears winking in the corners of her eyes. 'Rusty's … Rusty was my best friend. I wasn't sure of the way so she walked with me to the bus stop in the High Street.' She paused again, overcome by her recollection. At her side, her father exhaled noisily. He looked overcome with emotion.

'What happened next, Shema?' Geraldine prompted her.

'The bus came and I got on it. My father was waiting for me.' Mr Malik looked up and nodded, urging her to continue.

'What happened to Rusty?' Geraldine asked.

They waited a moment, while Shema wept. Her father handed her a large tissue and she blew her nose noisily.

'She said she was going back to the party. I asked her, will you be all right? I didn't want to leave her but I had to get home. She said she'd be all right.' Shema gazed at the tape machine refusing to look at Geraldine.

'You've done the right thing coming to tell us this.'

Lost in her memories, Shema didn't seem to hear what Geraldine was saying. She was crying again. 'I asked her, will you be all right? She said she'd be all right but I shouldn't have left her like that.'

'You've done nothing wrong, Shema,' Geraldine reassured the girl. 'This has been a terrible shock for you, I know, but none of this is your fault. You're not responsible for what Jacqueline did or where she went.'

'You don't understand. I should never have left her alone. She was very drunk.' Shema glanced fearfully up at her father who shook his head, looking at the floor.

'You see where it leads, Shema.'

Geraldine thanked the girl for coming forward. 'What you've told us is going to be a great help to our investigation.'

Mr Malik looked up. 'Do you know who did this terrible thing?'

'Oh yes,' Geraldine nodded grimly. 'We've a good idea who we're looking for, and we're doing everything we can to find him as quickly as possible.'

55

Patience

Jim spotted the policemen straight away. He spun on his heel and hurried back down a side street. They were waiting for him, but he'd seen them first.

'Can't catch me,' he chanted under his breath. This was all her fault. He needed to shut that stupid bitch up once and for all. He knew her name and now he'd found her. He got cleverer all the time with all the thinking he was doing. Very soon he'd be cleverer than all of them. He had plans. Great plans. Miss Elsie liked it when he was clever but even she didn't know how clever he was. He was going to be very busy, being clever.

Miss Elsie was laughing. 'You're more clever than you know,' she told him but she went away before he could tell her that he *did* know. He'd tell her next time he saw her. Right now he was in a hurry. It was his turn and he was winning. He was the seeker and the finder. All he had to do was follow her. He was so close, and when he found out where she was hiding, he knew what to do. He'd done it before and it was easy. The only difficult bit was the waiting. He pulled on his gloves and clenched his fists, wishing he was doing it right now.

He took a can of beer from a newsagent's. No one saw him. He could do anything he wanted now he was clever. If they were mean to him, he knew what to do.

'It's easy when you know how,' Miss Elsie said. They'd never catch him. He was old enough to drink beer. He was old enough to do anything he wanted. That was what it meant to be a grown up and clever. They'd never stop him now.

He watched the children running out of school, afraid he might miss her in the crowd. He waited in the side street, careful not to be seen. It would be easy to follow her without being noticed because he knew how to do it. He was clever, and he was patient, and he'd found her. Even the police didn't see him. She should have known she couldn't escape. He was no fool. He knew her tricks. She wouldn't go running to the newspapers to tell on him again. He'd make sure of that. He remembered the picture of him in all the papers. They made his scar look ugly. He licked his moustache with the tip of his tongue and shuddered. Then he giggled to himself because he'd seen her. She walked quickly out of the school and he followed her down the road. She didn't know he was there. No one knew.

She disappeared round the corner and he hurried after her. He was worried he might not be able to see her when he turned into the next street but she was there. He watched her go round another corner. He was almost running to keep up with her. She was walking fast on purpose to make his legs hurt. He followed her until she went into a house. He stood under a tree across the road and hugged himself. He knew where she lived. He laughed softly and settled down to wait until it grew dark. No one knew he was there, watching and waiting in the shadows.

As it grew dark, a car drove up and a man went into the house. Jim felt his face tighten. She had to be alone. It was all her fault. She shouldn't have spoken to him in the park. She knew he wasn't allowed to talk to strangers.

'You're a dirty sneak. You told. You got to be punished,' the children screeched and he felt a tremor of fear.

'Don't worry, they can't hurt you,' Miss Elsie whispered.

'What if he never goes away?' he asked but Miss Elsie

wasn't listening. No one ever listened to what he said, not even Miss Elsie. They talked to him, but no one ever listened to him. That was because they didn't know how clever he was. Only someone very clever could be the hider and the seeker. When he'd finished he was going to tell Miss Elsie how clever he was. She'd listen to him then. Everyone would listen to him. He waited patiently but the man never went away. When it was dark, Jim turned and walked away. He'd come back and find her when she was alone. It was his game now, and he was going to win.

'It won't be long now,' he whispered to himself as he disappeared into the darkness.

56

Hideout

Jim Curtis had to be somewhere. Geraldine stood up and sat down again. There was no point going home. She fiddled with her pencil. She glared at her phone. She had to admit, when Kathryn Gordon went into action she made things happen. They'd set up a huge search. Every uniformed officer in the area had been sent to sweep the park once more. They'd examined every inch of turf, beaten their way through every leaf and shrub and searched the gardeners' huts again. The lake had been dredged, throwing up old cans and bottles tops, coins and condoms, cigarette packets and plastic cartons, more garbage than anyone would have thought possible. None of the detritus shed any light on the case. Even the letter Heather Spencer had received had drawn a blank. No postmark, no prints. It had been posted through the door by hand during the night. Whoever delivered it must've crept in under the car park barrier and slipped along the wall under the security cameras.

From the park, they'd moved outwards, conducting house-to-house enquiries. The search was widening.

'Have you seen this man … a man with a scar … a man with a moustache … anyone suspicious … a stranger …' Despite the public outcry against the killer, no one had come forward with any leads. They'd pulled in the odd tramp or drugged up kid, but the Woolsmarsh Strangler remained elusive. Poring over maps and cruising the area, Geraldine had joined the quest to discover where he was hiding.

Shema told them Jacqueline had intended to return to the party when she'd left the bus stop. According to Ella's statement, Jacqueline had never returned. They were concentrating on the area between Queen Street, where Ella had her party, and the bus stop on the High Street where Jacqueline had last been seen alive.

Not far from the park, there was a row of empty terraced houses waiting for demolition in Mortimer Street. The site had been bought by a property developer who was going to knock it down and put up flats. Opposite the derelict houses a block of flats had already been built, set back from the road. Geraldine sat in her car and gazed thoughtfully at the empty properties. A man could come and go there unseen. The DCI had already sent a team of uniformed officers to check out the empty houses.

Two hours later, Geraldine was sitting at her desk trying to read through a file when an announcement was relayed to everyone. The search team had stumbled across a shed where someone had been sleeping rough. Jacqueline Ross's mother had recognised the description of some clothes found there.

'No marked cars in Mortimer Street,' the DCI said, rushing through an emergency briefing. 'We need to maintain an invisible presence. I don't want any sign of unusual activity. A forensic team's going in at once but they're to stay hidden. All phones silenced. Complete blackout. I'm on my way. Carter,' she added with sudden ferocity, 'keep the press away.'

'A shed?' Geraldine repeated, her frustration forgotten. Summoning Peterson, she hurried out to the car park where Carter was addressing a cluster of reporters. From what Geraldine could hear, he seemed to be giving an impromtu press briefing.

They drove to Mortimer Street. Neither of them spoke. The only sound was the low hum of the engine. There were several rusting cars parked along the kerb in Mortimer Street but no one stirred as they drove past. Peterson parked round the corner and they walked quickly back past derelict houses, their downstairs windows boarded up. Tiny front gardens lay untended, most of them paved over, weeds sprouting between the flagstones; the few that still displayed grass and flowerbeds had run completely wild. The flats across the road were concealed behind a tall hedge. Geraldine led the way along a narrow side passage into an overgrown wilderness of a back garden at number 73. It was like an open landfill site littered with empty cans and food cartons, old newspapers and bottles. Everywhere they looked discarded clothes were heaped in damp piles: trousers and jumpers, coats and vests, all jumbled together. It was past five o'clock and would begin to grow dark soon.

'Must be overrun with rats,' Peterson muttered, gazing around in disgust.

At the far end of the garden they saw a shed nestling among gigantic nettles and brambles. It reminded Geraldine of the shrubbery in Lyceum Park where Angela Waters and Tiffany May's bodies had been discovered. She felt a prickling sensation at the back of her head. This had to be the killer's hideout. As she opened the door of the shed a foul stench hit her. Inside the shed the police had found Jacqueline Ross's party outfit neatly folded on top of a jumble of old clothes. The DCI was there, whispering into her phone. Lookouts had been posted in empty properties all along the street to alert them if anyone approached. The net was closing in.

'I want officers out of sight keeping front and back access under surveillance at all times,' the DCI had said when the team had gathered at the station to receive their detailed instructions. 'Officers posted in the back gardens on either side and over the back fence. Everyone out of sight. No marked cars anywhere. No uniforms visible. As soon as he sets foot on the property, detain him.'

They staked out the area while inside the shed two white-coated forensic scientists worked on, gathering minute samples. Geraldine stood in the garden for a moment imagining their measured movements inside the shed, before following Peterson back to the car. They waited but Jim Curtis didn't appear.

'What now, gov?'

'We wait,' she said, folding her arms 'We wait and we catch him.'

57

Home

Heather put her mark book away and left without pausing to say goodbye to anyone. Unnerved by the note she'd received two days earlier, she longed for the security of home. William was spending the evening with his father who lived just under an hour's drive away, on the way to the coast. Sometimes Heather accompanied him on these weekly visits, but William's brother was putting in a rare appearance and Heather had agreed it would be better for her to stay at home while they thrashed out their family issues. She'd been looking forward to the luxury of having some time to herself. She kicked off with a long bath. Lying back in warm water she felt the tension of the past few days soak slowly out of her neck and shoulders. She'd done her duty. The horrible business was nothing to do with her any more. She'd have time for a microwaved dinner in front of the telly before William came home. As a final indulgence she might go to bed with a mug of hot chocolate.

As she came downstairs, towelling her hair, her eye was caught by something white on the doormat. She was certain it hadn't been there when she'd gone upstairs for her bath. She picked the envelope up by one corner, telling herself she was being neurotic because she was alone in the house. Ridiculous, she thought, a woman of her age reacting like a hysterical teenager instead of walking past the envelope without a second glance. But she took the first glance. Familiar handwriting stared up at her.

Heather couldn't breathe. She was alone in the house and he knew where she lived. He could be outside, watching. Or worse. Too terrified to move, she listened for footsteps on the path.

Detective Inspector Steel had told her to call straight away if she remembered anything else. Fighting her panic, Heather ran to the kitchen to fetch her bag. The card the inspector had given her was in there somewhere, but she couldn't find it. She tipped everything out and scrabbled frantically through her purse, scattering coins. She shook her diary. Nothing fell out. She felt about in the bottom of her bag. It wasn't there. She must have left it by the sink in the toilets at school. Her hesitation was only momentary. The killer might be outside. She ran back to the hall, reached for the phone and dialled 999.

'Fire, police or ambulance?'

'I need to contact Woolsmarsh police station.'

'You'll have to call them directly, madam. This is an emergency line.'

'This *is* an emergency,' she protested. 'My name's Heather Spencer and I need to contact Woolsmarsh Police urgently.'

'I'm sorry, this is an emergency line only.'

'Wait! Please, I need to speak to Detective Inspector Steel at Woolsmarsh police station,' Heather gabbled. 'She's in charge of a murder investigation and I think the murderer's outside my house right now. It's the Woolsmarsh Strangler. He's here. I'm not imagining it, he's here. You've got to believe me.' She failed to control the panic in her voice. 'Inspector Steel gave me her direct line but I can't find the card she gave me and I don't know the number of the police station. My name's Heather Spencer. Please, you've got to help me …' She froze, hearing a window smash. 'Oh my God, he's here,' she whispered, 'he's broken a window and he's in the house.'

Dizzily, she watched a dark shape floating towards her across the kitchen. She felt as if she was drowning. He reached the kitchen door. Someone whimpered as she turned and raced up the stairs. She thought she heard feet pounding after her but it could have been her heart. She ran along the landing and shut herself in the bathroom, the only door that locked. Too late, she realised her mistake. She should have escaped through the front door while she had the chance but, wrapped only in a towel, it hadn't occurred to her to run out into the street. Now she was trapped upstairs. The house was silent. Perhaps it was a chance burglar and she'd scared him off. He didn't look like the man in the park, but there was something familiar about the figure. She knew it was him. What was he doing? The house was silent. He might be waiting for her to open the door. He'd killed repeatedly and now he was in the house, threatening her. She had to control her panic and think.

He'd killed the other women with his bare hands so he might be unarmed. She needed a weapon. Glancing round she grabbed the showerhead, weighed it in her hand, and tried to rip it from the bath. It wouldn't budge. She heard the stairs creak and panic flooded through her again. Razor blades. William used an electric shaver but she occasionally shaved her legs in the summer with disposable plastic razors. There must be a packet somewhere. She scrabbled frantically through the wall cabinet. Toothpaste, shower gel and bottles of shampoo flew to the floor, cotton wool balls burst unexpectedly out of a plastic bag and spun in the air before falling softly on the tiles. She found a few green and white razors. Her hands shook and she cut her finger as she fumbled to remove one of the blades. She couldn't imagine what he was doing. She dropped the rest of the razors on the floor and tried to peel away a strip of green plastic to release the blade but couldn't detach it. She sat on the toilet, picking desperately at it.

There was a faint squeal. Heather stared at the door handle as it rotated slowly.

'Open the door, stupid! I know you're there.' The yell startled her and she leapt up, almost slipping on a patch of shampoo oozing from a bottle on the floor. She gazed round wildly. Her eyes fell on some shiny bath pearls lying in a decorative china dish. She seized it. Bath pearls bounced like pink hailstones as she smashed the dish against edge of the bath. It broke into jagged shards. Please let the edges be sharp, she prayed, clutching a pointed sliver so that it sliced into her palm. Blood dripped onto the floor. Shaking with shock, she pressed a flannel against the wound. She felt as though the top of her head had floated away and this was all a dream.

'What do you want?' she called, hardly recognising her voice, trembling with fear.

'You've got to come out, I've found you,' he answered. There was a loud thud and the door juddered violently. He was kicking the flimsy plywood.

'I'd like to help you,' she ventured.

'Liar!' he roared. The door shuddered, splitting and splintering.

A booted foot came through the crack and she clutched her weapon tightly. Above the boot a strip of dirty skin was exposed below a brown trouser leg. The boot vanished. She considered slashing at the leg if it reappeared. She risked further infuriating her assailant but a nasty cut might slow him down, giving her a chance to make a run for it. It was the best plan she could devise. Adrenaline coursed through her as she manoeuvred into position.

His voice was wheedling. 'I found your hiding place so you got to come out. It's the rules.'

'I don't want to hurt you,' she called out.

'You're a liar!'

'I'm not a liar, I'm a teacher.'

'You're not Miss Elsie!' he bellowed in a fury. Who was Miss Elsie? Frantic with terror she crouched by the side of the door, waiting for his leg to reappear through the gaping hole.

58

Brothers

William paced the floor. The old argument was brewing. He watched his brother, George, set a mug of tea in front of their father who nodded bleary-eyed thanks. George settled back in his chair and looked up at his brother expectantly.

'I don't know what you want me to say,' William shrugged helplessly. 'Nothing's changed. You refuse to face up to your responsibility.'

'You know I'd help more if I could,' George muttered. His father watched his lips. 'It's not as easy for me as it is for you, Will. You know my time's not my own. I spend little enough time with the children as it is.' William nodded bitterly. He'd been waiting for that to come up. 'If you had children—'

'It wouldn't hurt you to bring them to see him once in a while,' William interrupted brusquely. 'When was the last time they were here?'

'They're busy,' George looked away, avoiding William's gaze. 'They've got lives of their own. I hardly see them myself any more.'

'Sit. Drink your tea,' their father said suddenly. His voice no more than a dry wheeze, he was still their father; a vestige of authority clung to his wizened frame. William dutifully sat down and sipped his tea. 'Take a biscuit. Go on,' the old man urged. William glanced around. There weren't any biscuits. 'Cake,' their father added brightly. 'Have some cake. Your mother baked this morning.' He

311

grinned toothlessly. They drank their tea in silence for a moment.

'You need to take some share in the responsibility,' William said at last, putting his cup down. 'Things can't go on like this.' He waved his hands helplessly. 'You can see what he's like. We do what we can, me and Heather, and the carer's reliable, but dad needs more.'

'Heather and I,' his father corrected him, suddenly sharp.

William grinned back at him, startled. 'Heather and I,' he repeated obligingly.

'He seems perfectly content. Aren't you, dad?' George turned to the old man and William groaned in frustration.

'Now then, what's this all about?' their father demanded. His demeanour had changed. Shoulders hunched, he glared at William. 'You haven't been fighting again? Remember what I said to you last time? I won't have you pushing your little brother around, William.' His fingers clenched into knobbly fists. 'No pocket money,' he threatened in thin, reedy tones, 'and I'll lock your bicycle away.' William glanced at his brother who sat, face averted.

'Content, is he?' William growled. He wished his brother *was* still small enough to be pushed around. He took a deep breath and tried again. 'You asked to see me, George. Heather stayed at home because we thought you were ready to talk.'

'Talk?' George hedged.

'For goodness sake!' William burst out in exasperation. He glanced anxiously at his father. The old man's eyes had glazed over and he sat, oblivious to the row threatening to kick off.

'He looks fine,' George said firmly. 'Suzanne and I have talked about dad a lot, William. Despite what you think, we're very concerned about him. He's my father too. And just because you've got more time to visit him, doesn't give you the right to make decisions unilaterally.' William opened his mouth to protest but George held up a manicured hand for silence. 'At least hear me out,' he said. 'Suzanne and I don't agree it's a good idea to move him. He'd never adapt to a new environment. Not at his age.'

'He can't stay here on his own.'

'Suzanne and I think he can.'

'When was the last time Suzanne saw him?'

'I refuse to move him against his will. Do you want to move, dad?' He turned to his father who was staring at the ceiling. 'I didn't come here to argue, Will.' William dropped his head into his hands in a gesture of despair.

George stood up. 'It'll take me over two hours to get back to London, and I promised Suzanne I wouldn't be late.'

William thought of his own wife, at home by herself, 'Heather understands about responsibility,' he replied. He looked at his father. His head was flung back and he was fast asleep.

'He looks fine to me,' George repeated stubbornly.

'Are you going to put him to bed?' William asked. 'I gave his carer the night off. I said we'd get him settled tonight.'

'Love to help, but I've really got to make a move.' George replied, thrusting his arms into his coat sleeves. Defeated, William watched his brother briskly button his coat. His visit had changed nothing. The whole evening had been a complete waste of time. William might as well have stayed at home with Heather and let the carer put his father to bed.

59

Escape

Geraldine pulled into the police station car park. The empty shed was under round the clock surveillance. Jim Curtis wouldn't escape again. After several hours' vigil, they'd followed Kathryn Gordon back to the station. The door to the DCI's office was open. As Geraldine passed she heard Kathryn Gordon barking out orders.

'Call me as soon as you've got him.' Geraldine understood her wanting to be there when the arrest was made. Sitting at her desk, Geraldine looked around. Everyone was trying to keep busy. Carter was at his desk, flicking over the pages of a document, waiting for the call. Merton was in Mortimer Street. Peterson was on the other side of the room, leaning against the wall, talking to Sarah Mellor who was smiling up at him.

Carter came over and leaned against her desk. She'd never seen him so twitchy. 'You just come from Mortimer Street?' he asked. She nodded. 'Anything going on there?' She shook her head and he returned to his desk where he sat, gazing at a document. Geraldine knew he wasn't concentrating on his paperwork any more than she was. She tried to focus on a report but her thoughts kept wandering to Jim Curtis. What was he doing now, while they waited for him to return to his filthy hide out?

When the call came through to the police station, it wasn't what they'd been expecting. Jim Curtis hadn't gone back to his shed. Geraldine and Peterson drove in tense silence to Heather Spencer's house. The sergeant glanced anxiously at Geraldine as they careered round a corner. They were both keen to be at the scene when the Woolsmarsh Strangler was apprehended. Sirens were screaming ahead of them and she accelerated. They weren't the first on the scene. Geraldine drew up outside a house cordoned off with blue and white tape. Two police cars and a van were already there, blue lights flashing, and several officers in uniform were standing behind the barrier. A line of onlookers had assembled, craning their necks to see what was going on. There was an atmosphere of muddle and excitement as Geraldine raced up the path ahead of Peterson. A uniformed officer was barking at the neighbours to keep back, a paramedic ran up the path to the house, and DS Black charged out of the front door and down the path, bellowing into his phone.

'What's happening?' Geraldine shouted at him as he barged past her. He didn't answer but continued his frantic phone conversation.

'Where is he?' Geraldine yelled at the uniformed officer standing outside the front door. He raised his eyebrows and shrugged. Geraldine hurried past him, her face taut. Peterson saw the consternation on her face as he charged after her into the house.

'Up there,' a uniformed constable told them and Geraldine raced up the stairs. Heather Spencer was sitting on the edge of the bath, shivering. She was wearing a man's dark blue dressing gown and her right hand was wrapped in a bloody towel. There were splashes of blood on the floor and the door had been partially kicked in. A female constable was on the phone requesting medical support. There was no sign of Kathryn Gordon. The atmosphere was chilly with disappointment. Geraldine felt a horrible sinking feeling in her stomach.

'Where is he?' Peterson repeated, coming in behind her.

'Mrs Spencer, Heather,' Geraldine said gently. She knelt beside the woman who stared at her unseeing, her hair dishevelled, her face bloated from crying.

'She's cut her hand,' the WPC explained unnecessarily.

'Where is he?' A note of desperation had crept into Geraldine's voice. The police constable shrugged helplessly. Geraldine raced in and out of the rooms upstairs. Uniform were everywhere. In the bedroom the wardrobe doors hung open. There was no one there. She ran downstairs. Peterson met her in the hall and shook his head.

'He's not here. We're searching the grounds,' a uniformed officer said tersely.

They stepped out into the cool of the evening. No one could slip out of the front door now. Several DCs were searching through the watching crowd but there was no one matching the killer's description, no unidentified male skulking in the throng.

'Can anyone vouch for you?' she heard a voice was asking.

'He's my husband,' a woman answered indignantly. Geraldine and Peterson went back into the house. The atmosphere was despondent after the excited bustle outside. In the back garden several officers were trampling through flowerbeds. A beam of light from a helicopter swept across the garden and away to the east, like a sudden burst of daylight. The Woolsmarsh Strangler had gone.

Geraldine ran back upstairs. Someone was bandaging Heather Spencer's hand and she was holding a mug of tea.

'Inspector,' she whispered, 'where is he?' her voice a soft echo of Geraldine's thoughts.

Geraldine answered with her own question. 'What happened?' In a disjointed narrative, Heather Spencer explained. Geraldine was shocked. The killer had been there, in the house, and they'd let him slip away. When Heather Spencer had received the first letter from him, it never occurred to them that he might follow her home. 'He's clever, Mrs Spencer, but we'll find him. Mrs Spencer – Heather – why didn't you call me straight away?'

Heather Spencer was shaking violently. 'I lost your card, the one with your phone number,' she explained. 'I called 999 and they came. I heard the sirens. He's gone, hasn't he?'

'Did you get a closer look at him this time?'

'No. I'm sorry, I didn't really see him at all. Not clearly. As soon as I caught sight of him coming out of the kitchen I ran away.'

'Of course you did. You did the right thing. You're safe now, Mrs Spencer. DC Mellor will stay with you.' Sarah nodded brightly and Geraldine gave her a wan smile. 'Don't worry, Mrs Spencer. There are constables outside. He can't come back here and he won't get far. We'll find him tonight.' Geraldine was on her feet, phone in hand.

'Inspector.'

'Yes?'

'Inspector, you've got it wrong.' Geraldine stared down at her. 'He's not clever. He's backward. Not right in the head. What he said made no sense and he sounded odd. Like a child.'

'What did he say?'

'He was talking about someone called Elsie. He said I was Elsie, or I wasn't Elsie. I can't remember exactly, because none of it made any sense. He said he'd found my hiding place so I had to come out. That was the rules. As if it was a children's game. I know it sounds silly, but I think he was playing hide and seek. And when he found me, I think he was going to kill me.' She began to sob. Geraldine took hold of her uninjured hand and tried to reassure her.

'DC Mellor will be here,' she repeated helplessly. 'Would you like us to try and contact your husband?' Heather shook her head.

Despondent, they returned to the car. Back at the station,

the DCI was barking out instructions. 'I want every available officer combing the area. He can't have gone far. Leave a presence at the Spencer place, front and back. No one is to be allowed in the house – apart from William Spencer. Keep the press away. The suspect left there at—' she checked her notes, 'between six and six fifteen. On foot.'

'As far as we know,' Carter added grimly.

'We've got officers on foot, cars, helicopter sweeping the entire area. Leave a surveillance team in Mortimer Street.'

'Where do you want me, ma'am?' Geraldine asked. 'Mortimer Street?' The DCI nodded uncertainly. Geraldine and Peterson drove off down the dark streets. Once the bright light of the helicopter swept by. They passed several patrol cars cruising slowly, and a small knot of youngsters gathered on a corner. Otherwise the streets were deserted. As they drove, Geraldine radioed Mellor. There were constables on guard at the front and back of the house.

'All quiet, gov,' Sarah Mellor assured her. 'Mrs Spencer's fine.'

At last the house was quiet. Heather made her way shakily downstairs. A nice young policewoman sat with her and brought her a fresh cup of tea. The inspector had promised she was safe, but they still hadn't caught him.

'Who is he?' she asked the constable. 'Do you even know?'

'Yes, we know who he is. Don't worry, Mrs Spencer, the DCI is onto him. She'll catch up with him very soon.'

'It's the Woolsmarsh Strangler, isn't it?' Heather whispered. The policewoman hesitated. 'If you don't stop him, he'll come back, won't he?' She could hear her voice rising in panic. 'Where do you think he's gone?' she whispered.

The policewoman beside her smiled uneasily. 'Don't worry, Mrs Spencer,' she said. 'We'll find him. Now, shall I call your husband for you?'

Heather shook her head. William would be home soon enough. She needed the interim to gather her thoughts and decide what she was going to say. In the aftermath of police cars, ambulance, blaring sirens and flashing lights, the neighbours would alert him to the drama that had taken place while he'd been away. It was bound to be in the papers. She blushed hotly. The children at school would read about her ordeal, making her the centre of whispered attention for days. Her sister would ring the doorbell, newspaper in hand, demanding the right to dispense unwelcome sympathy.

William would know about it long before all that. As soon as he came home he'd see the police, the bloodstains, the broken window temporarily boarded up, and her bandaged hand and she'd tell him everything. Afterwards she'd do her best to forget. Life would return to normal. But first the police had to find the man they called the Woolsmarsh Strangler – the man who wanted to kill her.

60

Hair

Melanie was surprised how easily she managed to forget about Terry and slip back into her former routine, spending her evenings at home listening to music in her room or going out with friends. During the day she worked in a small art gallery in West Parade. She loved the atmosphere when they held exhibitions, which happened about six times a year, but in between times the job was fairly dull. Today had been typically quiet and, in an idle moment, she'd called her hairdresser to book a late appointment. As soon as the gallery closed, she drove to the town centre and left her car in the main car park, a short walk from the salon.

It could all have turned out a lot worse. She'd cancelled her stolen credit cards before Terry had a chance to use them and her parents hadn't given her a hard time about the jewellery. In fact, they'd been surprisingly calm about the whole affair. Her father had contacted his insurance company and reported the theft to the police. After that he'd seemed, if anything, strangely cheerful about it. Melanie's mother had been elated when the stolen jewellery was recovered. Melanie suspected her father was more gratified to learn about Terry's arrest.

'Haven't seen you for a while, Melanie,' her hairdresser smiled at her through the mirror. 'You been away somewhere nice?' She began combing Melanie's dripping hair.

'No, just busy,' Melanie replied. She gazed at her reflection. Wet hair hung down on either side of her face, emphasising her angular features. Although it was straight, her hair always looked longer when it was wet and now it reached down nearly to her waist. She'd been considering having it restyled into a short bob.

'You've got lovely hair,' the stylist commented and Melanie smiled. She liked her hair and decided against having it cut short. She leaned back comfortably in the chair and reached for her coffee. The hairdresser waited, comb poised.

'The usual trim?' she asked, 'or d'you fancy something different this time? Some caramel lowlights would look nice. What's it to be?' She stepped back and gazed at her client's long blonde hair appraisingly.

'Just the usual,' Melanie answered with a lazy smile.

'Right you are,' the stylist agreed amiably. She picked up her scissors and began combing and snipping, talking all the while about the Woolsmarsh Strangler. 'Makes you scared to go out on the streets alone, doesn't it?' Preoccupied with her own thoughts, Melanie barely listened to her chatter. One thing was certain, she wasn't going to fall for a waster like Terry again. Although she'd never tell him so, her father had been right about Terry all along.

By the time her hair was finished it was nearly half past six and dark outside. As Melanie hurried back to her car it began to rain, big fat drops that splattered on the pavement around her suede shoes. She hadn't thought about the women's meetings for days so was pleased when her phone rang and she heard Julie's voice.

'Melanie, it's Julie. Are you coming on Tuesday?'

'Tuesday?'

'We're holding another meeting to talk about police inaction, seven thirty next Tuesday at my place. Can you make it? We've decided it's time to lobby our MP. Although it's hardly likely to be top of *his* agenda. We're all sick of the way our lives are controlled by men. Every way you turn it's the men in charge, and when there's a threat to *us*, what do they do?' Slightly taken aback by Julie's intensity, Melanie reminded her that a woman was running the police hunt for the Strangler. 'Yes, but she's not really in charge, is she? It's the men at the top who make the decisions. They're the ones with the real power. And some of us think it's time we women took control of our own lives.'

Melanie thought about her father and felt her jaw tighten. 'I'll be there,' she promised, resolving to be independent, like Julie. She threw her head back, thrust her phone forcefully into the pocket of her jeans and strode along the road, a strong, confident woman. When a patrol car drew into the kerb beside her and a middle-aged policeman called out, she bristled.

'You all right, miss?'

'Fine, thank you,' she replied sharply and turned away, in case he recognised her. She wasn't a child. She didn't need protection. 'My car's just round the corner,' she added brusquely. But as the police car drove away, panic ran through her like a jolt of electricity. Her mouth felt dry and she was suddenly so light headed, she thought she wouldn't be able to walk straight. The hairdresser's words reverberated in her head: 'Makes you scared to go out on the streets alone, doesn't it?' She glanced around, but the pavement was empty.

She turned off the main road and her alarm faded. The side street where she'd left her car was deserted. In the silence, the sudden shrilling of her phone startled her, making her heart beat wildly.

'Mel, it's Julie again. I forgot to say, it's your turn to bring cake or biscuits.'

Melanie forgot her isolation while she was chatting with Julie but when she hung up, the darkness of the street seemed to close in on her. Ahead, she could see the metallic paint of her car glimmering beneath a street lamp. Without looking round she quickened her pace.

She'd almost reached the car when she heard someone breathing.

61

Girl

Jim walked quickly along the road. He couldn't go far without seeing a patrol car. When he saw a pair of policemen walking along the pavement towards him, he slunk into an alley and stood flat against a fence post, holding his breath, until they went past. Another time he sneaked into a front garden and waited behind a tall hedge until he heard their footsteps fade away. After that he kept out of the light and walked along alleys and across dark lawns. In one garden he nearly slipped into a fishpond. Some of the houses had lights that came on when he approached, or dogs that barked hysterically so he nearly yelled out in fear. He stayed out of gardens after that.

He couldn't go back to the shed. He knew they'd be there, waiting for him. He'd go away, find another park and start all over again. He smiled. It was a clever plan. He heard the loud whine of a helicopter and watched as a huge beam of light swept across the street. He kept very still, pressing himself against a tree trunk. It was lucky he was so clever. He knew they were looking for him but they wouldn't find him. He was clever at hiding.

He was hurrying so fast, he nearly didn't see the girl, walking quickly in front of him. She had long hair. He hoped she was pretty but he couldn't see her face as he came up behind her. There was no one else around. He hesitated because she was talking to someone on her phone. As she walked past the entrance to an alley he heard her say, '…

thanks again Julie.' She put her phone in her pocket. No one was listening to her any more. He waited until both her arms were swinging freely and smiled because he knew what to do. She was only a few paces away. A street lamp threw a faint light over the opening to the alley; beyond lay darkness.

His hand was over her mouth, her wrists safe in his strong grip. She wasn't heavy. It was easy to drag her into the alley. Her feet bumped on the ground so he lifted her up. He tried not to laugh because he didn't need the park any more. He could go anywhere. They'd never find him. In the alley, she began to struggle. She could only make muffled grunty noises because his hand was pressing down on her mouth. He knew what it felt like when you couldn't say the words but it didn't matter. He wasn't listening. That was fair. It was his turn now.

He jerked her head backwards, wrenching it round so he could see her face. She wriggled and strained against him. He moved her wrists sideways to let her shoulders follow her turning neck. He didn't want to twist her neck too far. Not yet. First he wanted to see if she was pretty. Quickly, he took a step back towards the end of the alley and the faint light from the street lamp. It didn't matter if she saw his face. He looked at her and his hands released their hold. He was almost too shocked to speak.

'I didn't know it was you,' he stuttered as her arms swung at him, shoving him back against the fence. A loud siren screeched from her hand, drowning out her screaming as he turned and fled along the dark alley.

He ran and ran, keeping to the shadows. When he couldn't run any more he lay down under a hedge to think. Branches poked into his eyes. A police car drove past. He lay very still. He had to speak to Miss Elsie and tell her he was only playing. He was scared she wouldn't believe him.

'How was I to know it was you?' he asked her. She didn't

reply. It wasn't his fault. She should have told him. Another police car sped past and he pressed himself against the earth under the hedge. It was dirty. He was alone and very frightened. They were looking for him. He wanted to run away, but he couldn't. Not now he'd seen Miss Elsie. If he left Woolsmarsh he might never find her again.

62

Alarm

Geraldine was summoned by Kathryn Gordon. She stepped over the files surrounding her desk and made her way to the DCI's office where she knocked, careful to wait before opening the door.

'Ron Rogers has been on the phone. His daughter's been attacked. She managed to escape. It sounds like Curtis.' She nodded at Geraldine. 'Go and talk to her. Take DS Peterson.'

'Right away, ma'am.' Geraldine hurried from the room.

They set off for the Rogers' estate. Peterson started to say something, then stopped.

'What is it?' Geraldine asked.

'Nothing.'

She frowned. 'If you've got something to say, I'd rather you came out with it. I suppose you've been waiting for me to apologise for having a go at you the other day. All right, I'll apologise, if you want, but bear in mind we are working on a particularly difficult case. Everyone's stressed. You shouldn't take it personally.' She looked away, aware that she hadn't actually apologised, and unsure if she wanted to continue the discussion while they were both so edgy.

Peterson shrugged. 'I'd forgotten about it,' he replied. 'How's your new washing machine?' he added unexpectedly. Geraldine was taken aback. 'Delivered 27th September, the day after you moved in.' There was a pause. Geraldine hesitated, uncertain where this was heading. 'You never mentioned it to anyone.'

'My washing machine? Why would I mention it? It's a washing machine.'

'One of the delivery men was called Arthur Ramsden,' Peterson went on. He leaned forward speaking in a low voice so she could barely hear him above the whine of the engine. 'Arthur's got a brother, Norman Ramsden. Went down for armed robbery. Arresting officer, DS Geraldine Steel. Not long before your promotion to DI.'

Geraldine opened her mouth to protest, but Peterson went on. 'Thing is, gov, a few days after your washing machine was delivered, someone graffitied the fence at your flats. A week after the delivery, the same graffiti appeared on your garage door. Five days later, the lock on your garage door was smashed and your car was scratched.'

'How the hell do you know that?' She raised her voice in surprise.

'Jesus, gov, I am a detective! Give me some credit.'

Geraldine smiled in spite of her alarm. 'What are you going to do, now you know?' she asked. It was a relief to share her problem, but she was worried about the consequences if Peterson reported her trouble. She imagined him, busy on her trail. He might even have called her last station to check the background, giving some story that he was phoning on her behalf. Once he had Ramsden's name and had worked out his connection to Geraldine, it would have been easy enough to find out that Arthur Ramsden had delivered her washing machine. Easy enough for someone with the wit and the will to uncover the truth. What bothered Geraldine was the sergeant's motive.

'Why didn't you report it?' he asked.

'You know perfectly well why. They might've started fussing about special protection measures. The DCI would've complained about distractions. I might even have been moved, taken off the case.'

'So instead you decided to risk your own safety.' He

sounded angry.

'I can take care of myself.' She was riled. 'If I'd thought I was in any real danger—'

'You're not,' he interrupted shortly. 'Not any more.'

Geraldine glanced at him but he turned away from her. 'What have you done?' she asked. Suspicion shook her. He'd reported the situation to Kathryn Gordon.

'I paid a visit,' Peterson replied.

'To the DCI?'

'No.' He looked round at her, surprised. 'To Arthur Ramsden—'

'You did *what*?'

'I simply pointed out that any disruption to your work would be considered wilful obstruction of a murder investigation. He won't be bothering you again, gov.'

'So what did the DCI have to say?' she fumed.

'Why? Did you tell her?'

Geraldine took a deep breath. 'Taking a bit of risk there yourself, Sergeant,' she said. Gratitude swept through her so strongly she struggled for breath. 'Thank you,' she muttered ungraciously. 'Not that I needed you to step in like that,' she added quickly.

'Of course not.'

'I was sorting it out myself. I didn't need your help.' She fell silent, aware that she sounded petulant. She looked up again. This time Peterson grinned straight at her and she looked away, irritated. He'd behaved like a thug, warning Ramsden off with threats. It was hardly professional. 'In future, I advise you to stay well away from things that are none of your business.' But she couldn't deny she was glad he'd done it.

'In future?' he asked, with a quizzical expression. Geraldine opened her mouth to retort, but thought better of it. They travelled the rest of the way in frosty silence.

Lynda and Melanie Rogers were sitting side by side on a

leather sofa, holding hands. Even though Melanie's eyes were swollen from crying, the resemblance between the two women was striking. Peterson was staring at Melanie Rogers as though he hoped to see an image of her attacker reflected in the girl's eyes. A housekeeper set down a silver tray with an elegant tea set.

'Thank you, Nora. Can you take some tea and hot toast in to Ron before you go? Don't worry about us, we'll sort ourselves out later.' Lynda Rogers turned to Geraldine. 'My husband can join us if you like, but he was rather upset. We all thought Melanie could talk more freely without him in the room.'

Geraldine thanked her before speaking to Melanie. 'Tell us exactly what happened.' It had to be him: hands held behind her back, a palm slapped across her mouth, her lower jaw and wrists bruised from rough contact. Melanie Rogers described how she'd been walking to her car when she'd been attacked and dragged into an alley.

'He grabbed my arms, here, and then got both my wrists into one of his hands, and he put his other hand over my mouth. It happened so quickly I didn't even call out. His hand was over my mouth before I realised what was happening. I was too shocked to react at first. By the time I tried to struggle, he was holding me so tightly, I could hardly move. I thought he was going to twist my head off.' Geraldine saw Lynda tighten her grip on her daughter's hand. 'It's all right, mum, I'm OK,' Melanie said. Mother and daughter exchanged a glance charged with emotion.

'Go on,' Geraldine urged.

Melanie stared straight ahead, concentrating. 'He got me fast and twisted my head round. It was dark. He pulled me over towards the street lamp so he could see me. And then he let me go.' There was a pause. 'Mum had put a rape alarm in my pocket. She's obsessed with them. She keeps a cupboard full of them and slips them in all my coat pockets.'

She gave a half-hearted smile.

'It's just that with a serial killer about …' Lynda Rogers said softly.

'Don't apologise for being careful, Mrs Rogers. You probably saved your daughter's life—'

'No,' Melanie interrupted, 'it wasn't like that. I put the alarm on *after* he let me go. My hands weren't free till then. He just let go of me. He looked at me, and then he let me go.' The girl was bruised and battered, still in shock, but lucid. 'And his voice was funny. A kind of whispery lisp.' She frowned, biting her lip.

Geraldine looked up from her note taking. 'He spoke to you?' Melanie nodded. 'What did he say?'

'That was funny too. He said, 'I didn't know it was you,' when he saw my face. And then he let me go. I pushed him away and got out the rape alarm. I was yelling for all I was worth by then and what with the alarm and me screaming there was a hell of a racket. He just ran.'

Geraldine stared closely at the girl. 'Think carefully, Melanie. Had you ever seen him before?'

'I don't think so.'

Geraldine took a copy of the e-fit from her wallet. 'Melanie, I want you to look carefully at this artist's impression of a man called Jim Curtis. Was this the same man that attacked you tonight?'

Melanie shrugged. 'It could be. It's hard to say. He had a beard.'

'You're not sure?' The girl nodded uncertainly. 'But you'd be able to identify him if you saw him again?'

'I don't know. That's the thing. I saw him looking at me, but I only got this impression of a hairy face. It was hideous. Like something out of a werewolf movie.' She gave a shaky laugh.

'Would you recognise him if you saw him again?' Geraldine repeated the question.

Melanie began to cry quietly. 'I don't know. I just don't know. He smelt disgusting. Like an old dog.'

'Don't cry,' Lynda said softly. 'It's over now. They're going.' She looked at Geraldine, a silent entreaty in her brilliant green eyes. Peterson closed his notebook.

As soon as they were in the car, Geraldine was on the phone. 'We're on our way back. I want her clothes examined as a priority so stand by. And if SOCOs haven't put the whole scene under a microscope by now, I'll want to know why. I want their report in ten minutes ... An interim report then, as far as they've got. We need to work quickly ... Yes, that's right. We'll see you in five minutes.' She turned to Peterson. 'We'll drop her clothes off, report to the DCI and then take a look at the alley.' The initial stages were crucial in any investigation, before evidence could be contaminated, but there was another reason to move swiftly in their search. Jim Curtis had already attacked two women that night without success. Frustrated in his attempts, he was bound to try again. While the police were scouring the streets, he was out there, stalking his next victim. And the next woman might not escape.

'Funny thing about Melanie Rogers,' Geraldine said as they drove towards the station. 'Mrs Lewis at the B & B told me he had a picture of her.'

'What sort of picture?' Peterson asked.

'Just a picture torn out of a newspaper.'

'You mean he was interested in her?' Peterson asked. Geraldine shrugged. 'I didn't know it was you,' he repeated. 'Do you think he was looking for her all along?'

'I wonder what he meant when he said 'I didn't know it was you.'' Lynda gazed anxiously at her daughter, lying stretched out on the sofa, her head on her mother's lap. 'They said their suspect was called Jim. I wonder. It was all so long ago.'

'What was?'

'Before my career took off, I used to help out in Gina's unit,' Lynda said. Melanie nodded. Her Aunt Gina had worked in a special school for years. 'I thought I could be useful. I wasn't, of course. I was a complete disaster.'

Melanie raised herself up on one elbow. 'What was it like?'

'You want the truth?' Melanie nodded and her mother grinned. 'It was awful. I wasn't much use at all. I think they would've asked me to leave, only they were too nice, and too short staffed.'

Melanie pulled herself upright. 'What was wrong with the children?'

'Oh, all sorts. I didn't really understand much about it. The teachers were very strict with the children and I think I let the side down, trying to be nice. I thought it was the right thing to do.'

'I bet the children liked you.'

Lynda frowned. 'There *was* this one little boy who took a shine to me. I don't think he had any family of his own. No one who took any interest in him, anyway.'

'Except you.'

'Yes. I became a sort of a mother figure to him, I suppose. He used to follow me around everywhere.'

'That's sweet.'

'No, it was awful. And weird. He became obsessed with me. He thought I was an angel and he remembered everything I said to him. When he couldn't see me, he'd climb up on a chair and shout my name. He called me Miss L.C. because he'd read my initials on a bag and I told him that was clever. He wasn't clever, of course, he was slow, and he had a speech impediment.'

'Miss L.C.,' Mel repeated, laughing. 'I bet you liked him following you round, like a little puppy.'

'No, it wasn't like that. He was vicious, and very possessive. He nearly killed one of the other children when I admired her drawing. He wasn't small, and he was incredibly strong. He lifted her up bodily, and she wasn't slight. He was going to hurl her through the window. Luckily there were three teachers in the room and they managed to restrain him.'

'My God.'

'It wasn't his fault,' Lynda went on. 'He was disturbed. But I think he got away with a lot too. The other children were always complaining that he hurt them when the teachers weren't looking. It was difficult to get to the truth of it. Then my career took off and I never went back. Only I remember his name was Jim and I wonder ... No, that's ridiculous. It's a common enough name, and it was all so long ago.'

'How come you never told me about him before?'

'Oh, I haven't thought about it in years. It's not important.'

63

Vigil

Jim Curtis hadn't returned to his shed. The search continued throughout the night. They couldn't sit at the station typing up reports and there was no question of going home, so Geraldine and Peterson went back to Mortimer Street. They parked round the corner and received clearance to enter the site. Although she knew the suspect wasn't in the area, Geraldine felt a tremor of anticipation as they approached the abandoned property. She imagined Curtis was there, already handcuffed, ready to be driven to the station. He must have returned by now. Perhaps her phone wasn't working, or the team at the shed wanted to surprise them.

'We got him, ma'am,' she mouthed to herself, as though thinking the words might make them come true. The place looked deserted as they hurried across the front garden and crept into the passageway but Geraldine knew officers were in position all around them, out of sight. As she emerged into the back garden, Peterson at her heels, a dark silhouette acknowledged them.

'Any news, Constable?' Geraldine asked softly.

'Nothing yet, ma'am.' Geraldine felt a stab of disappointment.

They crossed the dark garden. Peterson stumbled once on a bramble before he slunk into the shadows behind the shed. Geraldine tapped softly at the door. It opened a sliver. A thick curtain hung inside the door to black out the light. Inside, the work of the forensic team went on silently.

Geraldine twitched the curtain and slipped into the brightly lit shed where white suited officers were busy. One of them held up a plastic bag and Geraldine saw it held a delicate strand, a few ginger hairs that might have been picked off a jumper.

She nodded and left, pulling the curtain across quickly and closing the door without a sound. She joined Peterson, concealed behind the shed wall. They could establish that Jim Curtis had been sleeping in the shed. They were convinced he'd killed Jacqueline Ross in there, but they had no proof. Geraldine swore under her breath, wishing either Heather Spencer or Melanie Rogers had been able to identify their attacker. They were so close. They couldn't track Jim Curtis down only to see him acquitted in court. A canny lawyer could dress a felon in a clean suit, put credible words in his mouth and create reservations about anyone's guilt. Questions would be raised about whether the victim, or only her clothes, had ever been inside the shed. There must be no room for doubt.

Two hours passed. Still they waited in the freezing dark. Geraldine's feet ached with the cold but she hung on. With every moment that passed, the chance of Jim Curtis returning to the shed grew more remote. They heard rustling in the grass.

'Rats,' Peterson mumbled. Geraldine didn't budge. She knew the DS wanted to go back to the station but she clung on, determined to be there when Jim Curtis returned to his hideout. She wanted to handcuff him herself, his hands behind his back.

They waited. The forensic team worked in the shed, unseen. Peterson kicked silently at the dirt with the toe of his shoe. A thick mist was beginning to glow with early morning light when she spoke again.

'We've lost him,' she said, no longer trying to muffle her voice. It seemed to boom in her ears after the silence of their dark vigil. 'Something's wrong.' She looked around the garden, eerie in the early mist. 'If he was coming back, he'd be here by now. He knows something's up. We're wasting our time.'

They returned to the car where Geraldine told Peterson about the hair.

'It doesn't change anything,' she pointed out when he punched the air in triumph. She suddenly felt very old. 'They found her clothes, that's all. It doesn't even prove she was here. The whole place is littered with old clothes. He's like a magpie. He's been collecting bin bags from outside charity shops and bringing them back here. He could've found Jacqueline's clothes and brought them back to the shed, with her hair clinging to them.'

'Forensics will find evidence she was killed in there,' Peterson replied. Geraldine smiled, but she felt uneasy. Jim Curtis should have been back by now. They still didn't know where he was. If they'd scared him off with the police patrols and the chopper, they might not find him before he moved away and killed again. And again.

'He won't get far, gov. He'll be picked up. We've got the whole town covered,' Peterson said.

'That's what I thought. But he must know we're searching for him. He would've seen patrols on the streets, couldn't have missed the helicopter.' She shut her eyes. Peterson waited. 'Let's focus on what we know about him. He's got mental problems'

'He's paranoid,' the sergeant said. 'He's been on his own, sleeping rough. He doesn't trust anyone.' He glanced at Geraldine.

She was sitting perfectly still, eyes shut, thinking. 'Heather Spencer said he's like a child. His records confirm low IQ. He's gone to hide, somewhere he feels safe. He took Jacqueline Ross to the park. Maybe that's where he feels safe.' She opened her eyes.

'The park? Are you sure? I would've thought that was the last place he'd want to —'

'No. I'm not sure,' Geraldine interrupted him. 'Let's go.' She stared straight ahead as Peterson drove off, muttering under his breath.

Geraldine felt sick with despair, but she had to do something. She couldn't just return to the station and sit around. They'd discovered his hideout too late. Jim Curtis must have fled the area at the first sight of a police presence. He might have a car – he could be anywhere by now. They'd lost their chance to catch him. Working in the shed, SOCOs were standing on the same floor the killer had trodden, searching the stinking pile of old newspapers and clothes he'd slept on, breathing the killer's stale air. They'd come so close to finding him.

They drew up by the park gates.

'Don't make a sound,' Geraldine warned Peterson. They closed the car doors as gently as they could.

They nearly missed him, lying down gazing into the water. In a glimmer of cold moonlight that cut through the swirling mist they caught a glimpse of movement in the reeds by the lake. If he hadn't moved his head slightly from side to side they might never have seen him. A low mumbling reached them. He was talking to himself. Peterson bent over to whisper in Geraldine's ear. She couldn't catch what he was saying. She nudged him and they walked swiftly down to the water's edge. They were too slow. The figure had vanished, aware of their silent approach. Peterson swore under his breath.

'Cover the main gate,' Geraldine hissed. She turned and hurried towards the back exit. They couldn't let him slip away, not now they'd found him. She was on the phone, summoning back up. He wouldn't get far. She hoped he'd slithered into the water, or ducked into the bushes but she knew he might already be racing silently to the perimeter fence. If he reached it before back up arrived he'd be able to climb over, concealed in the mist. Once out of the park it was still possible he might give them the slip. He knew how to hide in the shadows, like an animal.

Peterson had disappeared into the darkness. Geraldine walked silently across the grass. Jim Curtis had been there, a black shape in the moonlight. She felt her ears and eyes straining in the mist. She heard water lapping. In the distance a car sped by. The minutes seemed to stretch endlessly. She tried not to imagine how it would feel to read about his next victim in the news.

When strong hands seized her arms they held her so hard it hurt. She yelled but already both her wrists were clamped in a vice like hold, and another hand was slapped over her mouth. She felt a rough texture on her lips. A pungent stench of leather and sweat was in her nostrils as she struggled to breathe. Adrenaline rushed to her head, making her dizzy. Even if Peterson had heard her stifled scream, he'd never find her in the shadowy morning mist. She was alone with the killer.

Swiftly she manoeuvred one foot behind her assailant's calf to trip him up, but lost her footing as he dragged her across the grass. Her arms felt as though they were being wrenched from their sockets and she was afraid her neck would snap. Through her pain and terror, she found herself analysing the assault. He was using only his gloved hands. There was no time for anything else. She thought of Angela Waters, Tiffany May and Jacqueline Ross and was glad it would be over quickly. DI Geraldine Steel killed in the course of duty. Geraldine Steel, lying naked on a table in the mortuary. Panic gave way to rage and she kicked out in a violent frenzy. Her assailant yelled. Good, she thought as she kicked him again. At least she could hurt him before she died. He cried out once more and tightened his grip on her face.

She was pushed backwards onto the grass, her arms

339

pinned beneath her, crushed by the weight of his body. One hand continued to press against her mouth, forcing her lower jaw painfully backwards. His other hand felt for her throat. Frantically, Geraldine's fingers scrabbled at the earth and she managed to wriggle one arm free. Ignoring a sharp pain in her shoulder, she seized a handful of greasy hair and yanked it as hard as she could. Her assailant hollered, and loosened his grip on her throat. She gasped for breath.

She tried to gather her energy for another tug when the load pressing down on her suddenly lifted and her jaw was released. There were sounds of a scuffle immediately above her. She rolled to one side, and struggled to her knees, propping herself up on shaking arms. One shoulder jarred painfully as her palms slid on the wet grass.

'You all right, gov?' a familiar voice grunted somewhere above her head.

'You took your time,' she croaked, her thoughts spiralling out of control with shock and pain. Shivering and sobbing she clambered to her feet, struggling to control her hysteria. She couldn't breathe. She'd dropped her torch in the struggle and could barely see Peterson holding her assailant in a headlock, one arm twisted behind his back. Jim Curtis was crying like a child.

'Let go,' he sobbed. 'I hate you. I'm not playing any more.'

'Easy, Serge, you'll strangle him.' Her voice sounded hoarse and distant in the darkness.

'No more than he deserves. Slap the cuffs on him for God's sake. He's strong as an ox.' Fumbling, Geraldine handcuffed the man's hands behind his back. In the darkness his features were shrouded in hair. He remained a shadowy figure.

They heard the chopper circling overhead, bathing the scene in light, as dozens of uniformed officers charged towards them out of the dispersing mist. Geraldine nursed her sore shoulder. It was all over.

'We got him,' she began but had to stop. Shaking uncontrollably, she turned her back on the melee of uniformed officers and walked away, struggling to regain her composure. She hoped her outburst had passed unnoticed in all the commotion. It was hardly appropriate conduct for a DI.

A thin voice whined from the dark huddle of figures on the path. 'You're mean. I'm going to tell on you. It's not fair.'

The words checked Geraldine's hysteria like a slap in the face. Jim Curtis was right. It wasn't fair. She took a deep breath and stepped forward. 'James Curtis,' she called out. The babble of voices fell silent. 'I'm arresting you on suspicion of the murders of Angela Waters, Tiffany May and Jacqueline Ross, and the attempted murders of Heather Spencer, Melanie Rogers and …' She paused. Her mouth felt dry. 'Geraldine Steel. You do not have to say anything, but it may harm your defence if you do not mention, when questioned, something which you later rely on in court.'

Behind her, in the gathering light, she heard cheering.

64

Interview

'What the hell do you think you were doing, running around in the park like that, before back up arrived?' Kathryn Gordon stormed at Geraldine. They were in the DCI's office with the door shut, but Kathryn Gordon was shouting so loudly they could probably hear her upstairs in the canteen. Geraldine clenched her fists, pressing her nails into her palms, and winced as the tension in her arms caused a painful spasm in her neck.

The DCI lowered her voice. 'Your carelessness could've got you killed. Don't you realise the danger you put yourself in?' Geraldine lowered her head gingerly. She'd been to casualty, at the DCI's insistence, and was mortified at having to wear a neck collar despite her assurances that she felt fine. 'I'm going to keep a very close eye on you in future, Geraldine Steel,' Kathryn Gordon went on. She sat down, red faced with fury. Geraldine wondered if the DCI intended to put in a request for Geraldine to work on her team again. Right now, it didn't seem a pleasant prospect.

'Yes, ma'am,' she replied, trying to sound repentant. 'Thank you ma'am and I'm sorry for being ...' she paused, lost for words. With a disgruntled murmur, the DCI gave a nod at the door, allowing Geraldine to make her second escape of the day. At least her encounter with Jim Curtis had made the reprimand from Kathryn Gordon seem relatively tame, Geraldine thought ruefully. Avoiding the curious and sympathetic glances of colleagues, she scuttled to the relative privacy of a toilet cubicle. Perched on the edge of a seat she wept silently and without restraint, until her neck ached from the violence of her sobbing.

When she returned to the Incident Room she found her colleagues huddled in groups, reading the local newspaper with varying expressions of amusement or outrage. The *Woolsmarsh Chronicle* ran an outsize headline above a photograph of a police helicopter.

STRANGLER ARRESTED

<u>Killing Spree</u>

Notorious Woolsmarsh Strangler arrested after killing spree claimed three lives.

She scanned down the subheadings. There was a comment from Kathryn Gordon whom the paper was now praising. 'My team has worked tirelessly,' she was quoted as saying. Geraldine smiled at the editor's eagerness to share the glory.

DCI Gordon acknowledged the co-operation of T*he Chronicle* whose public awareness campaign played an important role in helping to protect local residents.

Inside were features including interviews with the victims' families and friends, and a map showing the route the killer might have taken between the park and the alley. A table of victims read like a list of the wives of Henry VIII. Brief and mainly accurate biographies of the dead girls followed, accompanied by pictures.

The story overshadowed news about the leader of the local council. A heading announced: 'COUNCIL LEADER CON.

Geraldine caught Carter's eye and smiled as they turned to face the Incident Board where Kathryn Gordon stood, her pale face stretched in a broad grin.

'Congratulations everyone, on a job well done.' There was a general murmur of appreciation. 'You've been a great team to work with.' Muted whispers swelled into loud cheering. Kathryn Gordon beamed and nodded her head as everyone dispersed to type up reports and clear their desks.

A solicitor was on hand for the DCI to start the interview. The forensic team were gathering evidence for a watertight case. Clothes found in the shed had been identified as those worn by Jacqueline Ross on the night she died. DNA hadn't yet been confirmed, but a strand of her hair had been discovered in the shed and Jim Curtis's fingerprints were found on her shoes. The similarity in method was compelling proof that one man had committed all three murders. Melanie Rogers and Heather Spencer might identify him, forensics were re-examining the letters Heather Spencer had received, and he'd been arrested in the act of attempted murder.

Geraldine should have been typing up her final report. Instead she sat, stupefied with relief. She thought about all the things she could do that evening: have an early night, make a start on unpacking the boxes still stacked on the floor of her living room, watch TV, or read. Or she might just sit in a chair and do nothing. She could rest. She wondered whether to call Craig, but decided against it. He wouldn't understand her uneasy triumph. Geraldine closed her eyes. Her shoulder ached and her neck hurt when she leaned forwards. They'd nailed him, and she didn't have enough energy to feel pleased. Her fingers sat motionless on the keyboard. She'd never been so tired.

'Gov.' Geraldine opened her eyes. 'DCI wants you in the interview room.' Geraldine saved what little she had typed of her report. 'Coming for a drink after work, gov?' Sarah Mellor asked as she passed her in the corridor. Forgetting her neck collar, Geraldine nodded and swore as the collar dug into her. Then she set off to meet the Woolsmarsh Strangler face to face in the harsh light of an interview room. Outside the door she paused. She was about to confront the man who had killed Angela Waters, Tiffany May and Jacqueline Ross. The terror she'd felt in the darkness of the park flooded through her and she clenched her fists until her short nails pressed into her flesh.

'It's just another interview,' she told herself, knowing her effort to appear blasé wouldn't fool anyone, least of all Kathryn Gordon.

A stale odour hit her as she opened the door.

'He won't tell us who he is,' the DCI said. 'Tells me he doesn't give his name to strangers.'

'Just strangles them,' Geraldine replied as she faced Jim Curtis across the table. Eyes glared wetly at her through a straggly fringe. She couldn't see a scar but knew they'd find it under his moustache. Staring him straight in the eyes, she sat beside Kathryn Gordon.

'DCI Kathryn Gordon. Also present DI Geraldine Steel. And – state your full name clearly for the tape, please.' Kathryn Gordon paused. 'The suspect is shaking his head.' The DCI pointed out that it was futile to try and obstruct the police at this stage. Jim Curtis didn't answer. Kathryn Gordon's face contorted with mock anger as she leaned forward. Geraldine wondered if the DCI's anger with her had also been assumed.

'All right, Mr Curtis. Let's stop playing games. We know who you are, so there's nothing to be gained by these delaying tactics. It won't help your case.' She paused. Jim Curtis stared at her, silent. She gave an exaggerated sigh. 'We've got you and you know it. So let's get a move on, shall we?' The man's lips moved under his scruffy moustache. Kathryn Gordon sighed and raised her eyebrows at Geraldine. Here we go: 'You can't talk to me like that. I know my rights.' Geraldine wanted to tell him he'd forfeited his rights the moment he laid his hands on Angela Waters, but the tape was running and the solicitor sat, mutely observing.

The Woolsmarsh Strangler didn't insist on his rights, nor did he try to protest his innocence. Stinking like a drain and crawling with lice, in a dry crackly voice he asked for a hot shower.

'But first I want my hair and nails cut short. It helps to keep them clean.' He nodded his head and the solicitor shifted uncomfortably in his chair.

'This isn't a hotel,' Kathryn Gordon burst out. 'And where you're heading, you're not going to be relaxing in the showers. You won't want to set foot outside your cell. No one likes people like you.'

The man's voice was hoarse and indistinct. 'Miss Elsie likes me,' he said. With a gurgle that might have been laughter he added, 'I think she loves me.'

Geraldine's tone was very gentle. 'Why did you stop taking your tablets, Jim? Don't you know three women have died because of it? Why did you do it?' Curtis appeared to be thinking. A smile stirred the hair on his face like a breeze rippling through grass.

'It's all right,' he said, suddenly eager to talk. 'I seen Miss Elsie. I didn't know it was her. Not at first. But it was her all right. I seen her. I seen Miss Elsie and she says I'm more clever than anyone. You don't know how clever I am. Miss Elsie knows it's not my fault. It's not my fault, Miss Elsie says. Miss Elsie's pleased with me.' His voice rose in a guttural shout of triumph. 'She's going to give me a merit star.' His eyes blazed, daring them to disagree.

Geraldine started to repeat her question but changed her mind and fell silent. Even if she could persuade Jim Curtis to explain himself, she didn't want to understand him. She only wanted to know he was securely behind bars so he couldn't destroy more lives. She didn't have the strength to think beyond that.

The DCI nodded at the officer standing by the door ready to escort the suspect back to the holding cell. As Jim Curtis clambered to his feet, Geraldine saw the hands that had crushed the life out of three women and almost ended her own life. They were unusually large, with long fingers that twitched as though playing an imaginary piano. Geraldine swallowed hard, resisting the urge to reach protectively for her throat.

In the doorway, the Woolsmarsh Strangler twisted round and stared straight at Geraldine. 'I seen her,' he repeated rapturously, 'I seen Miss Elsie—' the door closed on his hoarse babbling.

The DCI looked at Geraldine. 'You look worn out. You could do with a good sleep. But I need you to finish all your reports tonight before you leave.'

'Yes, ma'am. And … thank you, ma'am.'

'Better to confront him face to face,' Kathryn Gordon replied as she rose to her feet. She spoke brusquely, but there was understanding in her eyes. 'You'll sleep better for it,' she added, and left the room without a backward glance.

65

Celebration

As she walked into the pub Geraldine regretted joining the team for a drink at the end of the case. Her neck was aching and she was too tired to think straight, but they'd all seen her and she couldn't back out without looking churlish. Forcing a grin, she joined her colleagues. Several officers who'd been drafted in from other stations had already gone home, but Peterson was there, and Sarah Mellor, and the other DIs. For once, Merton was smiling. It was the first time Geraldine had seen his uneven yellow teeth. Kathryn Gordon was laughing.

Geraldine didn't feel like celebrating. She hadn't paid attention to a telephone message and, as a result, Tiffany May and Jacqueline Ross had died. If only Geraldine had listened more closely, those two teenagers might still be alive. However hard she tried to block the image of Mr and Mrs Ross from her mind, she couldn't forget their reaction on hearing of Jim Curtis's arrest. She'd found them sitting side by side on a sofa, locked together in solitary misery.

'We've made an arrest,' Geraldine had spoken as brightly as she could but had faltered almost at once, her words an intrusion in the silent house. 'His name's Jim Curtis. He's mentally ill. He didn't want his victims to suffer … it was over very quickly … she wouldn't have known …' She'd stopped. There were no words. If she closed her eyes she was powerless in the dark, hands trapped behind her back, one leather glove pressed, unyielding, over her mouth, while another closed around her throat. She could try to put it out of her mind but it would be there, waiting to catch her in restless dreams. There was no comfort she could offer them. She knew their daughter's death had not been easy. Mr and Mrs Ross had stared at her with empty eyes. 'I'll let myself out,' she'd muttered and left them disconnected, side by side.

'What's yours, gov?' someone asked; a brief reprieve from memory.

'This one's on me,' the DCI butted in. 'Name your poison, Geraldine?'

'A half, thank you, ma'am.'

'Get her a pint,' a voice called out.

Carter manoeuvred his way to her side. 'Don't beat yourself up over the victims, Geraldine,' he muttered. She could barely hear him above the hubbub. 'We'll never know how many lives we saved. Look over there.' He nodded at a boisterous group of young women occupying a corner of the bar. One of them was wearing a flashing headband with a small veil attached to it, announcing: 'BRIDE' in bright pink letters. Several of her companions had long blonde hair. All of them were laughing. Geraldine turned to Carter but he was already moving away from her. Over the top of his glass his eyes met hers for an instant. Then the DCI was back, thrusting a pint at her.

'Cheers, Geraldine,' she bellowed, 'and well done. You have the makings of a good officer.' Rare praise from the DCI. 'I'll be keeping an eye on you,' she added. Geraldine smiled, hoping she wouldn't be assigned to Kathryn Gordon's team again straight away. 'Just watch your step,' Kathryn Gordon added, 'and you'll be all right.'

Angela Waters, Tiffany May and Jacqueline Ross hadn't watched their step. But perhaps Carter was right. The noisy group out celebrating their friend's wedding were safe because of the team who'd worked tirelessly to find the

Woolsmarsh Strangler. None of the girls at the hen party looked in her direction as Geraldine raised her glass. She drank to them.